The Trail of a Songbird

Jayesh Bhaware is an author and poet based in Pune. Alongside his professional work in marketing and strategy with senior business leaders and CXOs, he writes on themes of love, healing and intimacy. He was born and raised in a small village in Maharashtra and has published a collection of poems, *Silk and Petals*. *The Trail of a Songbird* is his debut novel.

JAYESH BHAWARE

The Trail of a Songbird

Published by Westland Books, a division of Nasadiya Technologies Private Limited, in 2026

No. 269/2B, First Floor, 'Irai Arul', Vimalraj Street, Nethaji Nagar, Alapakkam Main Road, Maduravoyal, Chennai 600095

Westland and the Westland logo are the trademarks of Nasadiya Technologies Private Limited, or its affiliates.

ISBN: 9789371978880

10 9 8 7 6 5 4 3 2 1

Typeset by Jojy Philip, New Delhi
Printed at Thomson Press India Private Limited

To anyone who has felt lost in life and needed a bit of light to survive.

Prologue

Faceless. That's how she appeared in my dreams.

'It's better for both of us if you never know who I am,' she had written in her last letter. But no, she doesn't get to decide that. It's not her choice to make.

I lean against a tree, catching my breath. The cold wind flings tiny flakes against my cheeks, each one stinging like a needle. I stamp my feet, desperate to bring them back to life, but it's useless. My legs, my face, my arms—they've all started to go numb.

What if she's not there? What if every step I've taken leads to nothing?

That insistent voice inside my head starts again, telling me to turn back, to find warmth, to rest, to wait for her to return.

But no. I can't stop. Not now. Not when I'm this close.

I drag my feet forward, each step heavier than the last. I've spent too many nights lying awake, thinking about her, turning her letters over and over, searching for any clues that might lead me to her.

And now, when I'm finally this close, I won't let anything stop me: not the frozen limbs, not the aching lungs.

But what will I even say when I see her?

How will I explain everything I've wanted to tell her—how her letters saved me, how I've kept each one of them, and how I've read them night after night as if doing so will convince my mind that it was all real?

Because sometimes, it starts to doubt. Sometimes, my mind tells me it was all an illusion—that she never existed, that her words, her kindness, the comfort her letters gave me, were all just fragments of my imagination.

But no. She is real. And deep down, I know that if it hadn't been for those letters, I might have given in and accepted that it was all just a dream.

I exhale deeply, trying to push away the thoughts that are clawing their way back in, the voice that says I'm chasing a phantom, a dream—chasing which would be the end of me.

My boot sinks deep into the snow and gets stuck. I pull and twist until it breaks free. I lurch forward, and it sets something loose inside me, a flicker of panic I've been trying to bury.

What if she doesn't want to see me?

What if she says she never wanted me to come?

What if she tells me to leave her alone, the same way she left me and disappeared?

No ...

I have to try.

I have to tell her how I feel.

I have to show her how much she means to me.

The snow crunches beneath my boots as I move forward, the only sound besides my heavy breathing, breaking the silence around me.

1

A screeching sound, a sharp jolt, and the bus lurches to a sudden stop, slamming my forehead against the steel bar attached to the seat in front of me.

'Fuck!' The word escapes before I can stop it. *Did I say that out loud?*

Dizzy and disoriented, I slide back into my seat, rubbing my throbbing forehead. No one but me, I notice as I look around, seems affected by the abrupt stop. They're perfectly steady, their grip firm and their faces calm. Unlike me, they seem used to this, the sudden brakes, and the manic driving of the local bus drivers.

Across the aisle are two college girls, about my age. They had been talking about bunking classes. Not anymore. Now, their attention is on me. They're whispering, their eyes darting towards me and then back to each other. And now ... they are laughing.

Are they laughing at me?

Whispering about how I don't look like I belong here?

My chest tightens. I can't be sure, but my mind doesn't wait for proof. It fills in the blanks on its own. I turn to the window, trying to escape their stares and let the cool wind calm the ache in my forehead.

Maybe they're not even talking about me. Maybe it's just my throbbing forehead making everything feel worse.

Don't think about them.

But then they laugh again, a soft, muffled sound that somehow manages to cut through the noise of the bus.

My stomach twists. *They're definitely laughing at me.*

Maybe they're laughing at how lost I looked earlier, fumbling with the change while buying a ticket from the conductor. Or when he'd asked for my destination and I had to check my phone—which took forever to unlock—just to read him the name of the place she had sent me. Or maybe at how—

Don't overthink it.

I grip the steel handle in front of me, steadying my trembling hand, my knuckles aching.

You'll never see them again.

You are okay.

They might not even be laughing at you.

And even if they are ...

It's okay. You are never going to cross paths with them again.

Stop thinking.

The words don't help. They never do. It's like trying to calm a storm by telling it to be gentle, to stop breaking things, to quieten down. But storms don't care. They only want to tear through everything in their path. It doesn't matter to them that you've just begun rebuilding.

I try to breathe—steady, constant, deep—just like my therapist taught me.

Breathe in, hold, exhale.

I turn to the window. The glass is cold against my forehead. I let it bite into my skin. It helps, a little. The world outside moves fast, a blur of green, full of trees, tall and wild, reaching for the skies. I focus on them, anything to stop my mind from spiralling again.

Good, keep doing that. Focus on your surroundings, my therapist would say.

So, I do. I keep watching until the world becomes more vivid, until the chaos inside me slows down enough to let me notice the details—the milestone by the road showing the distance to the next city, the grass bending as the bus speeds past, and the sunlight filtering through the trees in flashes, appearing and disappearing, like it's playing hide and seek with the bus and its passengers.

It's strange how this world is nothing like the one I know.

Back there, it's all concrete and smoke—tall, cramped buildings packed close together, the air thick with horns, gossip, and endless noise that never seems to stop.

But here, it finally opens up. The hills stretch wide and silent, dressed entirely in green, with wildflowers scattered here and there, adding gentle bursts of colour.

It feels as if this is the place nature chose to sit down with her brush, wanting to paint a masterpiece—and succeeded.

I draw a deep breath. And for a second, I forget it all.

I forget the whispers in the college. The glares. The judgement.

No. Don't go there.

Not now. Not when it's finally getting quiet.

But the thoughts crawl back in anyway—fast, loud and cruel—dragging with them the faces, the voices, the night I keep trying to forget.

Don't think about it. Why the fuck does my mind love ruining things the moment they start to get better?

Breathe in, hold, exhale.

They must be talking about you.

Breathe in, hold, exhale.

Everyone must have heard about it by now.

Breathe in, hold, Exhale.

What if they ...

Stop bloody thinking.

I bang my fist on the rod, not caring about the stares from all around, they are nothing compared to what I am running away from.

That stops it.

I close my eyes and breathe again, deeper this time. *No one knows you here. None of them can reach you here. And these hills ... they don't know what you are running from, and they don't care. You are safe with them.*

It takes a while—several slow breaths, counting to four on every inhale, holding for two, exhaling through my mouth—before I stop feeling trapped inside my own head.

Once the storm quietens, there's nothing but silence.

I don't know how long I sit there, breathing, lost somewhere between calm and exhaustion, before the world comes rushing back. The bus screeches, jerking to an abrupt stop yet again.

This time, I'm ready. I brace myself against the handle, managing to stay in place.

But my olive-green backpack, the one that barely fit into the overhead rack, crashes into my lap with a heavy thud.

'Damn it,' I mutter, wincing.

'Your stop!' the conductor shouts just then, loud and impatient.

What timing! I shove the bag off my lap, arms protesting as I wrestle with the weight.

The kid in the next row, who is travelling to Manali with her mother and had become a good friend of mine while we were waiting for the bus, laughs as I struggle to stand up. She probably thinks this is another one of my tricks to make her laugh.

No, kid. This is real. My thighs hurt like hell, my forehead's still burning, and this damn bag just won't budge.

When I finally manage to free it—its buckle had got stuck behind the rod—I try to hoist it up, but it's heavier than I remember. The conductor, who is clearly not used to clumsy travellers like me, glares in my direction. I lift the bag with all my strength, and it swings wide, nearly hitting one of the girls across the aisle.

'Sorry,' I stammer, avoiding her eyes. She mutters something under her breath—something I don't understand, but don't need to. Her expression says enough.

Apologising again, I rush forward, glancing back once to make sure I haven't left anything behind.

'Get off! I don't have all day!' the conductor, his mouth red with tobacco, yells again, his voice grating.

I want to ask him about the change he'd promised to return, but one look at his flushed cheeks and clenched fists tells me it's not worth it. The college student in me hates losing money—I could've easily had two samosas and two cups of tea with that. But at this point, all I want is to get out. Away from the conductor, away from the passengers, who are now shooting daggers at me, clearly annoyed at me for the delay.

I step off, my bag nearly pulling me down.

A sweet, high-pitched voice calls out behind me.

I turn.

The little kid, her hair tied on top of her head and sticking out like a tiny antenna, is waving goodbye with a big smile on her face, her mother holding her close to the window.

I wave back. Her innocence is so endearing.

The world has not yet affected her soul, but it will. It always does.

I have never been much of a traveller. My world has always been small—my room in the hostel, the campus and the bookstore where I work part-time. That's about it. I've barely stepped out of the city in years. The farthest I've gone is maybe a bus ride away—never mountains, never beaches, never anywhere that needed more than a few hours of the day to reach.

Yet, here I am today, climbing down a mountain, with a heavy bag on my back that I bought just a few days ago, all because a complete stranger suggested it.

You need it, and besides, how hard can it be? I had thought at first. But as I step over rocks sharp enough to slice my skin and loose enough to send me rolling down with one clumsy step, I realise just how wrong I was.

'You will find a small pathway that will guide you to the spring,' she had written in her message.

I doubt if one can call what I am walking on a pathway.

The ground is uneven, covered in dried leaves that crackle underfoot. Some leaves are still wet with dew, making the rocks beneath treacherously slippery. My boots skid now and then, and I have to keep adjusting my balance under the load of my backpack—which, despite my attempts at packing light, is quite heavy.

The only sign that this is a pathway is the stunted growth of grass in places, worn down by occasional footsteps.

Despite all of this, I can't help but fall in love with nature. Unlike where I come from, tall green trees with needle-like leaves cover the hills here. Pine or deodar, maybe? I'm not sure, but I'm mesmerised by their short branches stretching almost parallel to the ground. They're so tall that just trying to spot their tips hurts my neck.

I stop as my eyes catch sight of a small yellow wildflower swaying gently at the edge of the trail. I crouch down and pluck it, careful not to crush the stem, and slip it into my pocket. A little something to carry back with me. A souvenir.

As I rise, I close my eyes and listen. To the birds, to the rustling wind, to the soft song the forest sings. And just like that, a realisation settles in me, gentle and certain.

I'm in love with this place.

2

The trees have all started to look the same. The wildflowers I had admired so much at first sight—captivated by their bright yellow, stark against the green and brown—have appeared along my path more times than I can count on my fingers.

I stop, lean against a tree for support, panting, and shift the bag on my back. It's heavy. Too heavy. My shoulders ache. My lower back is screaming.

And my legs ...

I hate how much they hurt. How even one more step feels like a huge feat.

During our conversation on Instagram yesterday, she had laid out what felt like a treasure hunt for me.

> Get off the bus and start walking downhill. The land will start to flatten, and soon you will come across a spring. It's not that far. And once you cross it, walk north until you find a tea stall. Tell the owner your name and he will give you a package meant for you. Inside, you will find the next set of instructions.
>
> Happy hiking!

It felt exciting when I read it. Like a quest. Like something out of a *National Treasure* movie—Nicholas Cage on a mission.

But now, standing here, out of breath and alone, I don't feel like America's star treasure hunter.

I scan the area ahead. Nothing. No people. No sign of the land becoming flat. No sound of water. No tea stall. Even the pathway I thought I was following is gone. Like it was never really there to begin with.

And that's when it hits me.

I'm lost.

I sink onto a rock, wiping the sweat from my forehead, and slide the heavy backpack off my shoulders. Leaning back against the tree, I let out a long sigh, my back instantly thanking me.

I'm crazy. I really am. I set out on what seemed like an adventure that would help me forget everything that's happened in my life and magically heal me, all because a girl—who I know nothing about—said so.

Could this be a prank?

Could she have given me the wrong directions just for a laugh?

I can almost imagine her telling her friends: 'Haha, that guy actually went where I told him. Can you believe it? What an idiot.'

No. She wouldn't do that.

I was the one who reached out to her first. She talked to me when I had no one else. She was there for me when everyone had turned their backs. She even sent me photos from her own trek to keep me motivated, while helping me plan my own trip.

She's been kind, supportive and honest. She wouldn't do something like that.

And honestly, even if this somehow turns out to be a prank, it would still be the kindest one anyone's ever pulled on me.

After everything that's happened these last few months, I don't think the world has much left to hurt me with—or surprise me.

The thought lingers for a moment before fading, replaced by a dry sting in my throat. I reach for my bottle and tilt it over my mouth. Barely a few drops fall. I try to hold on to them for as long as I can—two seconds maybe—before they vanish, like drops on a heated roof in summer, leaving my throat just as dry as before.

A wave of exhaustion washes over me, heavy and slow. My eyes start to blur, the world softening as if it's being pulled gently out of focus. And I feel myself slipping ...

Something is moving against my leg.

My eyes snap open. My brain screams one word: *Snake!*

I launch myself up like someone has lit a fire under me—only to trip over my own bag and land on my elbow.

Pain. Dirt. A surge of panic and raw fear.

And then ... a bark.

A bark?

I look up.

A reddish-brown dog. Small and fluffy. Looking at me with the biggest, most liquid eyes I've ever seen. There's dried mud on his legs, and his tail is wagging like he's just found a long-lost friend.

'Where did you come from?' I whisper, rising slowly.

He lets out a low, throaty 'Bhow' like that's supposed to explain everything.

And for some weird, unknown reason ... it kind of does.

He comes closer and sniffs my boots. I reach out slowly to scratch behind his ears—and just like that, his face melts into a gorgeous smile.

'Oh, you are so cute,' I say, scratching under his neck. His closed eyes and wagging tail tell me he's loving it—maybe a little too much.

When I stop, he barks at me—his expression suddenly switching, like he's asking me a question. 'Bhow. Bhow?'

'Yeah ... I'm lost,' I tell him. 'Are you too?'

'Bhow ...' he responds.

'Mmm hmm ...' I nod like I understand him.

He circles me twice and sniffs at my bag.

'Nothing to eat there, my guy. Unless ... wait a second.'

I unzip the side pocket and pull out the sandwich I had packed last night—just holding it makes my stomach growl. I had kept it for later, in case I got hungry. And I really am.

I offer half to him. 'Would you like this?'

He pants happily, tail wagging with excitement.

He devours it like he hasn't eaten in days.

'Gosh, you really were hungry,' I say, running my hand over his head again.

I look at the half of the sandwich left in my hand. I really want to eat it, but the way he's looking at it—those big eyes fixed on it—makes me realise he needs it more.

My stomach protests, but I give it to him anyway and he wolfs it down, crumbs flying, tail wagging, as if I just gave him the world.

When he's done, he looks at me, places his paws on my chest and licks my cheek.

'Oh! Oh, gosh. Relax, it was just a sandwich.' I laugh, wiping my face.

He lets out another satisfied 'Bhow,' then turns and starts walking away.

'Hey, where are you going? Don't leave me alone,' I call out, seeing the only friend I've made on this trip trying to disappear on me.

He stops, glances back, then barks again—this time looking at something in the distance.

'Do you ... want me to follow you?' I ask.

Another 'Bhow' and a little tail wag.

'All right then.' *What do I have to lose?*

I've barely gathered myself when he starts running—not trotting, but running.

'Wait for me,' I shout.

He doesn't.

I take off after him, my heart pounding in my chest, my lungs already begging me to stop. But he keeps going—darting ahead with a strange urgency—then stopping, turning his head to check if I'm still behind him.

Each time I catch up, he takes off again.

Eventually, he slows down and comes to a sudden stop.

'Bhow!' he calls, tail wagging furiously, eyes locked on something ahead.

I'm still catching my breath by the time I reach him.

I follow his gaze. And there is it—the spring. Glistening with flashes of silver, blue and white, like it's carrying pearls and diamonds in its current.

For a moment, we just stand there, silent, before slowly walking towards it. *He's brought me where I was trying to go.*

He dips his head to drink, tongue lapping noisily. I kneel beside him, pausing as the still water catches my reflection.

The face staring back is familiar, but worn. Thick, dark hair I usually keep swept back has fallen over my forehead. My eyes look tired. Older than they should. Stubble covers my sunburnt skin, making me look like someone who's been thinking too much and sleeping too little. No surprises there!

With my palm I gently swirl the water, breaking the image apart. Then I cup my hands and drink, letting the cold, clear water soothe my parched throat and something deeper inside me.

'I'm going to call you Dodo,' I say, filling my water bottle and looking at him.

He lets out a soft 'Bhow' and wags his tail, like he approves.

'Dodo,' I murmur, 'do you know you're the only one I've spent any time with in months?'

We are walking together again.

'Bhow.'

'Yeah ... Like, I've lost all my friends. There's no one. And now there's this girl who has suddenly entered my life and somehow, I'm here because of her.'

'Bhow?'

'Oh ... I wish I could tell you who she is. But even I don't know. We've only spoken through texts. She's asked me to find a tea stall, says there's a parcel waiting for me. But honestly? I don't even know if I'm going the right way.'

Dodo tilts his head at me, ears perked. 'Bhow?'

'Yeah ... Bhow,' I reply.

Then, without warning, he bolts—this time faster than before. A full sprint.

'What the hell. Man, if you're bored of me, just say it. You didn't have to run off like that,' I say, chasing after him, struggling to keep up.

There's a slope rising ahead, thick with trees, blocking my view. He disappears over the top.

'Dodo,' I call.

No answer.

I scramble up the hill, heart hammering again.

'Dodo,' I shout his name when I reach the top, scanning the path ahead.

Silence.

'Dodo! Dodooo!'

The forest doesn't even stir.

He's just ... gone.

A sting rises in my chest, sharper than it should be. He was with me for only a little while, but he felt like the only friend I had out here—and now, even he's disappeared.

I curse under my breath, angry at the universe. And just then, I see it.

At the edge of the slope, a small tea stall. Its roof patched together with old sheets of steel—the place she had asked me to reach.

My furry friend helped me get here.

A wave of relief washes over me—finally, I've made it to my destination. But as I walk towards the stall, that sense of satisfaction is tangled with a sharp pang of loss. The emptiness at my side presses in, reminding me that I've lost a friend.

In front of the stall, an old man wearing a faded grey kurta is bent over a wooden bench, wiping it clean with a worn cloth.

'Hello, baba,' I greet him, forcing a smile.

He looks up, pausing mid-wipe. His sharp yet warm eyes light up the moment they meet mine.

'Ah, hello there,' he says, his voice radiating joy. 'You look like you've had quite the journey.'

'Yes, baba,' I say, lowering myself onto one of the benches with a long exhale. 'I was lost, actually. If it hadn't been for Dodo—umm, he was a dog—he just came out of nowhere and guided me here. If it hadn't been for him, I'd probably still be wandering around.'

'A dog?'

'Yeah. He had reddish-brown fur.'

The surprise on his face is instant and intense, and almost reverent.

'You should consider yourself lucky,' he says, his voice soft, filled with something that feels a lot like awe. 'He was not a dog ... but one of the mountain spirits. They appear for the kind-hearted who are lost. They guide them to safety and vanish, just like that,' he says, snapping his fingers.

Spirit. Blessing. Vanish? What is he even saying?

'But you should be happy.' He gives me a knowing smile. 'The mountains have blessed you. They've welcomed you into their kingdom with open hearts.'

Was Dodo really a mountain spirit? Did he show up just to guide me? Or is this just something the old man has made up; a story they tell the kids?

God, I can't process any of this right now. I just want to ask about the parcel, get my next set of instructions and leave. The overthinking can wait for the night.

But my stomach speaks first—growling, loud and desperate—reminding me just how hungry I am.

The old man hears it too, and smiles again.

'Ah, forget about it. Let's not ponder over an old man's tales. Would you like something to eat or drink?'

I glance around. The stall is made of bamboo sheets plastered with soil for stability. A kerosene stove sits on a small table, a blackened kettle and jars of cookies resting beside it. A rack stands at the back of the stall, holding various packets of biscuits, instant noodles, and some travel essentials like soap.

'Tea would be nice,' I say. The thought of something warm and soothing is irresistible.

He smiles and rolls up his sleeves. 'Anything else?' he asks, pointing at the packets of snacks dangling from a rope overhead, swaying gently in the breeze.

'Just a Parle-G, please.'

He hands me the packet, and the moment it touches my hand, a wave of nostalgia hits me—pulling me away from all the mystical talk of mountain spirits.

Parle-G always takes me back to my hostel days.

Anurag and I had become best friends in our first year at the hostel, and by ninth grade, we were inseparable.

The first time a girl rejected him, I was there—handing him tissues for his dramatic reaction.

And the second time.

And the third.

By the fourth, I had a routine: listening to him vent while trying not to laugh.

After every rejection, we'd sneak up to the roof of the hostel, slipping past the rector's office like it was some top-secret mission from a Hollywood action movie. We always carried a pack of Parle-G biscuits, saved from breakfast and broken in half to make them last longer.

Up there, under the open sky, Anurag would let loose, waving his hands as he ranted.

'Girls don't respect good guys like us. It's always the bad boys who get the girl.'

He'd pause dramatically, take a bite of the biscuit, then continue.

'You know what? I'm going to become a bad boy. Just watch, then I'll get girls. Girls don't care about loyal guys, or the ones who have eyes only for one girl.'

Barely five minutes later, he'd say, 'Did you see that girl in the library today? The one who had the prettiest eyes? I'm going to talk to her tomorrow. I'm sure she's the one for me.'

I'd roll my eyes. It was always the same script.

Just stick to one and make an effort, I'd want to tell him. How can you jump from one to another and still call each one *the one*?

Sometimes, I'd even open my mouth to say it. To tell him that, while I hadn't exactly found love myself, I was pretty sure it didn't work that way. That maybe he should slow down, actually get to know someone. And that he definitely shouldn't be gifting the same thing to two girls on the same day and expecting one of them to say yes.

But he never stopped long enough to listen. He would move on to the next story, the next theory about girls, the next grand plan to win someone over.

So, I stopped trying.

I can still picture him, legs dangling off the edge as he sat on the parapet, crumbs scattered on the cement, talking animatedly about his latest heartbreak, while I just stood there, listened and laughed.

We were brothers, always standing by each other's side—until it changed, until everything changed.

'Living in memories, huh?' Baba says, handing me the cup of tea. 'It's dangerous business, I tell you. Ours is an age for dreaming, loving, going on adventures, and making lots and lots of mistakes. Brooding over memories ... not a good thing.'

He returns to the counter and inhales deeply. 'We young people should focus only on living every moment to the fullest.'

I can't help but *almost* laugh at the 'we young people' part. He's clearly older—wrinkles cover his face, his deep eyes seem to notice everything, and that gentle, friendly smile ... it's the kind you only see on people who've lived long enough to understand life.

And yet, something about his words—and the way he says them—touches something deep inside me.

'Don't judge a book by its cover,' he says, as if reading my mind again. 'I may be old, but I'm still a lot younger than most of today's youth. While you are all stuck behind glowing screens day and night, I'm out here meeting travellers like you, sharing stories, climbing hills every day and herding my sheep for hours.'

'Remember this, young one,' he says softly, his eyes meeting mine as if piercing my soul. 'A man hasn't truly lived if he hasn't loved with his whole heart ... or chased daring adventures that remind him just how lucky we are to be born in a world this beautiful.'

And with that, he turns back to cleaning, leaving me to ponder over his words. I take a slow sip of the tea and stare into the cup. He is so young at heart, so full of life.

Something that I have been missing for years.

I dip a biscuit into my tea. I get distracted watching him—the ease with which he moves, the life flowing through his words—and before I can pull the biscuit out, it breaks and sinks into the cup with a soft plop. I sigh.

When was the last time I felt like this—alive?

Between classes, deadlines, trying to make enough money to survive, and *everything* that has happened, I stopped living and started surviving instead. If I look back, I can't ever remember living fully. Ever seeking any adventures, just for the sake of finding a new thrill. Just to feel alive.

I've always been in survival mode. And lately ... I've almost failed even at that, with the thought of ending it all crossing my mind more times than I like to admit.

Don't think about it.

And somehow, this time, my mind listens.

Instead, I focus on Baba. I envy him a lot. I envy his way of living, his radiating youth and his bright smiles.

When I finish the last of my tea and the pack of Parle-G, the size of which has drastically reduced from how I remember it from my childhood, I clear my throat and ask, 'Did anyone leave a parcel here for me?'

As soon as I say the words, his expression changes. He sets down his cloth and stares at me, carefully eyeing me from head to toe. 'What's your name, boy?' he asks.

'Arjun,' I reply.

His face lights up as if he's been waiting for this moment. 'Ah, so you're the one!' he exclaims, the smile on his face—which I thought couldn't get any brighter—now gets ten times brighter.

He disappears behind the counter and when he returns, he's holding a parcel wrapped in brown paper, its edges neatly folded. 'She told me you'd come. A green boy named Arjun.'

Green boy? I raise an eyebrow. Did she really call me that, or is he adding his own flair? Either way, I decide not to ask.

'She was here two days ago,' he continues, placing the parcel gently on the counter. 'Off on another adventure with some new friends, some of whom I had never seen before.'

She was here.

So close. Just two days.

'Umm ... if I may ask ...' I hesitate, trying not to sound too eager. 'What's her real name?'

His laughter bursts out, warm and amused. 'She said you'd ask that.' He grins, handing me the parcel. 'And she also told me not to answer any questions you ask about her.'

I try my best to hide my disappointment behind a soft smile. I was really hoping to know more about her.

All I know are fragments.

That she loves travelling, climbing mountains, chasing sunrises. And she has this way of seeing life—soft, light, full of magic hidden in the smallest things—that makes you want to live life the way she does.

And all of this I learnt only from her Instagram—hundreds of pictures of her adventures, yet not a single one showing her face.

I offer a soft smile to Baba, holding the parcel carefully. It's heavier than I expected. I shake it gently, but the parcel doesn't make a sound. What could she have left for me? I resist the urge to open it. I want to be alone when I do that, away from any stares.

I pay for the tea and biscuits, but Baba pushes some change back into my hand with a knowing smile.

'She has already paid for your tea,' he says. 'She always starts her journey with Abdul miyan's chai, and she wanted you to have the same start.'

3

I sit in the farthest corner of the dhaba. The sign above the counter reads Jassi Da Dhaba, which is odd, considering this place gives off no typical dhaba vibes. For one, there are wooden tables with sleek 'A'-framed legs instead of the usual charpais. Two, there are no trucks parked out front. Three, the cooks are wearing aprons and hats. And four, the kitchen is spotless—clean, visible to everyone and extremely well-organised.

Reasons three and four are why I chose this place for lunch over all the other restaurants I passed. I guess I get that from my dad. Even though we've barely spent time together, I am obsessed with kitchen cleanliness, just like him.

I pick up the menu card, noticing that the prices are surprisingly reasonable. The sub-heading at the top, printed in gold just below the name of the dhaba, catches my attention: 'Be different from what the world expects you to be.'

Why would anyone put that on a menu? Just a clever tagline, something to sound cool and modern? I think at first. But as I glance around, it's hard not to notice how this place actually lives those words. From the polished wooden tables to the neatly dressed cooks in their spotless aprons, everything about this dhaba defies the stereotypes people expect. It's not what you'd picture when someone says 'dhaba'. And somehow, it's better for it.

Maybe I would be better too—if I stop playing by the world's rules.

The past few months, I've spent living exactly as everyone expected—alone and locked in my room. Just hiding, keeping away from the cruel whispers, and desperately trying to avoid those judging stares.

'Be different from what the world expects you to be.' I feel the menu card is addressing me. And maybe it's time I listen. Maybe it's time I stop acting the way they expect me to.

I take a picture of the menu card and the dhaba and save it in the 'I need this' album in my gallery. Once done, I glance around the whole place with sudden admiration, realising everything it's doing to break the rules of this world.

My stomach growls just as the waiter approaches to take my order.

'One Punjabi Thali, please,' I say. It's the most affordable option, cheaper even than the standalone vegetarian dishes that come without rotis. But they cost fifty to sixty rupees extra.

'Would you like to order anything from the starters?' the waiter asks with a practiced smile. I wonder how many times he must rehearse that expression every day.

'Uh ... no, thank you,' I reply, trying not to look at the tempting dishes on the nearby tables.

'It might take a while to prepare your order, sir. I can get you some starters in just a few minutes.'

'No, I'm good, really,' I smile politely, dismissing the offer.

He walks off, his smile faltering just enough for me to notice. My stomach grumbles again, protesting my decision. But I don't regret it. Starters have always felt like a scam to me—a clever ploy by restaurants to make you spend extra on food you didn't even come for. An easy and quick cash grab.

Once the waiter has left, I take out the parcel from my bag, holding it gently like it's something sacred. Even though I've opened it before, my heart races just as hard as it did the first time. Carefully, I unwrap it again. Inside is a folded piece of white linen cloth, bordered with a black rectangular frame.

I smooth it out gently, running my fingers over its delicate texture, and read the words woven onto it in golden thread: 'May this be your key to slipping off into a world of fantasies.'

I just stare at the words for a while, feeling a mix of warmth and surprise. *She remembers.*

I place it aside gently, on the still-intact wrapping paper, and pick up the item beneath it—a journal. Its brown leather cover is soft yet sturdy, with a leather strap fastened by a golden buckle. I release the buckle slowly, staring at the intricate design etched on the cover. There is a guy walking through dense woods, guided by a small bird flying ahead.

This has to be her work, I'm certain of it. I've seen her Instagram posts—paintings of mountains and rivers, sketches of trees, even close-ups of intricately carved wooden ornaments. But this is different. I run my fingers across the design and feel the shallow grooves in the leather, the fine cuts made by a blade.

I can only imagine how many hours, days even, it must have taken her to shape every intricate detail.

I open the journal to its first page, a thick, charcoal-coloured sheet with golden ink gleaming in elegant calligraphy: 'For the time when you find the story you want to share with the world.'

I reread the words, feeling a lump rise in my throat. Two days before this journey began, she had asked me what I like to do, my hobbies, my ways of escaping. I'd told her about my writing, half-expecting the usual responses people give, like *nice, great, that's cool*, when they don't really care. But she asked me if I could send her something that she could read.

I ended up sending her two pieces, a poem about dreams and a short story.

She read them both, and for a long time, the chat stayed on 'typing...' before her reply came through.

'These are beautiful,' she said. 'You really have a tender way of observing life.'

Then she asked, 'Why do you write?'

It took me a while to type back a response.

'To slip off into a world of fantasies,' I finally wrote. 'Because the real world ... it is too cruel sometimes. Too unfair. Everyone is always rushing to judge, to belittle, to win—even if it means breaking someone else along the way. But in stories, I can slow things down. I can build a world where kindness isn't mistaken for weakness, where good people don't have to get hurt. A world that lets you breathe freely for a while.'

After staring at the blinking cursor for a long time, I added another line: 'In fiction ... I guess I get to make it fair.'

She saw the message and replied a few minutes later, maybe taking her own time to form a response:

'That's a beautiful thought.

Thanks for sharing that with me.

And I could see that in your words—that softness, that gentleness of your heart.

I'd love to read your work if you ever decide to publish.'

'One day, for sure. I'll send you the first copy if I do,' I typed back instantly.

I remember smiling when I had sent that message, not knowing she would actually remember any of it. Now, holding her gift, I find that soft smile returning to my face.

It's been a long time since someone has made me feel this way.

It's not that I haven't received gifts before. My parents still remember to send me something on my birthday.

Just last year, Mom sent me a card with my name spelt wrong and an online coupon. Dad's assistant sent a cheque for a bike. Dad, probably seeing the reminder on his phone, must've told him to arrange it. He would've asked Di what I might want, and she must've said, 'He has been dreaming of getting a bike.'

I'd returned it all, the cheque, the misspelt card and the coupon. A small act of rebellion, even though a part of me really wanted to cash it in, get that cruiser bike I had my eyes on.

If I've managed on my own all these years, I can keep doing it for a few more, I had reminded myself.

But deep down, I still don't know why I did it. Who was I trying to prove a point to? And why? Because obviously, it doesn't matter to them. They don't give a fuck. They haven't for a long, long time.

But it wasn't always like this. They weren't always so distant, so unaware of what their own son would like. There was a time, back when I was little, when things were ... happy. Before the fights. Before everything changed.

One birthday, when I was barely nine or ten, they'd gifted me a guitar—small enough to fit perfectly in my hands. Every note I played, no matter how off it sounded, made them smile. You have a gift for music, they would say.

That was the last birthday we celebrated together. The last one not affected by the fights.

So, when tears gather in my eyes now, after holding the journal close for too long, I don't wipe them away. For the first time in years, it feels like someone truly sees me.

Even though I don't know who she is, I know this ... she cares.

My eyes are heavy, and I have stuffed my stomach so much that it feels like it would explode with a single gulp of water. I gather my things, packing everything back into my backpack. Just before leaving, I glance at my phone again—no messages. Has she forgotten to send me the next set of instructions?

I double-check the table to make sure I haven't left anything behind. Just the brown wrapping paper from the gift remains. As I pick it up to fold it neatly, something falls out—a sky-blue envelope I hadn't noticed before.

My fingers brush over the textured paper. On the front, there's a small drawing of a bird in black ink. Its wings are tucked in, its tiny curved beak giving it a calm, watchful look. My heart skips for a moment. *How did I miss this?*

I glance around. The waiter is still nearby, wiping another table but throwing me curious looks. I can't open it here. Not now. I tuck the envelope into the front compartment of my backpack and head out.

The road ahead is long and deserted. For the last twenty minutes, I've barely seen a soul, apart from a group of bikers riding in synchronised unison on their sleek cruisers. No houses, no noise—just the quiet hum of nature. I reach into my bag, pulling the envelope out.

Carefully, as if I'm unwrapping a treasure, I open the envelope. Inside are two pages folded neatly. I pull one out, unfolding it gently, and begin to read.

Hey Hiker,

Hope you have enjoyed your journey so far. It might have been a bit tiring, maybe even a little challenging—but what's a life without a few challenges, right?

Speaking of challenges, I have one for you. So far, you've probably spent your nights in hotels or hostels. How about trying something different tonight? Spend a night in the woods. Don't worry, the spot I've marked for you is perfectly safe.

No dangerous animals in this area, I promise.

Also, you'll find a map inside the envelope. Follow the directions and it'll lead you to where you can camp tonight. By tomorrow morning, I'll send you instructions for the next part of your journey.

Oh, and one more thing—after tomorrow, I won't be on Instagram as much. It's difficult to find good network around here, and honestly, I kind of prefer the old-fashioned way of communication. There is something magical about these handwritten letters that the un-sendable digital messages will never have. You can still send me updates on Instagram though. I would love to hear more about your journey as it continues. I will keep checking your texts anytime I get decent network.

Have fun out there.

Wishing you the best adventure of your life,

Birdie

PS No pressure if you're not up for it. But I've found that when you're out there, under that big, infinite sky, all your problems feel smaller somehow. And suddenly, you feel like you have the room to breathe. It's the best reset I've ever found, and I hope you give yourself the chance to feel it, too.

4

Birdie's letter keeps replaying in my head as I walk through the forest, her words looping like a song I can't turn off. 'A night in the woods,' she had written. 'It'll be a beautiful experience.' I wasn't sure when I read it, and I'm even less sure now.

I keep looking up, staring at the dark, infinite sky Birdie had described. I want to feel small. I want my problems to shrink until they're just dust under the celestial weight of it all. But the forest floor is uneven, and my boots keep catching on roots that are impossible to make out. It's hard to welcome a life-changing perspective when you're trying not to trip in the dark.

After the fifth smack, my steel torch—my supposedly 'indestructible' steel torch, which the salesman had assured me would never die—flickers to life. Its light unsteady and barely there.

I clutch it, my breath clouding in the air. The temperature has dropped, and I still need wood for the fire. I should've done this earlier. But no, let's waste daylight wrestling a tent instead.

Despite watching all the tutorials I had saved, pitching a tent was still a disaster that took me hours. Now it's lost somewhere behind me, and I just hope my shaky sense of direction can lead me back to it later.

I'm not completely alone, though. The constant chirping of crickets follows me—judging me, perhaps, or collecting gossip to share with their family. I can already imagine them turning this into a dinner-table story. 'There was this human we saw, a guy with a torch so weak that even my neighbour, Steve—the firefly who's come last in the 'Glow Firefly Glow' competition for seven years in a row—gives off better light than it. Poor thing thought he could beat the forest with that torch. LOL.'

The torch's faint light catches a branch hanging from a nearby tree, thick and dry—perfect for my fire. I grab it with one hand and tug, but it doesn't budge. Clenching the torch between my teeth, its metallic taste sharp against my tongue, I grip the branch tighter and heave with both hands.

One hard pull ... nothing.

Second ... still nothing.

Third ... this time with my full weight behind it.

The branch cracks free with a violent snap that sends me staggering backward. The torch tumbles from my mouth, hits the dirt, and dies.

A thick, heavy darkness swallows everything. The world is gone. And somewhere in the distance, an owl hoots, its call ripping straight through the silence. It sounds exactly like an effect from the horror series Di and I used to watch together, hiding under a blanket.

I drop to my knees, frantically searching for the torch in the dead leaves and dirt. In the absence of sight, my other senses decide to overreact. Every rustle of a branch feels like a footstep; every whisper of the wind a warning from some ghost. I tell myself it's just a forest—*just a really, really dark, forest*—but my brain doesn't listen. It's remembering all the supernatural stories I have read. They all have one thing in common: first goes the light, then goes the character.

My fingers finally brush against the cold steel. I grab it like it's the only thing keeping me alive. After countless panicked hits and a desperate attempt to rearrange the batteries, the torch finally flickers back to life. The beam is pathetic, but it's something.

'Never again,' I mutter. Next time, I'm bringing two torches. Hell, next time I'll use my phone's flashlight, no matter how much battery it drains. I sigh, cursing that stupid brain cell which thought it was a smart move to leave the phone charging in the tent.

Back at the campsite, I arrange the firewood and dry leaves I had gathered into a neat pile between three rocks I had set up earlier. The scattered leaves from my earlier attempts are quickly gathered and stuffed into the base.

The bottle I bought this morning is almost empty. I drain it, grab the spare bottle, and this time take my phone too. I'm not trusting the torch alone again.

The sound of water rushing over rocks takes me back to the scout camp in sixth grade. I can almost hear the gruff voice of my old scoutmaster, his words a mix of caution and ridicule: 'Always set up camp close to a water source. A hundred metres, no closer. Unless you want to wake up as bear food.'

Back then, Anurag had turned the scoutmaster into his favourite impression. He'd stuff a pillow under his shirt, waddle around, and in that exaggerated tone say, 'And remember, a big belly like mine isn't fat—it's survival. Store enough food in your belly and you'll never starve.'

Everyone would burst out laughing. He liked that—the noise, the attention, the way people looked at him. When it stopped being funny, he switched to the math teacher, chasing that same reaction. It didn't matter who the target was, as long as people laughed.

It was my first year at boarding school, and everything felt foreign—the smell of the dorms, the long corridors, the mornings that began with whistles instead of my mother's voice. Within days, everyone had found someone to sit with at lunch, someone to whisper to during roll call.

Everyone except me.

I'd never lived away from home before. The noise and the rules I could handle; it was the pretending to be fine that broke me a little each day. Back home, everything had already been loud, and this place felt like more of the same—just that nobody here knew me.

Two weeks later, they sent all of the sixth graders to scout camp—probably thinking it would help us bond or forget our homesickness. I had barely got used to the way the hostel's stairs felt beneath my shoes before I was thrown into another new place. Another set of rules. Another version of me trying to survive.

We learnt how to tie knots, light fires, follow trails—but none of it really stuck. I just remember staring at my hands, wondering how any of it was supposed to help me in the real world. I wish they had taught us how to pitch a tent instead of keeping us under concrete roofs. It might've helped me tonight.

On the third day of camp, our scoutmaster had declared me 'the worst scout' he'd ever seen. I wanted to yell at him, to cry, to say, *You don't understand what I'm dealing with.* But I didn't. He wasn't wrong—I had failed at everything.

Only a week before camp, during a call on my rector's cellphone, my parents had told me they were getting divorced. They had been fighting for months—shouting, slamming doors—but I never thought they'd actually get a divorce. When they did, it felt like a punch to the gut. I didn't even know what it really meant, not fully. I just knew it was bad. I remember holding the phone and nodding, even though I didn't know what to say. I didn't want them to take away my home.

Building campfires and tying knots felt pointless when things that really mattered were falling apart.

And the thing that scared me most was the thought that they would take my sister away from me, like it happened in some movie I'd seen. I didn't want that. I didn't want them to take away the only person who didn't shout.

Those days were tough, and I was a mess. If Anurag hadn't shown up when he did, I don't know how I would have managed.

Even now, when I think about that first time we talked, it feels like I'm right there again.

'You need help?' A voice had interrupted my spiralling thoughts. I looked up to see Anurag, his blue scout uniform slightly crumpled.

'No, I've got it,' I muttered, hurriedly gathering the pile of wood and leaves in front of me.

'I know you do,' he said with a grin. 'But Doublechin said we're supposed to work in pairs, and I'd rather not get another lecture. Maybe we can help each other?'

Reluctantly, I nodded. Anything was better than running laps as punishment. We worked quietly, arranging the wood and stuffing leaves into the gaps.

'I heard the winners get to skip evening PT,' I said, glancing at the other pairs. Everyone hated PT, especially the endless laps around the ground.

'Yeah, and Raj and Yogesh would have been the ones to win,' Anurag replied, nodding towards the pair who were off in their own corner, arguing about something.

'They should've finished by now,' I said, frowning. 'They were always the fastest during practice.'

Anurag smirked and pulled a lighter from his pocket. 'That's because they've been cheating. But not today.'

I stared at him, then burst into laughter. It all made sense. While the rest of us struggled with sticks and softwood, Raj and Yogesh had secretly been using a lighter.

'What are you going to do with it?' I asked, eyeing the shiny object.

'Use it for us,' he said with a shrug, as if it was the most obvious thing in the world.

'No,' I said firmly. 'It's against my morals.'

'But they cheat every time. And that a-hole Yogesh had the nerve to tease me today. Acting all smug, like he's some genius—when all he is, is a dirty cheating pig who should just go and roll in some filthy gutter.'

'God. You really hate him. But no ... we're not them. We will not cheat.'

Anurag sighed, but eventually tossed the lighter into the woods. 'You better have a plan then.'

I smiled, pulling out my pocketknife and carving a groove into the softwood. Anurag grumbled but helped me find the perfect stick. Together, we ploughed it into the groove with newfound energy. Within minutes, smoke curled up from the wood, followed by a faint flame.

That evening, every pair of eyes in the camp had been on us. And for the first time in what felt like forever, I had smiled.

I suddenly miss my gang. If I'm being honest, they were mostly Anurag's friends, not really mine. I just sort of tagged along. Still, it was nice—being around them, feeling like I was part of something.

I can almost see Anurag cracking jokes he probably stole from the internet and passing them off as his own. Shree would be sitting next to him, trying her best to understand and failing spectacularly, as always.

I wish I could call them, but I've already tried. Every time, it's the same. The call connects, rings once, and then an automated voice chimes in: 'The number you are calling is currently busy. Please try again later.' Busy. Right. I wish the lady would just say, 'The person you're calling blocked you, dude. Keep trying if you want, but it's not going to change.'

I shake my head, trying to shrug off the thought. No use dwelling on what's already happened. The only thing I need to focus on is reaching the stream ahead. My shoes squelch with every step, the damp ground announcing my presence to anyone—or anything—listening. Up ahead, the beam of my torch catches the faint glimmer of water tumbling over rocks. *Finally*.

I quickly fill the bottles, using a net to filter out the debris.

On my way back, I stay alert, listening for anything out of the ordinary. Birdie assured me there wouldn't be any dangerous animals here, but YouTube says otherwise: 'Always use your ears as much as your eyes in the woods.'

Thankfully, no animal, except for maybe a rat, crossed me. When I reach the campsite, the fire pit is waiting.

I pull out my lighter and click it three times before the flame finally comes to life. The dry leaves catch fire quickly, the flame crackling to life and casting dancing shadows across my tent. I place a pot of water on the fire to boil and grab my bag.

The waiter at the dhaba had tried convincing me to take parathas for dinner. 'Wouldn't take long to pack them,' he'd said. But I had refused. *This is my first night in the woods,* I had said to myself. *And I want to cook my own dinner.*

Now, staring at the three packets of Maggi, I can't help but laugh and doubt if they fit the definition of a self-made dinner.

When the water boils, I empty two packets of noodles into the pot and let them cook. Once done, I scoop them onto a plate, rinse the pot, and fill it with water again, to boil for drinking.

Switching on my phone, I glance at the network bars. Nothing. Not a single one. I open Instagram out of habit. The only thing on my feed is an old post—a doodle of a coffee cup, a tiny figure drowning in it while holding a book. It hasn't refreshed. No new content.

I don't know if Birdie has seen my message. I must've spent half an hour after leaving the dhaba, typing a line, deleting it, typing again, then staring at the screen like it could somehow tell me what to say.

In the end, I sent: 'Thank you for the gifts. They mean so much more than you can imagine.'

Now, sitting here, I wonder if I should've said more. Should I have told her how grateful I really am? That it's the first real gift I've ever received? That I almost cried when I held it?

Maybe not ...

I can't really stop thinking about her. Even though it's been less than a week since I started this journey, it feels like my life has shifted. Every morning now feels like an adventure. I wake up not knowing where I'll go, who I'll meet or what I'll see.

And she's been doing this for years. Her Instagram is filled with breathtaking landscapes, towering cliffs and serene lakes. But never a picture of herself—except maybe one. Even that doesn't reveal her face. The rest are just glimpses of her life: her purple bottle on a rock, her boots beside a cliff, a funny rock she painted a face on.

I finish the last of my noodles, the spicy broth warming me in the cool night. The water in the pot starts to boil again, so I take it off the fire and set it aside to cool. Unlocking my phone, I open the screenshots album and scroll to the picture from her feed that I love the most.

It doesn't take long to find—a pink hiking bag, covered in hand-drawn cartoon stickers, hanging from a tree branch. The caption reads: 'Every princess deserves a hiking bag on her back, not just a purse slung across her shoulder carrying her lipsticks.'

I smile at that. Trust her to make even a hiking bag sound like a reminder to live a little bolder.

Next is a screenshot from one of her medical camps—the only picture where she's actually there. She's in a white coat, a laughing kid in her lap, and the only thing you can clearly make out about her is her curly hair. There are a few more photos from different camps, posted months apart.

They're the only clues that got me closer to knowing who she is: a medical student. Maybe my age. *I hope.*

I really wonder how she'd react if she knew I stalk her feed every day. Maybe she'd laugh. Maybe she'd say she's used to it. She probably has dozens of people doing the same. There's just something about her posts—they pull you in, leave you in awe, and inspire you to fall in love with life.

Will I meet her soon? I don't know. But the thought of it alone makes me nervous. What would I even say? How do you thank someone who changed your life without ever meeting you? I'd probably end up freezing, staring at her like an idiot.

Her Instagram handle, @super.birdie, hovers above the post. Why @super.birdie? I've turned that question over in my mind countless times, never finding an answer. I even asked her once, but she had to rush off before she could explain.

Maybe I'll ask her the story behind the username when we finally meet.

I take out the journal she gave me and begin to write. I don't know where to start—there's too much to say. About her, first, of course. Her texts, her letter, the way she gave me hope when I had none. Then about everything else—the hike, the thoughtful gifts, the tent that refused to cooperate, and the unexpected beauty found in moments I hadn't planned for.

I make sure not to leave out Dodo—my magical spirit guide, Abdul miyan, his chai and his wise words. Finally, I write about this being my first night ever in the woods.

Once my bottle is filled with boiled water, I douse the dying fire and gather my belongings. Back in the tent, I zip up the entrance securely. Without the fire, the cold creeps in, its iciness wrapping around me even through the tent walls. Using my phone's torch, I carefully tuck the journal into the front pocket of my bag. That's when I see it—the khaki envelope, peeking out from the same pocket.

I freeze.

I must've thrown it in while packing, unknowingly dragging it here, to the one place I wanted to escape from everything. The past I've fought so hard to leave behind has been walking with me all along.

Don't open it. Don't ruin this night.

My heart pounds in my chest as I pick it up. My hands tremble, struggling to hold the envelope steady. The past few months flash through my mind like a horror movie on repeat. Tears blur my vision, but I find my hands opening the envelope.

Just breathe. You didn't do anything wrong.

But my chest tightens as the words on the paper sharpen into focus.

> You are suspended from the college until further notice. Your parents will be informed of your disgraceful actions which have led to this decision. Following a discussion with the disciplinary board, we will inform you of our final decision.

I drop the letter, my hands shaking uncontrollably. My phone slips from my grasp, the flashlight landing sideways and casting eerie shadows in the tent. My breathing becomes shallow, each gasp feeling like it might be my last. My chest burns, and I clutch at it, trying to steady myself.

No. Please no. Please.

I fumble with my bag, desperately searching for my medicine. My hands, slick with sweat, struggle to unscrew the lid. It takes forever, each second stretching unbearably, but it finally comes loose. The pills spill out, scattering everywhere, and I manage to grab just one.

I swallow it quickly, only to start coughing violently as the pill lodges in my throat. Grabbing my water bottle, I take a desperate gulp, spilling most of it down my front, but it's enough. The pill goes down, leaving a raw, burning sensation in its wake.

I fall back onto the sleeping bag, my chest heaving, throat raw, heart still pounding so hard it hurts. My hands won't unclench. My body is shaking uncontrollably.

Four days. Four fucking days. Did you really think you could escape it? That your broken mind would just let you go?

My eyes sting. The tent walls blur and twist as tears spill over. I press the bag to my chest, as if holding on to something solid might stop the shaking.

The edges of my vision darken. My breaths turn to shudders. I can still hear the ringing. I can still feel the pounding in my skull.

It's been two months. The same nights. The same shaking. The same begging for it to end. I thought this trip would help—I thought I could breathe again—but it's all still here.

It never leaves. It never fucking leaves.

5

I wake up to the chirping of birds. I lie still in my tent, listening, trying to recognise their calls, but it's useless. The only call I recognise is the sparrow's.

It's been years. Back at Grandpa's house, mornings began with sparrows hopping on the verandah. He'd scatter grains with his wrinkled hands, and they'd flutter down fearlessly, even peck directly from his palm while he laughed like it was no big deal.

I push myself up onto my elbows, and a dull ache runs through my shoulders and back—effects of sleeping on the ground. This soreness I can handle. It's the fog in my head that feels heavier. The memories of last night ... the letter.

No. I don't want to think about it. Not now. Not ever—if I could.

Deep down, I know I can't outrun it forever. But for now, I can at least keep moving. That's something.

When I unzip the flap, a rush of cold air slips in, brushing against my face. The light outside is blinding—sharp, almost like it's punishing me for missing the sunrise. I'd promised myself the day I had left that I'd catch one at least. So far, I haven't managed to do that even once. I squint, waiting for my eyes to adjust. 7 a.m. Not sunrise early, but early enough.

I stretch my arms, letting the sunlight warm my skin. It's strange how quickly light can change things. Just a few hours ago, I couldn't even breathe without feeling like the world was caving in. And now, it's just ... quiet. The same forest, but somehow softer.

A bird tweets nearby, then another, and soon more join in. I close my eyes, letting the chorus pull me back to happy childhood memories. For a moment, I let myself believe I'm okay. Just breathing. Just listening.

Then the music stops.

'No, no, no,' I whisper, almost without realising it. 'Just once more.' The words sound silly as soon as they leave my mouth. I am sure birds don't take requests.

For the next few seconds, there's only silence. Then, out of nowhere, a bright, sweet melody cuts through the air. I look up and spot it—the most beautiful bird I've ever seen. Its head a shade of soft blue, its body a mix of red and rust, white feathers standing upright like a tiny crown. Maybe this one rules this part of the forest.

It sings again a couple of times, then goes quiet, leaving the forest—and me—hanging in a silence that feels cruel.

I try imitating its call. Hoping it would answer. It doesn't.

Grandpa never had that problem. The birds always answered him. They would even go back and forth as if they were having an actual conversation.

'You're a magician,' I'd say.

'Anyone can do it if their heart is pure,' he'd reply. 'But it only really works when their heart is at peace.'

I cup my hands and whistle again, doing my best to calm my mind by focusing on the leaves rustling around me. I wait, imagining the wind carrying my call to every hidden bird. But after a minute, nothing. I whistle once more, hoping for even a single reply. Still nothing.

Maybe I don't have Grandpa's magic. Maybe I'm nowhere near at peace. No surprises there.

I pack my tent first, then my bag. A few crushed pills lie where the tent's entrance was—last night's mess staring back at me. I look at them for a moment, then brush the dirt over them. I can't use them now. Hopefully, I won't need to.

I lift my heavy backpack over my shoulders and start walking. It's easier this time—no half-dead flashlight, no eerie shadows, no panic rising at every sound. Just light and quiet.

The trees ahead are bathed in gold, the mist still clinging low to the ground. I take out my phone and click a picture—a quiet reminder that mornings like this can exist, even after nights like that.

Just then, I notice the battery level: 15 per cent. I must've forgotten to switch off the torch. Thankfully, the OS killed it at twenty. Thank you to whoever wrote that piece of code.

The messed-up part? The power bank's dead too.

My phone's still searching for a network. And before the battery gives up, I need to find a spot with a decent signal.

I need to know where I'm going next.

I kick a small stone resting on the edge of the road. It skids forward, rolling unevenly, and I jog after it.

What could she be doing right now? If she were like my classmates, she'd still be asleep, her phone clutched in her hand after a night of scrolling through reels, or maybe recovering from a hangover.

But from the way she writes, from the little glimpses on her feed, I know that she isn't like them. She's unlike anyone I've ever known.

I kick the pebble again, watching it bounce ahead before stopping near the bend. She would probably be scaling a mountain, capturing the morning light over the forest with her brush, or planning her next adventure.

Or maybe she's off on one of those medical camps she posts about.

Being an engineering student, I have no idea what a medical student's life looks like. Do they too, like us, have endless assignments? The kind that make you write pages upon pages until your hand starts to hurt instead of actually learning something useful?

That'd be weird. Imagine a doctor who's mugged up exactly how many millilitres of medicine to administer, but has never actually held a syringe. Or doesn't even know how to find the right vein.

Up ahead, the road curves around a patch of bare earth, all the green stripped away, like the mountain's lost a piece of itself.

A landslide, maybe. It looks like someone took a brush dipped in brown paint and dragged it across a perfect green canvas.

It's a sad sight, like the mountain's been hurt. And even though I wish I could help it—from one broken thing to another—there is nothing I can do. I barely know how to fix myself.

Then something catches my eye—thin green blades pushing up through the mess. Tiny plants growing here and there. It's like the mountain is healing, slowly, one inch at a time.

I wonder how long it took to get this far; and how much longer until the scar disappears completely.

Healing, even for nature, seems to take forever.

Is it the same for us? Do we heal with time, too? I kick another pebble next to me. I hate not knowing the answer.

I hate not knowing if I'll ever heal, if it's even possible. And I hate how I'm pinning all my hopes on this trip to heal me.

I kick another pebble. It rolls off the edge, disappearing down the slope. That's when I remember I have had this conversation with her before.

I scroll through my phone, dim the brightness to save battery, and find the screenshot.

Me: *Do you think people can heal?*

I'd sent it one evening out of nowhere.

She'd replied an hour later. That's what I liked about her—she never ghosted. She wasn't like those people who thought disappearing or not replying makes them look cool.

Her: *They can.*

Me: *A lot of people say some wounds never heal. That sometimes, no matter how hard you try, you just can't move on with your life. That getting back up is impossible.*

She went quiet for a while. I thought maybe I said too much. Then her message popped up.

Her: *I've heard that too. Too often. But trust me when I say this—wounds do heal. Sometimes completely. Sometimes just enough to teach us how to live alongside them.*

And you know what, Arjun? Time helps. Even the oldest scars fade, eventually.

I remember typing back slowly:

Me: *I hope they do.*

Her reply came almost instantly.

Her: *They do. They will. But, Arjun, most people give up on healing too soon.*

They stop believing in it. They convince themselves they'll never be whole again.

Things break us, I know. One moment we're laughing, and the next, everything's gone. The whole world comes crashing down, and we think we'll never rise again—not with the weight of it on our back.

But we do.

The problem is that many times we keep wishing things would go back to how they were, not realising the universe is trying to send us something new—a new way to live, to see, to grow. And when we don't accept the new things coming our way, that's when the healing stops.

Her: *To heal, you have to stay open to new positive experiences—to small joys, to new beginnings, to the idea that life can still be kind. Because healing doesn't mean going back to who you were. It means learning to live again as a new version of yourself.*

I stared at the screen, rereading her words, not sure how to respond. Then, before I could even type anything, another message came in.

Gosh, I'm sorry if that sounded too heavy. I just ... hope it helped.

It had. That night, I'd managed to sleep without the anxiety closing in.

My phone starts chiming, notifications flooding the screen. First, a ton of WhatsApp messages—birthday wishes for someone in the class group. Then there are messages from the student council group, probably about an event I should be helping with. I'm shocked they haven't kicked me out of both yet.

Mixed in are texts from random brands I don't even remember signing up for, offering discounts on things I don't need. WhatsApp spam—just what I need. I swipe those away without a second thought.

But no messages from her. My stomach tightens. Did she forget?

I'm about to give up when I see it—a notification from Instagram. My heart skips. 'Four new messages from @super.birdie.' I open the app quickly, but the messages don't load right away.

The screen stays frozen on my last message: the simple 'Thank you for the gifts ...' My fingers tap the edge of the phone impatiently, and I curse under my breath. Come on. Come on.

I refresh the app, my chest tightening with every second that passes.

I'm glad you liked the gifts, Arjun.

The messages finally appear.

I can't wait to read the stories you'll write someday.

I'm kinda hoping this trek will give you a few to write about.

And always know that I'm rooting for you.

Rooting for me. I lean back against the tree, letting the phrase settle in my chest. How long has it been since someone said that? Since someone genuinely believed in me?

I read the next text.

Oh, before I forget ...

Here's a location link for where you need to go next.

You'll find another letter waiting there.

I stare at the message, a smile tugging at my lips—then my phone dims for a second. And a message pop up:

10 per cent battery remaining.

'Shit!'

Thank you for everything.

When will I get a chance to meet you?

I quickly type out a reply.

My thumb hovers over the 'send' button. *Will she think I'm desperate?* The fleeting thought crosses my mind. But I don't care. I want to meet her. I want to ask her so many things. I want to see the face behind the letters and texts. I hit 'send'.

I open the link she has shared. The location pops up—nearly a two-hour drive from where I am. I need to find a ride.

Yesterday, I waited over an hour, only to end up walking two miles before a bus finally stopped. I hope today will be different.

I finish my second packet of chips and shove the empty wrapper into the side pocket of my bag. No trashing the mountains.

The walk along the endless asphalt road is already wearing me down—my legs are aching, my throat feels dry, and there's still no sign of a ride. Just as I'm lowering my bottle after a long sip, an engine rumbles behind me. My head snaps up.

It's a pickup truck. I wave my arm in a frantic 'lift please' gesture, but it speeds past before I even have a chance to be noticed. 'Damn it,' I mutter under my breath, watching it grow smaller in the distance.

But then, something miraculous happens. The truck slows down, coming to a gradual stop a few metres ahead.

For a moment, I can't believe it. A hand appears from the driver's window, waving me over. I fumble to shove my water bottle into my bag and sprint towards the truck with every ounce of energy I can gather.

'Where you headed?' the driver asks, his voice casual, matching his clean-shaven face and the easy-going vibe he gives off.

I'm panting so hard I have to wait a second before answering.

'Hop in,' he says with a wide smile. 'Going there myself to collect some supplies.'

'Thank you ... really.' I'm still catching my breath. Even running a few steps with this bag feels like dragging a cart full of rocks. I open the door, and my eyes catch a local newspaper sprawled across the passenger seat, with a stainless-steel tiffin box perched on top.

'Sorry for the mess,' he says, before quickly clearing it away, making room. 'I don't usually have passengers.'

I smile, thanking him again as I get in.

The cab smells of sandalwood, courtesy of incense sticks wedged near the AC vents—the scent strong but pleasant.

The driver turns the key. The engine sputters, coughs and then dies.

'She's an old girl,' he says with an apologetic grin. 'Throws tantrums now and then, but once her drama's done, she listens. Watch this.' He strokes the dashboard affectionately, almost as if coaxing a pet. 'Come on, baby. Don't embarrass me in front of our new friend.'

He tries again. Nothing.

'Okay, I'm sorry. I am sorry that I called you an old girl, and I promise I won't wake you up so early next time. Happy now?' He mutters an exaggerated apology, almost like he's talking to a moody partner. On the third try, the engine roars to life.

'See?' He glances at me triumphantly. 'She just likes to act out. But it's my fault. I'm the one who spoils her. No eating inside, cleaning her up daily, new tyres every year, fresh oil all the time. And still, she troubles me.'

The truck jolts over a rough patch in the road, making me grab the handle above the door for balance.

'Whoa, girl!' he exclaims, gripping the wheel tighter. 'No need to be so mean to me.'

I can't help it—I laugh. It's the kind of laugh that escapes in spurts because the ride is so bumpy.

'She's offended,' I say between chuckles.

'Like a newlywed bride,' he replies. 'Always upset over the tiniest things. But hey—sorry again, okay?' He directs his apology to the truck, blowing a kiss, which grumbles as if forgiving him.

As the road smooths out, I let go of the handle and sink into the seat. The truck settles into a steady pace, and the ride feels less chaotic.

'I'm Rishabh, by the way.'

'Arjun,' I reply.

'So, what do you do, Arjun?' he asks, glancing at me briefly before focusing back on the road.

'Engineering. Third year,' I say. There's something oddly fascinating about Rishabh—his carefree demeanour, the way he talks to his truck like it's alive.

'Good. Starting to travel young, then. I keep telling my nephews to get out and explore, but they'd rather stay home playing those shooting games on their phone.'

'Haha, thanks,' I reply, hesitant to admit that this wasn't my idea.

'Been a while since I've seen a solo traveller around here,' he says after a pause. 'Usually, you guys are in groups.'

I nod, trying to avoid the sympathy that usually comes with being alone. 'I started solo, but I've got a group waiting for me at the next stop.'

'Good call. Some things are better experienced alone,' he says, then adds, 'but some moments happen only when you're around people. They can change you, give you a new perspective.'

I nod again, hating myself for lying.

'Mind if I charge my phone?' I ask, noticing the dangling wire near the dashboard.

'Go ahead,' he says, handing it over. Relief washes over me as the charging icon flashes to life on my screen.

He turns on the radio.

The RJ talks about the beauty of songs from the '70s and '80s, and soon a few old classics of Lata Mangeshkar and Mohammed Rafi start playing. It's a lovely vibe—beautiful songs, the hum of the engine, the road stretching endlessly ahead, and Rishabh singing along to every word.

Then Kishore Kumar's *Ek Ajnabee Haseena Se* begins, and Rishabh's face lights up.

'Ah, this song. Classic!' he exclaims. 'You know this one?'

'Yeah. But I don't know the complete lyrics.' I've always loved old songs—their lyrics have meaning, emotion. They tell stories. Not like most of the modern ones that are made just for the sake of going viral on reels.

'Who cares? Give it a try,' he urges.

I resist at first, but his enthusiasm is infectious. I sing a few lines—just the chorus—but it feels good, freeing even, to sing with a stranger on an unfamiliar road.

When the song ends, Rishabh glances at me, a wistful smile on his face. 'This song reminds me of something ... someone, actually.'

I lean forward slightly, sensing a story coming.

'Of a girl from foreign lands,' he says, his voice softening. 'I was driving once—just like this, this very song playing on the radio—and I gave a lift to a group of foreigners. There were six of them, all from different countries. But one of them, the girl who sat right where you are now ... she was the prettiest woman I'd ever seen.'

I lean forward, intrigued. A story like this isn't something you stumble upon every day.

'She was Italian,' Rishabh continues, navigating a bend in the road with care. 'She had these piercing blue eyes that hypnotised me the moment I looked at her. And tattoos—her whole arm was covered in them, disappearing under her clothes. I couldn't stop staring, though I tried to be polite about it.' He chuckles at the memory.

'They needed a ride to a town a few hours away, and I told myself, "Forget work for today." Dad yelled at me for months afterward. But you know what? I didn't care. I was a man in love—or at least something close to it.'

He glances at me, a playful twinkle in his eye. 'You ever done something crazy for a girl? Just dropped everything because you couldn't wait another second to see her?'

I shake my head, the truth spilling out before I can stop it. 'No.'

'Don't say no, kid. Say "Not yet". One day, you might meet someone who makes everything else fade away, someone who makes you feel like being with her is the only thing that matters.'

'Anyway, we spent five days together,' he continues. 'We went everywhere we could, climbed every hill in sight, and stole moments just to be near each other. I struggled to understand her words, and she had a hard time with mine. But we kept listening to each other. She held my hand for support during climbs, and I went crazy feeling the softness of her touch. By the third day, I knew I had fallen in love with her. By that evening, she had kissed me, and by the night, we had made love under the stars thrice.'

I blink. Once. Twice.

There's something in the way he says it—like it's no big deal. Like that kind of thing just ... happens. I look out the window, not sure what to say, or if I'm even supposed to say anything at all.

Rishabh laughs, producing a deep, hearty sound. 'So sorry, I tend to over share.'

I manage a small smile. I don't know what to say. But somewhere inside me, a quiet voice whispers, *I want something like that someday*. A love that feels like an adventure. A love worth leaving everything behind for.

'She came back to India once after that,' he adds a while later, his tone sad. 'Just to see me. But a few years later, she got married, and that was that. Life moves on, you know?'

I just nod, keeping my eyes on the road. My chest feels heavy. I don't know why, but I was rooting for them. Maybe because I want to believe stories like theirs get happy endings.

'Why am I telling you this?' Rishabh leans back in his seat, his hands relaxed on the wheel. 'Because anything can happen when you travel. You meet people who change your life. Maybe forever, sometimes just for a while. And sometimes, a while is enough. Don't be afraid to take risks, kid. Fall in love. Sing with strangers. Make mistakes. That's what makes life worth living.'

Take risks ... Fall in love ... Make mistakes ...

I keep replaying his words in my mind. He's stirred something in me, deep down. Something that feels like a quiet nudge, telling me to be open to experiences, to make the most of this trail Birdie has put me on.

Anything can happen when you travel.

If that's the case ...

I glance out the window, the passing scenery blurring into shades of green and brown.

Then maybe ... just maybe ... there's still hope for me.

For the first time in a long time, I feel like I'm exactly where I'm supposed to be: on a road that helps me meet people who have lived and known life a little more than me.

6

The letters 'T&T' are carved in cursive on the dark wooden board above the glass door. Just below the letters is the full form, 'Trails and Traditions'. I am right where she asked me to be.

Looking back, I can vaguely see the spot where Rishabh dropped me. My eyes almost make me believe this was an easy climb. But my sore back and tired legs assure me that it wasn't.

I drop onto one of the wooden tables outside the store. There's a big open space around it, with picnic-style benches scattered here and there. Not too far away, some stones are arranged in a circle—blackened with soot, half-burnt logs still in the centre. Someone had a bonfire here. Not too long ago.

I take off my backpack, feeling the burn where the straps had dug into my shoulders.

I should go to the counter. Ask if someone there knows Birdie. If she has left anything for me. But my legs feel too heavy. My whole body does.

I decide it can wait a few more minutes.

I lean back, looking up at the leaves overhead. I watch them sway and twist in the wind, sunlight slipping through like it's playing hide-and-seek.

And slowly, without meaning to, I start to drift.

'Helloooo.'

'Hey. Can you help me here?'

Someone is calling out.

'Hello?'

It takes me a second to realise ... They're talking to me.

Still half-asleep, I turn my head towards the voice without lifting it fully. At the far end of the store, I spot a tall guy in a greasy grey shirt, sleeves rolled up.

He's looking right at me. 'Hey, can you lend me a hand?'

'Su—sure!' I call out, pushing myself up. Every muscle in my body protests.

'Sorry to disturb your little nap,' he says, scratching his thick beard. He's got a rugged look—hair tied into a bun, strong jawline, the kind of guy who probably chops firewood just for fun.

'It's nothing. I just sat down,' I reply. Total lie. I'm sure my face still has sleep written all over it. But I try to smile anyway. 'Really, not a big deal.'

He nods, returning the smile. 'Thanks, boy.'

I walk over to him. As I get closer, something shifts. His eyes widen, and he just ... stares. Doesn't blink. Doesn't speak. His gaze slowly moves across my face, as if trying to figure something out.

Do I have something on my face?

'Umm ... you needed help?' I say, trying to break the awkward silence.

'Oh—yeah, yes,' he snaps out of it, wiping his hands on a stained cloth. 'Just back here, if you could follow me.'

Without another word, he turns and starts walking towards the back of the store. I have no idea what just happened. But whatever it was, he does not seem okay.

I follow. For someone who must be in his mid-forties, he is well-built, with wide shoulders, and walks way faster than me. I have to practically jog to keep up.

A few seconds in, he slows down. Just enough to let me catch up.

He glances over—and for a moment, his eyes linger on me.

He doesn't speak. Just stares for a beat, then offers a faint smile.

It feels off. Not unfriendly—just like there's something behind it. Something I can't quite read.

Then he turns and walks on.

We stop at the back of the store—built like a wooden cabin—where a small farm stretches out, roughly the size of two or three mini trucks parked side-by-side, with plants of the same kind grouped together.

Thanks to all the time I spent with Grandpa when I was a child, I can name almost all the plants that are here, even though many of them are not laden yet. Tomatoes, cucumbers, ladyfingers, potatoes, brinjals and more.

'My ... uh, my wife. She likes to save money wherever possible,' the man says, noticing me looking around. His voice is deep and gravelly. I catch him staring again. But he quickly looks away.

It's starting to feel ... weird.

He clears his throat, 'One day ... well, she—my wife—came back from the market furious about a merchant who charged her more than usual. She went on and on about it all night.'

He speaks warmly, eyes fixed on the neat rows of vegetables as if he's reading the story from the leaves. 'The next morning, she decided she was going to grow the crops herself.'

He picks up a bottle of oil lying on the ground, turning it over in his hands.

'I didn't think she would if I am being honest,' he continues. 'But a day later, she was reading up on how to grow vegetables and the nutrients they need.' He laughs then, a genuine sound that slightly dissolves the awkwardness. His eyes meet mine, shining with pride. 'And it's been three years since we've been eating mostly what we grow.'

'She's done a great job, really,' I say, noticing how there are no dry leaves or dead plants and how the farm is free from any weeds. 'Back home, we also have a garden and a small farm. We have people to look after it, but I always liked working in it.'

'That's nice,' he says, guiding me into a large garage with its wooden door already open. A strong odour of oil and grease welcomes me inside.

'Some people are naturally drawn to the wild. For example, I fell in love with the mountains when I was just a child in primary school. I used to bunk my classes and wander in these valleys. My parents hated that,' he says with a laugh. 'You wouldn't believe it, but my dad used to actually run behind me with a stick, to force me to go to the school. But I never listened.'

I find myself picturing him—not the broad-shouldered man with a deep voice standing in front of me, but a small, stubborn boy darting through the trees as his father trailed behind with a stick.

I let out a small laugh.

The man's eyes crinkle at the corners, his own smile widening. He seems relieved, as if my laugh was the sound he'd been waiting to hear.

'Aye, he had a good arm, too. Almost never caught me, though,' he says, his voice losing its awkwardness. He shakes his head, a distant memory flickering across his face.

'But on the rare days he did ... well, I'd rather not think about that part.' He lets out a full, hearty laugh, the sound bouncing off the wooden walls of the garage.

I laugh with him. There's something funny about it—this broad, strong man still flinching at the memory of a childhood beating.

We pass a wall lined with tools and wrenches, each one arranged with almost obsessive precision—looking damn cool.

But my jaw actually drops when I see him kneeling in front of a bike.

It's a regular commuter, or at least it used to be. Now it's been modified so much that I can't even tell the brand. A large windshield towers in front—something I've never seen on a bike before. Saddlebags hang on both sides, and even the rims look custom.

'Wow.' The word slips out before I can stop it.

He looks up, eyes glinting with pride.

'Did a lot of work on this one,' he says, doing some adjustments near the engine. 'She helped me get out of the most difficult times of my life.'

I walk around the bike, not being able to stop admiring its condition. While I don't own a bike, Anurag used to let me drive his bike sometimes. He even forcefully took me to a bike rally during the annual function. He needed someone to hold the black flag he had created, which had a skull painted on it. He was sure it was going to help him get a girl—it hadn't.

I keep admiring the bike. I've never seen one in such great shape—no scratches, no dirt spots, and shining as if it's brand new.

He lets out a victorious groan, drawing my attention. 'This might do.'

'Can you do me a favour and kick-start it for me?' he asks. I nod and shift to the other side.

'Just wait for my signal,' he says, crouching on the other side of the bike. I see him fiddling with something near the cylinder head—probably the spark plug.

'Now.'

With the clutch pressed between my fingers, I kick the starter. The bike comes to life with a thunderous roar, and then, with a dying groan, goes back to sleep.

'No problem,' he says, doing some adjustments near the engine, which I can't see from this angle. 'Just try it again.'

I place my foot on the starter and kick it. The bike roars to life, and when I turn the accelerator on high, it feels like I'm taming a wild animal eager to leap on its prey.

'You see how desperate she is to run free?' he says proudly, his eyes gleaming and his chest puffed out.

'She wants to fly,' I say, feeling the vibrations and turning the accelerator on high just to hear the loud noise.

'She seems like you,' he says. 'And you should take it for a ride.'

I hesitate. I've ridden before, but this is someone else's bike—and in *this* condition? The last thing I want is to risk scratching it.

'Oh, don't overthink now, boy,' he says, his voice flooding with energy and enthusiasm. 'Take it for a spin. She wants you to.'

I nod, being unable to resist my smile.

He steps back, giving me space. I climb onto the bike, feeling its weight settle beneath me, my fingers wrapping around the handlebars.

'You ready?' he asks as I fasten the helmet.

'More than ever,' I say with a grin and kick-start the engine.

'That's the manly way to do it,' he laughs. 'Never liked those button-start ones. Now, I'm sure you know this, but just in case—first gear down, the rest up.'

I nod. It's just like Anurag's bike. Shifting down to first, I ease off the clutch. The machine surges forward with a deep, throaty roar.

I take it slow, steering towards the front of the shop. He jogs a few steps behind, cheering me on.

The thrill begins to build, washing away the hesitation. I circle the open space, careful to avoid the benches.

Then I hear him shout, 'Take her to the highway! Let her run wild!'

I am happy to oblige. I turn downhill. The road opens up before me. I shift gears, release the clutch, and let the bike glide on its own.

Wind whips through my hair; my shirt flutters like I have wings. The rush of adrenaline makes my heart race, urging me to go faster. But it's not my bike, and as tempting as it is, I hold back. He probably wouldn't mind—he'd probably *want* me to—but honestly, I'm just happy I even got the chance to ride it.

I shift gears again, smoother this time. Around the next curve, a group of kids is crouching on the road, playing marbles. I press the horn urgently, and they scatter, laughing as I pass.

Reaching the base of the hill, I make a sharp U-turn, wind cutting against my face. That's when it hits me—I've just crossed off something from my bucket list: riding solo on a hill.

I let out a shout of pure joy, not caring about the few heads that turn my way.

Grinning, I ease off the throttle and ride back towards the store, the engine humming steady beneath me.

'Hurray!' he shouts, clapping wildly, his enthusiasm contagious. I pull the bike to a stop in front of him and turn off the ignition.

'So, how was the ride?' he asks, raising his hand for a high five.

'Liberating,' I reply, meeting his palm with a solid clap. My heart is still racing, adrenaline coursing through me. 'Never driven on a hill before.'

He gives me a warm smile and a heavy pat on the back. 'That's the thing about life, boy,' he says, in his deep voice. 'Just when you think you've seen it all, it finds a way to surprise you.'

'So, how can I help you?' he asks as he pushes the bike back into the garage and puts it on the stand. I had completely forgotten about Birdie and why I am here.

'Umm ... actually, Birdie sent me. My name is Arjun.' The man freezes, his hand holding the key only halfway to his pocket. A look of sudden realisation crosses his face. He smiles briefly, his eyes holding back so many emotions. For a moment, I think he is going to hug me. He takes a good look at me and says, 'I should've guessed.'

'Did she tell you I would come?'

'She mentioned you before leaving yesterday,' he says. My heart sinks at that. If I had been here just a day earlier, I would have been able to meet her. Or maybe I still can, if I manage to leave early.

'Arjun,' he repeats my name under his breath, slowly.

'Yes, sir. That's me.'

'Don't call me sir,' he says quickly, a hint of warmth in his voice. 'You can call me Sharma Uncle, like Birdie does.'

'Okay, Sharma Uncle,' I repeat. He smiles and then we walk towards the benches in silence. He insists on helping me carry my bag inside.

As I enter the store, I notice a Tibetan praying flag hanging on the door which moves as the wind comes in.

We leave the bag at the counter. The store is bigger than I had thought from outside. To my left, there is a neatly arranged display of camping gear, tents, sleeping bags, hiking boots and backpacks. There are racks filled with woollen socks, gloves and hats, perfect for all those who travel farther north and encounter chilly nights.

To my right, there is a section dedicated to local handicrafts. There are colourful rugs on display along with some beautiful purses made of hemp, some shawls as well as some beautiful stoles and scarves. I'm sure my sister would fall in love with all of this. I make a mental note to ask her to visit the store.

I move further inside, taking in everything neatly arranged on the racks. One corner feels almost like a mini-museum—Tibetan artefacts displayed on wooden shelves, intricately carved prayer wheels, mandala paintings, Buddha statues, and prayer flags covered in Tibetan symbols.

I stop next to a rack. Some beautiful leather diaries line the shelf, same as the one Birdie gave me. There are three or four sets. Diaries in each set have similar designs, created by using small knife to carve out the detailed patterns and images.

'My wife has the skills for that,' Sharma Uncle says. I hadn't even noticed him standing behind him.

'She gave me one. I mean Birdie gave me a similar diary,' I tell him, shuffling through the diaries, trying to find one that resembles the one she gave me. But there is none. None of them carry any pattern similar to the one I have.

'She did?' The man seems surprised. 'Well, she has always loved art. When she was a kid, she would sit with my wife for hours, trying to mimic everything she created. And now, when she shows me something she has created, I can't help but feel like she's even surpassed my wife. She is too possessive about the things she creates, though.' He guides me towards the counter. 'And you should count yourself really lucky if she gave you one.'

'I do count myself lucky,' I say, running my hand over the cover of a diary, feeling all the grooves and the cuts that make the elaborate design. 'And hey, your wife is a great artist too.'

'Would you like to tell her that directly?' he asks, quite eagerly.

'I would love to,' I reply. Even though I really want to ask him about Birdie and if she has left anything, I stop myself. I know how much it means to artists when someone compliments their art.

'I'll be back,' Sharma Uncle says and disappears through a door behind the counter.

I unlock my phone and see dozens of unread texts from my sister. She doesn't know what happened—no one does.

I had given the wrong address and phone number to my college. Hopefully, they haven't managed to reach my parents.

I had informed Mom and Dad's personal assistant about this solo trip, though. I didn't want them to hear about it from someone else and turn it into chaos.

At least they don't know where I am. I didn't tell them. And honestly, I don't think they'd even care.

I call my sister. Barely two rings—one and a half, to be precise—and she picks up, her voice slicing through the speaker like a sharp needle.

For the next few minutes, her frantic mix of worry and anger pounds in my ears. I'm pretty sure I'm about to go deaf.

When she finally stops to breathe, I seize the moment.

'Don't panic,' I say, though I know it won't work. Predictably, she starts shouting again. When she pauses to breathe this time, I quickly lie, telling her I'm with a professional travel group—eight to ten people, with three experienced guides who won't let anything happen to me. 'Please don't worry, Di. I really need this trip,' I add, using my most desperate voice.

It works—just a tiny bit.

She makes me tell her where I am. I beg her not to share my location with Mom and Dad. She agrees—but only if I promise to call her every single day.

Argh. We negotiate like lawyers and finally settle on once every two days. I know I have to agree; if I don't, she'll probably show up here herself before I even go to bed tonight.

After listening to her endless instructions on safety, I end the call with 'I love you, Di. You're the best sister in the entire world.' Which I hope will be enough for her to manage things with Mom and Dad, if they go wrong.

My stomach growls. I haven't eaten anything today apart from the chips in the morning and I am famished.

I turn. Sharma Uncle is waiting for me at the counter.

'I'm really sorry to keep you waiting.' I push the glass door open to enter. 'It was my sister. She was worried.'

'Family comes first.' He gives an *I-can-understand* smile, and just as he does, the backdoor opens and a lady wearing a red shawl over her white kurta and salwar comes out. She has oval eyes, a long face and her cheeks are accentuated with high cheekbones.

'Meet my beautiful wife, Tenzin, the goddess behind all things beautiful you can find in this store.' He plants a kiss on her cheek.

'Oh, stop that, Tarun,' she says, turning her face away. It took just one compliment from her husband and her pale cheeks have turned red. 'He keeps doing that,' she says, looking at me for the first time, and when she does, her eyes stay frozen on my face.

'You ... y ... you seem ...' The colour drains from her cheeks, turning her face even more pale as if she's seen a ghost.

'Familiar, yes!' Sharma Uncle says, cutting her off and wrapping his arm around her shoulder, rubbing it gently. 'He's the same guy Birdie said would join us today. See how perfectly she described him? My thoughts were the same as yours when I saw him. She painted such a vivid picture that it feels like we've seen him before.'

Sharma Aunty's lips are trembling, and she is looking at me without blinking. Something isn't right.

'Yes ... familiar,' Sharma Aunty says, her soft voice quivering. 'That's ... that's what I meant. Birdie told us about you. And ... and ... welcome to Trails and Traditions.'

'Thank you,' I reply, pretending as if I didn't see her hide her trembling hands under her shawl.

There is a thick silence in the air.

'Arjun wanted to compliment you on your designs he found in the store,' Sharma Uncle says, breaking the silence.

'Yes!' I had completely forgotten about it. 'They are really pretty. I mean all of them. One of these diaries has those flowers carved on it and it is the most beautiful thing I have ever seen. I can't even imagine just how long it must have taken you to complete it.'

'Thank you for your kind words, son,' Sharma Aunty says, 'but it was nothing.'

'Oh, don't be modest,' Sharma Uncle says, 'For pieces like that, she works for like tens of hours. She could get away by doing those minimalistic designs. But no, she doesn't. She keeps taking time and makes sure there are finer details that a non-artistic eye can't even notice. But that's my wife for you. She just can't help but make things beautiful.'

'You are too much, you know that?' Sharma Aunty says blushing, the colour slowly returning to her face.

'Yes, I am. I am too much in love with you,' Sharma Uncle brings her palm close to his lips and kisses it.

I look away for a second, heat rising to my face.

'I'm sorry for his behaviour, son,' Sharma Aunty says, freeing her hand and hugging him from the side. 'He's crazy.'

'If crazy is what this world calls lovers these days, then I am crazy,' he replies.

'Stop it! You're embarrassing me,' she gives him a gentle push. 'It's been twenty-four years since our marriage, and he's still the same.'

'You're insulting me by saying that. I'm not the same. I love you more every year we spend together,' Sharma Uncle says, and the way they look at each other makes me feel like I am in some romantic Bollywood movie.

'You two look beautiful together,' I compliment them. And I mean it. I try to remember if my parents have ever been this good. They haven't. Not that I've spent any time with them together in the last decade.

'Thank you. And you have beautiful eyes, son,' she says, raising her hand and bringing it closer to my face. Her palm is just inches away when Sharma Uncle gently holds it and brings it down.

Things were just starting to feel less weird.

'I'm ... I'm sorry. Did he offer you any food or drinks yet?' she continues without waiting for my answer. 'Tarun! You really don't have any manners left in you,' she says, slapping Sharma Uncle's arm. I'm sure it must have hurt, but from his expression, I can tell he's very much used to it.

'Come inside, son. Have something to eat. You must be hungry,' Sharma Aunty says, and my stomach growls again.

I want to ask if there was any message from Birdie, but for now, I'm just really hungry, and some food would be really nice.

Sharma Uncle stumbles as his wife pushes him aside and guides me into the house through the backdoor. He doesn't even complain, just laughs.

I remove my shoes near the door. The house is bathed in natural light, thanks to the big windows along the walls opposite the entrance. Prayer flags hang across them, fluttering gently. We walk past the living area. Cream sofas. A wooden coffee table with a few books and a vase of fresh flowers. A light rug that blends with the room.

Opposite the sofas, there is a small bronze statue of Buddha, surrounded by incense holders. There are also a few indoor plants scattered around the house—one just beside the statue, another near the sofas, and a bigger one by the window.

This place is way more beautiful than I expected. And all of it proves what Sharma Uncle had said earlier: 'That's my wife for you. She just can't help but make things beautiful.'

Sharma Uncle says he'll show me a room to freshen up. Aunty nods, tells me to rest, to feel at home, and that she'll make something for me to eat. I thank her. Sharma Uncle then leads me down the hall. To a room that used to belong to their son.

He tells me to get some rest, points me to the bathroom if I want to take a shower, and leaves.

I definitely need a shower and would love it more than anything else right now.

The room inside carries the same warm, aesthetic vibes as the hall. To my right is a bookshelf stacked with novels—many by my favourite authors. Whoever Sharma Uncle's son is, he has surely got a great taste in books.

Near the shelf, a few framed photos catch my eye. Most are family pictures—Uncle, Aunty, and their son through different stages of his life. Him in a graduation gown. Him in front of his college gate. Him as a kid in school uniform. Him hiking with his parents.

There's something about these pictures that pulls me in, maybe because they remind me of what I never had. A family that's there for each other.

Then one photo stands out. A black-and-white one. It's different from the others. There are two couples in hiking gear. I recognise Sharma Uncle and Aunty from their younger days. Sharma Uncle looks as well-built as he does now, and Mrs Sharma ... she looks even more beautiful. I haven't seen many films from Northeast India, but she looks like she could have easily been a lead actress in one. They have their son with them, barely five or six years old.

Beside them is another couple, the woman holding a child in her arms. I wonder who they are. Their little girl is wearing a floral dress and has one of the brightest, happiest smiles I've ever seen—the kind that pulls your attention without even trying.

I don't think I've ever felt as good as I do when I lie on the bed. My whole body sinks into the mattress, grateful for the rest. I close my eyes and let the day replay in my head.

I can still feel the bike beneath me, the wind tearing through my hair, the road opening up like it belonged to me. I can see Sharma Uncle's face lighting up when I rode back, the way he high-fived me like we'd been friends for years.

I'm never going to forget today. I'm sure of it.

But ... but why did Sharma Aunty react the way she did when she saw me? And even Sharma Uncle looked shocked the first time he saw me. They're both so nice—too nice, actually. And the problem with that is, no one really is.

The notification tone of my phone snaps me out of my thoughts. I pick it up, and there are two new messages from @super.birdie. I quickly open Instagram, my heart skipping a beat.

'Soon, maybe.' She has replied to my 'When am I seeing you?' message. Soon? What does soon mean? Today, tomorurow, in an hour? When?

There's another text below that.

'Could you please do me a favour and stay with Sharma Uncle and Aunty for a day?

It would mean a lot to me if you could.'

Why?—I want to ask her. But after everything she's done for me, I don't. If this is important to her, then it's the least I can do.

'Sure. You didn't even have to say please,' I reply.

Before I can send another message, another text notification pops up on my screen. It's from Shree, one of my closest friends in college.

'How could you do it, Arjun?! I didn't want to text you, but I couldn't sit comfortably, not having confronted a monster like you.'

'I haven't done anything, Shree. You have to trust me.' I type back, my fingers trembling slightly. I'm sure she will trust me. After Anurag, she was the only one I felt closest to.

The animated typing indicator appears, and my heart starts racing. I need her to say she believes me. That she doesn't believe the lies. She keeps typing, taking way longer than she should. My heartbeat quickens with each passing moment. Then the animation disappears. She's no longer typing.

'You have to trust me.' I type again with trembling hands, my anxiety creeping in. I hit send, praying she'll respond. She wouldn't be like the others. She wouldn't judge me without hearing me out. She knows what kind of a person I am. I know she'll listen.

And then the reply comes in.

'You disgust me, Arjun.'

The phone slips from my hand. The world stops. Everything goes silent, and tears start gathering in my eyes, making everything blurry. I can't believe what I'm reading.

After everything we've been through?

After all the times she chose me to talk to when she thought no one would understand?

After all the times she thanked me for being there for her in her lows?

After all those times ... she has chosen to trust them instead of even asking me what really happened.

I try to pick up the phone, but my hands are shaking too much. I wipe my tears, trying to pull myself together. I have to make her understand.

'How could you say something like that? You know me.'

'Truth is the hardest thing to digest, Arjun.'

'Please, I can explain everything.'

'Really? What's left to explain! I'm just happy I got to know who you really are.'

Tears fall from my eyes, blurring the last words of her text. How could she think that? How could she just turn on me like this?

I open her contact and tap on the call button. She has to pick up. I need her to hear me out. She has to understand. She's the only one who can.

My heart pounds in my chest, each beat echoing the panic rising in me. I dig my nails into my leg to stop it from shaking, to distract myself from the pain in my chest.

Please, Shree, just pick up. Pick the damn phone. *Please!*

The call connects, but it rings only once before she disconnects. I hit the call button again, desperately hoping she'll pick up this time. But again, it rings once and she disconnects. The pain in my chest intensifies, like a thousand needles stabbing me at once. There's a message on the screen. I can't see it through my tears. I wipe my eyes, focusing hard to read the words.

'I'm blocking you, Arjun. No matter what you say, nothing will justify what you did. I hate choosing someone like you to be friends with. Don't show me your face ever again!

'Bye.'

'Shree, don't do this. Pls just hear me once.'

I quickly type and send.

There is no *seen* written below the text. I tap on her profile.

Instagram User.

The phone slips from my hand, clattering to the floor. I grab my head with both hands, trying to steady myself, but the spinning won't stop. Not Shree. Not her too.

She knows me. She was supposed to listen.

I didn't do anything. I didn't do anything. *I didn't!*

I try to stand, to make my way to my bag where my pills are. My knees give out, and I collapse, losing all sense of direction. The tears blur everything, and my chest tightens with each rapid, uneven breath. My heart pounds so hard it feels like it's going to burst. My head throbs like it's caught in a vise, every beat of my pulse adding to the pressure.

I curl up on the cold tiles, pulling my legs tightly to my chest.

Just let me explain. Just listen to me.

Why won't anyone ask me what really happened? Why won't anyone give me a chance to speak?

Flashes of that day float in front of my eyes. Anurag is pushing me and punching me, accusing me of so many things. 'I didn't do it, man! I wouldn't! You are my best friend.'

'Yet you did. You should be ashamed of yourself.'

'I did not! Trust me.'

He punched me hard in the face, and I remember the taste of blood in my mouth.

'I don't want to see your face ever again in my life, Arjun. Get lost.'

'Stop it! Please,' I scream, my voice echoing in my head. I crawl towards my bag, desperately searching for the pills, but they're not there. I open all the pockets, emptying their contents on the floor. They aren't here. I must have left them somewhere last night, but I can't remember where.

Panic surges through me as I lie there, clutching my legs to my chest, feeling the weight of everything crashing down on me.

Just let me explain. Just hear my side of the story.

I close my eyes, trying to shut out the chaos in my mind, but the memories keep coming back to haunt me. Anurag's words replay over and over, each one like a blow to my gut. And now Shree ... Shree, of all people. How could she just believe what they told her without even asking me?

My body starts to tremble uncontrollably. I need to find those pills. I need something to stop this feeling.

But they're not there. They're not anywhere.

A wave of helplessness washes over me, and I sink to the floor, my back against the wall. The room feels like it's closing in on me and I can't breathe.

Nobody asked me. Nobody bothered to know if I really did it.

Tears flow freely down my face as I hug my knees to my chest, rocking back and forth, trying to calm the storm inside. But it's no use.

Why did this happen? How did everything get so messed up? I didn't do anything. But now, it feels like the whole world is against me.

I bury my face in my hands, trying to make sure my sobs do not leave the room.

7

After what feels like forever spent staring blankly at the wall, I finally push myself to get in the shower. Sharma Uncle will probably be here soon and I don't want him to see me like this. I let the cold water run through my hair, my thoughts spiralling as it washes over me.

Shree. Just another name added to the growing list of people who judged and left without knowing the truth. If even the ones closest to me don't believe me, how can I expect anyone else to? How am I supposed to go back to college, walk in the corridors and avoid those stares which look at me as if I am a monster?

I dry myself and change into a grey T-shirt and black tracksuit pants. The room is a mess. The crumpled bed sheet rests in one corner of the bed, and the spilled contents of my bag are scattered on the floor. I straighten the bed sheet, put everything back in my bag, and make sure the room looks exactly like how it was before. I am nowhere close, but I am hoping they won't suspect a thing.

There is a knock on the door.

'Can I enter?' It's Sharma Uncle.

I quickly scan the room again. 'Yes. Please.'

He steps in.

'You ready for lunch? I actually came by earlier, but I heard the shower and figured I would wait.' He is watching me carefully, and I silently pray my eyes aren't too red or swollen from crying.

'Tenzin has been after my head for too long,' he chuckles. 'I am her husband and the woman hasn't even asked me if I'm hungry. She just wants to make sure you are fed, no care for her poor husband.'

We both laugh. 'I'm sorry for taking so long, Uncle. I fell asleep for a bit,' I say, hoping that explains my eyes, 'And then I went for a shower.'

'That's fine. And hey, I know I suggested it earlier, but please no more uncle. Call me Tarun.'

'I will try, Tarun,' I say. It feels weird calling him by his name, since he must be my father's age or something.

He must have sensed the discomfort in my voice, 'You know, Arjun, you can still call me Sharma Uncle if that makes you feel better.'

It does.

'Thanks, Uncle.'

He smiles. 'Now, let's head to the kitchen before Tenzin comes in here, enraged, with flames bursting through her hair, and kills me.'

I can't help but laugh. But when I realise he is actually serious and is terrified of his wife, I just follow him out.

As we pass through the living room, he leans in conspiratorially. 'Just wait until you're married. Then you'll understand the true meaning of fear.'

'Long time for that,' I reply, smiling.

We step into the kitchen. Sharma Aunty is bustling around, her face glowing with happiness, and humming a cheerful tune as she sets up the table. She has a really good voice.

'The food smells incredible,' I say, genuinely appreciating the aroma.

Sharma Aunty looks up at us with her face lit up. 'Oh, thanks. I mean, yes, I hope it's good—I mean, I know the smell is nice, but I hope the food is nice too—I mean I just want you to enjoy it, I haven't really cooked like this in years, to be honest, so, I'm a bit nervous.'

She starts picking up the plates excitedly and nearly drops one, but Sharma Uncle is quick to catch it. 'Got it!' he says, his eyes twinkling as he looks at her. 'Don't worry, I've got it all under control.'

'You always do,' she says, with a warm smile, and takes off her apron while eyeing him with affection.

She feels so different from the version of her I met just a while ago. She is smiling more, seems excited rather than simply nervous and shocked, and her voice is cheerful too.

'You know, you don't have to wait until you're married to know fear,' Sharma Uncle says, as she turns, continuing our previous conversation. 'You must have a girlfriend, right? Aren't you scared of her?'

'No, I don't have one.' As soon as I say it, I feel sad and weird. I have never had a girlfriend.

Sharma Uncle looks genuinely surprised. 'Really? You're a fine young man, good-looking too. That jawline should've caused at least three heartbreaks by now. How come you don't have a girlfriend?'

He glances at his wife, who's now placing the last of the dishes on the table. 'Tenzin, can you believe this? No girlfriend!'

She turns around, beaming at me. 'That surprises me too. You're such a sweet boy, dear. Do you have a crush at least?'

Her question catches me off guard. I've never really opened up about my feelings to anyone. The last time I did, back in eighth grade, Anurag told everyone about the girl I liked, even though he had promised he wouldn't. After that, I always kept my feelings to myself.

'Umm ... I do have a crush on someone,' I finally admit.

Sharma Uncle's face lights up. 'Aha! Now we're getting somewhere. Does she know? What's she like? Have you told her?'

I shake my head. 'No. I mean, I've never told her. And I don't think I ever will. She's just ... too incredible."

I pause, needing a breath to hold myself together.

'We worked together on a bunch of events. Whenever we're planning something, she always comes up with the most amazing ideas—but still makes sure everyone else feels heard first. And if someone has plans, even when there's work left, she'll tell them to go, saying she'll handle the rest.

'I usually stay back too ... not because she needs me or anything, but just for a chance to talk to her. Maybe have a cup of tea in the canteen afterwards.'

An involuntary small smile tugs at my lips. 'We run into each other sometimes. In the corridors. When we do, we walk together. Not always saying much. Just ... walking.'

I glance down at my hands.

'I kind of freeze up around her, though. Like ... sometimes when she smiles at me, I just forget how to function.'

God, why am I telling them all this?

The realisation that I have shared too much crashes over me like a bucket of ice. I can feel the heat crawling up my neck. 'I—sorry,' I stammer, my voice cracking slightly. 'I overshared ...'

A soft smile appears on Sharma Aunty's face. She walks over to me and places her warm hand on my shoulder. 'That's so sweet, Arjun. I really hope when you go back, you'll find the courage to tell her. She'd be lucky to have someone like you.'

I smile, but on the inside, I'm scared. What if she's heard the rumours too? What if she is one of those who have already believed them and think of me as some kind of monster? I can barely face anyone anymore, let alone her.

But I just nod and smile.

'Honey, you were after my head for not bringing Arjun in, and now that I have, aren't you going to show him what all you've cooked for him? He must be starving,' Sharma Uncle says, nudging her gently.

'Oh, yes! I am sorry, I am so so sorry, you must be starving. Oh god! What was I thinking?' Sharma Aunty suddenly springs to life and starts placing various containers on the table.

'You are going to love it. Kheer is her specialty. You will be left licking your fingers,' Sharma Uncle says, his voice brimming with pride, as he serves.

'Oh, don't jinx it. Let him taste it and decide for himself,' Sharma Aunty counters, but I catch the faint blush on her cheeks.

I take a bite of the kheer and puri first.

It's too freaking good.

'Aunty, this is the best food I have ever had in my entire life,' I say and Sharma Uncle gives me a *I-had-told-you-so* look proudly.

I eat quietly, trying not to seem greedy, but each bite makes it harder to stop.

Sharma Uncle tries to serve me four more puris, and I stop him. 'I don't think I can finish all this,' I say.

'Oh, come on,' he says, a grin spreading across his face, as he puts them in my plate anyways. 'She had me go all the way to the town centre to get groceries so she could make her best dish. You have to eat it all.'

'A young lad like you needs to eat, Ashu. Who knows if you've even been eating properly these days,' Sharma Aunty says, her voice filled with concern.

Who is Ashu? Maybe her son. I don't react or correct her. She seems very happy right now and I don't want things to get awkward.

What surprises me even more than Sharma Aunty's cooking is how effortlessly she tells stories.

'No one knows these valleys and mountains better than us. It was Tarun who first started gathering enthusiasts for camping in these valleys,' she says, her eyes softening with love as she looks at him.

'His dad hated it, though,' she adds, laughing. 'Going down this path right after college ...'

The image of Sharma Uncle's father running after him with a stick flashes in my mind again. I fight hard to hold back my smile.

'But once the money started rolling in, he didn't care,' Sharma Uncle cuts in, piling another bowl of kheer into my plate along with two more puris. I don't protest. The kheer is ridiculously good.

'And honestly, I'll never regret it,' he says. 'Because that's how I met her.'

'Just two or three years into the business, we hosted this group of college grads from the North-East,' he continues.

'They were here to explore the valleys. And among them was this stunning girl in her early twenties—in love with the mountains, the trees, the springs. From day one, every guy in the group was hitting on her, trying to win her attention.'

Curious, I ask, 'How did you win her heart, then?'

'I wrote her anonymous poetry,' he replies, a playful gleam in his eyes.

'Anonymous?'

'Let me answer that,' Sharma Aunty cuts in, clearly excited to share. 'On the very first night of the camp, I found a note in my tent: "If the universe is god's canvas, you are his masterpiece." I thought it was some kind of prank or that maybe everyone had received one. But no one else had. And then, every day, I started finding these beautiful messages everywhere.'

I pick up my plate, and even though she's eager to serve me more food, I place it near the sink.

'And then?' I ask, caught up in the story.

'That drove me crazy,' she continues with a laugh. 'I wanted to find the person who was writing such beautiful lines for me. I stayed alert, searched everywhere, but I couldn't catch the one behind the notes. He wasn't that easy to find!' Sharma Uncle raises his glass of water, as if to toast his younger self.

'When did you finally figure it out?' I ask, leaning in.

'On the very last day! We were all sitting around the campfire. He took out his guitar and started singing a song he had written for me. I knew the words because he had slipped it into my tent just the night before.'

'And then she joined in and sang with me,' Sharma Uncle continues. He stands up, helps his wife to her feet, pulls her close and starts swaying with her, their hands intertwined. 'We danced together until dawn, and at daybreak, I asked her to marry me.'

As they move in unison, their faces light up with pure joy, their eyes never leaving each other. They're so beautiful together. I've always been scared of love and finding a partner because of what I've seen growing up. But as these two dance together, with so much of love in their eyes, I feel like there is more to love than I have ever known. I feel this sudden desire to find what they have.

'Someone seems to have forgotten they have work to do,' she teases him, her tone playful.

'It's not every day we take a trip down memory lane, is it?'

Sharma Aunty gently tries to free herself.

'You need to go out and get everything ready, honey. It's getting late. The campers will be here in a few hours.'

'I know,' he whispers. As he lets go of her hand, I see something else besides love ... *pain.*

'Do you have any plans for the night?' Sharma Uncle asks, cleaning the plates along with his wife.

'Not really,' Birdie asked me to stay here for the night, but I haven't yet found a way to ask him.

'Would you like to stay here for the night? I mean if you can. We are going to receive a few returning campers today. And we could really use an extra pair of hands.'

'I would love to,' I respond eagerly, without waiting a second.

'That would be just great,' he says, his face muscles relaxing.

I'm soaked with sweat by the time Sharma Uncle and I finish setting up all the tents and chopping wood for the fire. The sun is about to set, and Sharma Uncle is making a final round to ensure that the tents are secure. I can't wait to see how the fairy lights we have put around the tents look when we turn them on.

'Need any more help?' I ask, placing the last of the wooden logs on the bench.

'Nope, just making sure we're all good here. Be careful with those,' he says, just as one log starts to roll off the bench. I catch it at the edge of the table and set it back.

'Thank you. Let me know if anything else remains.'

'I think we are done for now. Thank you, son.'

'Don't mention it. I enjoyed working with you.' I mean it. Sharma Uncle knows more about camping and mountaineering than anyone I've ever met. The whole time we worked together, he told me various stories of his adventures, and also taught me how to tie a knot in twelve different ways, each with its unique purpose.

What truly amazed me was how quickly he could set up a tent. He had pitched his tent perfectly by the time I had just unpacked and figured out which side was up. He even gave me tips on setting up a tent faster and securing it against strong winds.

He smiles, a trace of weariness in his eyes. 'Thanks for this,' he repeats, heavier this time.

'It was really no big deal, Uncle. You and Aunty have been very kind and welcoming to me, and I've hardly done anything. You did most of the heavy lifting.'

'No, you don't understand.' He sits down on a bench. 'Thank you for making Tenzin smile.'

A pause.

'I don't understand.'

He motions for me to sit beside him on a nearby bench, his hands trembling slightly as he pulls two cans of soda from a cooler. Popping the tabs, he hands me one, avoiding my gaze.

'Tenzin hasn't really been herself for a long time. Seeing her today—laughing, humming, being present in the moment ... it means more to me than you know.' His voice cracks, and he takes a long sip to steady himself.

He sets the can down and looks at me with a sad smile. 'I wasn't going to tell you any of this. I thought maybe it was better this way. But I see the way you look around, at her, at me, with those questions in your eyes, trying to figure things out.' He sighs deeply, 'You sensed something was off, didn't you?'

I nod.

'The thing is ...' he says, voice low, almost a whisper. 'We lost our son. Three years ago.'

My chest tightens. I stay still.

He keeps going.

'He had a medical condition ... the details I'd rather not get into. Not because they hurt—they do—but because I want to remember him for the life he lived. Not for the disease.'

He swallows hard. His voice wavers.

'He loved these mountains. Lived for them. Hiked every trail, even when his body refused to cooperate. He was in pain ... a lot of it.'

He wipes his eyes quickly. Clears his throat.

'Sorry. I ... I still can't always hold it in.'

I don't reach for words. I know that any 'I'm so sorry' I could offer would be too small, too weak against his grief.

So, I just sit with him.

I want him to know he doesn't have to apologise for sharing—for letting out what he's held back all this time, all the ways he's been brave. I just want him to know that I'm here, and I'm listening.

He exhales shakily.

'But he never let her see it,' he says, his voice dropping to a whisper. 'Even when the condition made him so weak he could barely sit up, he'd find a way to smile the second she walked into the room. My boy ... he kept it all in. All the sickness, all that hurt, all that pain. He was a brave boy. He was being his bravest just so his mother didn't have to see him breaking.'

He pauses, and the silence stretches between us. I swallow, feeling a lump form in my throat. I can't begin to imagine the pain he must have gone through. I want to say something, anything that might help, but what can I even say?

What can anyone say to a parent who has survived his only child?

He draws in a slow breath, as if gathering the strength to go on.

'Since he passed away, Tenzin had forgotten how to smile,' he resumes, his tone breaking a little as he looks away, trying to mask the quiver in his voice.

'We were both in pain, but I had to bury mine to care for her. She busied herself in her art, trying to use it as a way to deal with her grief. Earlier, when she used to do that, she would always keep humming some tune—but she wouldn't anymore. She would just sit there, with no expressions on her face, and try to create things.'

He pauses, then looks at me.

'But today ... today was the first time I heard her humming in years.'

A shaky breath escapes him.

'Today, I could see my old Tenzin again.'

He swallows hard.

'And it ... it was all because of you.'

He looks at me, his hand resting gently on my back, his eyes stay glued to my face. 'You look like him, and he was your age when we lost him.' He laughs, embarrassed, 'I hope that explains the weirdness in our behaviour.'

I just nod. A heavy sadness washes over me, sinking deep inside. Sharma Uncle and Aunty are the kindest people I've ever met, and it's heart-wrenching to know that they've gone through so much.

We sit in silence for a long time, neither of us saying anything. Even the wind, as it blows, feels heavy, and the darkness has slowly started to take control.

'I noticed you seemed a bit off earlier,' he says. I feel a jolt of panic. My mind starts racing, frantically scrambling for any fake story or excuses to hide behind. I open my mouth—the first lie already forming on the tip of my tongue—but he gently cuts in before I can speak.

'No need to explain.'

I freeze. The half-baked excuse dying in my throat.

'Just know that if you ever want to talk about anything, I'm here for you.' He gives me a warm, reassuring smile, pats my back, and stands up to leave.

'Think of me as family.'

Family.

I've never really grasped what that's supposed to mean. But maybe, just maybe, it's that feeling of warmth which washes over me when Sharma Uncle smiles at me kindly like that.

The campers start to arrive as night falls. The area is softly lit by fairy lights, with the major attraction being the bonfire at the centre. I am stationed at the grill, managing the potato wedges that Sharma Aunty taught me to prepare earlier. She said it was easy as long as I keep an eye on them.

I am glad to be working on them. I am glad to be working on anything that can keep my mind busy.

I flip the wedges, their sizzle joining the chorus of laughter and chatter that fills the air.

Aunty comes over to check on me. 'How's our chef doing here?' she asks, peeking over my shoulder at the golden-brown wedges.

'Trying not to turn them into charcoal,' I quip, showing her the batch that looks suspiciously darker than the others.

She laughs and reassures me, 'A little char adds flavour. Don't worry about it.'

She is laughing more now and looks really pretty when she does. I get why everyone in her camp, including Sharma Uncle, was hitting on her.

'With some practice, you could really become a good chef, you know?'

'Really?'

She picks up a wedge, blows onto it once, and takes a bite.

'Se—seri—seriously,' she stammers, her words interrupted by quick puffs of air as she tries to cool her mouth. She still manages to smile and laugh along with me as she chews it down. 'When it was my first time on the grill,' she takes another few quick puffs of air, 'I had burnt everything. I mean everything. But you have managed to get them just right, nice and real crispy. You're already ahead in this game.'

'Thanks,' I chuckle, feeling really proud. I have been enjoying her company a lot more after my conversation with Sharma Uncle. The awkwardness I had felt is long gone.

She offers me a wedge. I bite into its satisfying crunch. It's too damn good.

'Should we start serving?' I ask.

'Yeah,' she smiles, glancing towards the crowd. 'They must be starving.'

We carry the platter towards the bonfire. Fairy lights twinkle overhead, strung between trees and tents. The fire burns bright at the centre, its glow dancing across faces—some talking in small groups, others sitting cross-legged on the ground, laughing over half-told stories. The air smells of food and smoke and something warm, something alive.

We start passing around plates and someone thanks Sharma Aunty for the food. She just waves them off, smiling.

The guitarist by the bonfire strums a lively tune. Laughter bubbles up from the crowd, plates pass from hand to hand, and the night hums with an easy, joyful rhythm.

I watch from the side, smiling, but my gaze lingers on the guitar. It's not about the attention he's getting—though the girls nearby, all extremely pretty, can't seem to take their eyes off him. *It's the music.*

My last guitar broke years ago, and I never replaced it. Maybe I should have. I miss the weight of it—the strings beneath my fingers, the way a tune could pull me in and quieten everything else.

The song shifts, slower now, and the group begins to hum along. The air feels softer, warmer somehow. By the fire, Sharma Uncle and Aunty join in, shoulders brushing as they laugh together.

They look like the happiest, prettiest couple I've ever seen.

And as I watch them, a sudden realisation washes over me.

That night had music too. Laughter. A handful of friends. A reason to celebrate.

And if someone had paused it right there, just before everything shifted ...

If someone had told me what was coming ...

Maybe I could've stopped it.

Maybe I could've run.

Maybe I could've saved myself.

The noise, the laughter, even the fire—it all starts to feel a little too much.

I need to get away.

I head to my room, close the door behind me, and let out a slow breath. The silence feels heavy, but it's easier to sit here than with the triggering noise outside.

I check my bag for tomorrow's journey—one last glance to make sure nothing's missing—and then pull out the diary Birdie gave me.

I sit down on the edge of the bed and start to write. I write about Rishabh and the ride, about Sharma Uncle and Aunty—their warmth, their laughter, the way they looked singing together—and how, for the first time in a while, I felt a part of something that almost feels like family.

When I close the diary, my eyes rest on the art on its cover. It's beautiful. Thoughtful.

I haven't met Birdie yet, but I already know she's a wonderful person. No one puts that much heart into a gift for a stranger.

No one is kind to a stranger the way she was.

I still remember the first time I texted her.

I was running away from everything—anxiety clawing at my chest, therapy sessions that didn't help, panic attacks growing worse with each passing day.

And then I came across her feed by chance—a post on Explore that led me to her profile. Pictures of mountains, her words about freedom, the way she seemed to belong to the hills, the rivers.

It made me think—if I could just get there, maybe the mountains could teach me how to live again.

So, I texted her:

'I wish I could live the way you do. I'm going through a lot, and it feels like it would have saved me.'

I never expected a reply.

But she responded.

A simple message that changed everything:

'Why don't you join me then? I'm going on a trek next month. Maybe you could follow in my footsteps?'

That single text became my lifeline. The only thing that felt like it could stop me from this constant drowning.

And I had decided: *I'm going.*

Now, holding the diary, I realise again how much she's done for me. How she's saved me. And I find myself wanting to give something back—something from the heart, something that needs efforts to make.

That's when the idea comes to me, and I rush out to find Sharma Aunty.

'Can you help me?' I ask after explaining what I have in mind.

Sharma Uncle is talking to a few campers near the bonfire. Its glow has dimmed, the flames low and soft, their occasional crackle blending with the quiet laughter around us.

She looks at me for a moment, her face lighting up with a bright smile.

'I ... I'd love to,' she says, her voice filled with warmth.

She even seems happier. I understand *why* only when we begin working on it.

'She's too special for me and Tarun, you know,' she says, her eyes softening. 'We've always treated her like a daughter—our Birdie. It fills my heart with joy to see someone doing something so thoughtful for her.'

'Can you tell me something about her?' I ask, unable to hold back my curiosity. I don't think anyone knows Birdie the way they do, and I don't want to waste this chance.

'I wish I could, Arjun,' she says gently. 'But she's asked us not to. Still, I'll tell you this—she's the loveliest, most magical soul you'll ever come across. Just like you.'

I smile—not because of the 'just like you,' but because somewhere I know she's right. *Loveliest and most magical*—that's exactly how she feels.

I take the wooden piece Aunty gives me and start grinding it. A few minutes later, Sharma Uncle joins us in the living room. Aunty quickly fills him in, and he looks at me with quiet pride, patting my shoulder before settling by the pillar with his back against it.

As Aunty guides me, she picks up her embroidery again. After a few stitches, she begins to hum—a soft, soothing tune that fills the quiet room.

I glance at Sharma Uncle. He looks away, wiping the tears gathering in his eyes.

Last night, Sharma Uncle told me I'd have to leave early, and that he'd drop me at the starting point of the hike.

Now I sit on a bench, admiring the still-sleeping world, the air dark and cold against my stinging eyes.

I yawn—barely four hours of sleep will do that to you.

I pull out the wooden figure from my bag—the one I spent half the night carving. Sharma Uncle and Aunty had stayed up with me, sacrificing their sleep to help me finish it. Aunty guided me through each step, her hands steady and graceful as she showed me how to add the delicate finishing touches.

Uncle had made tea twice, though he hadn't taken a sip himself. The way he kept watching Aunty—quiet, patient, his gaze never leaving her—made me think he didn't need tea or caffeine to stay awake. Watching his wife hum, create and smile was enough to keep him awake for a thousand nights.

At first, I wasn't sure if my idea was good, but as I trace the small wooden bird with my fingers, feeling the grooves I carved with such care, I think she'll love it.

Aunty had given me a few beads to decorate it—turquoise, blue, and one soft pink. They hang from a thin thread tied to the bird, swaying lightly with every movement.

I cup it in my hands, feeling the faint warmth of the wood against the cold air, and wish she'd meet me soon so I could give it to her.

Sharma Uncle steps out of the cabin, and Aunty follows close behind, holding a tiffin and a plastic bag.

'I told you not to,' I whisper, keeping my voice low so I don't wake the campers. Most are still asleep—some in tents, others under the open sky in sleeping bags.

When I'd woken up earlier, Aunty was nowhere to be seen, and I'd felt relieved, thinking my plan to sneak out quietly with Uncle had worked. We were supposed to wake her only for the goodbye.

'God, when did you even wake up?' I ask, taking in the sight of her—already dressed, eyes tired but smiling, holding a tiffin and a plastic bag in her hands.

'Oh, not that early,' she says, but her puffy eyes tell another story.

'I packed some aloo ke parathe for you,' she says, handing me the tiffin. 'Wrapped them in foil so you can eat them later, even at night. I really hope they're enough—I didn't have much time. And there's some achaar too. Oh, and I steamed some momo for breakfast. Don't give any to Tarun. I make them for him twice a week; he can survive one morning without them. These are just for you.'

'That's true,' Uncle laughs, 'but still not fair.'

'Oh, shut up,' Aunty says, swatting at him.

'You didn't have to make all this,' I say, taking the tiffin and the bag from her. 'And why both parathas and momos?'

'Momo, not *momos*,' she corrects, rolling her eyes. 'And please, it wasn't much, Arjun.'

Uncle heads towards the black truck parked a little away from the camp, giving us a moment.

'Okay,' I say, my voice catching a little, overwhelmed by her care.

'Good,' she replies softly. 'And promise me you'll visit us whenever you can, okay? We'd really love to see you again.'

'I will,' I say, meeting her eyes. 'I promise.'

8

Sharma Uncle drops me off at the starting point of the trail, a good two-hour drive from T&T.

As I get out of the truck, he hands me a map. The lines are delicate, almost artistic, and I can tell Birdie has drawn it. She's marked a few spots along the way, one of them circled in red with a little star beside it: *Tea stall and the best view of the valley.*

I can't help but smile when I read what she has written at the bottom, in her familiar, elegant handwriting: ☆ *Best place to eat the momo Sharma Aunty must've packed for you.*

Before leaving, Sharma Uncle gives me a firm handshake and pulls me into a side hug. In his fatherly voice, he tells me to take care, to stay true to who I am, and to not care about what the world thinks of me.

I promise him that I will try.

Then he adds that I should always think of him and Sharma Aunty as family.

I nod, feeling a lump rise in my throat.

'Thanks, Tarun. For everything,' I say. The smile he gives me when I call him by his name is one I know I won't forget anytime soon.

She wasn't lying.

It's probably been an hour since I left the tea stall Birdie had marked for me to have momo. The view was so worth it. Even now, if I close my eyes, I can still see the mist crawling across the valley like a slow-moving tide.

I'd sat there for a long time, devouring the momo Sharma Aunty had packed. *God, they were delicious!* Their taste—the kind that exists only in food made at home—still lingers on my tongue, making me wish for more. I could totally see why Sharma Uncle's obsessed with them.

I've been walking ever since, the map still folded in my back pocket. And now, at last, I think I've reached the final spot.

The yellow letterbox is barely visible, hidden beneath a mess of overgrown vines. Rust covers most of it, and it leans slightly on a weathered wooden post wrapped in frayed wires. I brush off some dust, revealing faded drawings of birds and flowers. Their colours are almost gone, with just hints of blue and red remaining.

I drop my backpack to the ground and wipe the sweat from my forehead. The scent of damp earth and wildflowers filling my lungs as I take a deep breath.

'Let's hope you don't fall apart on me,' I mutter, and lift its lid carefully.

The old and stubborn hinges creak in protest, flakes of rust falling as the lid gives way.

A small pile of books rests neatly inside, their edges curled and yellowed, spines faded from years of being passed around. Between them, someone has tucked dried leaves and tiny wildflowers, giving the inside of the letterbox total Pinterest-y vibes.

A note taped to the inner wall catches my eye,

Do take a book if you are in need of a companion. But don't forget to return it at the next letterbox.

I run my fingers over the spines. Most are familiar titles—classics I've read in school. In one corner, there's a tiny figurine of one of my childhood heroes, Shaktiman. He stands there, his arms resting on his waist in his signature pose, as if guarding the treasures of the letterbox from anyone who might try to steal them. It's too cute and instantly pulls me back to those simpler days—rushing home after school just to watch him on TV.

In another corner, there's a small stack of cards covered in handwritten notes. I pick up a few.

'Keep climbing, even if you're tired. The view from the top is worth it.'

The next one read:

'While you're aiming for the summit, don't forget to enjoy the path that gets you there.'

And a third, scribbled in messy handwriting, says:

'Note to self: Next time, don't trust the tea stall guy when he says "just fifteen minutes uphill".'

I smile, knowing he had said the same to me. Flipping through more, I find handwritten notes, small stories, and words of encouragement left by strangers who'd passed by before me.

But then I remember why I'm here. My eyes scan the contents again. No letter.

A knot tightens in my stomach.

'Did I mess up the directions? Reached the wrong letterbox?' But that can't be. I followed Birdie's map exactly. The tea stall with the faded red awning, the viewpoints overlooking the valley—everything was exactly as she had said.

It has to be here. It *has to.*

Unless ... someone took it.

The thought makes my heart sink.

Fuck. What am I supposed to do now?

I could text her—but will she even see it in time? What if she doesn't get network for a day or two? What if I end up stranded here?

I run a hand through my hair, trying to think, when something catches my eye.

A corner of a white paper—barely visible beneath the pile of books.

I push the books aside and pull it out.

Written on the envelope, in her familiar handwriting, are the words:

For Arjun.

I open it carefully. Inside, there is a hand-drawn map and a letter. I unfold the letter and start reading.

Hey Ranger,

Before anything else, I need to say this: thank you. Thank you for agreeing to stay with Uncle and Aunty. It means so much more to me than you could imagine.

They've been a big part of my world, and I thought you spending time with them might do them some good—and maybe you too.

There's so much to learn from them, and I hope, in some small way, you did.

Now, about this trail. There's something I want to tell you about it. It's not just another path through the woods. For me, it's the most special one. Mainly because it's the one where I didn't take a single step—I was carried the entire way.

This was my very first trek.

I was barely a year old when my parents brought me here. There's a photo in my diary that I've kept all these years. I'm in my dad's arms, wearing a dress with wings like a fairy's, my hair tied in two tiny ponytails. My mom is next to him, kissing my cheek. If you look closely, you can see this very letterbox in the background.

Yeah ... it's that old.

For my parents, nature was the truest form of god. They wanted me to be blessed by it. And I think I was. Ever since then, these trees, the air, the springs—they've always been there for me. I've told them my secrets, shared my pain, and in return, they've given me strength whenever I've needed it.

I hope you find that same magic out here. May your heart receive their blessings, just as mine has.

Yours,

Birdie

PS Open the map. It'll lead you to your next stop.

PPS The trail has a way of bringing people and moments together when you least expect it. Don't fight it. Let the trail surprise you.

I read the letter again, picturing one-year-old Birdie in her dad's arms, her mom kissing her cheek, and this old letterbox in the background. It's unbelievable to think I'm standing in the exact spot as they once did.

I close the lid of the letterbox, and as I do, it wobbles. One small push or careless attempt at opening it, and the entire letterbox could topple over.

I can't just leave it like that. Not when this place means so much to her.

The rusted metal creaks under my hands as I straighten it. The wooden post is loose, so I grab a sturdy branch, wedge it beside the base, and pack some stones and dirt to hold it steady. I loop a few vines around the post for extra support. It's not perfect, but it'll last.

Stepping back, I wipe the sweat off my forehead. The letterbox stands taller now, less likely to fall over. For some weird reason, that makes me feel proud.

On a whim, I pull out my phone. I don't usually take selfies, but this feels worth capturing. Standing beside the fixed letterbox, I try to frame us both in the shot. My hair is a mess, sticking out at odd angles, and I notice the dirt smudge on my cheek. Definitely not a perfect selfie.

I click the photo anyway.

Looking at the picture, I hesitate. Should I send it to her? I bite my lip, my thumb tapping the phone cover nervously. After a moment, I open Instagram, find Birdie's chat, and before I can overthink it, I type a quick message: *Found your letterbox. Tended to it with love.*

I attach the photo and hit send.

Sliding the phone back into my pocket, I feel a mix of nervousness and excitement. It feels good to share this moment with her—a small memory.

But then the thought crosses my mind: What did she mean by the line in the PPS?

Was it just motivational—or a hint of something waiting ahead?

'Hey there!'

I turn towards the voice. A tall, skinny guy waves at me from the bend in the trail.

'Uh, hello.' I slide the letter and phone in my bag.

'Have you seen any hikers go this way?' he asks between heavy breaths.

'Nope. You're the first person I've seen in about an hour.' His face falls. He kicks a pebble and it skitters towards me. I step aside just in time.

'Whoa, sorry. Didn't mean for that to happen.' He runs a hand through his short curly hair, making it stick up.

'It's fine,' I say, passing an *it's-alright-buddy* smile.

'It didn't hit you, right? Man, I'm really sorry. I always mess things up.' He sighs and kicks a larger rock near the letterbox. 'Ow!' He hops on one foot, clutching his toes. A string of muttered curses escapes him, mixed with a chanting of 'bad, bad, rock!'

'You okay?' I ask, worried if he will be able to walk again for quite some time.

'Not really.' He plops down on a nearby rock. 'Officer sent me downhill to grab some chips and said they'd wait here. But they're gone. And ... and ... I think ... I think they ditched me. We had a fight and ...' He hides his face as his voice quivers.

I glance at my map. Every minute I waste here, Birdie's getting farther ahead. But I can't just leave him. If I do, my guilt will show up at 3 a.m., knock on my conscience's door, and be like, 'Hey man, remember that hiker you abandoned?'

'Hey, hey, don't jump to that yet,' I say softly, trying to comfort him. 'Maybe they didn't leave. They could just be waiting somewhere else.'

He looks up, giving me a glimpse of more than just his curly hair this time. His eyes are red.

'You think so?' he asks, his voice small.

'Sure,' I say, keeping my tone light. 'Maybe it's just a mix-up.'

He nods, sniffling. *He's actually crying.*

I definitely can't leave him now.

'Yeah. That's gotta be it.' He suddenly springs to his feet, a spark of hope replacing the gloom. 'I probably just forgot where we were meeting. They wouldn't leave me—Officer wouldn't, and Huntress definitely wouldn't.'

Who the hell is Officer? And Huntress? Are these some sort of nicknames?

He grabs his oversized backpack and nearly topples backward under its weight. I reach out instinctively to steady him.

'Isn't that bag a bit heavy?' I ask.

'Nah, I might look skinny, but I've got muscles,' he says, flexing an arm that doesn't show much. 'This is nothing. Once, I hiked a mountain with a bag ten times heavier.'

'Impressive,' I say, biting back a smile as he wrestles with the straps, still wobbling like a baby giraffe.

'I'm Guu ...' he starts, then his eyes widen as if he's just realised he's about to break some unspoken rule. 'Uh, Loosepants!' he blurts out, visibly relieved he didn't slip up. 'We, uh, don't use real names on the trail.' *That explains it.*

I raise an eyebrow but shake his hand anyway. 'Loosepants?'

He nods vigorously, curls bouncing. 'Yep. And you are?'

'Umm ... you want my real name?'

'No!' he practically yells, waving his hands. 'No real names. Only trail names while you're on the trail.'

'Uh ... okay then,' I say, biting back a laugh. He's really serious about this.

'I don't have a trail name,' I admit.

His jaw drops. 'No trail name? That's a big no-no. We've got to fix that before someone gives you one you might not like.'

I decide to play along, partly for the entertainment and partly for the joy radiating on the guy's face.

'Alright, any suggestions?'

He taps his chin thoughtfully, a mischievous grin spreading across his face. 'Since you're hiking alone and seem kind of mysterious, how about "The Shadow"?'

I consider it. 'You are definitely creative. And I like it, but maybe not quite suitable for a trek? I mean, it would be good for let's say—online gaming?'

'Okay, okay ... Oh! How about "Curly"?' he suggests, then laughs. 'Wait, that doesn't make sense. That's me!'

I chuckle. 'Yeah, I think that fits you better.'

'Okay, hmm ... Batman? Superman? Wolverine?'

'Not really. Maybe we should drop the trail name thing. I really need to get going—'

'Wait!' He bounces on his toes. 'I've got it. I've got it. I found you alone, and you're hiking solo, right?'

'Umm ... yeah.'

'Then I name you "Lone Wolf".' He takes his water bottle and taps each of my shoulders like he's knighting me.

'Lone Wolf?' I repeat.

'Yes! It fits perfectly. From now on, you're Lone Wolf. But guess what? You're not *lone* anymore because I'm joining your pack. So, you are, from now on, just Wolf.'

'Alright man, Wolf it is,' I say, laughing. I kind of like the name.

He is grinning, looking ridiculously proud of himself.

'Thanks for the name, man. It was nice meeting you.' I sling my backpack over my shoulder and shake his hand. 'But I should really get going. I'm running late.'

His face falls slightly. 'Yeah, I get it. Goodbye, Wolf.' He waves awkwardly.

I start walking in the opposite direction. After a few steps, I glance back and see him still standing there, adjusting his heavy pack. *Was I rude to him? I hope not.*

I unfold the map, trying to focus on Birdie's directions. In neat black ink, she's marked the mailbox—my current spot. From here, a narrow road winds towards the base of a hill. To its right runs a river, and not far from it, she's drawn an X—that's where I need to go.

I'm tracing the route with my finger when I sense movement behind me. Before I can turn, Loosepants is suddenly right beside me, leaning in to peer over my shoulder.

'That's the same direction I have to go!' he exclaims.

I nearly drop the map. 'You can't just sneak up on people like that,' I say, my heart pounding. I quickly fold the map, shielding it from his view.

'Sorry! Didn't mean to startle you.' He steps back, hands raised as if surrendering.

'You did, though.' I tuck the map safely into my pocket, forcing my heartbeat to slow down.

He scratches his head, looking genuinely apologetic. 'I just wanted to ask where you're from so I could write it in my diary—but then I saw the map, and I got curious, and when I get curious, I can't help it, you know? So I peeked, and then I saw the hill and the river, and I remembered—my friends said they were camping there—and I thought maybe we could go together! I swear I didn't mean to scare you, but yeah, I totally did.'

'But can we ...' he continues, not even pausing for breath, 'tag along for some time?'

For a moment, I just stare at him—this fast-talking, skinny guy drowning in clothes two sizes too big. Then Birdie's words echo in my mind: *The trail has a way of bringing people and moments together when you least expect it. Don't fight it.*

I take a slow breath. Maybe this is what she meant. Maybe not.

Either way, I decide not to overthink it this time.

'Alright,' I say quietly, as if convincing myself more than him.

—∞—

'... And that's when I realised I love chocolate ice cream more than vanilla or butterscotch. But not all chocolate ice creams are the same. Belgian chocolate is my absolute favourite. I tried peanut butter chocolate once, but it wasn't for me. I didn't even know an atrocity like that existed. Two of my friends loved it, though. God knows how and why! Maybe their tastebuds were just born weird or had some mutation.' Loosepants pauses to take a breath. 'What kind of ice cream do you like?'

'Umm ...'

'Oh wait! Let me guess. You seem like a strawberry ice cream kind of guy.'

It's chocolate chip cookie. But I decide not to correct him—it doesn't really matter. We will probably be on our separate ways soon. Before I can even open my mouth, he's already off again, passionately debating the *best* flavours of potato chips and listing the ones he still needs to try.

I consider myself a patient person, but his constant chatter is wearing me down. With him talking non-stop, it's hard to focus on where we're going. My watch tells me it's been nearly two hours since we started hiking together. In that time, he's covered everything from his first bike, to how aliens are real, to the tragic tale of how he once stepped into a puddle and ruined his favourite shirt.

I've tuned out most of it

'... What do you think?' he asks, stopping mid-step. I catch only his last few words. If he hadn't stopped, I might not have realised he'd asked me a question.

'Sorry, what was that?'

'I think we might be lost.'

'It's too soon to say that.' I pull out the map. 'The hill is still to our right. We should be reaching the river soon.'

'Huh.'

'Maybe we've strayed off the path a bit, but we can adjust.' In two hours, we haven't come across anyone. That would have really concerned me if I had been alone. But Loosepants's constant chatter didn't even let me realise it.

'If you say so. What happens when we reach the river?' he asks.

'You'll find your friends, and I'll continue to my destination.' His expression shifts; disappointment flickers across his face.

'Where did you get that map?' He's walking beside me now.

'Someone gave it to me.'

'Is it a treasure map?'

'No.'

'Some secret spy stuff that you can't tell me about?'

'No.'

'A map leading to a Dragon's lair?'

'No.'

'Any nuclear bunker with hidden government secrets?'

'God, no.'

'Then what's it for?'

'It's ... complicated!'

'Okay ...' He looks hurt and quickens his pace, moving ahead of me.

Why? Like, God, why?

'Maybe ...' I begin, not wanting to upset him.

He stops mid-step and spins around, eyes wide, hopeful. 'Maybe what?'

I take a deep breath. 'Maybe, based on past experiences, this map will lead me to a place that will teach me how to live again, how to start over.'

He stands there, momentarily speechless. For the first time since we met, Loosepants is at a loss for words. After a moment, he speaks softly. 'I hope you find what you're looking for, Wolf.'

We exchange a brief smile.

We continue walking in a comfortable silence. The forest around us feels alive—the rustling leaves, the distant call of birds, the soft crunch of twigs beneath our boots. The sun is dipping lower, casting long shadows across our path.

'Did you hear that?' Loosepants suddenly stops, holding up a hand. The silence lasted for just five minutes.

'Hear what?' I listen intently, but all I catch is the rustling of leaves.

'Shhh. Listen.' He tilts his head. A moment later, a faint voice reaches my ears. Someone is shouting.

'Loosepants!'

'Loosepants, where are you?' another voice calls.

His face lights up. 'I'm here! I'm here!' he shouts back, waving his arms.

'Wait there, Loosey! We're coming!'

I scan the trees, trying to spot them, but the dense forest cover blocks my view. 'If we want them to find us, we should move towards them,' I suggest.

He nods vigorously. 'Yeah, let's go.' He adjusts his bag and starts moving quickly. He's practically bouncing with each step.

'Wait up,' I call after him. He breaks into a run, and I have no choice but to follow. Despite my regular jogging routine, keeping up with him while carrying a heavy backpack is challenging.

Finally, he stops in a small clearing. Three figures are approaching, silhouetted against the setting sun. I'm out of breath by the time I catch up.

'Let go of me already,' a girl shouts, struggling to free herself from Loosepants's overenthusiastic hug. Her curly black hair glint with greenish-blue highlights as she wriggles away.

'I'm so glad you came looking for me.' Tears stream down his cheeks.

'Get off me!' She smacks him on the head with a flashlight. This time, he releases her.

'I shouldn't have agreed to come find you,' she grumbles, her fair cheeks flushed red, matching her lipstick.

'I know you don't mean that,' Loosepants says, smiling widely.

Judging by her clenched fists and narrowed eyes, I know—*she definitely means it.*

'Where the hell did you wander off to?' she demands.

'Me? You guys *left* me!' Loosepants protests, pointing at her dramatically.

'Us? We were waiting for you. Right where we said we'd meet. You never showed up! We finally thought you'd headed straight to the camp—because that's what you *do*. You just run off without thinking. So we went there, waited, searched for hours—and you, you didn't come! And who the hell switches their phone off like that?' she shouts, smacking his arm a few times with the torch.

'Oh,' he says simply, rubbing his arm.

She blinks at him, stunned. Then throws her hands in the air. 'That's it? *Oh?* We've been running all over the mountain looking for you, and all you've got is "*Oh*"?'

He starts talking fast, like he's racing to get every word out before she explodes. 'I dropped my phone in water this morning, okay? So I put it in a bag of rice—you know, that phone-saving trick? And it *actually works*. This is, like, the third time it's happened to me. But you've got to leave it there for at least forty-eight hours, so obviously, I couldn't call you. Since it had been just half a day, and I didn't want my phone to go BOOM. And I know that I *should* have called you, I know! And I *would've.* I was gonna borrow someone's phone, but first, I was kinda upset—thought you guys ditched me—and then I met him.'

She just stares at him for a few seconds, then throws her hands up. 'Unbelievable. You're a walking disaster.' Her voice softens a little as she follows where he's pointing. 'And who's he?'

'We met on the way. His name's Wolf. I gave him that name!' Loosepants says in one quick burst, chest puffed out like he's announcing a superhero.

The guy beside her groans under his breath. Dressed in a white shirt, he's tapping impatiently at his sleeve like he has better places to be.

'I'm Arjun ... I mean, Wolf,' I say quickly, offering a small, awkward nod.

At the sound of my name, the girl's eyes widen. A squeal escapes her lips as she practically shakes with excitement.

'I *knew* you'd come. And I did feel like I had seen you somewhere. I told Officer you would, but he didn't believe me. You saw how he treated me, right? Well, now he's going to regret it.' She shoots a victorious glare at the guy in white. He merely shrugs, completely unbothered.

'Uh ... what?' I ask, lost. Her excitement, the way she says my name—it all feels strange. Was she *expecting* me? A wild thought crosses my mind.

Is she ... could she ... be Birdie?

'Officer would've made my life miserable if you hadn't shown up,' she says, turning back to me like I've just saved her from a villain.

Loosepants gasps dramatically. 'Is he the guy? I mean, is he *the* guy?'

'Yes!' she says, pulling out her phone. My stomach tightens. Her phone case—a bird hovering over a white daisy. My heart skips.

A *bird. Birdie?*

She taps the screen a few times before showing Loosepants something. There is a picture of a guy on her phone.

And that picture ... is mine.

'... And how could Officer say I don't know what I'm doing? I knew you'd come. My sixth sense is too good—it never betrays me.'

I study her for a moment. Even in the fading light, I can see she's quite pretty. She's carrying a white purse with blue highlights along its edges. A white daisy is stitched onto the bag, surrounded by several blue-painted birds with wings spread wide.

Could she be Birdie? The thought just won't leave my head. Even her hair—it's curly, just like Birdie's in that one photo she posted. The one I've stared at a hundred times, frustrated that it never showed her face. Her phone case, her purse ... everything about her seems to hint at it.

There's only one way to know.

'You guys didn't introduce yourselves,' I say, trying to sound casual even though my heart is suddenly racing.

'You already know me, Wolf. And don't worry, the others will introduce themselves when we're at camp. It's a tradition,' she replies, making my heart sink.

'We have to hurry,' she continues. 'The sun is about to set, and we'd want to reach the camp before dark, right?' She tugs at the sleeve of the guy in the white shirt, her eyes fixed on his face.

'Yeah,' he says, yanking his arm free with a sharp jerk that almost makes her stumble.

Asshole.

'You found your way back!' a tall guy in a tan jacket shouts, pulling Loosepants into a tight hug. 'I was starting to think you'd never make it.'

He lets go when Loosepants starts tapping his shoulder, clearly in pain. 'Didn't want to miss out on the chips. I hope you got my favourite flavour.' The guy laughs, giving him a playful shake before slapping his back hard.

Loosepants groans and almost loses his balance. I quickly grab his arm to steady him.

'You guys ...' the man in the white shirt mutters, looking annoyed. It's the first time I've heard him say more than one word. 'Call me when it's time for the campfire.'

He walks past us without another glance.

'I'll come get you,' the girl in the white sweater calls after him, almost standing on her toes as she watches him leave. There's a softness in her expression when she looks at him.

'Does he always have to be so cold and above it all?' the guy in the jacket says, glaring.

'He isn't cold or above it all,' the girl retorts, her face flushing as she meets his gaze.

'You'd notice if you weren't always drooling over him,' the guy in the tan jacket says with a loud laugh.

'Ugh.' Before I realise what's happening, he doubles over. The girl has punched him in the gut.

'Don't call him names,' she snaps, challenging him with her eyes before sharply turning and walking away. A pang of something—jealousy, maybe—hits me, seeing this girl, who might be Birdie, care so much for someone else.

'Did it hurt?' Loosepants asks, leaning towards the guy and supporting him from the side. 'You okay?'

'Of course I am.' He shrugs Loosepants off. 'I'm not a weakling like you.' He then turns his attention to me. 'And who might you be?'

'I'm Wolf—'

'I named him!' Loosepants interrupts. 'Found him near the letterbox by town. His name is Arjun, but since he was walking alone, I called—'

'Huh, didn't think you'd show up,' says the guy, cutting Loosepants off completely, and without any care. 'I even placed a bet on it.'

'Well, here I am,' I reply. I don't dislike people easily, but I already know I don't—and will never—like him.

'I'd introduce myself, but we'll wait for the campfire,' he says.

'I don't think that's necessary. I can guess who you are.'

'Humour me.'

'You're Officer, if I'm not mistaken,' I say.

He bursts into wild laughter. 'Indeed, I am. Seems like I'm famous.' He grips my hand in a handshake and begins to squeeze. A self-satisfied smirk plays on his face.

My knuckles ache as he increases the pressure. I flex my fingers, hoping he'll let go, but he doesn't. I grit my teeth and smile, refusing to let a bully win.

'I like you,' he says, finally releasing my hand. The muscles in my palm throb with relief. 'This camping trip is going to be fun.'

Loosepants keeps a hand on my shoulder. 'Let's go set up our tents,' he suggests, and we start moving. I'm grateful to put some distance between us and Officer.

There are five tents already pitched in a semicircle, leaving enough space in the centre that could fit two large vans. We find an empty spot and begin setting up our tents.

Loosepants has been unusually quiet since we left Officer, and his silence is unsettling.

'I don't like that guy,' I finally admit.

'Officer?' Loosepants asks.

'Yeah, him.'

'He's a great guy once you get to know him.'

'He bullied you,' I point out.

He remains silent. I decide not to push further. Sometimes it's best to let people process things on their own.

Thanks to Sharma Uncle's teachings, I set up my tent quickly. I glance over at Loosepants; he's still wrestling with his tent poles. I offer to help, and he accepts with a nod.

As we work together, the girl from earlier steps out of her tent across from us. In the soft glow of the lantern hanging nearby, I notice again how pretty she is.

'Falling for her?' Loosepants asks quietly.

'No, not at all,' I dismiss. 'I just observe things.'

'Not into girls?' He leans in, eyebrows raised.

'No, I definitely like girls,' I say, perhaps a bit too loudly. The girl turns towards us. I force a smile, pretending nothing happened.

'It's okay if you don't,' Loosepants whispers.

'I know. But I do like girls, no doubt about it.'

'Then, are you into her?' he asks. 'I wouldn't blame you. Lots of guys are.'

I can see why. Even out here, when everyone else looks kind of dusty and tired, she somehow doesn't. She's wearing a white fuzzy sweater and black ripped jeans, her curly hair—streaked with green and blue—falling perfectly over her shoulders. I even noticed subtle hints of makeup on her cheeks, just enough to enhance her features without overdoing it.

'So, are you attracted to her?' Loosepants presses.

'I don't know,' I say after a pause. She's beautiful, yeah—but it's not just that. Every time I look at her, I keep wondering if she's *her*. If she's *Birdie.* And maybe that's why I can't look away.

'Well, it won't matter anyway,' Loosepants says as we finish setting up his tent. 'You'll understand soon enough, if you haven't already.'

I look at him, puzzled. But deep down, I think I know what he means. I've seen the way she looks at the guy who was with her when we met.

'Take a nap if you want. I might finish off the last of my ice cream cup. I can share if you have a spoon. I only have one,' he offers.

'Thanks, but you enjoy your ice cream,' I say, though I can't help wondering how it hasn't melted by now.

'Oh, it's melted,' he replies, as if he has read my thoughts. 'Technically, it's more of a milkshake now—but that's how I like it.'

I blink at him. Once. Twice.

What the hell even is this guy.

'You should try it. It's underrated. And did you know there are more than a thousand flavours of ice cream out there?' he rambles.

'I didn't.'

'There are, and the number keeps growing. Want to hear their names?'

'Maybe another time. I'm just a bit tired.'

'Alright. You take a nap. We'll call you.'

'Thank you, Loosepants.' I head back to my tent, wondering if I'll ever get used to calling him by that name. I pull out my phone, the screen lighting up the small space, but there's no network here. No way to reach Birdie. No way to confirm if it's her.

I lie down on my bedroll, the image of the girl floats in my mind. *Could it really be her?*

'Wolf, hey Wolf, come out!' Someone is calling.

'Come on, Wolf.' The voice is familiar—the girl in the white sweater.

'Coming,' I reply. I pull on a dark green T-shirt. Debating whether to change out of my grey joggers, I decide it doesn't matter. Unzipping the tent, I step outside. The world that was bathed in the warm hues of sunset is now enveloped in darkness.

'Did you get enough rest?' She asks softly.

'Yes, I did,' I say. She's wrapped a brown scarf around her neck.

'Come on, let's get coffee. Loosey is brewing some for us.' She reaches out and takes my hand. Her touch is cold but soft. My heartbeat quickens. *She wouldn't hold my hand now if she didn't know me, would she?*

Loosepants is pouring coffee into mugs. He waves when he sees us. The guy in the white shirt is also there, sitting on a large wooden log.

The girl releases my hand and takes two mugs from Loosepants. She smiles at me before walking over to the guy on the log, handing him a mug of coffee. He accepts it without a thank-you or even a glance.

'Here you go,' Loosepants says, offering me a mug. 'Don't feel bad.'

'I'm not feeling bad,' I say, though my eyes drift back to her. She's talking to the guy beside her. Under the light of the lantern hanging near a tent, I notice she's reapplied her makeup. She reaches for his hand, but he pulls away, continuing to sip his coffee.

'Are you sure?' Loosepants asks again.

'Yeah,' I reply, taking a sip. I'm not feeling bad for me, but for her. More so, if she is actually Birdie.

The coffee is surprisingly good. My gaze returns to her; she's no longer talking and is staring at the ground. I feel a pang of sympathy. No one deserves to be treated like that. I wish I could go over and talk to her. I wish I knew if she is Birdie.

God. If you're Birdie ... please just reveal yourself.

We sit around the small fire Loosepants built for brewing coffee. I shift my seat to avoid the smoke.

'So, are you guys going to introduce yourselves now?' I ask, unable to wait any longer.

'It's tradition to wait until we light the main campfire, but since you already know most of us, I think we can start,' Loosepants says. *Loosepants, I could hug you.*

He stands up, clearing his throat like he's about to give a TED Talk. 'Hi, I'm Loosepants. I like ice cream, conspiracy theories about *everything*, and I once walked two kilometres backward—long story. Anyway, that's me!'

What a guy.

'Would you like to introduce yourself next?' The girl-who-might-be-Birdie asks the guy beside her.

'Whatever,' he says, setting his mug down. 'I'm Frost, and I don't like a lot of things.' Loosepants and the girl exchange a glance but say nothing.

'Your turn,' I say to the girl—the one person I've been most eager to learn about.

'Okay.' She smiles, adjusts her scarf and stands. 'You already know me by my real name, and we've even talked before.' *I don't know your real name.* But when she mentions we've talked, I feel a surge of hope.

'But since we don't use our real names on the trail, let me tell you my trail name. I am ...' She pauses. *Say it already.* '... Daisy. I love shopping, doing makeup, and lots of other things that I don't talk about. And I'm a social media influencer, as you already know.'

Daisy. My mind stumbles for a moment, trying to catch up. Clarity sweeps over me like a sudden gust of wind. *Daisy.* That explains the daisy on her watch and bag. The birds ... they must have just been part of the design. I feel a mix of surprise and disappointment.

I look at her face glowing in the firelight.

If you're not Birdie ... then who is?

And why does she even want me here?

'Did you enjoy the coffee?' Loosepants asks as I set my mug down.

'It was the best one I've ever had,' I reply honestly.

'Wait until you try my ginger tea,' he says, grinning. 'Huntress loves it.'

'Huntress?'

Loosepants throws his hands up dramatically, eyes wide with realisation. 'Did I really not tell you about her? God, how could I forget? Huntress is the best! She is like the sweetest and the most adventurous of us,' he says, glancing around.

'I wish you two had got a chance to meet. But I don't think she'll turn up for a few hours. She is always out there, hunting for new challenges. Even right now, she's probably doing something scary. Once, she scaled a cliff, nothing huge, but high enough to break your bones if you fell, and she did it without any ropes attached to her body.'

Officer passes by, struggling to carry an overloaded stack of firewood, bits of it trailing behind him. Loosepants watches Officer out of the corner of his eye, and it's clear that neither of us wants to jump up to help after our last encounter.

'She seems interesting. Who else is here?' I ask. Including Huntress, there are seven of us, but eight tents set up.

'There's also the Nerds,' Loosepants smirks. 'But you won't see them here.'

'Why not?'

'They're off somewhere in the woods, probably snogging all over the place,' he adds with a wink. 'They can't keep their hands off each other. It's kinda cute, actually, but a bit too much sometimes.'

'Sounds like you've gathered quite the group.'

'Oh, you have no idea. But they're great people. Just sometimes, you walk into the wrong place at the wrong time, if you know what I mean.'

I raise a brow. 'Yeah.'

'How did you get yourself to come on this camp?' Frost asks suddenly. It's the first time I've heard him speak voluntarily. His voice is low and steady, and his expression unreadable as he waits for my answer. I stare blankly, scrambling for a response, but I don't have any.

'Let me answer that,' Daisy chimes in, practically jumping out of her seat.

Yes, please do that. Even I would like to know.

'One morning, I was going through my emails, mostly brands wanting to collaborate with me, when I found an unusual one.'

'Let me guess, let me guess ... it was from Wolf!' Loosepants interjects excitedly.

'Exactly,' Daisy exclaims. 'He said he'd seen my Instagram stories about preparing for this trek, and he went on and on about how much he loved my posts, the beautiful photos I sometimes click of nature and put on my stories, and would really like to join. He was so sweet and polite. And, you know, I don't like disappointing my followers, so I agreed.' Her face lights up, either from the moon now peeking through the trees or from pure, radiating joy.

'Then why didn't he just message you on Instagram?' Frost asks. *A good question*, one I might've asked myself, but again, I have no explanation.

Daisy, however, jumps to my defence again. 'Isn't it obvious? He probably figured someone with as many followers as me gets loads of DMs, so he wanted to be sure I'd see it by emailing me instead. Right, Wolf?'

My mind races to piece together the puzzle. 'Ye ... s. Yes.' My voice wavers slightly, and I offer a hesitant smile, trying to convey my gratitude without revealing my own confusion.

'Whatever ...' Frost mutters, clearly unimpressed.

I ignore him, turning to Daisy with a smile. 'Thank you for letting me tag along, Daisy. And I love all your posts, reels and stories, by the way. There are so many creators on Instagram, but trust me, no one is as incredible, genuine and sweet as you. It's quite inspiring to be honest.'

'Thanks, Wolf.' Daisy's smile widens, her cheeks flushed.

And just like that, I know I've won her over.

God, I hate myself for it.

For lying.

For sounding like him.

Just like my dad—who always knows the right words to say, even when they're not true.

PPS The trail has a way of bringing people and moments together when you least expect it. Don't fight it. Let the trail surprise you.

You did this, Birdie. You reached out pretending to be me.

I clamp my hands over my ears as a loud metallic banging nearly deafens me. Spinning around, I see Officer hitting a steel plate with a serving spoon, a mischievous grin on his face.

'Would you stop it?!' Daisy shouts, her voice cutting through the noise. Even with my ears covered, I can hear her anger. When he doesn't stop, she marches over and snatches the spoon from his hand.

'Woah, woah, so feisty,' Officer chuckles.

'Were you planning on making us all deaf?' Daisy snaps, standing inches from him, her eyes locked onto his.

'Would you just calm down? Man, you try to be a good guy, and this is what you get.' He throws up his hands as if surrendering. Daisy doesn't budge, her glare unyielding.

'Alright, alright, I'm sorry for disturbing your evening.' He steps away, casting a quick glance at me. There's something unsettling in his expression, but I can't quite figure out what. Daisy still looks furious as he walks towards me.

'Wolf, Wolf, our dear new companion,' Officer calls out, coming closer. He places his hands on my shoulders, leaning in a bit. 'I gathered everyone here so I could apologise to you.'

I blink in surprise. 'Apologise?'

'Yes. Come forward, my fellow hiker,' he gestures grandly. 'Guys, let's give him a warm welcome!' He starts clapping, and after a hesitant moment, Daisy and the others join in. I notice they seem unsure.

I take a cautious step forward.

'Don't be scared, Wolf. I just want to make you feel at home,' Officer says, his tone surprisingly friendly.

'That's a nice thing to do,' Daisy remarks, though she looks a bit uncertain. Am I the only one sensing something's off?

'I'm really sorry for how I acted earlier,' Officer continues, pulling me closer by the arm. His voice drops to a low whisper. 'I hope you'll forgive me.'

'No hard feelings,' I reply with a small smile. Maybe this is my chance to make a friend. Considering I don't have friends, I don't want to waste this opportunity.

Officer picks up a wooden torch lying near a pile of wood and lights it. Flames spring to life, casting flickering shadows across his face. He raises it high above his head.

'To officially welcome you to the camp and accept you into our group, you will light this bonfire,' he announces, pointing to the large stack of logs arranged at the centre of the circle of our tents. 'It will symbolise our trust, friendship and togetherness as true campers.'

Cheers and shouts erupt from the group, though Frost remains silent, his gaze distant.

Feeling touched by the gesture, I accept the torch. Maybe I misjudged Officer. Perhaps I shouldn't be so quick to form opinions, after all, others have judged me too quickly before, and I hated that.

The warmth of the torch is comforting in the chilly night air. Holding it carefully, I step towards the bonfire.

'Go ahead, light it,' Officer encourages.

'Yes, Wolf. Light it up!' Daisy calls out, her eyes shining with excitement.

All begin chanting, 'Light it! Light it! Light it!' Their voices blend into a rhythmic chorus that fills the night.

As I approach the bonfire, I catch a quick glimpse of Officer's face—a sly grin that sends a small doubt through me. But I push it aside. Maybe it's just the firelight playing tricks.

I lower the torch to the dry leaves at the base of the pile. They catch quickly, flames climbing up to the kindling and larger logs. Satisfied that the fire is spreading evenly, I toss the torch onto the top. Bright orange sparks shoot into the sky, drawing cheers and applause.

I turn back towards the group, sharing a smile with Officer.

Maybe this is why Birdie sent me here, to make friends, to learn to trust again.

Just as I'm about to step away, a burst of bright orange and yellow sparks erupts from the bonfire, far brighter than before. My eyes snap back to the flames. Moments later, vivid blue sparks shoot out, followed by flashes of green.

'What the ...?' I mutter, a feeling of unease creeping in.

A sudden, deafening blast shatters the calm night, throwing me off balance. I stumble backward, catching myself with my hands before hitting the ground. Another explosion follows, a wooden log breaking apart and sends fiery pieces in all directions.

'Yes! Woohoo,' Officer shouts, his voice filled with wild excitement.

I scramble away on all fours, narrowly avoiding a burning piece that crashes where I was just standing. Panic surges through me. Around me, chaos erupts, Daisy and Loosepants are shouting, their words lost in the noise. The darkness is filled with blinding flashes of red, green and blue—colours so bright they burn into my vision.

Covering my ears does little to block out the relentless noise. My heart pounds erratically, and cold sweat covers my skin. I try to look away from the raging fire, but it's like I can't move.

It's okay. It'll stop. It has to stop.

Gradually, the explosions fade, leaving an eerie silence. The bonfire smolders, pieces of wood crackling softly. I stay crouched, hands still pressed to my ears, afraid to believe it's over.

A gentle hand touches my shoulder. I flinch but then see Loosepants's concerned face. He's speaking, but his words sound muffled, like we're underwater.

'Are you okay?' he asks, his eyes wide with worry.

I nod weakly, though every muscle in my body feels tense with fear. My legs shake as he helps me stand.

Flashes of a memory flood my mind.

Mom and Dad yelling downstairs. Me, no older than five or six, clutching a firecracker on the balcony. The sudden spark, the hanging clothes catching fire. The chaos that followed—the frantic rush to extinguish the flames, my screams echoing in the air. My father's hand striking my cheek, the sting of it, the force knocking me to the floor. The shouting, the noise, the blame, the fights—louder than the fire itself.

A loud clap on my back jolts me back to the present. Someone strolls in front, a wide grin plastered across their face. 'No hard feelings, man. Just a big welcome.' They say, their voice light, as though the scene from moments ago was nothing but a joke.

I stare at him, a mix of emotions swirling inside me—confusion, betrayal, anger. This wasn't a harmless prank; it was reckless and dangerous.

'Why ... why would you do that?' I manage to whisper.

'Lighten up. It's all in good fun,' Officer replies, brushing off my distress. 'Besides, everyone loves a good fireworks show.'

Around us, the others are trying to pull themselves together. Daisy glares at Officer, her earlier excitement replaced with anger. Someone keeps a steadying hand on my arm.

'I … I … I need to go back to my tent.'

'Of course. Come on,' Loosepants says.

As we walk away, Officer's laughter echoes behind me.

9

When you're camping and forget to roll yourself into a sleeping bag before you fall asleep, the cold does the job of waking you up. *What time is it?* I wonder, but I don't want to make the effort to check. The walls of the tent are still dark, so the sun hasn't risen yet. I stretch my numb limbs and wrap myself tightly in the blanket, shivering as the cold fabric touches my skin.

Each movement reminds me of where I am and, more painfully, of what happened last night. Loosepants, Officer, the bonfire, the firecrackers, my panic attack ... I'm wide awake now. What would they think of me? Did they notice? I hope they didn't. I had tried my best to hide the shaking until I reached the tent.

I turn onto my side, pulling the blanket closer as if it could shield me from my thoughts. Why did Birdie send me here? I've been following her blindly, but maybe I shouldn't this time. I don't want to be around people. I can't, not anymore. I can't try to make friends again.

This version of me, this broken state ... It's because of my friends. It's because of how they treated me when I needed them most.

I suddenly remember every call that I made, every text I sent—each one ignored.

A heavy weight settles in my chest. My hands start to tremble, and breathing gets harder. The darkness of the tent isn't empty anymore; it's thickening, pressing against my skin. It's reaching for me, trying to drag me back to that cruel night.

None of them trusted me. None of them gave me a chance to explain. It felt like everyone was just waiting to turn on me, to label me a monster.

If only they had listened, if only they had ...

Don't think.

Don't let your mind go there.

That night. If only I had—

Stop thinking, Arjun.

I clutch my chest. My heart pounding hard. I blink, trying to steady myself, but the thoughts keep coming.

They didn't wait.

They didn't ask.

They didn't care.

How they all looked at me when—

Stop thinking, Arjun! Just breathe ... Please.

I try. But it's like my body has forgotten how to breathe.

Each breath feels like a fight. An exhausting effort. I claw at my chest, dig my nails in until it hurts too much. I like that pain. I like how it drags me a little further away from that night.

Inhale, Arjun.

The breath breaks halfway.

Hold—

I can't.

Exhale.

Focus on what's here. Now.

Ground yourself.

I look at the tent walls, I look at my bag sitting in the corner. I look at the tent's zip, fully closed.

Breathe.

I run my fingers over the blanket, feeling its rough fabric beneath my palm.

Breathe.

I listen. A faint sound of rustling leaves reaches my ears. I hold on to it to ground myself. I manage to draw in a deep breath. The air is cold, and smells of damp earth and pine. It's different from the city air I'm used to. It helps. It helps me remember where I am. I am in the mountains. I am not there. I am not where it all happened.

For a long time, I let the mountain air, the soft sounds outside do their work. My heartbeat starts to ease.

And when it finally comes back to normal, the realisation comes rushing in.

I know what I have to do.

I have to leave.

In a few minutes, I've packed everything: my diary, my only pen, the torch, the blanket ... I double-check that I haven't forgotten anything. I'm ready to go. I just need to take down the tent and pack it.

'Hey, you awake?' I nearly jump, dropping my phone. Someone is outside my tent.

'Wolf?' the voice calls again, sweet and calm. Maybe it's Daisy, I think. But it doesn't sound like her. It could be one of the Nerds.

'Um ... yes,' I reply. There's no point hiding; they must have heard me moving.

'Would you like to take a walk?' the voice asks.

'I promise you'll like it,' she adds when I stay silent too long.

The instinct to say no is too strong to resist. But there is something about her tone ... there is no malice in it. There's no edge to it. No pressure. Just ... a little warmth. *Maybe even care?*

And if someone's awake, sneaking away unnoticed won't work anyway.

'Okay,' I say.

'Come outside when you're ready,' says the voice. It's oddly familiar but I can't place it.

I put on my shoes and my grey jacket, then unzip the tent. I shiver as the cold air hits me, and I immediately regret leaving my gloves behind.

Once outside, I look around, trying to find the source of the voice. But there is no one here.

'Don't turn around,' says the voice from behind me.

I want to argue, to turn and see who it is, but something in her tone disarms me.

'Why?' I can't help but think this might be another prank.

'You have to trust me on this, Wolf,' she says.

'Is this another prank?' I ask, trying not to turn.

'No. Just trust me for the next few minutes,' she pauses. 'Can you please do that?'

I hesitate. Every instinct tells me not to. But there's something in her voice—something honest, soft, warm—that makes me want to give in to whatever she is telling me to do.

I exhale slowly, my breath fogging in the air. 'Okay,' I reply.

'I'm going to blindfold you now,' she says. I open my mouth to protest but stop when I feel her fingers wrap around mine.

Her touch is reassuring and warm. 'Just trust me,' she says, even more softly this time, the words reaching my ears slowly.

She lets go of my hand, and I feel a soft cloth being tied over my eyes.

'Is this necessary? I can't see anything in this darkness anyway.'

'It is,' she says. I have definitely heard this voice somewhere.

'Just follow my lead.' She holds my hand again.

I shiver and grip her hand tightly as a gust of cold wind passes by. Closing your eyes makes you open to a wider world, I had read somewhere, and now I know it's true. I hear the rising birds chirping, mixed with the constant sound of crickets—that have not yet gone to bed.

As we walk, I notice the ground beneath my feet changing. The soft, even earth turns uneven. My steps become shorter as the path starts to incline. The air feels thinner, cooler. My breathing gets heavier.

'Are we going uphill?' I ask, feeling the strain in my legs and the slight pull of gravity against me.

'You've always been a smart one,' she says with a smile in her voice.

'Wait. Do I know you?'

'Shh, just move your feet. You don't want to miss it.'

And I do.

It should be impossible to hike blind, but with her guiding me, it feels strangely doable.

She warns me about a root, and I step over it perfectly. 'Duck your head,' she whispers, and I feel something like pine needles just graze my hair. 'Squeeze through here,' she says, warning me about the trees ahead, her shoulder brushing mine as she guides me through. 'Can I take it off now?'

'Just a little further.'

Eventually, the ground levels out and a strong wind hits us, but she holds me steady. I remember Anurag talking about his first date with Reecha. 'It's magical when you hold a girl's hand,' he'd said. 'It's like you never want to let go.'

I remember laughing and teasing him at the time, but now I get what he was talking about. Her hand is strong but delicate, her touch softer and warmer than anything I've felt before. And somehow, even when I am blindfolded, with her hand in mine—I feel completely safe.

'We're here.' She lets go of my hand—I kind of wish she hadn't—and says softly, 'Now, I need you to promise me something. Promise me you won't look at me but only look ahead when I take off your blindfold.'

I want to know who she is more than anything, but still, I say, 'Okay, I promise.'

'I'm taking it off. Don't open your eyes until I tell you to.'

Her fingers brush gently against the back of my head as she unties the blindfold. The soft fabric slips away, and the cold morning air kisses my eyelids, sending a slight shiver through me.

Even with my eyes closed, I can feel the world changing around me. The air is cooler here—crisper, lighter—carrying a scent of pine and damp earth. It grazes my skin, slides into my hair, moves around me as if trying to know who this new person in the mountains is.

'Just breathe,' she whispers. 'Feel the air around you.'

I take a breath, slow and deep. The cold air rushes in, fills my lungs, and leaves a sharp, grounding ache in my chest. I draw another breath, steadier this time, my lungs getting used to it, and with it comes a strange calm, like something inside me is beginning to quieten down.

For a moment, everything is still.

It's just me and my breathing now—slow and steady. There is nothing else. Just a silence so complete that the constant noise in my head—the one that hasn't left me alone for days—is simply gone. It is not haunting me anymore.

It feels strange at first. Scary, even. To find my mind so empty. I'm so used to the chaos that I keep waiting for the panic to come rushing back, like a predator watching its prey, before it sneakily attacks. But it doesn't return.

Then, slowly, the sound of my heartbeat reaches me. It's the old, familiar rhythm. It isn't racing or pounding; it isn't gripped by anxiety. It's just free.

I hear her speak then, her voice calm and just an inch from my ear.

'Now ... open your arms.'

I obey.

I open my arms wide, feeling the wind wrap around me. It rushes past my ears, wild and cold, brushing against my neck, my face. Its chill seeps deep into my skin—sharp at first, then strangely comforting. My jacket flutters against the pull of the air, like it's trying to take flight. I steady my feet, lean into it. For a moment, it feels like the wind is holding me, steadying me, telling me, *I've got you.*

And then, I almost imagine it whispering:

No one can chain you.

You're not meant to live caged by the whispers and judgements of others.

It feels like it's telling me I don't need anyone else to live, to move, to breathe.

That if I choose to, I can be the way it is—running wild through valleys, singing songs, carrying stories wherever I go.

'You can be free,' it whispers.

'You can be the wind—wild, untamed, unapologetically free.'

'Can I? Really?' I find myself asking it, holding onto that feeling for long.

'Now, open your eyes,' she whispers.

I slowly open them, and the world unfolds before me.

Mountains, endless, layered one after another, their peaks cutting into the sky. The horizon is painted in colours I feel like I'm seeing for the first time—deep purples fading into pinks, fiery oranges melting into soft yellows. The first rays of the sun peek over distant peaks, the snowcaps glowing as if lit from within. The sky stretches endlessly—vast, open, infinite.

Below us, a sea of mist blankets the valleys, only the tallest deodar trees piercing through like islands in a white ocean. The whole landscape is drenched in golden light—gentle, yet powerful—chasing away the last traces of the night.

I take a careful step forward. I'm afraid of heights, but I still sit down on the grass a few steps away from the edge. Dew soaking through my clothes. But I don't mind.

I keep staring, as long as I can. As far as I can.

It feels like the world has been reborn, and I'm witnessing its first morning.

Tears well up, blurring my view. I can't tell if it's because of the cold air or everything stirring inside me. All I know is—something's changing.

As the sun climbs higher, I feel it calling to me.

Reminding me how it rises every morning, fighting the darkness. And maybe it's my turn now—to forget, to let go, to fight through my own darkness ... and to begin again.

I hear soft footsteps behind me. The tears spill over, warm against my cold cheeks. I don't wipe them away.

For once, I'm not afraid of being seen—*really* seen.

She sits down beside me without a word. Together, we watch as the world wakes up. The mist begins to lift, revealing the lush green forests below. Terraced fields and tiny rooftops of distant villages start to appear as the sunlight reaches them. The trees sway gently, as if welcoming the new morning.

I take a shaky breath, feeling lighter than I have in a long time.

It's quiet. Peaceful.

Then, barely above a whisper, I ask, 'Can I look at you now?'

'Yes,' she replies, 'you can.'

I turn to face her, my heart pounding.

For a moment, everything around me blurs—the wind, the sunlight, even the sound of my breath.

And then our eyes meet.

I freeze. I know those eyes. I know that face.

And not even in my wildest dreams could I have imagined it to be her.

'Anjali?'

'Hello, Arjun.' She smiles, tucking a loose strand of her straight hair behind her ear. The whole world goes silent. Nothing else exists—not the mountains, not the cold, not the birds singing far away.

Just her. Her eyes. Her smile. The way the faint sunlight glows across her face.

And in that moment, I realise why everyone at college had a crush on her ... including me.

10

'You ... I mean ... How?' I ask, feeling as if the air has been sucked out of my lungs.

'I had the same look on my face when Daisy showed me your picture,' she says, glancing over at me.

I study her face. Anjali—the first name Anurag had written on the list of 'The Girls Arjun Can Date'. We had both agreed she was way out of my league and crossed her name off the list.

'I'm Huntress here, by the way,' she says, extending her hand playfully.

'I'm Wolf,' I reply, shaking her hand. Part of me wonders if she knows about everything that happened back at college, but she doesn't mention it. There's no hint of changed behaviour either—not even in her smiles.

Maybe she hasn't heard yet. She was away for the last few months, working at that high-paying internship at the big IT company—the one everyone wanted, but only she managed to get.

Maybe her being away worked in my favour.

'Loosey told me,' she says. 'The entire story of how he named you Lone Wolf, and then the transition to just Wolf,' she pauses. 'The name suits you, though.'

Her voice shifts—gentler now, almost careful. 'Even though you had a group, it kind of always felt like you were on your own.'

Her words hit deeper than I expect. I try to smile.

She's not wrong. I've always been surrounded by people, yet somehow always alone.

What surprises me more is that she noticed it.

As the morning air warms, she unzips her green sleeveless puffer vest, revealing a cream plaid long-sleeve shirt underneath. A charcoal knitted beanie sits snugly on her head, her hair perfectly straight, falling neatly over her shoulders.

Anjali.

I can't think of a girl more popular than her in college. She's easily the prettiest one there. Part of the student council, always buried in her textbooks or working on something on her laptop. I know plenty of guys who suddenly became regulars at the library just because she'd be there.

And when she's not working or studying, she's out there organising donation drives for underprivileged kids.

I've never really understood her, to be honest. No one has. As Anurag always said, 'How can a girl so pretty and so cool be so nerdy at the same time? I mean, shouldn't a girl that hot be out clubbing or something?'

'Never took you for a hiker, Mr President,' she says, breaking the silence. Mr President—that's what she always calls me, though my post in the student council is (or was—I don't know if I've been removed) general secretary.

'I hike all the time,' I lie, and she raises an eyebrow.

'You are such a terrible liar,' she says, laughing.

Caught, I smile.

'Do you come here often?'

'Always,' she replies, looking ahead.

We lapse back into silence, watching as the last remnants of fog lift from the valleys. Eventually, she stands and offers me her hand.

'We should head back.'

We walk side by side down the trail. Now that I can see, it's much easier.

'This place reminds me of the trek you organised for the student council and teachers—just outside the city,' I say.

Her eyes light up. 'And you arrived before anyone else, helping me carry breakfast and water. I was so worried about managing it all alone. But you were there, helping me, like always. Being yourself, the sweetest person.'

I feel my cheeks warm. 'It was nothing.'

'It meant a lot,' she insists, adjusting her beanie—it's a bit worn out, threads fraying at the edges. It must hold some special meaning for her to keep it all this time.

'It was a great day, and a bit scary too. Do you remember how Dean Bedi had nearly collapsed?'

She laughs. 'Oh, yes, I was really scared. The irony was that he was the one who had asked me to arrange it and had kept boasting about how fit he was and how he could easily run up the mountains.'

'And then he was absent for two days afterwards,' I add. 'He claimed he had to attend a conference, but everyone knew he could barely move.'

We both laugh.

It's not until we can see the camp that I realise I haven't thanked her. 'Hey, thank you,' I say, stopping.

'Don't mention it,' she says, giving me a wide smile. 'Everyone needs to witness the magic of a sunrise every now and then.'

The smile, the words, the way she is just here ... next to me. I can only try and pretend to be normal as my heart does somersaults inside.

'Hey, by the way,' she says as we enter the camp, 'let's keep the college connection between us for now. I'd rather not have everyone pestering us with questions about college life or asking us to share stories.'

I nod, agreeing.

Loosepants is the first one to spot us. He comes running and hugs me tightly.

'I was so scared for you, man. Frost said you'd come around since your tent was still here, but I was worried. I thought you were going to leave us.' His last words come out almost as a sob.

'Don't worry, Loosey. He was with me. Everything is fine,' Huntress says reassuringly.

'The next time you plan something like this, you take me with you,' he says, freeing me and hugging her. I wish I could do that.

'Okay, hon, next time for sure.' She pats him on the back.

By the time he finally lets her go, Daisy and Frost have joined us. Loosepants half walks, half drags us towards breakfast. I'm thankful; my stomach is growling.

The fire they've built is struggling but still has enough warmth to make morning tea. Loosepants doesn't let me help, and soon hands us all steaming cups. I bring out the packet of bread I bought yesterday at a tea stall and share it with everyone.

I'm truly happy no one has brought up anything about last night. I guess it was terrible for all of us, and everyone just wants to leave it in the past.

Daisy offers her share of bread to Frost, and he takes the slices without even saying 'thank you'. *Fucker.*

'I'm not really hungry,' she says to me, but I know that's a lie. She probably ate nothing last night either. I offer her some slices of bread from the remaining ones. She thinks about it for a moment, then accepts with a smile. Huntress is watching me and gives me an approving nod as I get back and sit next to her. There's a familiar warmth to her gaze that I have always admired.

'Boo!'

I nearly spill my tea. Officer has come out of nowhere and yelled in Huntress's ear.

'You don't scare me,' Huntress says, smiling, unaffected.

'One day, I will,' Officer says confidently, picking Huntress up from behind and spinning her around. Good thing she had finished her tea. I manage to get away just in time to avoid Huntress's long hiking boots from hitting me.

'Stop it! Please, please, stop it!' Huntress screams, but she's laughing hysterically like a little kid. When he finally puts her down, they hug.

I don't know if it's just my imagination, but she shoots me a look—the kind that makes you feel like that person cares and is worried about how things are affecting you.

'Give it to me,' Loosepants says as he takes my empty cup away. He too, I notice now, is staring at them. His cheeks are flushed, and the corners of his mouth are turned down. I can't blame him if he has a crush on Huntress and is sad or jealous to see her with Officer.

'You were nowhere to be seen this morning,' Officer says to Huntress, his hands still holding her by the waist. *It hurts. It shouldn't. She is just a crush. But it bloody does.*

'I wanted to go for a walk. And lucky for me, Wolf here was gracious enough to agree to come with me.'

'And that reminds me, you were going to apologise to Wolf,' Huntress tells Officer firmly. She has that authoritative tone—the kind that always makes everyone in college fall in line during events we organised.

'Alright,' says Officer, turning towards me. 'I'm sorry, man. I didn't mean any harm.'

I don't know how, but I manage to smile at him.

Officer ... Is he the reason Huntress always said no to every guy who asked her out in college?

I'd heard dozens of stories about guys approaching her—the richest, the most popular, even the nerdiest. She'd turned them all down.

Was it all because of him?

It's her personal life, I tell myself. You don't have any right to think about it. And even if they are together—and you don't like it—it's her choice whom she wants to be with.

Even if it's a bully like Officer.

Huntress leaves with Officer, going to another corner to sit down and talk. When she laughs at something he says, I do feel a pang of jealousy. She passes me a smile once when our eyes lock. It's a soft smile, almost sympathetic, before she looks away.

Daisy orders everyone to pack their stuff and get ready to move out, complaining that we are already late. My whole bag is packed and ready to be hoisted, but I spend some time inside my tent doing nothing. I don't want anyone to know I was already planning on leaving this morning.

I pull out my phone and check my notifications. I had sent Birdie a selfie with the letterbox, hoping she'd see it. But there's still no signal here. No way to check if she has even seen the message. What if she's replied with something important and I'm missing it—maybe my next steps? I stare at the empty signal bars, feeling a mix of frustration and impatience.

With a sigh, I slip the phone back into my pocket. A few more minutes pass before I start taking down my tent. It doesn't take long, and I'm done soon.

Huntress has finished packing too and is now helping Loosey with his gear. His entire tent floor looks like a mini marketplace—stuff scattered everywhere.

Daisy's done with her packing and has moved on to help Frost. At first glance, it looks like they're working together, but watching them for more than a second makes it obvious—she's doing most of the work.

She crouches, rolling up their sleeping mats and shoving them into bags. Frost holds a tent pole loosely, occasionally spinning it in his hand like a baton. When Daisy struggles with the tent canvas, he just stands there, nodding like some sort of supervisor.

'Could you grab that corner?' she asks, slightly out of breath.

'Sure,' he says, taking hold of the fabric with one hand. As soon as it's folded enough to manage, he lets go, leaving her to wrestle it into the carrying sack.

I take a step towards her to help, but she turns to me, smiles, and mouths the words, 'I'm fine'. I just nod and turn away.

I watch him from the corner of my eye—tall and lean, with fair skin and sharp features. Some might call him handsome, but to me, he's nothing but a piece of shit. An arrogant jerk who doesn't know how to appreciate anyone's effort—or maybe just doesn't care to.

Officer has packed up and is sitting on a big rock, studying a map. Probably deciding the next route. His bag leans against the rock, nearly flat. *Travel lightly.* He seems to have taken those words a little too seriously.

The only new face I spot is the guy sitting opposite me. I walk up to him. He still hasn't taken down his tent—must be one of the Nerds Loosey told me about.

'Need any help?' I ask.

He nearly jumps. 'You scared me there,' he says, catching his breath. Sweat shines on his forehead, and I notice he barely has a neck under his double chin.

'Sorry, I didn't mean to,' I say, not sure what else to add.

'No, it's not your fault. I just thought you were Officer,' he says, dabbing the sweat off his brow and glancing over my shoulder. I look back too—relieved to see Officer hasn't moved.

'I totally get why that would scare you,' I say. 'We haven't met. I'm Wolf.'

'I'm one of the Nerds,' he replies with a grin. 'They call me just Nerd when my hot half isn't around—and He-Nerd behind our backs when they want to talk about me.'

I hesitate, unsure how to respond.

'Don't worry,' he says, smiling. 'We picked the name ourselves. We like flaunting that we're, proudly, nerds.'

'Okay,' I nod. 'And really, let me know if you need a hand with it?' I offer. The guy looks tired.

Before he can answer, a girl steps out of the tent, arms crossed over her chest. Unlike him, she's incredibly thin, with a long neck and thick glasses perched on her nose.

'He doesn't need anyone else's help,' she says sharply.

'He was just offering, my eye candy,' He-Nerd teases, flashing a smile at her.

'Yes, I just thought to lend a hand,' I add quickly, trying to ease the tension.

'Why? Do you think that my Hulk cannot do it himself?' She glares at me from behind her round, thick glasses. 'And he has me to help him if he needs it. Do you understand?'

'I only wanted to help, nothing else,' I say, stepping back because she's nearly in my face.

'Oh, so now you think I cannot help him?' she accuses.

'I didn't mean that.' I look around, hoping for somebody to come and rescue me.

'Oh, I know your kind, mister,' she says, straightening the hairband she is wearing. The hair on her forehead is pulled forward, and maybe because the cut is self-given, the bangs are not in a straight line. They form a curve instead, with her hair being longest at both ends and shortest in the middle. 'Your kind thinks a woman can't do the same tasks you men do,' she says, baring her teeth and making her braces clearly visible.

Where did this come from?

'Oh, Pookie, he didn't mean it,' He-Nerd says, coming to my rescue.

'You are too innocent, baby. You don't know them like I do. Always belittling women,' says She-Nerd.

'I don't think less of women,' I protest, clenching my fists.

'Please, honey. He didn't mean anything bad. Besides, you know what you are capable of, everyone here does. So just calm down, my cutie,' says He-Nerd. As he utters the last words, She-Nerd bends down and pulls his face close to hers. I look the other way, hoping it will be over soon.

Ten, nine, eight ... I start counting backward from ten—the same way I used to when Anurag and Reecha had first started dating. By the time I used to reach zero, their kiss would have ended.

I turn back towards the Nerds. They are still kissing. I'm about to turn away when She-Nerd opens her eyes and stares at me. With her free hand, she points at their faces and slides her tongue inside He-Nerd's mouth. *Ew.*

I turn away, repulsed by the sight and struggling to keep my breakfast down.

Apart from being an influencer, I've found one more thing about Daisy—she doesn't like to be late. She spent nearly ten minutes scolding Loosepants for not being ready on time. She was like a raging storm. Even I was a little scared.

Loosepants had realised he'd packed his sunglasses and hat, which he wanted to wear, deep inside his bag. He emptied everything out, creating a mountain of gear, only to find them in the small front pocket—exactly where Daisy had suggested they'd be.

His victory dance only made the situation worse, with Daisy lecturing him for fifteen minutes before finally apologising to him ten minutes later. She was teary-eyed as she asked for his forgiveness, even though he'd already accepted her first apology.

'He doesn't deserve her,' Loosepants says as we watch Frost carelessly toss aside the small bouquet of wildflowers Daisy just gave him. 'She spent so much time collecting them.'

'Yeah,' I agree, watching Daisy walk with her head down, her steps slower than before. She-Nerd, walking next to us, deliberately steps on the bouquet, crushing it underfoot. I don't know how to react, but part of me feels a strange sense of satisfaction.

'Not everyone you meet is a nice person. It's sad but true,' Loosepants remarks, glaring at Frost.

I think about that. Not everyone is nice. I recall Reecha and how she made my life miserable.

'But not everyone is bad, either,' I say, glancing at Huntress. She's walking ahead with Officer, who is holding her hand.

Walking through the tall trees feels like stepping into another world. The air is thick with the scent of pine, and the trunks of the deodar trees are covered in moss—some a vibrant green, others dried to a weary yellow. The ground is a thick carpet of pine needles and leaves, cushioning our steps.

The forest is alive with the sounds of birds and the rustling of leaves, filling my heart with some much-needed peace. But it doesn't last long. One glance at Huntress, laughing and walking with Officer at the front, and the what-ifs start flooding my mind. *What if Huntress finds out about what happened? Will she also turn me away like my friends did, without hearing my side of the story?*

Behind me, Daisy walks alongside Frost. She's in a white crop top, a sky-blue sweater tied around her waist, black yoga pants and blue shoes.

She wasn't in blue this morning. Frost hadn't changed by breakfast either—still in black then. It was only afterward that he switched to a blue shirt, around the same time Daisy went back into her tent and reappeared in new clothes.

Never pour your heart and efforts where they're not appreciated, Daisy, I wish I could tell her. She's beautiful, has a lovely smile and she's genuinely nice. Any guy would be lucky to have her.

She just needs someone who sees her like that. Someone who isn't as cocky as Frost or Officer.

'We have network!' Daisy announces suddenly.

I fumble for my phone. *Birdie.* I need to see if she's replied. Has she seen the picture I had sent? Said where I should head next? Is she meeting me? Or am I just supposed to keep tagging along with this group?

Nothing. No text. No seen tick. Just silence.

'Damn. This pic is hot,' says Loosepants, practically shoving his phone in my face.

It's Daisy, and she does look amazing. Her curls, with faint blue-green streaks, look like they've borrowed their colour straight from the forest and the blue sky. She's wearing the same crop top she's wearing now, just posing differently. I barely glance before looking away.

'Yeah, kind of,' I say.

'*Kind of?* Honey, she's serving main character energy. Look at that angle—those curves could start a war,' he says, fanning himself theatrically.

I shake my head. 'You need help.'

'Please, you just need taste. What kind of a straight guy could look at this and ignore it?' he fires back.

I don't argue. Daisy is looking kind of hot, sure—but she's not the one my mind's stuck on.

The kind of mystery and curiosity I find when it comes to Birdie—the drive to want to know who she is and to meet her in person; or the kind of warmth and admiration I feel towards Huntress. There's none of that with Daisy. Just a deep concern, maybe.

She's too kind. And I notice how easily she gives so much of herself away, how much energy she pours into someone who doesn't meet her halfway. Someone who won't even acknowledge her efforts.

Maybe I'm wrong. Maybe it's none of my business. But still—if she continues like this, chasing a red flag, I'm scared she'll get hurt. And I don't want that for her.

She doesn't deserve that.

Loosey is still staring at me, completely baffled, and waiting for a response.

'I may have to test it,' I say, shrugging innocently. 'Maybe I really am gay then.'

Before he can respond, I reach out and run my fingers up his arm, slow and deliberate, crawling like a spider.

He yelps, jerking his hand back like he's been electrocuted. I burst out laughing.

'Ah, don't worry, Loosey, I'm not gay. And even if I were, I wouldn't jump on you without your consent. I'm a man of values and morals.'

'Good,' he says, first shocked, then breaking into laughter.

I've memorised Daisy's Instagram ID. I make a mental note to check it out later, to make sure I know everything about what she posts and doesn't. I don't want to get caught.

—————

We come upon a wooden bridge arching over a shallow stream. I have no idea who built it, but it's striking. The wood is worn and weathered, its once-smooth planks now roughened by time and the footsteps of passing travellers. Its boards creak softly under our feet, and patches of moss cling to the sides, giving it a mystical vibe.

Daisy stops in the middle of it. 'Could someone take a picture of me here?' she asks, her eyes lingering on Frost.

She tucks a strand of hair behind her ear, waiting for him to respond. But he doesn't even glance her way, striding ahead without so much as a glance in her direction.

She watches him go, disappointment flickering across her face. Before I can step forward, Loosepants jumps in. 'Sure, I'd love to!' he exclaims, his voice brimming with enthusiasm.

For a moment, Daisy seems caught off guard, but then she pulls herself together. It's like watching a mask slip into place. She straightens up, a charming smile spreading across her face. Her eyes sparkling, she moves effortlessly into different poses—twirling lightly, leaning against the railing, gazing thoughtfully into the distance. The wind catches her hair just right, and she laughs. Gosh, I would love to see the picture captured in that moment.

Loosepants keeps clicking photos without stopping. 'These are turning out great,' he calls out.

I stand off to the side, observing the scene. Her followers would never guess from these photos that just moments ago she had looked so sad. She's a natural in front of the camera, her sadness hidden behind practiced smiles and lively expressions. It's impressive, but also heartbreaking.

I wonder how many people will see that laughing picture on her Instagram and think she's living the perfect life. How many will compare their own lives to hers, and wonder why theirs doesn't feel as bright and happy.

'Hurry up!' Officer's voice cuts through the calm. Everyone's waiting for us. Frost checks his watch, impatience evident in his stance.

'We're coming,' Loosepants replies, handing Daisy her phone. 'Take a look—I think you'll love them.'

'Thanks,' she says, her smile softening into something more genuine as she glances at the screen. 'They're really good.'

As we start walking to catch up with the others, I notice Daisy steal a quick glance at Frost. He doesn't notice. Her smile falters for just a second before she catches me watching her. She gives me a small shrug, as if to say, *can't do anything.*

I really pity her. I make a promise to myself: *I am going to help her realise her own worth.*

11

'Do many people walk this trail?' I ask Loosepants, trying to sound casual but unable to hide the eagerness in my voice. Any clue that could bring me closer to Birdie is worth pursuing.

'Quite a few,' he replies. 'Last winter, we met nearly eight groups along this path.'

'Have you met any this time?' I ask, a bit too quickly.

He glances at me but continues. 'Actually, three groups so far. We ran into one just a couple of days ago. We were scouting for a good campsite and found them packing up. We ended up using the spot they left—and guess what, they had some firewood remaining! A bonus.'

My heart quickens. 'How far ahead are they?'

'Maybe just a day. They can't be too far. Really nice folks, about our age—four guys and three girls ...'

Three girls, a day ahead. Could one of them be Birdie?

'They even offered us some chocolates,' Loosepants adds. 'And even though we're not supposed to take candies from strangers, we did. They seemed really nice, and the chocolates were even nicer. But why the sudden curiosity?' He looks at me, eyebrows raised.

I shrug, trying to play it cool. 'Just curious.'

'Were they by any chance medical students?' I ask, not being able to resist the curiosity.

'Oh yeah, now that you mention it,' he says, snapping his fingers. 'They were. I got to know when I talked to this curly-haired girl in their group. She was really kind, you know? She actually listened when I told her about different ice cream flavours in the world. Then I started pitching her new ones—like Sitaphal with chocolate, or maybe mango with sea salt. She didn't interrupt me once! Can you believe that? She even said my Sitaphal-chocolate combo sounded *too delicious.*'

Curly hair. Kind. Medical student.

Birdie ...

Loosey's still talking, his voice running somewhere in the background, but I don't hear any of it. Everything fades into the rhythm of my heartbeat.

She's just a day ahead—a single day.

And he's met her.

He's talked to her.

If I move fast, if I don't stop tonight then maybe ... maybe I could find her. Talk to her. See her.

'Oh, hello? Wolf! Wolfie?' Loosepants's voice cuts through the haze.

I blink, snapping back.

'You with me?'

'Yes ... yes.'

'We're nearly there,' Huntress calls out from ahead, pulling me out of my endless thoughts of Birdie.

Travelling isn't something I've done a lot, but standing here now, I understand what people mean when they talk about magical places. As we reach higher ground, the view takes my breath away. Below lies a crystal-clear lake, its surface reflecting the sky like a perfect mirror. Near the lake, nestled among towering pine trees, are several wooden cabins, their wooden colour blending perfectly with the trees around them.

It feels like we've stepped into another world—one preserved with love and care.

'It's beautiful,' I whisper, unable to take my eyes off the scene.

'It's something else, isn't it?' Loosepants says beside me. 'This place has a special vibe. And trust me, it's not just about the scenery.'

As we make our way down the path, the sound of children reciting a prayer reaches our ears, growing clearer with each step. I glance at Loosepants, but he just smiles knowingly.

In front of the cabins, on a wide grassy field, about thirty kids of various ages sit cross-legged, eyes closed, chanting in unison. An elderly man stands beside them, wearing a crisp white kurta, a shawl draped over his shoulder. His grey hair is neatly combed, and a white beard frames his face. He turns slowly towards us, and gives us a warm smile that whispers *welcome home.*

He reminds me of my own late grandfather in a way—the gentle stare and the kind of smile that makes you feel instantly accepted.

The man's voice leads the mantras, each word resonating deeply. It's powerful, almost hypnotic. I find myself closing my eyes. For a moment, everything else fades away.

The chanting stops and footsteps approach. I open my eyes to find the old man standing before us. He adjusts his square brown glasses and smiles.

'It's nice to see you all again,' he says, his gaze resting briefly on each of us. His eyes linger on Huntress. 'You're late,' he says to her, a gentle reprimand with a hint of affection.

'Sorry, Grandpa,' she replies, stepping forward. She hesitates for a moment, glancing at the kids, but she is too close now. And goes on to wrap her arms around him in a warm hug.

Wait—Grandpa?

I blink, surprised. Huntress never mentioned her grandfather lived out here. Not that we have ever talked about her family.

I notice the children's faces lighting up, especially when they look at Huntress. Some wave at her subtly, hiding their gestures from Grandpa, and she gives a small wave back.

'And who is this new face?' he asks, when the hug ends, turning his attention to me.

'This is Wolf. It's his first time here,' Huntress says.

I bend down to touch his feet. It just feels like the right thing to do.

'He's got more manners than you, little one,' he teases, his laughter rich and deep. He places his hands on my shoulders, lifting me up before pulling me into a side hug.

'Ha-ha, very funny,' Huntress says, rolling her eyes but smiling all the same.

The children behind him are starting to chatter among themselves, their neat rows dissolving into clusters. They're too adorable—the shy smiles they give me, the playful faces they make at Loosepants. I'm so going to love being around them.

And then, as the moment stretches, I start noticing the smaller things. A girl in the front, maybe ten, wearing a kurta that's way too big for her—the sleeves almost swallowing her hands. The boy beside her has a shirt that's too tight, the buttons pulling across his chest.

Once I see it, I can't unsee it. Almost every kid here has clothes that don't quite fit—either hanging loose or clinging close.

Why?

Why are they dressed like that? I don't ask. Not now. I'll have to ask Loosey later when we are alone.

But what gets me—what really surprises me—is how they're still laughing. How are they shining in the sunlight as if none of it matters?

Their chatter grows louder.

'Children, back to your classes,' Grandpa calls out, his voice firm yet kind. 'Go on now, in lines!'

I expect some resistance—maybe a few grumbles, a bit of pushing, something. But to my surprise, they move quietly, forming neat lines before heading towards the cabins.

They must really respect him. Grandpa watches them until the last child disappears inside. Then he turns back to us.

'You haven't been eating properly,' he says, his eyes settling on Huntress and Daisy.

'We are!' they protest in unison.

'And I've already given up on you,' he says, chuckling as he looks at Loosepants.

Loosepants grins. 'I do eat a lot. Ask anyone. But I don't know why I still look the same. You know, since the last few months I have even—'

'It's so good to see you again, Grandpa,' Daisy interjects, cutting him off. She's put on the sweater she had tied around her waist earlier. 'I brought this for you.' She pulls out a brown muffler from her bag.

'Oh, I can't accept this,' he says, hesitating. 'It must have been expensive.'

'Please take it, Grandpa. It'll look great on you. Huntress, tell him,' Daisy insists.

'It will, Dadaji. Try it on ... please?' Huntress says softly.

'You don't want me to be angry with you, do you?' Daisy adds.

He chuckles, shaking his head. 'You two certainly know how to twist my arm.' He wraps the muffler around his neck and strikes a pose with his hands on his hips. 'How do I look?'

'Like a movie star,' Huntress says, smiling.

'Now, go get settled and be ready for lunch,' Grandpa says, smiling, gesturing towards the cabins. 'I'll be with you shortly.'

Huntress opens her mouth to ask something, but he stops her and says, 'I know what you are going to ask. Don't worry. The kids have eaten already.'

We start walking towards the cabins. Each one is built from sturdy logs with slanted shingle roofs, elevated slightly on wooden beams. Every cabin has its own small porch overlooking a grassy field dotted with wildflowers.

I pause at the garden in front of our cabin. Neat rows of wildflowers—blue, pink and many shades of white—sway gently in the breeze. Up close, they're even more vibrant than when I saw them from a distance.

We're sleeping in adjacent rooms. The girls take one, and the boys share the other. Inside, there are three wooden bunk beds. Officer, Loosey and He-Nerd rush to claim the bottom bunks. I'm fine with any spot, so I place my bag on the top bunk above Loosey. Frost doesn't seem to care either; he tosses his bag onto an upper bunk without a word.

The room has a cozy vibe, with the glass window providing a beautiful view of the lake. I open it, and a gentle breeze greets me.

'I always love coming here,' Loosey says softly, gazing out the window.

'And you should, always,' Officer chimes in. He drapes an arm around Loosey's shoulder, pulling him close. 'The money Dadaji gets from renting these cabins to hikers helps provide for the kids.'

Provide for the kids? But before I can think more on that, I watch as Officer's grip tightens. Loosey's smile fades; he looks at me—as if asking for help—and starts trying to wiggle free.

'Leave him alone,' I say firmly, stepping forward. I'm not going to let him bully Loosey.

For a few moments, nothing happens. Frost rises from his bunk, his eyes flickering with interest at the unfolding drama.

'As you say, Wolf,' Officer replies, drawing out my name. He gives me a mocking grin, but releases his grip on Loosey and backs off, hands raised in feigned surrender.

I place a hand on Loosey's back and guide him outside. *I hate Officer. God knows what Huntress sees in the guy.*

The fresh air outside feels good, and we seem to be the first ones out.

'Sorry about that,' I say as we descend the stairs.

Loosey shrugs, forcing a small smile. 'It's okay,' he mumbles, but the way he rubs his shoulder tells me otherwise.

'I wanted to ask you, Loosey ...' Maybe this is as good a time as any to ask, 'these kids ...'

Before he can answer, Huntress appears beside us, nearly making me jump. 'They're orphans,' she says. 'Dadaji takes care of them as if they're his own children. He never wants them to feel like they're alone in this world. And they aren't. They have Dadaji, they have me—their elder sister—and they have Loosey.' She wraps an arm around each of us, pulling us into a warm embrace. 'And now, they have you,' she adds softly, her voice filled with warmth.

'Yes, they do,' I reply, meeting her gaze. From up close, I notice how her eyes catch the sunlight—I have always heard that brown eyes look the most beautiful in the sunlight. I wonder if they started saying that after seeing her eyes up close.

Suddenly, I realise I've forgotten how to breathe. *She is truly remarkable.*

I look away, before it could get awkward.

'Loosey,' I say, nudging him gently. He's still quiet. 'Huntress is tall, but she's not as tall as us, right?'

He looks puzzled. 'Um ... if you think about it ...'

I wink at him. 'You know what that means?'

Huntress raises an eyebrow, a hint of suspicion in her eyes. 'What are you two plotting?'

Before she can react, Loosey and I exchange a quick glance and, in one swift motion, we each take hold of her and lift her off the ground.

'Hey! What are you doing?' she exclaims, laughter bubbling up despite her mock outrage.

'Transporting you, Your Huntress Highness,' Loosey says, his eyes lighting up.

'Yeah, can't have you walking all that way,' I add with a grin.

She kicks her feet playfully. 'You guys are ridiculous! Put me down!'

'Sorry, can't hear you over all this laughter,' I tease.

We carry her towards the cabin at the end of the pathway, the one with a wisp of smoke curling from its chimney. As we get closer, the scent of spices drifts towards us.

Her laughter is contagious, and soon all three of us are chuckling. When we finally set her down, she starts chasing us playfully. We dart away, laughing loudly, the sound echoing amongst the trees.

By the time we stop running, breathless and grinning, the others have joined us. They look at us with amused expressions, though Officer's gaze feels like daggers. Is it because of the earlier incident with Loosey or because I'm next to Huntress? I don't know. But I would be lying if I say it doesn't scare me a bit.

Inside, the wooden tables are set with leaf plates, and the air smells of spices and warmth. Dadaji serves steaming rice, dal and puris—with Huntress helping him.

I take a bite. It tastes better than anything I've had in a long, long time.

'This is amazing,' I tell him, and he grins, piling more onto my plate before I can stop him. He does the same for everyone, ignoring their protests. The joy in his eyes and the glow on his face only increases with every serve.

After everyone finishes eating, conversations start to pick up. Loosey shares that he has a funny story to tell—which actually felt scary to me—about the one time he tried cooking rice and the cooker's lid blew open. Daisy recalls their last time here and how the kids kept staring at her hair—wondering how she grew them green.

As the laughter fades, Dadaji stands up. 'Well, since everyone seems rested, how about I show you the classrooms?'

'Yes, please!' Loosey exclaims, the excitement returning to his face.

Huntress and I trail behind the others, our footsteps crunching softly on the gravel path.

'How long has he been doing this?' I ask her.

'For over a decade,' she says, a hint of sadness in her voice.

'That's a long time. He's been doing some great work.'

'Yeah, he is a great man.' She pauses. 'I used to hate him sometimes when I was a kid—wanting all his attention for myself. But as I grew up, I started realising the sacrifices he was making. When he started, there was nothing. Just that one small cabin.' She points to a small cabin at the edge of the clearing. Unlike the others, it's old, with an uneven roof. 'It used to be crowded with five or six children. I slowly watched him put his entire life's savings into feeding the kids, and as more started coming, in expanding bit by bit.'

'It must have been hard,' I say, softly.

'It was.' She gives a sad smile. 'I'd often find him awake at night, walking around the lake, worried.'

I look ahead at Dadaji, leading the group with a high energy that contradicts his age. The respect for him grows in my heart.

'Do you come here often?' I ask.

'Whenever we get long holidays.' Huntress plucks a white wildflower from a nearby plant, twirling it between her fingers. 'I always wish I could stay here longer,' she says, handing the flower to me. 'But it's difficult for him. He never says it, but I can see it in his eyes. So, I come with hiking groups, never staying more than a week at a time. Sometimes, only for a day, like we will this time.'

Why is it so difficult for him? I want to ask, but I hold back.

'Is he the only one who teaches the kids?' I ask, putting the flower she has given me in my shirt's pocket, not wanting to ever lose it.

'Mostly. A few teachers from the nearest village volunteer on weekends, but that's it. Dadaji teaches them the rest of the time.' She lowers her gaze. 'It's difficult to get permanent teachers without any funding. But lots of hikers come this way, and renting these cabins helps a bit.'

As we round the first cabin, some of the children stand at the windows, flashing us their brightest smiles. I think about asking my father to donate money to this orphanage under his company's CSR commitment.

I imagine calling him and how that conversation would go: *Hey Dad, it's me ... yeah, me, your son ...? So, there's this orphanage I visited. They're doing some really great work, and I was hoping you could donate some money to them. Yeah, I know we haven't talked in years. But still ... help them, okay? It would mean a lot to me. Thanks. And yeah ... I probably won't be calling you again anytime soon.*

He would help, I think. But I'm not sure Dadaji would approve. I will ask Dad the next time we meet.

My eyes settle on Huntress. In college, she was always the first to volunteer for anything that involved helping others. Half the time, she was the one coming up with those ideas herself.

Once, a nearby school for special children reached out, asking for support. Huntress immediately decided to start a fundraiser. She didn't want anyone to feel pressured—though no one would've said no if she'd asked—so she convinced the student council to set up donation boxes around the campus.

With the cultural festival coming up, most people weren't too keen on helping.

I volunteered anyway. We spent two days cutting cardboard, painting signs and placing the boxes everywhere. I told myself

I was doing it for the cause, but really, I just wanted more time with her.

When the time came to count the donations, it wasn't much.

Without telling her, I slipped in the money I'd earned from a freelancing gig. It wasn't a lot, but it felt like something. Then, for the first time in months, I cashed one of the cheques my father had sent—and added that too.

The smile on her face had made it all worth it.

Worth every rupee.

Worth swallowing my pride.

But she didn't stop at just donating. She kept going there on weekends to teach them. I often wanted to go with her, more than anything else, but the freelancing I was doing to pay for college and my job at the bookstore kept me busy, especially on weekends. I had explained how much I wanted to come but couldn't. She had told me she understood, that I'd already done a lot.

When we reach the cabins, Grandpa is ushering the students, who have come out, back inside. One of them, a girl of maybe six, runs up to Huntress with a rose in her hand. She offers it to her.

'Did you make this?' Huntress asks, picking her up.

She nods, playing nervously with her skirt. I'm stunned; all this time I thought it was a real flower. As I look closer, I realise it's made of paper.

Huntress kisses the little girl's cheek. 'It's beautiful.'

As Grandpa walks towards us, she gently sets the girl down. The child, noticing Grandpa, doesn't need any more prompting. She runs off, laughing and singing a beautiful song, the words of which I don't understand.

'She's getting really good at it,' Grandpa says, admiring the rose.

'Yes, she is,' Huntress replies, pride in her voice.

'So, what are you all planning to do today?' Grandpa asks the entire group.

'I was hoping to get them to play football with me,' Officer speaks up. 'I brought one with me, and I'll leave it here for them when we go.'

Dadaji's eyes soften. 'That's very kind of you.' *Indeed. And very unlike him.*

'You can take them out after some time,' he says. 'They haven't studied much today.'

'What if we each take a class?' Daisy suggests, her eyes gleaming. 'I can teach them painting, along with Huntress and Frost. The Nerds can teach science. Wolf and Loosepants can also, I'm sure, teach them something.'

Everyone nods in agreement, except Frost, who remains impassive. Dadaji smiles warmly at us. We split up, each heading to a different cabin. Officer, whom Daisy hadn't assigned a class, joins Loosepants and me. I cross my fingers, hoping he won't cause any trouble.

Before we can decide what we could teach, Dadaji approaches us. 'Actually, could you three help me with something?' he asks, looking at Officer, Loosepants and me.

'Sure, Dadaji,' Loosepants replies. 'Anything you need, this brave group shall put their lives down if need be to help you in your mission.'

'You honour me with your words, brave knight. But nothing so complicated as putting your lives down. I was planning to take the children to our small farm to do some quick harvesting. A few extra pairs of hands would be helpful.'

'We would love to help,' I say.

Officer shrugs. 'I'm in.'

The children eagerly gather around us. 'We'll show you the way!' a little girl exclaims, her pigtails bouncing as she jumps.

'Always the excited one,' Grandpa chuckles. 'But if you're going to show them, what will I do?'

We all turn to the little girl, curious about her response. She thinks for a moment, tapping her chin thoughtfully.

'Hmm ... I know! You can sit with Anjali Di,' she declares confidently. 'We'll take them to the farm and even teach them what to do.'

I can't help but grin. *Damn, I love her sassiness.*

'But I—' Grandpa begins.

'She'll teach us, Dadaji. We don't need you,' Loosey chimes in, winking at the girl.

Hearing this, the little girl jumps up and down, her pigtails bouncing with her. She turns and teases Dadaji by sticking her tongue out at him.

He gasps. 'Come here ... you!' he exclaims, starting to chase her. She squeals and dashes ahead, while he stops after a few steps, laughing aloud.

—ɯ—

The children are eager to lead the way, some even dancing as they set off.

We follow the winding path until it opens into a small field lined with tomato plants—tall, green, and neatly tied to wooden sticks for support.

'We keep some for ourselves and sell the rest in the village,' the same little girl says proudly. She can't be more than six, her hair neatly parted in the middle and tied into two pigtails with bright red ribbons.

'Nice hairstyle,' I say, smiling.

She beams. 'Dadaji did it for me. He said I look like a princess.'

'He was right,' I reply. She blushes as her friends giggle, everyone's shyness melting away.

'Do you sell the tomatoes yourselves at the market?' Loosepants asks, clearly fascinated.

She shakes her head vigorously. 'Nope. Dadaji takes them to a merchant in the market. He doesn't let us go—I wish he did! But he says he doesn't want us to worry about that stuff. He just wants us to learn how to grow things.' She twirls, her ribbons fluttering. 'He says when we grow up, we can grow thousands of them if we want. Can you imagine? Sooo many!'

'That would really be something!' I reply.

A gentle breeze carries a sweet floral scent. Before I can ask where it's coming from, she grabs my hand.

'Come with me,' she says, dragging me round a corner.

Rows of rose bushes stretch before us—red, pink and white blooms glowing under the morning light.

'Wow,' I whisper.

'Do you like them?' she asks eagerly.

'They're beautiful,' I say. I pluck one gently, careful to take out the thorns, and tuck it behind her ear. 'Now you really look like a princess.'

She giggles and runs back to show her friends. Loosepants grins, and to my surprise, even Officer is smiling—really smiling.

'So, what do we do now?' I ask as we rejoin the group. The kids demonstrate how to pluck only the ripe tomatoes and drop them gently into the buckets. We take off our shoes, letting the cool mud press between our toes.

I think of my father—how he would've scolded me for getting my hands dirty. But here, surrounded by laughter, it feels just right. *A soft rebellion even if he isn't watching.*

I glance at the cabins—small, worn and full of life. Back home, our house is three times the size and yet, it has none of this—no laughter echoing off the walls, no joy to be found in its corners.

—෴—

An hour slips by, though it feels like no time at all. My hands and legs are smeared with mud, but despite being a cleanliness freak, I feel surprisingly okay with it.

We head to a nearby handpump to wash up, the splash of cold water over my skin feels refreshing after all the work.

Suddenly, someone sprays me with water. I look up, droplets trickling down my face. It's Loosey, grinning mischievously, his hands cupped and ready for another attack. 'Here it comes!' he yells, and I dart away, narrowly avoiding another splash.

The kids start running too, shrieking with delight as Loosey playfully aims at them. Officer is the only one who approaches him bravely, not caring about the splashes coming his way.

'No, Officer! Don't come any closer. I swear I'll drown you in a tsunami,' Loosey shouts, but he's running soon as Officer takes control and splashes water at him, both of them laughing uncontrollably.

I guess even bullies become a better version of themselves around kids.

—෴—

We head back towards the cabin and put the buckets near the kitchen.

'Who wants to play some football?' Officer shouts just then, biting into a tomato.

The children erupt in cheers and chase after him as he gets a ball from the cabin, his chin smeared with tomato juice. Wiping it off, he leads them towards the open field in front of the cabins.

As we follow, I secretly hope Huntress is around.

Children pour out from all three cabins, led by Dadaji. He asks to inspect the ball first, pretending to test if it's safe for the kids—then suddenly bolts away with it, laughing like a mischievous kid himself. The kids swarm around him, laughing, jumping and trying to reclaim the ball. Despite his age, he's surprisingly quick, dodging everyone with ease.

Finally, he tosses the ball high into the air, and the real game begins. Dadaji waves me over, and Loosey and I join him. Officer starts showing off, juggling the ball with his feet—the guy is really good at it. He kicks it repeatedly with his knees without letting it touch the ground. He even manages to balance it on his forehead, not letting it drop.

He then passes the ball to Loosey, who deftly kicks it over to me. I take off running, teasing the kids by keeping the ball just out of reach, kicking it forward again every time they close in. Officer tries to steal it, but I fake left, dodge right, and leave him grasping for air.

A moment of satisfaction.

But it barely lasts a second as out of nowhere, someone swoops in and kicks the ball away from me. I turn, surprised to see Huntress sprinting away with it.

'Show-off!' I call out.

'Come and get it,' she taunts, flashing a mischievous grin.

I chase after her, but she's too quick and skilled. Dadaji and some of the children stop playing to watch, clapping and cheering her on as she effortlessly evades all my attempts to steal the ball. She pretends to pass, then rolls the ball back in one smooth move, leaving me standing there like a total fool.

It's the only time I am happy looking like one.

Accepting defeat, I run back to the cabins and sit on the stairs, catching my breath. Huntress passes the ball to one of the girls and steps out too.

I notice Daisy, who hadn't joined the match, moving around the field with a DSLR camera. She's capturing some candid moments, dodging the ball, moving through the chaos, pausing just long enough to click.

Huntress walks over to Dadaji and wraps him in a tight hug. As they part, after a long time, I catch a glimpse of her wiping her eyes.

Even after the game is over, Daisy keeps taking pictures. A huge crowd gathers around her—some kids are singing songs, others are showing off dance moves, and one even does a backflip. She moves effortlessly amongst them, her camera clicking with ease.

There's something different about her now. She feels lighter, freer as she keeps clicking. As if she was born for this. To be behind that lens, capturing happiness in its purest form.

I find Frost, who didn't participate, sleeping under a tree, and the Nerds are nowhere to be seen.

I haven't seen Huntress either since she was with Dadaji. I ask Daisy and Loosey if they've seen her. They haven't. *I need to find her.* The last time I saw her, she was wiping tears from her eyes. Is she okay? The thought keeps circling around in my head, refusing to leave. Maybe it's none of my business. Maybe she wouldn't even want me there. But still ... something in me wants to find her. Just to know she's alright.

I find her packing something into the back of a red pickup truck with another elderly man. She seems completely okay.

'You walked in at just the right time. Can you give me a hand?' Huntress says, smiling as she notices me.

'Absolutely,' I reply, rolling up my sleeves. As I step closer, I try to read her face—looking for any trace of what I saw earlier. But there's nothing. Maybe I imagined it. She hands me a crate full of tomatoes. It's heavier than I expect, but I manage to lift it and place it gently beside the others in the truck bed.

'Make yourself useful,' she says with a playful grin.

'Yes, ma'am,' I reply, grabbing another crate. Together, we work in a steady rhythm—lifting, carrying and stacking the crates neatly. Before long, we've loaded all the crates. I wipe the sweat from my forehead, a slight ache settling into my arms.

'I'm heading out now,' Huntress says. 'I need to take them to the market. You stay here and get some rest.'

I hesitate. I don't want to leave her alone if she's even remotely upset. 'Actually ... you might need some help at the market, right? Like ... someone to unload? I could come along.'

She pauses, eyes narrowing slightly, the corner of her mouth curving into a teasing smile.

'Sureee,' she says, drawing out the word. 'I'd *love* that. Always good to have an extra pair of hands.'

'Great,' I say, a little too quickly, hopping into the passenger seat before she can change her mind.

She shakes her head, amused, climbing in beside me, still smiling.

On the fourth try, the truck roars to life and lurches forward with a jerk. Its whole body rattles, and the hood shakes as we drive down the bumpy road. I grip the edge of my seat, trying not to look nervous. This truck feels like it's held together by duct tape.

'I won't let anything happen to you—*ever*,' Huntress says softly. She skilfully swerves to avoid a massive pothole.

I truly love how comforting her voice can be at times.

'I trust you,' I reply, still gripping the handle above the door as we hit another bump.

She laughs, glancing at my white-knuckled grip. 'I can see that.'

We both join in for a laugh.

'Those bowls and plates back there—they're impressive,' I say.

'The children make them,' she replies, her eyes on the road. 'We sell them to raise money for the school. Dadaji believes every child should learn something practical. He knows he can't send them all to college, so he finds people who can teach them trades. At least something that'll help them earn later.'

Another pothole. Which she again skilfully avoids. I can't help but admire the way she is driving, not rushing, not too slow, and avoiding every single pothole.

'He regularly asks professionals in these fields to come down and train them; they never say no. Once, he asked the barber from the village to teach them how to give haircuts. Another time, he asked a doctor, who respects Dadaji a lot, to teach them how to do first aid. And many times, he even takes them to visit our milkman and his farm, to show them how to milk a cow and to learn more about farming.'

'That's amazing,' I say, genuinely impressed.

She smiles softly, eyes still on the road. There's a warmth in her voice whenever she talks about him.

My respect for Dadaji grows even more. And for her, too. Huntress has always been a mystery to me. During college events or the volunteer drives she led, I'd tried to learn more about her, but she never really let anyone in. Sitting here now, listening to her, I feel happy, feeling as though I'm finally a small part of her world.

I steal another glance at her. The sun is beginning to set, its golden light kissing her face. Coming here was a good idea—not just because I care about her, but because being with her like this, even without speaking, feels like a dream come true.

We reach the highway, and she turns on the radio. A song from the '90s fills the truck, and she hums along softly. The wind rushes through the open windows, playing with her hair. She tucks a few rogue strands behind her ear and I lock that image safely away in my heart.

She parks the truck near the entrance of the market. Around us, vendors are packing up for the day. The ground is strewn with wilted leaves, crushed tomatoes and scraps from the day's trade.

Huntress walks over to a nearby stall. Large cooking pots, their exteriors blackened from use, are stacked high—utensils that could easily cook for hundreds at once. She approaches a man wearing a neat kurta, jotting something down in a small pocket diary. He greets her with a big smile, and after a brief conversation, orders his men to unload the pickup.

I try to help, but they ask me to step aside. They unload everything within minutes.

She didn't need me here. She knew that.

And still, she let me come.

When she glances over, there's a small smile she tries to hide. I don't really know how to feel about that—not with the butterflies fluttering in my stomach.

The man asks his men for a final count, then hands Huntress some money. They don't negotiate; she doesn't even ask about the price. He just hands over the cash—perhaps a regular arrangement. Bidding him farewell, we drive through the city.

We stop next in front of a narrow tailoring shop that stretches deep like a railway coach. I follow Huntress inside. The walls are painted a faded green, and the steady hum of sewing machines fills the air.

Behind the counter stands a man with a measuring tape draped around his neck, his shirt straining against his round belly. He's carefully cutting fabric along faint chalk lines, completely absorbed in his work.

'Do you have the order ready, Master-ji?' Huntress asks.

He looks up over his half-moon spectacles. 'Have you told Dadaji yet?'

'He'll find out tonight,' she replies, tapping her fingers lightly on the glass counter. 'You didn't talk to him about this, did you?'

'No, I didn't,' he says, setting his scissors aside. 'But I still don't understand why you're keeping it from him.'

Huntress doesn't answer. He calls one of his men over, who steps away and returns with two other men carrying six bags of clothing. Three bags contain sets of peach shirts with black pants, and the other three have peach dresses for the girls.

'And ...' Huntress says, tapping the counter again, 'do you have the other order as well? The one we talked about?'

He ducks beneath the counter and comes up holding a neatly folded white kurta and pyjama, along with a coffee-coloured vest.

'You have no idea how many old notebooks I had to dig through to find his measurements. It's like he hasn't had any new clothes made in years,' Master says, shaking his head.

'Thank you so much. It will look great on him,' Huntress says, running her hand over the vest's intricate, traditional design. 'Thank you, Master,' she adds, her voice full of gratitude.

She takes out money from her pocket and pays the tailor. The money we got from the sale is in the glove compartment of the pickup. She hasn't used any of it.

The tailor gives her a curious look but accepts the payment. His assistants help us carry the clothes to the pickup.

'I want to get something for the children as well,' I say just as Huntress starts the engine.

'You don't have to,' she says, avoiding my gaze.

'But I want to.' She stares at me blankly.

'They love to draw, right?' I ask. She nods, looking at the steering wheel. For the next ten minutes, we drive around the city to get to its biggest stationery shop. When we leave, we have bags full of notebooks, watercolours, brushes, crayons, pencils, pens, slates and drawing books. I also pick up as many storybooks as I can find, wanting to give the kids some beautiful stories to read.

'You didn't have to do it. I kept telling you,' she says in a detached voice as she drives.

'I wanted to. I can't explain it, but I feel a special connection with them,' I reply. 'One that is very likely to never go away.' I'm down to the last few thousand in my savings account, but that's okay. The smiles on the kids' faces will be worth it—and I can always pick up a few more content writing or web designing gigs when I get back.

The whole drive back to the cabins is filled with silence, except for the creaking of the car. She had turned on the radio earlier, but now it's off. She seems to prefer the quiet. I think I understand. Maybe she feels obligated towards the kids and doesn't want me to feel the same—or maybe she doesn't want me to do it just for her. But I'm not doing it for her. I hope she'll understand.

The darkness has fully settled, and the roads are nearly empty as we drive back. In the distance, I spot the soft glow from the cabin lights, flickering like guiding beacons against the night. As we pull closer, the warm lights grow brighter.

The children come running towards us. They must have heard the loud noise the pickup makes. Huntress honks a few times, telling the kids to be patient and let her park. It takes nearly five minutes for us to park the pickup. The children are at the back, trying to jump into the truck bed.

'Did you bring something for us?'

'Did you get us candies?'

'What's in these boxes?'

'There are so many of them!'

'Can we open them, please?'

All the kids are talking at the same time. Huntress tries to answer them one by one, asking them to be patient. But many of them have started climbing into the truck bed.

'Little help here?' she says, holding two squirming kids in her arms. It's the first time she's looked at me since we left town. I grab a couple of them and set them gently down, but three more are already climbing up.

'I'll return everything if you don't behave,' she warns. The effect is instant, everyone freezes, then hop off without needing another word

'Officer, Loosepants, Nerds, Daisy ... Help!' she calls. They rush over. He-Nerd starts walking towards us but stops, looking at She-Nerd as if asking for permission. Only when she begins moving does he continue.

Huntress apologises to the kids for scaring them earlier and asks them to wait near the cabins where there's light. She assures them we've brought something special, and that they'll love it. Their faces brighten instantly. They race off, eyes wide with excitement.

Once they're gone, Huntress opens the boxes. Inside are paper bags marked with sizes—shirts and pants for the boys, dresses for the girls. She hands us the stationery and tells us to slip one of each item inside. Officer finishes his stack first, grinning proudly. The rest of us take a bit longer.

Out of the corner of my eye, I can still see the children. Many are standing on their tiptoes, trying to see what we're doing, while others are bouncing with excitement.

'All right,' Huntress says, tying one last bag. 'Each of you take one and hand it to a child. Guess the sizes as best you can.' She quietly points out a few matches, just in case.

Daisy asks if she can take pictures. Huntress nods.

We step out, carrying the bags. The kids run towards us again, unable to hold back their excitement. We start handing out the gifts, one by one. Their laughter fills the air as they tear open the bags, pulling out clothes and crayons like they're treasures.

'Didi has brought me a new dress!' someone shouts.

'Also, colours!'

'A pen too!'

The next few minutes are pure chaos—in the best way. Laughter, squeals, little feet jumping all around. Some of the kids even start dancing. A few rush to hug Huntress, their arms barely reaching around her waist.

'It wasn't just me,' she tells them, smiling. 'Many of these gifts are from Wolf as well.'

'Thank you very much, Wolf Bhaiya!' a little girl says, running up to me.

Loosepants immediately bursts out laughing, his palm hitting his knee. 'Wolf Bhaiya!' he repeats. I glare at him. I'm honestly a little worried thinking about how much he's going to throw that around.

The little girl throws her arms around me. She is the same one who had shown us the farm earlier. I pick her up, and before I can react, she plants a quick peck on my cheek.

I freeze for a second, then manage a smile, fighting through the surprise—just in time to hear Loosepants make a very loud 'aww' sound.

Huntress claps her hands lightly. 'All right, everyone—go keep your things safely.'

I put the kid down and they all sprint towards the cabins, clutching their treasures. I doubt any of it is going to end up neatly packed.

That's when I notice Dadaji stepping out of his cabin, watching the kids swarm towards him, proudly showing off their new gifts. He listens to each of them, smiling. One girl holds out a pen, and he bends down, drawing something on her hand. She turns to show me—a butterfly.

Daisy, now using a low-light lens, catches the moment perfectly. She shows me the photo. The girl's grin, the butterfly, Dadaji's near watery eyes—it's all there.

It's getting darker by the minute. The children have finally let Dadaji be, and have gone back to the cabins. Dadaji, too, has gone inside. Huntress picks up the outfit she bought for Dadaji and starts to walk away.

'Park the truck for me,' she says to me.

As she starts leaving, Officer holds her hand for a moment. 'I'm proud of you,' he says softly. 'I'll be waiting.'

Huntress glances briefly at me, then looks away and walks off. A tightness builds in my chest before I can stop it. I stare at Officer—muscular, confident, everything I'm not—and though I know it's unfair, something inside me burns. It's stupid, I tell myself. It's her choice. She chose him.

But reason doesn't help.

Jealousy isn't logical. It just sits there, heavy and bitter, eating you from the inside, refusing to leave.

I get inside the pickup truck and find that Huntress hasn't left the key in the ignition. She took it with her. I walk towards Dadaji's cabin—the old one with its sagging roof—to retrieve the keys. I'm just outside the closed door, about to knock, when I stop.

'You didn't have to spend all your savings on them,' Dadaji says.

'They deserve it, Dadu,' Huntress replies. Her voice carries a mix of determination and tenderness.

He sighs deeply. 'I know they do. I work hard every day to keep them happy, to provide for them. But you don't need to keep putting their needs before your own. You don't need to keep on sacrificing.'

'I'm not sacrificing anything,' she says softly.

'But you are. You've been saving up all year to fulfill your dream—to visit the place your mother and my son always wanted to take you. But every time, you give that money away for them. It's admirable, noble, and I'm most proud of you, but I don't want you to lose sight of your own dream while you're helping secure theirs.'

'I'm not giving up on my dream, Dadu,' she insists. 'I'll go there next year. I set aside a little bit each time. And by next year, I should have enough.'

'You're so stubborn,' he says, his voice losing its strength. 'I just want to see you go there while I'm still here to hear all about it.'

'Don't say things like that,' she snaps, her voice sharp. 'Nothing is going to happen to you. You're healthy and will continue to be for many, many years.'

Silence fills the room.

'Dadu, I promise. I'll go there next year. I've planned it. I'm not giving away everything I earn. Now, please, can you smile for me and tell me if you like the jacket I got for you.'

I don't hear a response.

I step back from the door and head towards the pickup. I shouldn't have eavesdropped. What dream was Dadaji talking about? Where are her parents? Is this why she's always busy in college, always trying to study, and why the internship was so important for her?

For the first time, I realise just how little I know her.

Daisy is standing near Frost, showing him the pictures she clicked. He is barely looking at the photos, and when she doesn't stop, he shouts at her.

Bastard.

I want to step in, say something, but I don't. There is too much going on in my head right now.

But I will talk to her when my head is clear. Maybe tomorrow.

While we were out, the others had dinner with the kids. Loosey explained it's their routine—early dinner and early to bed—but tonight ran a little late. The kids have been tucked in, and Loosey and the others have returned to their cabins. Now it's just me, leaning against the truck, the cold metal biting into my back through my shirt. My legs ache from standing too long, but I don't move. Not yet. Not until she comes out.

Dadaji came out and joined the others earlier, gathering the kids as they settled in. But Huntress ... she's still inside.

The night feels heavier now. The lively hum of children has given way to the steady chorus of crickets. The moon's soft glow mixes with the cabin lights, creating a scene that looks like it's straight from Pinterest. It's beautiful, but I can't seem to focus on it. All I can think about is her—what's keeping her so long, and whether she's okay.

Then I see her.

She slips out of the cabin quietly, her head bowed, her steps slow. The warm glow spilling from the doorway seems to hesitate, not daring to follow her into the night. Her shoulders are hunched, as if she's carrying something too heavy.

I hurry towards her.

'Huntress,' I call softly.

She doesn't stop.

'Anjali ...' I try again, my voice barely louder than a whisper.

This time, she pauses. She turns her head slightly, just enough for me to catch a glimpse of her face. 'Oh ... Hi,' she says, her voice flat, distant.

'You forgot to give me the keys,' I say, trying to read her expression. Her face, usually so alive with warmth, feels guarded now, plain and unwilling to reveal anything.

'Oh.' She pulls the keys from her pocket and hands them over. Just like that.

'Are you okay?' I ask gently.

'I was just going for a walk,' she replies, her gaze fixed on the ground.

'I see,' I say, slipping the keys into my pocket. I hesitate for a moment before falling into step beside her. She doesn't tell me to leave, so I stay.

The night feels colder as we walk. The air around the lake is damp, laced with the faint smell of moss. The moon hangs low, its reflection trembling in the rippling water. The sound of our footsteps mingles with the occasional rustle of leaves, but otherwise, it's quiet. Too quiet.

'It's cold,' she says finally, her arms wrapping around herself.

'Should I grab you a jacket?' I offer, glancing at her.

She doesn't answer. Her eyes stay fixed on the water, her gaze far away, as if she's looking at something I can't see.

We walk a little further, the cabin lights behind us shrinking into faint, flickering dots. Finally, I stop. 'Anjali ...' I say softly, reaching for her hand.

Her fingers are freezing. She stops too, turning to face me. In the moonlight, her face looks pale, and her eyes glisten with crowded tears.

Her voice wavers as she speaks. 'Can you hold me?'

I don't hesitate. I step closer, wrapping my arms around her. She leans into me, resting her head on my shoulder, and for a moment, we're just two people standing in the middle of the night, the world around us fading away.

Then I feel it—her tears, warm against my shirt. A small, broken sob escapes her, and my chest tightens. I don't say anything. What could I say that would make this better? That would take this pain away? When I don't even know all that she has been through.

So, I just hold her tighter, as if holding her against me can shield her from whatever it is that's hurting her. My hand brushes gently over her hair, trying to whisper a promise.

You're not alone. You will never be. I'm never letting go.

Her sobs then come in waves, and I let them. I let her lean into me, cry into me, because it's the only thing I can offer her right now. I wish I could tell her that she doesn't have to carry everything on her own, that she doesn't have to be so strong all the time. I want to tell her that if it's the kids, or the orphanage, or even the fucking weight of the world, I'll help her carry it. Whatever it takes.

Eventually, her sobs subside and her breathing steadies. She pulls back slightly, wiping her face with trembling fingers. 'I ruined your shirt,' she says, her voice small, barely audible.

'No, you didn't,' I reply gently, still holding her hand. 'Besides, it's just a shirt. You can ruin as many as you want.'

That earns me the tiniest laugh from her—more of a breath than a sound, but it's something.

She looks at me then, her eyes soft and searching, the faintest smile breaking through her tears. 'You're a good guy, Arjun.'

When we return to the cabin, Huntress heads inside to sleep, her footsteps soft on the wooden stairs. I stay back, leaning against the railing, her words playing over in my mind: *'You're a good guy, Arjun.'*

Would she still think the same if she gets to know those rumours? The whispers, the allegations, what all of them are saying about me. My chest tightens. What if she finds out? What if *everyone* here finds out? People who once thought I was a good guy now look at me as if I'm some kind of a monster. What if she, too, starts looking at me that way?

My heart pounds, my breath catching painfully in my throat. I reach for the railing and grip it so hard my knuckles ache. The world blurs at the edges, the distant lake becoming a dark, shifting smear. I rub my forehead, trying to ground myself, but my spiralling thoughts already pulling me under:

What if she doesn't believe me? What if she doesn't even give me the chance to explain?

She's the only one from my old world who still sees me without any hatred or disgust. If she turns away too ...

How will I survive that?

If she turns away too, it will be the last piece before everything falls apart; before I do too.

A sharp chime cuts through the static in my brain. I reach into my pocket, my fingers still clumsy and shaking, and pull out my phone. The light from the screen is blinding for a second, but then I see the notification.

It's Birdie!

She's replied to the photo I sent earlier—the one of the letterbox I spent the afternoon fixing.

Birdie: *Hey, thank you so much!*

It's in a much better shape now. Honestly, I have often thought of fixing it myself but could never bring myself to touch it. Maybe the thought of breaking it scared me more.

Birdie: *But seeing it in such good shape today reminds me how much it needed that. Thank you!*

I stare at the words, and the tightness in my chest begins to loosen, just a fraction. I focus on the text, letting the letters ground me. I take a shallow breath, then a deeper one, the cool night air finally reaching my lungs.

She's typing again.

Birdie: *Now that I look at it again, it looks so much like it did in the picture I have with it. Thank you again.*

I feel a strange, quiet warmth spreading through me, chasing away the anxiety. I start typing quickly.

Me: *It was nothing, really. I just knew it meant a lot to you, and I couldn't just leave it like that.*

Seen. She's still online.

I type another message.

Me: *Also, I now have a trail name. Just like you.*

Birdie: *Can't wait to hear it. What is it?*

Me: *Wolf.*

Birdie: *That's a good one. Arjun—sorry, Wolf! That's a really great choice.*

Me: *Thank you! It wasn't my idea, actually. It was bestowed upon me. But yeah, I love it too.*

Me: *And thank you for putting me with this group.*

She reacts with a heart.

Birdie: *I hope you're enjoying this journey, Wolf.*

Me: *A lot. I need to thank you.*

Birdie: *You don't need to.*

Me: *No. I do ...*

I take a deep breath and type.

Me: *I was lost, broken and felt so alone in this world. And it was you who saved me. A stranger who helped me when the people I knew wouldn't. You talked to me when I had no one to talk to. You stayed when everyone else left. And you never once asked for anything in return.*

Me: *I'll always owe you.*

She starts typing.

Birdie: *Wolf, life takes us through many twists and turns that make us feel like nothing can save us again. We find ourselves hurt, wounded, all alone in the dark, and we think we'll never find a way out. But that's never the case. There's always light to be found. We just have to reach out for help. And you did. The universe decided to help you, using me as the medium.*

I'm sure someone else might be praying for some magic in their world right now, and maybe the universe is helping them by putting you in their lives.

I read her message again and again, thinking of how she gives credit to the universe, not accepting that she was the magic that entered my life and helped me—not the universe.

I type back.

Me: *I've never believed in the universe.*

She replies.

Birdie: *That's okay. The universe believes in you.*

—∞—

The sound of something low and rumbling wakes me, pulling me from the kind of sleep that leaves your mind foggy. For the next half hour, I try to go back to sleep, pulling the cushion over my head. But sleep refuses to return.

I roll over and peek through the small gap in the curtains. It's still dark outside, the world is wrapped in silence. A sigh escapes me. Too early.

Reaching for my phone, I use its faint glow to find the ladder and climb down carefully. The wooden floor greets me with a sharp chill that crawls up my legs. I pull on my sweater—thin, but better than nothing—and glance around. The room is quiet except for the steady rhythm of soft breathing. Everyone's still asleep.

There's no point staying here.

I grab the diary Birdie gave me, along with a pen, and slip outside. The cold air hits me, crisp and refreshing. I make my way to the porch and lean against the same railing where I sat last night, texting Birdie. Her words replay in my mind, each one comforting.

Flipping open the diary, I begin to write. First, I jot down her words, copying them as they are from my phone:

'There's always magic to be found. We just have to reach out ...'

Then, I write another line:

'You're a good guy, Arjun.'

Seeing Huntress's words on paper makes them feel more real. That one sentence validates what I've always known deep down—I am a good person.

'Boo!' A voice cuts through the quiet, and I nearly drop the diary.

'God! You scared me.' I clutch my chest, slamming the diary shut as I turn. Huntress is standing there, grinning like a mischievous kid.

'Mission accomplished,' she says, her eyes twinkling in the faint porch light. 'What's that?' She nods towards the diary now pressed against me.

'A gift from a friend,' I say, still catching my breath.

'A friend, huh? Sounds like someone special,' she teases.

'It's not like that,' I stammer. 'I mean ... special, but not like ...'

She chuckles, cutting me off. 'Relax, Arjun. You don't have to explain.' She starts walking away, then glances back over her shoulder. 'Come on. I know a good place for you to write.'

Curiosity gets the better of me, and I follow her down a wooden ramp that stretches into the water. At the end, she crouches to untie a rope. As I step closer, I realise it's a boat—small, weathered, but sturdy—rocking gently against the dock.

'A fisherman's family gave it to Dadaji,' she says, working at the knot. 'Their eldest moved away, and the father couldn't manage it anymore.'

She straightens up, gesturing to the boat, 'Get in.'

I hesitate for a second before climbing in. The boat creaks under my weight but feels solid enough. The inside is painted white, though the paint is chipped in places. I sit on one of the planks, but Huntress shakes her head.

'Not there. You're rowing.'

'As you command,' I reply with a mock salute, moving to the middle seat where the oars rest. I push off from the dock, and we glide smoothly onto the open water.

Out on the lake, the cold gets sharper. The darkness begins to soften as the first hints of dawn appear on the horizon.

'You didn't sleep much,' I observe, noticing the faint shadows under her eyes.

She shrugs. 'I don't sleep well many times. Been that way for a while.' She pauses. 'Stop here,' she says before I can respond. 'This is a good spot.'

I want to ask her why—what keeps her up at night, what thoughts claw at her heart—but something in her tone tells me not to. I really hope she tells me one day, voluntarily, trusting me enough with her story, her pain.

I let the oars rest, and the boat drifts gently. Huntress lies back, gazing up at the fading stars.

'Do you ever think about your life and the turns it takes?' she asks.

'Sometimes,' I admit, settling into my seat.

'How does it go for you?' she asks, her eyes still on the sky.

I take a moment to think. 'Honestly? It feels like it's mostly bad turns and terrible twists,' I say. 'But every now and then, something good happens. Those good, happy moments don't always stay for long. But I'm slowly learning to appreciate those moments while they're here, instead of worrying about what's next.'

This is one of those good and happy moments for me. I wish I could tell her.

She nods slowly, sighing deeply. 'I wish I could do that. Not worry about the future so much. I've felt what good feels like recently, and now I'm scared of when the bad will come.'

I start to say something, but she waves me off without even looking my way. 'No ...' she says, sitting up slightly and pointing to my diary. 'You write, Wolf. Do what I brought you here for.'

I hesitate for a moment, then open the diary and pick up the pen. Then, I write. I write about everything—the lake, the swaying boat, the cold air that makes my fingers stiff, and her, lying there with her thoughts spilling into the breaking dawn.

—w—

We return after some time and find Daisy and the others awake, rubbing sleep from their eyes. The quiet morning buzz has begun to stir.

Daisy wastes no time. 'We need to leave soon,' she announces. 'Let's get ready before the kids wake up.' Her tone is calm but firm, and everyone nods in agreement. Loosey leans over to me and whispers, 'Last time, the kids wouldn't let Huntress go. They cried so much, it was painful to watch. Daisy is probably trying to save us from that.'

We quickly pack up and meet in the kitchen for a light breakfast. Grandpa is already there, wearing the clothes Huntress brought him yesterday. His transformation is simple but striking. Daisy immediately hugs him, grinning. 'You look so handsome in these, Grandpa!' she exclaims.

Grandpa chuckles, 'Thank you so much!' He looks over at Huntress, even giving a small turn, showing her the outfit like a small kid, 'What do you think? How do I look?'

Huntress barely glances up. 'Good,' she replies, her tone dry.

We sit down for tea and girda—a soft, chewy flatbread with a mild sweetness that's impossible to not love. It's my first time trying it and I savour each bite, letting the warmth of the bread and the spiced tea settle into my bones.

But even as we enjoy the meal, I notice the tension between Grandpa and Huntress. He keeps looking at her, his eyes filled with a quiet ache. He pours her more tea, serves her an extra girda, and even tries to crack a granddad joke or two. She doesn't meet his gaze, focusing instead on her plate.

When breakfast wraps up, Grandpa hands each of us a small bundle wrapped in cloth. 'These are parathas for lunch,' he says with a warm smile, 'and some girda for later. You can have it even in the evening—it keeps well.'

As we prepare to leave, Huntress leads us towards the kids' cabins quietly. She slips inside and, one by one, plants a soft kiss on each child's forehead. The kids stir but don't wake. I notice her wipe a tear from her cheek as she steps back out.

We start walking back to the truck, but before we leave, Huntress turns to Grandpa. 'Take care, Dadu,' she says, pulling him into a tight hug. 'And don't worry about me, okay? You've got enough to handle here. You just take care of yourself. I can take care of myself.'

Grandpa holds her close for a moment, his voice steady but thick with emotion. 'I know you can, my sweet little girl. But you'll have to forgive your old Dadu for worrying anyway.'

He pauses, reaching into his jacket pocket and pulls out a beige knitted beanie. 'Before you go,' he says, handing it to her, 'I made you a new one. The old one looked like it has seen a hundred winters.'

Huntress takes the beanie, her lips curving into the brightest smile as she pulls it over her head. 'Thank you, Dadu,' she whispers, hugging him again.

As she steps back, Grandpa looks at her with a mix of pride and sadness. 'Stay safe.'

'I will,' she says, her voice firmer now, as she bids him goodbye.

12

We finally break free from the woods, our muscles aching with every step after what feels like an endless walk. Ahead of us, a small town peeks over the next hill, rooftops catching the warm noon sunlight.

While the rest of us are tired, Officer is still buzzing with energy. 'Let's scale that mountain,' he suggests, pointing at a towering peak nearby, his eyes practically shining with excitement. 'We can climb down the other side!'

Everyone, except Huntress, immediately shoots down the idea. Even the Nerds—who've spent most of their time with their tongues down each other's throats whenever they got the chance—pause their snogging long enough to voice their disapproval. Officer then spends the next fifteen minutes trying to convince Daisy, Frost and the Nerds to join him.

Frost, who I have barely seen utter more than three words at a time, starts giving him a detailed explanation about why the other side of the peak is way too steep and dangerous. But Officer, fuelled by adrenaline, doesn't seem to care.

The Nerds, meanwhile, suggest heading into town and relaxing in a hotel. 'We've been walking forever,' She-Nerd complains. 'A comfy bed sounds perfect.' Everyone knows they just want privacy—not that being inside a room or outside it matters to them.

Loosepants perks up, eyes wide with excitement. 'There's an adventure park nearby! I googled it, and they have bungee jumping, zip lining and so much more. And it would be exciting. Plus, the reviews are so good. Nearly two hundred of them, and almost all of them are praising the place. We should totally go, come on, please, I mean seriously, who wouldn't want to go zip lining?!'

I have to give it to him—the guy can speak for ages without taking a breath.

It does sound fun, though, watching them take part in adventure sports. My fear of heights will never allow me to participate, but cheering them on will be exciting. Just then I remember—I need to find the letter from Birdie. The one she told me last night she has left at the next letterbox.

While I'm caught up in my thoughts, Daisy is busy trying to convince Frost about something. Before I can hear what they have decided, Officer walks past me, his shoulder slamming into mine. 'No sorry,' he mutters, not even glancing back.

Asshole. Somehow, even that word doesn't seem strong enough to describe him.

'He's not that bad, you know,' Loosepants says, surprising me.

I raise an eyebrow. 'Really? Isn't he the same guy who made me light a bonfire filled with firecrackers? And who keeps giving you a hard time every chance he gets?'

Loosepants shrugs, shifting from one foot to another. 'Yeah, he's a lot, but you saw him with the kids. He was so good with them. And you weren't with us last time.'

Since we left the campsite, he's been telling me stories from their past treks—but this one, he's told three times already. 'We ran into another camping group,' he says, eyes lighting up. 'They had this giant guy—twice my size. He threw the javelin so far, we thought we'd lost for sure. But then Officer stepped up. The other team was already celebrating, and he just picks up the javelin and launches it twice as far! He saved our asses.'

'Okay, but how does that make him any less of a jerk?'

Loosepants just shrugs.

Daisy walks back over, a slight frown creasing her forehead. 'I'd love to go to the adventure park, but Frost wants to go to this restaurant he saw on Instagram reels, and I promised I'd go with him. You guys can go ahead without us.'

Chaos erupts as everyone starts pitching their plans all at once, voices overlapping, each person trying to out-talk the other. Huntress raises her hands, cutting through the noise. 'Hey! Let's calm down,' she says, her voice firm. 'How about we split up? Pair off, do what we want today, and meet up tomorrow evening in town.'

There's a collective murmur of agreement. 'I'll join Officer on the mountain,' Huntress adds.

My chest tightens, and I force myself not to react. I would have loved for her to say, 'I'll go with Wolf.' But of course, it's not like she'd choose me over Officer just because we've shared a few special moments. It stings, nevertheless.

The Nerds couldn't be happier. They're already drifting away, She-Nerd planting a sloppy kiss on He-Nerd's lips before they leave. 'Ew ...' Loosepants mutters beside me. *Ew* ... I agree.

Daisy looks content enough as she heads off with Frost, even if visiting a restaurant isn't exactly her idea of fun.

That leaves me and Loosepants.

I turn to Loosepants, ready to suggest we hit the adventure park. Maybe I can slip away at some point and find Birdie's letter. But before I can speak, Loosepants turns to me.

'I'm sorry, Wolf,' he says quietly, eyes shifting away. 'There's something I need to take care of on my own. But you have fun! Here, take my pocket radio.' He tosses it to me. 'It doesn't work most of the time—I tried fixing it during our last trek, but gave up. Who knows, though? Maybe you'll have better luck.'

I catch the radio and nod.

'And I'm really, really sorry,' he says, his words tumbling out. 'I know I shouldn't leave you alone, but there's just ... something I need to do, otherwise—'

'That's okay,' I cut in before he finishes. 'Really, it's fine.'

He hesitates, scratching the back of his neck. 'We're still a pack, right? You won't kick me out just because of this?'

I can't help but smile. 'No way, buddy. You go do your thing—and have fun.'

He grins, relieved, and jogs off down another trail.

As everyone else scatters, I start walking alone. The silence hits harder than I expect. No Loosepants talking a mile a minute, no random jokes breaking the quiet. The trail feels wider, emptier. It stings a little—him choosing to go off without me—but maybe it's better this way. No distractions. No need to come up with excuses.

I focus on the task at hand. The letter from Birdie—that's what matters. I need to find out what's next. The trail splits ahead, and I remember her instructions: take the left path. She'd even sent me a map pin. I pull out my phone, confirming that I'm headed in the right direction.

Thank god, the network works here.

The forest is calm, the only sounds coming from rustling leaves and the occasional birdcall. Sunlight filters through the canopy, painting patterns on the ground. After a while, I spot it—a weathered letterbox nailed to a tree trunk. Its paint is faded, the colours peeling, but it's unmistakably the one.

My heartbeat picks up as I approach and I brush my fingers over the rough wood. I open the small door, and there it is: an envelope with my name written across it in Birdie's familiar handwriting.

There are two letters inside, along with a hand-drawn map. One of the letters has 'Do not open' written in big letters. I open the other one and start reading.

> Hey Wolf,
>
> Before you beat your head, yes, I was here last night. I had to come back to replace the old letter. I wanted to address you with your trail name. As I told you last night, it suits you.
>
> You described yourself as lost and broken when we texted. Lost? Maybe, yes. But broken? No. Perhaps even tired, too exhausted, but you were never broken, Wolf. Since the first time we interacted, I have always found you to be a wonderful person with a beautiful heart, whom the world and destiny have acted cruelly towards.
>
> Which has been the case with me too, a couple of times.
>
> But I held on, as you have.
>
> I can't help but wish we had found each other earlier; I can't imagine how life would have been, to have someone so good at heart as you along with me.
>
> Too heavy? Sorry for laying it on you.
>
> One of these days—and I know you've been asking about it—I will tell you how I got my trail name. It's a

beautiful story, one that very few people know, and one that I haven't told anyone in maybe over a decade.

Anyway, I've put up a challenge for you today, completing which might change you as a person. You must have seen the other letter. Open it when you reach the spot I've marked for you on the map.

Yours,
Birdie

PS There's this bakehouse in the next town. Visit it tomorrow early morning if you can. I have some fond memories of it. Hopefully, you will make some too.

Behind the letter, she has written the name of the bakehouse—*you can find it easily on Google*, she's added.

I keep staring at the small bird she has drawn at the bottom of the letter. I reread the line: *I wish we had found each other earlier.* Even I can't imagine how life would have been, to have her along. What it would have been like, being close to her. Someone who has such a beautiful heart and is one of the kindest souls I've ever come across.

Maybe I wouldn't have been broken—not broken, not that word—exhausted then. I also can't help but wonder what life has put her through. What's her story? What has she gone through that made her such a kind person, even towards a stranger?

I find the tree with a circle drawn on its trunk in white. The trail has been quite straightforward so far, but Birdie has asked me to take a narrow pathway leading down from here. It feels weird going away from the main trail, but I know better than to challenge her plan.

The sound of water reaches me, faint at first, but growing louder with every step. The trail curves, and I see it—a stream cutting across the path. The water is clear, rushing over smooth rocks, its surface glittering in the sunlight. The spot she has marked on the map is still a bit far, but the sound of a nearby waterfall is too tempting.

No, Arjun, you need to go to the marked spot first. See what Birdie has planned.

But curiosity wins.

When I reach the place, the sight steals my breath away. A waterfall spills from a rocky ledge, crashing into a clear pool below. White sprays burst upwards, cool and sharp against my skin. Trees with low, sweeping branches cover the place like they're guarding a secret. It feels untouched—as if nature itself doesn't want anyone to find this beautiful place.

And then I freeze.

I'm not alone. Just along the edge of the pool, someone steps in. It's a girl, and she starts taking off her shirt. My brain screams, *Turn around!* and I do, whipping my head away so fast, I almost lose my balance. I step back, only to catch my arm on a vine. It tangles around me and I stumble into a nearby tree.

'Who's there?' The voice is sharp and familiar. The noise from my clumsiness has surely given me away. 'I've got a knife, and I know how to use it,' the voice threatens.

'No need for that,' I say, taking a moment to recognise the voice. 'It's me, Huntress, Wolf.'

There's a pause. 'Wolf?' The voice softens, then sharpens again. 'What the hell are you doing here? Come out where I can see you.'

I step out hesitantly, hands raised slightly. And there she is—Huntress. Her shirt is still on, thank god, but she's holding a knife, a hunting knife, glinting in the sunlight. 'Okay,' I say, my heart pounding. 'Girl? Are you seriously carrying a knife?'

She tosses it in the air and catches it effortlessly. 'Always. It's been with me for years. I like a little protection.' She smirks, slipping it back into her bag.

'You are scary.'

'I know,' she says proudly, with a wink.

'Are you following me?' she asks, narrowing her eyes. God, she looks dangerous, and, weirdly, it makes her look even more beautiful.

'What? No!' My voice cracks a little, and I clear my throat. 'I was just passing by. There is a ... a thing that I want to do. And I heard the sound of water and got curious.'

'Really?' She's now glaring at me, widening her eyes. I've never noticed how big her eyes are—or how terrifying they can look when she's angry. My throat goes dry. I can hear everything—my own breathing, my racing heart, the rush of the waterfall, the rustle of leaves.

And then she laughs. 'Just pulling your leg, Wolfie. I wish you were following me. That would have been nice.'

Wait, what?

My brain short-circuits for a second. *What did she just say?*

'You really scared me,' I say finally, hoping my voice doesn't betray how fast my heart's racing. 'It's like behind that pretty face of yours lives the devil.'

'Do you have any doubts about that?' she grins.

'What are you doing here?' I ask her, hiding the map in my hands, hoping she hasn't seen it.

'I was going to have a bath and started undressing for it, but then you popped up,' she replies. 'But it's good. Had you been a little late, it would have been embarrassing for you.'

'Why only for me? Why not for you as well?'

She just smiles, her eyes sparkling with mischief.

My heart jumps.

God. Girl. Are you trying to kill me or something?

'So, since you've ruined my long bath, what are we doing instead?' She picks up her hiking bag and starts walking ahead of me. Completely unaware of what her statement put me through.

'Weren't you with Officer?' I catch up to her and ask.

'Yep, I was.'

'Where is he?'

'Do you always ask so many questions?' She starts humming, and I don't know what to reply.

What version of hers is this?

We follow the stream for a while. The water is fighting its way through the creeks and rocks, and the droplets splash us every once in a while.

'Chill,' Huntress says when I stay silent for too long. 'We were travelling together, but he wanted to do rock climbing and I didn't want to. We had a small fight and parted ways.'

'Okay,' I reply, trying to hide any signs of satisfaction on my face. I'm sad that she had a fight, but happy that she's with me now. Also, I despise Officer even more now for having a fight with her. She really deserves better. Someone who is kind and loves her with all of his heart.

Sunlight spills across her face as we step into a clearing, and it makes her entire face glow.

'Stop staring,' she says, catching me with a sideways glance and a teasing smirk.

'I wasn't staring at you,' I lie, horribly. 'I was just ... noticing your bracelet,' I say, pointing at her arm. *Lame.* 'I've never seen you wear one before.'

'You're quite observant,' she says. 'Tell me, Wolf, do you take an interest in observing girls a lot?' I can see her lips fighting a smile.

God, why does she have to say things like that? Can't she see the effect it has on me.

'No,' I say, fighting for a word or two to come out. 'I just ... I mean ... I notice everyone.'

'So, I'm not special?' She stops and turns, her gaze sharp. Before I can move, she steps closer—too close—and my back hits a tree. Her hand comes up, resting on the bark beside my head. Suddenly, there's nowhere to go.

God, I can't breathe. And I can feel her breath on my skin. *Fuck.*

'I didn't ... I didn't say that.'

'So, I *am* special?' she presses, voice playful, confident, and way too close. *She is just inches away from my face.*

'I ... I am not answering that.' I swallow the lump rising in my throat. 'You're too good with your words.'

'Not as good as you,' she replies, finally stepping back. I manage to breathe after a moment, but my heartbeat clearly doesn't get the memo. It's not slowing down.

God, she really does have an effect on me.

It's like my entire body forgot how to function—breathing, blinking, existing—just because she stood too close.

'What do you mean?' I finally manage to ask when we start walking again, my legs wobbling at the start.

'Your anonymous story for the college magazine.'

I freeze mid-step. 'How do you know about that? I wrote it under a ...'

'A pen name,' she finishes for me.

She grins. 'I know. Remember that old wooden box near the library? The one we used for submissions? I saw you drop a folded paper in. Later, when I checked all the entries, there was only one with a pen name ... and yours was the only missing article. Didn't have to be Sherlock to figure that one out.'

I stare at her.

'You read that?' I ask, trying to sound casual, but my voice cracks halfway through.

It's weird—writing something and then knowing someone's actually read it. Especially someone who you have a huge crush on.

'I didn't think anyone would,' I add quickly, eyes on the ground. 'It was just ... something I had to get out. I didn't expect it to matter.'

'Of course I did.' Her tone is sincere. 'It was beautiful. That part about an artist stuck among machines—god, that hit hard. I thought it would inspire a lot of people. It definitely inspired me.'

I look away. I don't want her to see my face, which already feels hot enough to start a campfire.

Calm down. It's just a compliment. But a compliment *from her.*

'Thank you,' I manage to say. 'That means a lot.'

I almost hadn't submitted it; had kept staring at that folded page for hours, wondering if it was even good enough.

'I also liked the pen name,' she says, laughing. 'Masked Lord? It has a nice ring to it, but we can—*and we definitely should*—find a better one for you.'

'I couldn't think of anything else,' I admit. 'So, I just used the name of a character from a short story I was working on.'

'Would love to read it someday,' she says, smiling softly, walking backwards, facing me.

'Su ... sure,' I manage, half distracted by the way she's smiling softly. 'You're going to fall if you keep walking like that.'

'Maybe I trust you to catch me,' she says lightly, her lips curling into the prettiest smile.

God, she's dangerous when she smiles and says things like that.

And my heart—my poor, stupid heart—I don't know how long it can survive this.

We walk long enough for me to start wondering if we're lost. And just then, through the gaps in the trees, I see it—a shimmer of blue.

'Wow,' Huntress says, stopping in her tracks. 'How did you know about this?'

'An online friend told me about it,' I say, which isn't entirely untrue. It just leaves out a few details. 'They'd been here before and thought I should see it.'

'That's cool,' she says, smiling. 'You've got great friends.'

I nod, not trusting myself to speak more.

'I'll be back in a moment,' I tell her. 'Uh ... quick nature break.'

'Okies,' she replies.

As soon as I'm out of her sight, I pull out the second note Birdie left for me and open it.

The title reads: *'Chance to win over your fear.'*

Beneath it, her handwriting continues: *I hope you haven't cheated and opened this before you got here.*

'It was tempting,' I mutter to myself, though she's not here to hear it.

The letter goes on,

If you've followed the map correctly, you're at the open side of the lake—not the one with the long cliff wall.

I check—yes.

Do you remember the time I asked you about your biggest fears? And you replied, heights?

I remember. I've told her things I've never told anyone else. It's strange, really—how the people closest to you aren't always the ones you can be honest with. How sometimes it's strangers who make you feel safe enough to say the truth out loud.

This is your moment to face that fear, the letter reads. *Look at the cliff ahead of you. It's a bit tall, isn't it?*

A bit tall? Really? That cliff is massive, towering like an untouchable fortress. My gaze follows the sharp edge all the way up, and I feel a shiver go down my spine.

You are going to climb up the cliff, and you are going to take a dive into the calming waters of the lake.

No way! I nearly scream. Heights have always terrified me. Diving from there seems impossible.

I know you must be calling me crazy or something. And I totally leave it up to you whether you want to do it or not.

But once, when I felt like I was at my lowest, I decided to face a fear I had. Mine was driving. Even being in the passenger seat scared me beyond belief. I know you may think that's not as scary as heights, but trust me, nothing frightened me more than being in a car. It would always bring shivers, trembling, and leave me fighting for breath, and so much more.

But one day, I decided I was done letting it own me. I started slow. I practised. And the first time I drove on my own,

I cried afterward. Not out of fear—but relief. One ride changed everything. It taught me that if I could face my worst fear, I could face anything.

It gave me a sense of control over my life again. And I think it could do the same for you.

'Wolf! Where are you?' Huntress's voice cuts through my thoughts, pulling me back to reality. Alarmed, I shove the letter back into my bag. *She can't see this.*

'Coming!' I call out, trying to sound casual. I force myself not to look at the cliff as I walk back, pretending it isn't looming over me like some giant, merciless monster.

When I return, Huntress is standing near the water, hands on her hips. 'You took your time,' she says, eyeing me suspiciously. 'What were you doing?'

'Just ... umm ... nature,' I say, waving vaguely at the woods.

She raises an eyebrow, but then a mischievous grin spreads across her face. 'You're acting weird, Wolf.'

'Am I?' I try to play it off, but my voice cracks slightly.

'Anyway, what are we going to do?' Huntress asks, her eyes glinting with excitement.

I swallow hard, draw in a breath, and meet her gaze. *Don't show fear.*

'I was thinking we could go up that cliff,' I say, pointing at the rocky wall. 'Watch the water from above.'

The lie slips out before I can stop it. I'm not sure I even believe it myself.

'That would be cool!' she says, practically bouncing. If only I felt the same.

We drop our backpacks near the base. I tell her we should take the longer trail—'more scenic,' I say. Truth is, I just need time.

Every few steps, my heartbeat quickens. My palms get sweaty and start trembling. I shove them into my pockets, hoping she won't notice.

I once read that every fear has a cause.

It was true for my fear of firecrackers. But heights? I've never figured that one out. They just paralyse me.

When we finally reach the top, Huntress walks straight to the edge. One misstep and ... *Fuck, don't think like that.* I stop six steps behind her—that's farther than I'd usually dare.

'It's beautiful,' she says softly. And she's right. The sun is directly overhead, making the water below shimmer like a sea of diamonds.

'Come here,' she says, grabbing my arm and gently walking me towards the edge.

'That's enough,' I say, pulling my hand free.

Do things you normally wouldn't. I remind myself of the words Birdie had told me before starting this journey. I've followed her advice so far, but this feels different. I can't.

I glance over the edge and freeze. From down below, the cliff seemed high, but from up here, it feels like it stretches without an end. My knees feel weak; I stumble back, my breath shaky.

Breathe. It's fine. You can still go back.

But I can't breathe.

The fear feels alive inside me—pressing hard against every inch of my conscience, heavy and loud.

'What happened?' Huntress's voice pulls me back. She's holding my arm, her other hand pressed against my cheek as if checking for a fever. Then she gently cups my face. I look into her eyes. They're so warm, kind and full of concern.

'Hey, you okay?' her voice quivers ever so slightly.

I nod too fast. 'Yeah. I'm fine.'

She doesn't buy it. Her hands linger another second before slipping away, and I instantly miss their touch.

'What happened?' she asks again, her eyes still searching mine.

'I don't know. It was nothing.' I try to steady myself, but the fear still lingers in the pit of my stomach.

She doesn't look convinced.

'What happened?' she asks again, quieter now.

'I ... I'm scared of heights,' I admit. Her expression softens, the corners of her mouth tugging into a small, understanding smile.

'Then why did you come up here?'

'I thought maybe I could face my fear by jumping into the lake.'

'And what do you think now?'

I look down again. The water glimmers far below, rippling like it's alive—teasing me, daring me. The wind brushes past my ears, whispering at me to let go of my fear. My throat tightens. My hands are starting to tremble. My heart's pounding so loud I can barely hear anything else.

'I don't know,' I finally say. My voice sounds small, swallowed by the wind. 'It looked easier from down there.'

For a moment, neither of us speaks. She just holds my trembling hands, trying to ease my anxiety.

'Should I do it?' The words slip out before I can stop them.

'Sometimes,' she says gently, 'all you need is one leap.'

'Have you ever done this before?'

'I have, yes. Many times.' She comes even closer to me, the proximity steadying me.

'Any tips for a first-timer?'

'Sure.' She smiles, and it's enough to bring a flicker of calm into my chaotic thoughts.

Over the next couple of minutes, she explains how to jump—how to go feet first, keep my arms close, and what to do once I hit the water.

'You can do this,' she says, placing a hand on my shoulder. I attempt a smile. Thanks to her, I know the mechanics, but this isn't like cramming for a college exam where I can memorise the facts and pass. My heart races and my hands shake openly now. I feel the familiar tightness in my chest—the onset of a panic attack. My breaths come quicker, each one shallower than the last.

'Watch me,' she says suddenly, taking a few steps back.

'What?' I ask, but she's already moving.

She winks at me once—her face fearless—and sprints forward.

Before I can say anything, she's gone, vanishing over the edge.

I rush to where she just stood, my pulse hammering in my ears. I reach the brink just in time to see her slice through the surface of the water below. Time slows.

She doesn't resurface.

My stomach twists.

Where is she?

Why isn't she coming up?

Is she okay?

And then—she breaks through, water spraying around her as she gasps for air. Relief floods through me so hard I almost laugh. She waves from below, already swimming towards the rocks.

'I'm coming!' I yell down to her.

My heart pounds harder than ever, but something's different now. I feel alert, alive. Adrenaline surges through me. I take a deep breath and start running, just like she taught me. As I near the edge, I push off and leap into the open air.

For a moment, everything is still. I'm weightless, suspended between the sky and the water. The wind rushes past me, whistling in my ears, and there's a moment of silence that feels almost sacred. I'm floating, just for an instant, as if nothing can touch me—not fear, no doubt, nothing. It's exhilarating.

And then, gravity takes over. The fall becomes faster, more intense. The lake below rushes up to meet me. And I hit the surface.

The impact is stronger than I anticipated—a shock that surges through my body, awakening every nerve. The water is cold, biting against my skin, and bubbles explode around me—the air from my lungs escaping—creating a veil that blurs my vision. For a split second, I am suspended in the depths, completely enveloped, being pulled by the lake to its core.

Swim upwards. Find the light. Keep moving. Her instructions echo in my mind.

I kick, push, fight against the pull. My chest burns, my arms ache, but I keep moving. I keep pushing. And then, finally, I slice the surface of the water.

The noise of the world crashes back into me, the rush of water, the echo of my own desperate breathing. I tip my head back, gulping in deep breaths, my chest heaving. My heart is still racing, but now it's exhilaration—pure, unfiltered exhilaration. There's no fear here, only the thrill of having done something I never thought I could.

The sky above looks different—brighter, clearer, as if the colours have deepened, become more vivid. Everything feels sharper, more alive.

I feel more alive.

I let myself drift onto my back, my arms spreading out as I float, letting the water carry me. It holds me gently, like an embrace, rocking me back and forth. My breaths slow down, each one deeper and calmer. And for the first time in a long time, I feel at peace.

I lose track of time, just floating, feeling the water cradling me, the sun on my face and the coolness of the lake beneath me.

Eventually, I turn my gaze to search for Huntress. She's there—watching me from afar. Her smile is wide, and even from here, I can see the pride in her eyes.

'You did it!' Her voice echoes across the water, and a grin breaks across my face, unrestrained.

'Yeah, I did.' I laugh, the sound of it pure, born out of joy and unburdened by anything else. She swims closer, her hair floating around her and the sunlight catches the droplets on her skin, making them sparkle.

'How do you feel?' she asks, her eyes locked on mine, her smile softening.

I pause, replaying the moments—the fear, the courage, the leap, the rush of air, the cold shock of the water, the rise to the surface, and finally, seeing the sunlight again.

'Like I have just learnt how to breathe,' I reply.

We swim to the shore together, the water around us rippling with every stroke. The air feels warmer now, wrapping around me like a reward after the lake's cold bite. My body buzzes—

half from the adrenaline, half from the quiet satisfaction of what I just did.

As we climb out, water streams from our clothes, forming tiny puddles that sparkle under the sun before fading into the dirt. I take a deep breath, filling my lungs with the clean mountain air.

'Thank you,' I say to Huntress.

'It was nothing,' she says, giving me a soft smile.

I give a gentle nod—and inside, I'm thanking someone else too.

Birdie. For this. For pushing me.

The list of things I am grateful to her for keeps growing. And she was right—I needed this.

Huntress picks up her backpack, glancing at me with a teasing smile. Her wet hair clings to her face and her eyes glint with mischief.

'Don't you dare look,' she warns, heading towards the trees.

'Wouldn't dream of it,' I say, turning away, though I can't stop the grin tugging at my lips.

I grab my bag, feeling its familiar weight, and glance back at the lake. The surface is calm again, the ripples from our jump long gone. The sunlight dances across the water, turning it gold.

I take a moment to absorb it, this place where I faced my fear and won.

A place where I took a leap—literally and figuratively.

Huntress is taking a nap in the tent we set up earlier. 'I know a great place where we can see the most beautiful sunset,' she had said. Now, as I sit outside, watching the valley be bathed in the golden hues of late afternoon, I know she wasn't lying. Even with time left before the sun dips below the horizon, the view is breathtaking.

There is silence everywhere—the kind of silence that lets you hear everything clearer, the distant calls of birds, the soft rustling of leaves as the wind weaves through the trees and the occasional hum of an insect.

Or maybe it's my mind that is finally quiet, letting me hear everything clearly for the first time in forever.

And I have an anonymous, magical stranger to thank for it.

I pull out my phone and type a message.

'I did it,' I write to Birdie.

And the world seems to have changed for me.

To be honest, I don't even know how to thank you anymore. You've inspired me, given me moments I never thought I'd experience, opened up a world that feels so new, welcoming, comforting. And now ...

I hesitate. Would it sound desperate? But then I think to myself: I don't care anymore.

Now, I just want to meet you. I want to know who you are. I want to give your words a face. I want to thank you in person. Maybe over tea somewhere quiet. I'll tell you everything about this trip, all my experiences, and you can tell me your stories—in person.

I pause, take a deep breath and type again.

'When are we meeting?'

The message sits there, sent. Birdie hasn't seen it yet. Not that I expected her to reply right away. She's probably out adventuring or sprinkling magic somewhere in the world.

I check her profile. The number on top—the total number of posts—has gone up. I check her feed quickly. There's a new picture she's uploaded: a line of ants carrying a leaf above their heads.

I smile. I like this about her—how she notices things. How she pauses for small moments like these, stops to really see them and treasures them in pictures.

That's the only new post, but the count is still higher. Maybe she's unarchived a few. I keep scrolling—thank god there's network here.

I know her feed by heart now, so I spot it instantly.

An old photo—she's sitting near the edge of a hill, her curly hair flying wild in the wind. The sky behind her looks endless.

Even there, she hasn't shown her face.

But something about that picture pulls at me, like she's right there, yet out of reach. And I wish I was beside her, sitting in that same silence, watching the world stretch out in front of us.

Then there are two more pictures.

One from what looks like a blood donation camp—rows of people on folding chairs, sleeves rolled up, smiles that say *doing something selfless feels good.*

I can almost picture her moving through them in her white coat, stethoscope around her neck, focused but calm. She'd be checking vitals, scanning for early signs of a drop in blood pressure, making sure no one's feeling dizzy.

And knowing how she is—caring and gentle—I am sure she would be making sure the donors don't feel even the slightest hurt.

And then there's another one—a skeleton hung on the inside of a tent. I almost laugh out loud.

She's drawn eyelashes on it with coloured pencils, shaded the cheekbones in pink, and even added lips.

It should look ridiculous. But somehow, it doesn't.

It just looks ... adorable. Not something I ever thought I'd say about a skull.

How can someone be this creative? It's like she saw something lifeless and couldn't help but bring it back to life.

I keep scrolling—misty mountains, medical camps, her curls flying wild in the wind.

I stare at her posts for a long time.

It feels strange—how much warmth a screen can hold.

How someone I've never met can feel so close.

I finally tuck my phone away and whisper under my breath,

'Who are you ... and when are you going to let me meet you?'

Huntress emerges from the tent a little while later, stretching her arms above her head.

'I hope I didn't leave you alone for too long,' she says, her voice still a little groggy as she sits down beside me on the mat I spread out.

'Not really,' I say, smiling. 'But I was going to wake you up soon.' I nod towards the pot on the stove. 'I made tea.'

'God, you're a lifesaver,' she says, wrapping her hands around the cup as I pour tea for the both of us. She inhales deeply, eyes closing for a second.

'Boy, this smells good. Whoever ends up with you is going to be the luckiest girl on the planet.'

I blink.

'I ... uh ... thanks,' I manage, trying not to sound as thrown off as I feel. I hand her a piece of girda that Dadaji packed for us, avoiding her eyes.

She grins, taking a bite. 'To be honest, I'd even fight her for that spot if you're going to take such good care of her.'

My brain short-circuits.

Why do you say things like that? Don't you see what they do to me?

And ... And why do you think that you will have to fight?

'Can you grab a shawl?' she asks quickly, as if realising what she just said. 'It's getting cold.'

I get up, grabbing the shawl from my bag—along with the old radio Loosepants gave me. Her words keep replaying in my head: 'the luckiest girl on the planet ... I'd even fight her for that spot.'

She was joking. Of course she was. She's with someone—someone who is taller, muscular, and maybe ... maybe even more good-looking than me.

I drape the shawl over her shoulders. She looks up at me, a soft smile tugging at her lips. 'Thanks,' she says.

I sit beside her, and she moves closer, pulling the shawl around both of us. Her shoulder brushes mine, just barely, but it's enough to awaken every nerve in my arm.

We sit like that for a while, silent, watching the sun slip lower, the valley below turning gold. For a moment, everything feels still. No noise, no rush—just warmth, and her beside me.

As the last edge of the sun disappears, I reach for the radio.

'It doesn't work,' Huntress says softly, watching me fiddle with the radio. 'We've tried fixing it so many times.'

'Maybe,' I say, twisting the old dial, 'but I don't know ... feels like the universe has been kind to me today. Maybe it'll listen one more time.'

I keep messing with it, trying to tune it up, give it a slap or two.

'It doesn't work,' Huntress repeats, her voice soft, trying to save my efforts.

'Hmm,' I mutter, not giving up yet.

I sigh, take the battery out, wipe it on my shirt and slot it back in. 'Come on, work with me,' I whisper, as if it has life and can understand me. Then I pat it again, firmer this time.

And suddenly—

A faint melody crackles through the static.

We both go still. The sound is broken but familiar—a '90s love song. Slowly, the sound clears, the faint melody slipping into the calm of the evening.

Her lips part slightly in surprise. 'You actually got it working?'

'Guess the universe really *is* being kind to me,' I reply.

She gives me a gentle smile. Then, slowly, she leans her head against my shoulder.

My heart skips a beat. Butterflies rise in my stomach—a feeling I've heard and read about so much, but never experienced until now, not like this. I keep still, trying not to move in the slightest, not wanting to cause her discomfort. The urge to wrap my arm around her shoulder, to brush it slightly, to tuck her hair—those strands covering her face—slowly behind her ear grows stronger with every passing moment.

But I can't.

Not when she is with someone else.

Not when every part of me knows it would be wrong.

So I do the only thing I can—sit in silence. I let the song play. Let her rest, without trying to imagine how it would feel to hold her close, to feel the warmth of her breath against my skin.

And I try not to wish for the universe to be kind to me just one more time.

As the last of the sunlight disappears, I light up a small fire. The flame flickers weakly at first, then steadies, its warmth brushing against our faces.

'You better stop that by the way,' she says suddenly, breaking the long silence.

'What?' I ask, glancing at her.

'This habit of slipping things into boxes,' she says, nudging me lightly.

'I have no idea what you're talking about.'

'Dumbo,' she teases, her shoulder bumping mine. 'You hide in plain sight. You pretend you're invisible, but you're not. I know the magazine article wasn't the first time you did that.'

She looks down at the flames, her expression softening. 'I know about the donations you made to the charity.'

'I ...' I trail off, not knowing what to say.

'It meant a lot to me,' she continues, her voice gentle. 'But I never knew how to thank you for it.'

'You don't have to thank me,' I whisper.

'I do,' she replies.

She looks up, her eyes meeting mine—warm, steady and full of something that feels dangerous yet enticing enough to give in to. The fire's glow paints her face in a soft orange, her hair catching the light and her lips part ever so slightly.

My heart is racing.

She leans in a little.

I do too.

Her warm breath mingles with mine and for a moment, I forget the rest of the world even exists.

And then—

A sharp screech bursts from the radio, slicing through the quiet.

We both jerk back.

Fuck you, radio. Or ... or maybe ... thank you, radio!

She bursts out laughing, hiding her face in her hands. 'God, talk about timing,' she says between giggles that seem forced.

I manage a weak laugh too, still trying to catch my breath. 'Yeah ...'

She glances up at me, her smile faltering for a second before she looks away. 'Umm ... well ... the sky's pretty tonight, huh?'

I clear my throat, desperate for something normal to say. 'Yeah ... yeah, it really is.'

Awkward smiles, awkward breathings, awkward silence.

There's a lot left unspoken, and yet, the quiet between us doesn't feel empty. It feels like there's more there, more to say, more to come. And I secretly hope it's true.

When we say goodnight, I catch her eye. 'Hey, wake up early tomorrow, okay? I've got a place my friend recommended we check out. We should go.'

She nods, her smile reflecting in her eyes. 'Sounds good.'

I smile back, pretending that my heart isn't still racing for her.

—∾—

Inside my tent, I check my phone. Birdie still hasn't seen the message.

For a while, I just stare at the screen. It feels strange—how a message can travel miles to that one person who you know nothing about, with just a single tap. But you cannot. No matter how badly you want to meet them.

I sigh, rolling into my sleeping bag, my thoughts swirling. The jump. Huntress guiding me, helping me overcome my fear. The sunset, sitting side by side under the shawl. *The almost kiss.*

And then, I feel scared. *What if she finds out?* The thought returns, pressing in, sharp and relentless. *Will she believe their lies? Their version of me? Will she give me a chance to explain before she decides who I am? Or will she, like the others, close the door before I've even had a single chance to speak?*

God, I am terrified. I have so much more to lose now—more than ever. A friend, a close connection with my crush, and parts of me that are only just beginning to believe in the possibility of healing. I've only just learnt how to stand again. How to breathe without feeling like the ground might give way beneath me.

If she doesn't believe me, if she looks at me the way the others do and pushes me away without listening—god, I don't know if I can survive that.

I turn in my sleeping bag, exhaling deeply, hoping the thoughts will settle if I stay still long enough.

They don't, not for a long time. And then, slowly, Birdie drifts back into my mind.

Her letters. Her calm, steady voice that always found me when I was lost.

She is the one who told me to take the leap. She is the one who talked to me when the thoughts of giving up, of ending everything wouldn't leave me. When the panic attacks would leave me crawling to a corner of the room, holding my knees to my chest, tears spilling down endlessly.

If it weren't for her, I would have just ...

No. Don't go there.

But it's the truth.

I wouldn't be alive if it were not for her.

I pull out my diary, jotting down the day's events—every little detail I can remember. I run my hand over the cover when I'm done, thinking of Birdie. Then my mind shifts to that almost kiss. Guilt pricks at me, and I push it away, too tired to dwell on it.

If Birdie were here, maybe she'd know what to say. Something that would tell me how to untangle this.

But she isn't.

I wake up early while Huntress is still asleep and slip out of the tent. I need to make things right, especially after last night's awkwardness.

I want things to feel normal again—just two friends hanging out together, camping, without any complications.

The mist clings low to the ground as I walk, and I remember the apple tree we passed yesterday. It doesn't take long to find it. The branches hang heavy with red apples, their skins glistening with dew. I pluck four of the plumpest ones, wiping them clean with my sleeve.

On the way back, I spot a patch of herbs growing near a line of rocks—fresh, green, full of scent. I gather some that I know carefully.

Maybe it's silly, but I want to make her something.

Something small.

A thank-you for the way she cheered me on yesterday, for her warmth, her laughter, for the shared sunset.

I build a small fire, feeding it with bits of dry wood, and start boiling water. The faint hiss of the pot fills the quiet. I crush the herbs and add them to the water.

I remember a line I once read: *It's the smallest things that paint the canvas of love.*

I'm hoping that this slight gesture, this soup, will at least start painting the picture of our friendship—something simple and unbreakable. Strong enough that if things get messy, and she hears about everything, she would give me a chance to explain my side of the story. *Unlike others.*

The soup begins to simmer, its aroma filling the air.

I smile faintly.

Maybe it's not much. But it's something.

And sometimes, that's enough.

'Good morning,' I hear Huntress's soft, sleepy voice from behind me. She's blinking slowly, her eyes half-closed, her hair tousled from sleep. There's a playful innocence in her demeanour, as if all her usual defences are nowhere to be seen.

'Morning,' I say, smiling at her.

She yawns, stretching her arms above her head before plopping down cross-legged on the mat beside the fire. 'It's so cold,' she mumbles, rubbing her palms together.

'It is,' I reply, though I'm barely aware of the air. My eyes are fixed on her.

She catches me staring and giggles. 'Stop staring,' she says, hiding her face behind her hands. 'I probably look like a total mess.'

This is the first time I've heard her voice like this—unguarded, raw. It's different from her usual confident tone, and I like hearing it.

'Quite the opposite,' I whisper before I can stop myself.

Her hands lower, eyes flicking towards me—wide, curious—her lips forming a smile. I want to tell her how beautiful she looks, even now, just after waking up. But I keep that thought to myself. *She's with someone else, Arjun. Remember that.*

I hand her the bowl of soup. 'I made you this.'

Her eyes widen as she takes it and breathes in the aroma of the soup. 'This smells so good!' she exclaims, taking a sip and sighing with a bright smile. 'God, I needed this. Wolf, you are the sweetest.'

'It's just some soup,' I say, trying to shrug it off.

'Nope. This is just too good,' she insists after another gulp. She looks at me, her eyes warm and filled with genuine appreciation. 'Wolf, you cutie, you're the best.'

I feel my face heating up. 'Uh, thanks,' I mutter, looking away. I bet if the apples could talk, they'd be teasing me about how red my cheeks look right now.

13

'The map says it should be just around the corner,' I tell Huntress.

We'd walked to the highway earlier, caught a minibus to reach this quiet village, and since then have been wandering its narrow lanes in the chilly morning air.

'Cool,' she says, her voice soft, her eyes tracing everything around us—the low walls, the painted doors, the smoke curling from a chimney in the distance. She looks completely lost in it.

I can't blame her.

The village feels untouched, like time here moves differently—slower, kinder. Houses sit neatly along the slopes, their roofs catching the playful dance of shadows and sunlight.

We keep walking. Every turn brings us something new—a burst of green from the trees, glimpses of some old stone houses wrapped in vines, and the curve of the path disappearing into the next bend as if leading us deeper into a secret.

'You've arrived,' the map lady suddenly announces.

It's a beautiful place made of stone, like an old cottage converted into a bakehouse. The frames of its glass windows are painted green, with wooden supports criss-crossing between them, giving it a charming, welcoming appearance.

It's not open yet, but there's already a family waiting outside—a couple in their mid-thirties, with a little girl dressed like a fairy, maybe just a year or two old. She's holding her father's hand while trying to eat her fist.

The dad wears khaki shorts and a buttoned-up shirt, paired with bright blue shoes. The mom is wearing a pink shirt and pink pants decorated with floral patterns, matching her pink clogs. The kid smiles at us, giggling as she babbles something incomprehensible.

'God, she's so cute,' I say to Huntress, smiling.

Huntress, who is staring at the family—watching how the mom and dad interact with the little girl, playing with her, making her laugh—looks lost.

'Huntress,' I say softly, placing my hand on her shoulder.

She blinks, as if waking from a dream. 'Ah—yeah. Sorry. Did you say something?'

'You okay?' I ask, keeping my voice gentle.

'Yes. It's just ...' She pauses her eyes still following the family. 'It's lovely to see them,' she says finally. She raises a hand to wave at the little girl.

'How old is she?' Huntress asks the mom.

'Around a year and a half,' the woman replies with a warm smile.

The girl lets out a high-pitched giggle.

'She's full of energy,' the dad says, chuckling. 'Ever since we came to these hills, she's been waking up before daybreak. She wakes us up too—wait, let me rephrase, she screams until we're all up—and then just wants to rush outside.'

'It's like she was born for the hills,' the mom adds, bending down to kiss the girl's chubby cheeks.

I watch them, and my mind drifts to Birdie. I can almost picture her as a kid, hiking with her parents, filled with curiosity and adventure. Maybe she was just like this—an energetic, cute, little girl, who was born for the hills, born for exploring.

When the bakehouse door finally opens, the family gets up first. The mom gives us a warm smile as they step inside. We follow them in.

Huntress lingers at the entrance for just a moment, her eyes sweeping over the stone walls and the rustic charm of the place. There's a look on her face—something fleeting, almost wistful. It's gone before I can place it, replaced by her usual bright smile.

'This place looks so good!' she says, her voice flooding with excitement. 'I can't wait to order.'

I feel the same.

'What would you like to have?' I ask as the family starts placing their order.

She's glued to the glass display, eyes wide, following the warm yellow light as it dances over croissants, pastries, cupcakes and fresh loaves of bread.

'A carrr ... carrot cheesecake ... I mean, pastry,' she says, stumbling over her words, then laughs at herself. 'God, there are too many options. I can't even decide.'

'A carrot cake it is,' I smile. 'And a blueberry cake for me.' I add two garlic croissants too, mostly because the baker swears they are the best.

Inside, the bakehouse is softly lit by old-fashioned yellow lamps, the stone walls and wooden pillars giving it a nostalgic vibe, like something out of a fantasy book.

'This place is amazing,' I say to the baker as he hands us our order. 'The variety, the feel of it—it's all perfect.'

'Thank you,' he replies with a warm smile. 'It's been in the family for nearly four decades, passed down from generation to generation.'

Huntress and I find a seat by the window, which is nearly as tall as I am and just as wide. The view beyond is breathtaking—pine and deodar trees carpeting the valley, touched by the morning sunlight. Huntress doesn't stop staring at the view for even a second. I can't blame her; the place feels like it's suspended in time. The rustic charm and the serene atmosphere—it's unlike anything I've ever seen.

'Let's eat now,' she declares suddenly, scooping up a generous bite of her cake. Her face changes instantly, her expression softening as if all the noise inside her has been silenced by that one bite.

'This is so good, you should try it,' she says, her voice gentle as she holds out a spoonful towards me. I lean in and taste it. The sweetness, the texture—it's perfect.

'God, this is unreal,' I say. In my mind, I am already thanking Birdie for sharing this place with us.

'Yes!' she exclaims, grinning as she steals a bite of my blueberry cake. She nods approvingly, cheeks puffed. 'I still love my carrot cake more, though.'

We laugh. Then she takes another bite of her cake and does a tiny dance in her seat—shoulders wiggling, eyes closed in bliss, a smile on her face. A universal sign of a girl loving her food—or at least that's what Instagram reels have told me.

When we finally finish and step out of the bakehouse, the air feels cooler, softer. Huntress turns to me, her eyes glimmering with an idea.

'Can we take a picture here?' she asks, her voice filled with enthusiasm.

'Of course,' I reply.

The father we met earlier, overhearing us, steps forward with a smile.

'I'd be happy to take it,' he says, pulling a small camera out of his bag—the kind that prints photos instantly. When I offer him my phone, he just waves it off.

'These are far better than digital,' he says.

Huntress looks nervous, her arms fidgeting a little. 'I'm not good at posing,' she says, her voice low.

The mom chimes in, smiling, 'You can hold his arm—don't worry, you both look lovely together.'

'We're n—' I start, but stop mid-sentence when I feel Huntress's arm slip around mine. Her touch is light, but enough to send a storm through me.

'Smile!' the man calls.

We do. The camera clicks and the film slides out with a soft whirr. A few seconds later, he hands us the photo.

I look down at it—her arm around mine, both of us smiling, the bakehouse in the background.

I know I'm going to treasure this photo.

No matter where life takes us, I'll make sure nothing happens to this picture carrying a brief, precious moment frozen in time.

After lunch at an inn we had come across, Huntress and I decide to keep walking along a random trail we found, curious to see where it might take us. The path is lined with wildflowers and tall grasses that sway softly in the afternoon breeze, creating a picturesque setting that feels both exciting and peaceful.

'Do you have a crush on anyone at college?' Huntress asks out of nowhere, as I duck under a fallen branch that is propped up against a nearby tree. Thick moss grows all over its bark.

My heart stops. *How do you tell your crush you have a crush on her?*

'Umm … why do you ask?' I try to sound casual, but my voice cracks halfway through.

She shrugs, 'No reason. Just curious.'

Curious. Gosh, If only I could tell you.

'Uh … kind of,' I say, after what feels like too long. My throat feels dry. I keep my eyes on the dirt path, pretending to study the uneven ground.

'Aha! Who is she?' her voice perks up immediately, her eyes widening in excitement.

I look at her and wish I hadn't. The way she's looking at me—wide-eyed, excited—it almost hurts. I wish I could tell her the truth. That it's been her since the first day of college when she boarded the same bus as me.

I couldn't believe how someone could be this beautiful.

'You can trust me,' she says, crossing her heart. 'I promise not to tell anyone.'

'Nah,' I mumble, forcing a smile. It's not her telling anyone that scares me. It's how she might react. If she'd asked me this a few months ago—before everything happened—maybe I could've told her. But now? I just can't.

'Okay,' I say, stopping to face her. 'I'll tell you if you tell me about yours first.'

'Nice try,' she says, laughing, brushing past me as she keeps walking.

A few minutes later, she slows down. 'You go ahead,' she tells me. 'I need a short break.'

'Alright,' I say, walking ahead. Trying to imagine how she would respond if I told her.

Sorry, Wolf, but I'm with someone else.

Wolf, I am sorry, but I've never thought of you like that.

Wolf, you're kidding, right?

I pull out my phone, desperate for a distraction. Maybe Birdie's finally seen my message. Nothing. Still unseen.

Argh, what is she even doing? It's been weeks of talking—texts, letters, late-night messages—and yet, she's still a mystery. No pictures, no clues. Just words. Words that I haven't been able to give a face to.

There's a text from my sister though—she's upset with me for not telling her where I am and not calling her as we had agreed. I text her quickly, my fingers tapping the phone fast. I can't have her get too worried and upset.

I even tell her the next town that I am going to be in—which Huntress had mentioned to be more than just a small town.

I walk a bit further and stop when I hear a voice up ahead.

It's faint at first—a low grunt, like someone's hurt. That can't be Huntress; she's just behind me.

I take a few careful steps forward, listening. The sound comes again, sharper this time, half a groan, half a sigh. The voice ... it sounds familiar. *Loosey? Is he okay?*

My pulse quickens. I push through a patch of tall grass and duck under a branch, following the sound deeper into the trees. For a moment, I lose it completely. Then, just when I'm about to call out his name, I see him. And he is not alone. He is with someone. His eyes are closed. His shirt unbuttoned. Someone is kissing his bare skin. I step back, wanting to give them privacy. But then the person stands up, coming into view, and I stop.

My stomach twists.

No. That can't be who I think it is.

But it is.

I take a slow step back, careful not to make a sound. My head feels heavy, my thoughts scattered and loud. I don't know what shocks me more—what I've seen, or whom, or the realisation that ... *Huntress can't see this.*

I turn and walk quickly, branches snapping under my feet, trying to shake off the image. When I reach the trail again, my breathing is uneven and my palms have gone cold.

How?

Huntress is standing right where I left her.

'And here I thought I was going to have a hard time catching up to you,' she says with a grin.

'Nah ... I stayed nearby. Figured you'd get lost without me,' I try to be witty—hoping it will not let her in on my thoughts. She laughs, a genuine, hearty laugh.

Will I be able to protect that smile? Will I be able to save it if she uncovers the truth?

'Can we take the main road?' I ask her, wanting to take her away from here as soon as I can. 'I would like to see more of the town.'

'Umm, okay. Sure,' she says, eyeing me curiously. I try to fake a smile, hoping she wouldn't guess that something is wrong.

'You act weird sometimes,' she says to me as we take the main road.

'I know,' I say, without even realising.

My mind is busy interpreting what I have just seen.

—w—

We reach the village market before dark. It's small but full of life—rows of wooden carts covered with handmade crafts, colourful scarves, small painted figurines. Huntress lights up instantly, pulling me along from one stall to another.

And I try to match it. To keep up.

To not let the image replay in my head.

But it does.

For a split second, I'm back in the woods ... *No!*

I blink hard, forcing the thought out. I *don't* want to think about that.

A man stands near a wooden plank dotted with balloons, holding a toy rifle. Perfect. Something to aim at, something to focus on.

I take her there.

'Let's see if you live up to your name, Huntress,' I say, forcing a grin. 'Bet you can't beat me.'

She raises an eyebrow, smirking. 'Ah, a challenge. Get ready to lose.'

'Only rule: you've got to call out the balloon before you shoot it.'

She nods, and I go first. I steady the toy rifle, pretending it's heavier than it is.

Then I shoot. *Pop. Pop. Pop.*

Seven out of ten.

'Not bad,' she says, patting my shoulder.

'Not bad? That was legendary!'

'Watch and learn,' she says, stepping forward.

She's good. Too good. Each shot lands, smooth and effortless. By the time the last balloon bursts, she's grinning wide, her hair catching the fading sunlight.

'So?' she asks, half proud, half playful.

'So ... the name suits you,' I say, trying to sound casual. *Is there anything this girl can't do?*

Just ahead, a cart catches my eye—filled entirely with jhumkas of all shapes and colours. They're some of the prettiest I've ever seen. I try to remember if I've ever seen her wear any. I don't think I have. I haven't even seen her in traditional Indian clothes before.

We move closer, scanning through the collection, but my attention stops on one pair—oxidised silver, delicate and detailed. It has floral centres with crescent moons beneath and tiny silver beads hanging from fine chains. I pick them up.

'Can you face me for a second?' I ask her.

When she does, her eyes aren't focused on the jhumkas but locked onto mine. I lift the earrings, holding them near her ears, just to see how they suit her.

And gosh, she makes them look so beautiful.

'Can you pack these?' I ask the shopkeeper, not addressing Huntress directly. She's still staring at me and I don't dare to meet her eyes. I don't think my heart will be able to take it.

'I don't have the clothes to match them,' she says, flustered. 'And ... I ... I don't wear traditionals.'

'I know. But keep them as a memory,' I tell her. She gives me a soft smile, holding the jhumkas close—too carefully—as I hand them to her.

My eyes pause on another pair. They're like feathers, golden, with parts painted in shades of blue. My hand instinctively reaches for them.

'Can you pack these too?' I ask the shopkeeper. *Birdie might like them.* 'It's for a friend,' I tell Huntress, and she nods with a soft smile.

14

The sun has begun to set, and we start walking towards the camping site where we had planned to gather.

My footsteps feel heavy, unsure how I'll face everyone now that I've seen what I saw. But I keep walking and smiling, trying to ensure Huntress doesn't sense it.

The thoughts rush back again.

Should I tell her? No. I can't. It's not my secret to tell.

The doubts are still swirling in my mind when a minibus slows down ahead of us. A vehicle has broken down in the middle of the narrow road, blocking the way, and a cart is wedged sideways beside it—blocking the other part of the road. No way to move. If this doesn't clear soon, it'll turn into a full-blown traffic jam.

I glance at Huntress, about to suggest that we take a detour—when something on the bus catches my eye.

A blue medical cross painted on its side. Inside, a few medical students wearing white coats.

Before I can stop myself, my eyes start scanning the windows.

It's foolish. Impossible.

She can't be here.

Not here, at this exact moment. The universe can't be that kind to me.

And yet, I keep looking. Window to window. Face to face. Searching.

And then—

Through the window, glowing against the golden light of the setting sun, I see her.

A girl in a white coat, a scarf wrapped around her face, a few curls escaping and glowing in the light. And her eyes ... her eyes are fixed on mine.

Birdie?

Everything else—the noise, the shouting, the engines—fades away. I stand frozen, staring at her. And her eyes don't move either, don't go away, just stare back—like time itself has stopped between us.

I don't blink. I don't breathe. Afraid that if I do, she'll vanish.

And then, before I can move, before I can take a step or call out her name, the car in front starts speeding away, and the bus lurches forward, following it.

'Bir—' I almost call, when Huntress holds my hand.

'Are you okay?' she asks me.

I don't have a response. I don't know how to react. I want to run behind that bus, leave everything behind, climb it up and talk to Birdie. But the bus is already turning, disappearing around the bend, taking her away from me.

'Yea ... yeah,' I manage, the words coming out with a struggle. 'I am.'

She looks at me, her expression full of concern, with a hint of fear beneath.

'I'm okay,' I tell her again, this time trying to keep my voice firm. I'm not sure who I'm trying to convince—me or her.

She doesn't force me to explain. But I can see that she doesn't buy it.

I walk beside her, pretending everything's normal. But inside, I'm somewhere else.

The minibus. The scarf. The glowing curls.

Could it really have been her?

15

Frost and Daisy are the first ones at the camp. Daisy, who hasn't seen us yet, sits quietly in her tent, eyes fixed on the camera in her lap, her face clouded with sadness. *Did Frost do something again?* He's a few feet away, headphones on, scrolling through his phone, barely acknowledging our arrival.

I'm almost grateful the others aren't here yet. My mind is too tired from thinking about everything that has happened just in a day and needs some alone time to process things.

Everything that follows is a blur.

Setting up tents. The Nerds arriving, pitching their common tent, retreating into it. Loosey coming in, bringing a burst of energy. Officer arriving from the opposite direction, waving food parcels in his hands.

The second he spots Huntress, his face lights up. He runs straight to her and pulls her into a hug.

The sight makes something twist inside me. I look away, pretending to adjust a tent rope which doesn't need adjusting.

What kind of twisted game is he playing?

Loosey waves at me excitedly. I force a smile back and busy myself collecting sticks for the campfire—anything to keep my thoughts from spiralling.

Later, we enjoy a hearty meal of carrot and beetroot soup alongside cheese toasts that Loosey prepares. He proudly declares them 'the best we will ever have'. They're good—not the best—but they're satisfying.

Throughout dinner, I notice Loosey glancing towards Huntress and Officer who are sitting close, too close—their shoulders touching, his hand holding hers for long stretches of time. Loosey's expression keeps shifting between irritation and confusion.

There's something different about Huntress, though. Her laughter—the one I've grown used to seeing—never comes. She looks quieter tonight, distant. A few times, our eyes meet across the fire. There's something in her gaze, something searching.

As if she's trying to read what's going on inside me.

I push the thoughts down and focus on Loosey. He is my friend and I need to be there for him.

'You okay?' I ask, sitting beside him, near the campfire.

He looks startled, then shrugs. 'Yeah. I'm fine. Never been better.' But his voice betrays him. I can't even imagine what he must be going through.

The images of him from earlier flash in my head—pinned against the tree, eyes closed. I push it away.

We talk for a while. Loosey asks me what I was up to. I dodge the details, especially about my time with Huntress. And I return the question.

'Did you do the thing you said you had to do?'

'What thing?' he asks, puzzled.

'You mentioned you had something to take care of.'

His expression shifts, realisation dawning. 'Oh, the *thing*! Yes, I did it. Of course. How could I forget? It was fun. I'll tell you about it later.'

He continues, saying he spent the morning exploring and met some local shepherds. According to him, their sheep were twice the size of a tiger and incredibly feisty. That's how I know he's lying—he's just not good at it. His downcast eyes and the ridiculous story only make it clearer.

And I know he's lying—because I know what really happened.

The question keeps echoing in my head, over and over.

Should I tell her? No, I can't. But god ... what if she finds out on her own? How will I protect her then?

My chain of thoughts snaps as Daisy suddenly stands up and declares, 'I've decided—I'm going to be a stand-up comedian after college.'

For a moment, there's silence. Then the group bursts into applause, even Frost—whom I didn't think capable of being excited about anything—joins in.

'You should try telling some jokes here,' Officer suggests. Daisy nods eagerly and steps forward, clutching a pink diary.

'She's been writing jokes she finds online in that diary for days,' Loosey says, turning to me. 'Probably because Frost loves comedy shows.'

'Okay, everyone, just be silent. Here is my first joke for you,' Daisy begins confidently. 'What did the traffic light say to the car?'

I know better than to answer. These jokes rarely go as planned.

'I made you stop!' Huntress guesses.

'No! Wrong answer, Huntress. Anyone else?' Daisy remains cheerful.

'I'm a green flag?' Loosey guesses.

'Nope, Loosey. Good one, though! But it could just as easily be a red flag—or yellow,' Daisy says with a grin. She pauses, waiting for anyone else to try, then adds, 'Alright, since no one's got it ... here's the answer.'

She clears her throat, reading from her notebook. 'What did the traffic light say to the car? "Hey, don't look, I'm about to change."'

He-nerd laughs, I chuckle, and even Huntress shares the amusement.

'That was the lamest joke I've ever heard,' She-Nerd declares, glaring at Daisy. 'I haven't witnessed anything this bad.'

'You sure have,' Officer chimes in. 'The cheese toasts Loosey made. They were the worst. I'm sure vomit would taste better.'

Frost laughs along with She-Nerd, while Loosey freezes. His expression hardens for a moment—hurt flashing across his face—but he swallows it down. He doesn't say a word. Just blinks a few times and looks away.

Huntress glares at Officer, a sharp look that clearly demands an apology.

Loosey suddenly stands up. 'I'm heading out,' he mutters. When I try to rise, he gestures for me not to follow.

The group falls silent. Moments later, Huntress is still talking with Officer, and the Nerds have retreated to their tent.

Daisy towers next to Frost, attempting another joke. As she finishes, Frost looks up, stands and walks away.

'God, you are irritating,' he mutters loud enough for everyone to hear.

Her smile drops instantly. In the wavering firelight, I can see her eyes glistening. She turns quickly, so no one can see. But I do. She swipes her cheek once and takes a step into the dark, walking away from the camp.

Huntress starts to follow, but Daisy shakes her head, silently asking to be left alone. For a moment, I just stand there, torn. *Should I go after her?* I don't know her that well. But maybe that's exactly why I should.

From my own experience with Birdie, I know that sometimes it's easier to talk to a stranger than to someone who knows you too well.

And while I may not have the right words for Loosey, I know exactly what Daisy needs to hear.

'I'll go,' I say when Huntress looks at me.

'I can come with you,' she offers softly.

I shake my head. 'I've got this. And maybe you should stay here—talk some sense into Officer.'

She nods.

The moonlight trails over the path ahead, and with every step, the memory of what I saw in the woods creeps back in.

It was Loosepants's voice. I couldn't see him at first—just the rough bark of a massive tree. Then, when I was about to call out his name, I realised he wasn't alone. Someone else was with him.

I froze.

I still remember the other person's face. The one who had him pinned against the tree. The one who was kissing him.

Officer.

For a moment, I thought I was imagining it. But no—it was them. Unmistakably them.

Officer and Loosey.

Now, having seen Officer besides Huntress, acting like nothing's happened, the memory twists in my mind. Loosey must be breaking inside, pretending he's fine.

What am I supposed to do with this? How do I help him? How do I protect Huntress?

Stop. Not now.

One thing at a time. Right now, Daisy needs me.

Daisy pauses when we reach a flat stretch of ground lit under the moonlit sky. She stops and sinks down, her gaze locked on the distant mountains that glow in the dim moonlight. I settle beside her, and she startles—she clearly didn't realise I was behind her. Quickly, she wipes at her eyes, trying to hide her tears.

For a while, she just sits, sobbing quietly, as if she's trying not to fall apart. And I let her, knowing how sometimes it is important to just let go, let everything out.

'I just wanted him to notice me,' she finally says, her voice trembling. 'I did everything I thought he'd like.'

'I know,' I manage to say. It hurts to see her like this.

'He really loves comedians, so I decided I'd become whatever he wanted.' She lifts a small diary, pages filled with her handwriting. 'I spent hours googling jokes, writing them down, hoping it'd make me ... worth seeing. And when She-Nerd called my joke lame, I thought he'd have my back. But he didn't.'

She breaks down again, covering her face. I hesitate, then place my hand on her shoulder, patting gently.

'I'm sorry,' I whisper.

After a moment, her sobs slow down, and wipes away her tears with the back of her hand.

Silence falls. The mountains loom in the distance, their peaks piercing the darkness. I look up at the sky, where stars scatter like flecks of silver on black velvet. The image reminds me of when I used to stargaze with my grandpa—those peaceful nights I wish I could go back to.

'Do you know its name?' I point at the bright spot near the moon.

'That bright star near the moon?' she asks.

'Yes,' I reply. 'But it's not a star actually.'

'Really?' She is intrigued. *Good.*

'It's actually a planet.'

'I didn't know that.'

'Most people don't. My sister and I had a debate over whether it's a star or a planet. Then I asked my grandpa, who told me it's a planet.'

'Who won then?' she asks.

'My sister.' I smile, glad she's not crying. 'But she didn't know its name either. So at least I could use that as a defence when she teased me. It's Venus, by the way.'

'It's the brightest in the sky,' she says, her eyes now exploring the open sky.

'You wanna know a nerdy fact?'

'Uh, huh.'

'It's named after the Roman goddess of love and beauty.'

'Love and beauty ...' she chuckles softly.

After that, silence.

'Daisy ...' I say softly.

'Yes?'

'I've seen you both online and here—in person—and I just ... I think you're one of the sweetest, kindest and most beautiful people I've ever met. And maybe it's not my place to say this, but ...'

She looks up, eyes red. 'But?'

'But you deserve someone who sees that. Someone who sees *you*—who falls in love with who you are, who knows your worth without you having to prove it every single time.'

Her gaze drops to the ground. I can see her fingers tightening around her little diary.

'The way you've been putting in efforts for him,' I say gently, 'if he can't see your worth, if he doesn't understand how rare it is to have someone put in that kind of effort ... then ... then he's not worth it.'

She doesn't speak for a long while.

'I don't have the courage to accept that,' she admits finally, her voice trembling.

'But you need to, Daisy. For the sake of your own heart ... you have to.'

Her eyes glisten again, but this time she doesn't hide them. 'I just wanted to be what he would like me to be, you know,' she says, her voice weak.

'I know. But love isn't love if it changes who you are.'

She sighs, the weight of the words settling between us.

'Can you give me an honest opinion?' she asks, opening her phone.

'Sure.'

She opens the gallery and passes her phone to me, showing me pictures she's clicked of the kids at the orphanage.

'Copied to the phone just today,' she says.

I can't help but admire the pictures. Each one captures the raw essence of the kids' childhood—laughter, smiles, moments of playfulness. They're beautiful, worthy of an art gallery.

'These are too good.'

'You're being kind,' she says.

'No,' I respond, quickly. 'I've never seen someone click pictures this good, Daisy. You're a natural with a camera.'

'Thank you, Wolf,' she says. 'I have always wanted to be a photographer. Started my Instagram page just for that. But I realised, guys and the algorithm loved it far more when the pictures were of me, and not of what I saw. Soon, I forgot why I started and got caught in the race for likes and followers.'

'But maybe it can change now,' I say quietly. 'I'd love to see the world through your eyes again. Sure, some people might be disappointed. Some might unfollow. But that's okay—because the ones who will stay will love the real you. They'll fall in love with how you see the world.'

I give her hand a small squeeze. 'Do it for yourself, Daisy. Fall in love with your art again. Let it remind you of who you are, let it help you realise just how much you are worth.'

—∾—

The air turns too cold and we decide to head back to camp. As we approach, I see Huntress feeding wood into the campfire. She smiles at us and we wave back.

Daisy pulls me by the sleeves of my jacket and whispers, 'Though you called me one of the most beautiful girls, I know she's the one you have your eyes on.' It feels dangerous, as if she's seen some naked truth. 'When are you going to tell her how much you like her?'

Before I can say anything, she plants a kiss on my cheek.

'Thank you for tonight,' she says, offering me a small smile before heading to her tent.

'It wasn't like that,' I blurt out, suddenly aware that Huntress saw it.

'Chill,' she says with a small smile. 'Her face said enough. Whatever you guys talked about, it seems to have helped her a lot. So, thank you for that.'

She steps closer, her lips finding my other cheek and staying there—warm, steady, soft. Softer than anything else in the world.

And I dissolve into nothing. I don't know where I end or where she begins. I forget the fire, the night, even myself—everything except for the part of me where her lips are.

She pulls back, her eyes catching the firelight—warm, unreadable—then she turns away to feed another log to the flames.

I just stand there, useless, the silence in the night filled only by the crackle of burning wood and my own racing heart.

It takes me an impossibly long time to finally move.

'You're still awake?' I finally manage to ask, sitting next to her, my voice unsteady.

'There was a fight after you left,' she replies casually.

'A fight? Really? Who fought?'

'The Nerds,' she says, tossing another piece of wood into the flames.

'The Nerds?' I repeat, unable to believe it. 'What could they possibly fight about?' I picture them as their usual selves—him agreeing to her every word, and the two of them blissfully oblivious to anything that wasn't snogging.

Huntress must have caught my expression because she elaborates. 'He finally called her out. Said she should've treated Daisy better. Apparently, he hated how cocky she was tonight and told her to be nicer. She didn't take it well.'

I blink. 'That doesn't sound like him.'

'Exactly. She got mad—really mad. They argued for a long time. Then she asked if she could sleep in my tent.'

'And that's why you're out here?'

'Yep,' she sighs. 'I tried sleeping next to her, but barely ten minutes in, and she was snoring like a freight train.'

'You can take my tent,' I offer quickly. 'I'll sleep out here by the fire.'

She shakes her head. 'The fire won't last all night. You'll freeze.'

I don't have a counter. My mind scrambles for another solution, but Huntress beats me to it. She hesitates for a moment, looking at me with an awkward but determined gaze.

'Maybe,' she starts, her voice soft but steady, 'we can both sleep in your tent?'

I should be thrilled. I'm lying right next to the prettiest girl I know. But my mind is split—half of it still stuck on the moment from earlier today, when the minibus stopped and I saw her.

Birdie.

Those eyes.

The sunlight in her hair.

For a few seconds, the world had gone completely still, like everything had paused just so I could look at her. The thought that she was *right there*—close enough to reach out, to finally meet—and the fact that I missed that moment ... it kills me.

And now, here I am—lying in a quiet tent with my crush right beside me. Our sleeping bags don't touch, but her presence feels close enough to set every nerve in me on edge.

Her breathing, slow and steady. The cold fabric separating us.

It's ridiculous, how restless it makes me.

Has she fallen asleep yet? I have no idea. And I'm too nervous to turn and check.

What did the peck on the cheek mean? And now this—her sleeping in my tent? Are these signals? Am I missing something? My thoughts spiral as I try to make sense of it all.

'You should be asleep, Wolf. Is me being here making you uneasy ... or maybe, a little excited?' Her tone is playful, but her voice—low, near my ear—sends a quiet shiver through me.

I turn slightly towards her. 'No, it's not like that,' I stammer. 'I thought you were asleep.'

'Not really.'

I scramble for words, but none come. The silence stretches between us, until she finally says, 'Wolf, my cutie,'—it's the second time she's called me that—'sleep now. We have a big day tomorrow. Goodnight.'

'Goodnight,' I murmur, closing my eyes.

The memory invades my mind like a storm.

I'm back in the garden of the villa Anurag rented for Reecha's birthday. The music is loud, spilling out into the garden where everyone's drinking heavily—everyone except Reecha, who's surprisingly sober.

After a while, I decide to leave. It's all starting to get too much for me—the music, the smell of smoke and alcohol.

Reecha stands too, saying she should head back and that I can drop her off. She mentions she doesn't like driving alone at night—and it's too late.

Anurag, drunk and grinning, waves us away. She kisses him goodbye, light and careless. We start walking, the cool night air a relief after all the noise.

She suddenly stops mid-step.

'Shit. I left my purse upstairs,' she says, turning back. She asks me to come with her, claiming she's scared to go alone.

Something in her tone feels off. I hesitate. *Don't do it, Arjun. This is where everything will go wrong. This is where it all happens.*

Against my better judgement, I follow her.

The music muffles as we climb the stairs. The air inside feels heavier, quieter. My footsteps echo faintly against the marble.

At the turn of the hallway, she stops abruptly. Her hand presses against my chest, firm, pinning me to the wall. She steps closer, eyes locked on mine.

'Reecha … what are you doing?' My voice comes out low, uncertain—disbelief and dread tangled together.

'We can have a little fun, can't we?'

'This isn't right.'

'Oh, come on, Arjun. You've wanted me for so long—I know it.'

My stomach turns. 'No, Reecha. I told you before, I'm not into you. I don't want this.'

'Argh, who cares, Arjun? It's just a party. Everyone deserves to have some fun. You can kiss me, and no one will know.'

She steps closer.

'Reecha, stop.' I take a step back, but she moves with me. 'You're drunk. You don't mean this. And I don't want this. You are my best friend's girlfriend.'

'Well, I chose him after *you* refused me, didn't I?' she says, her voice trembling between anger and hurt. 'But I've always liked you, Arjun.'

Before I can reply, she leans in and kisses my cheek. Her hand slides down my chest.

'Reecha, *stop.*' My voice breaks. I grab her wrist and push her back gently. 'I'm not doing this. You need to get your purse, and we're leaving.'

But she doesn't move. Her eyes harden, and suddenly she's on me again—her hand reaching lower towards my pants, her lips trying to force mine.

That's when something in me snaps. I push her away, my voice shaking but loud this time.

'I said stop!'

Silence.

Her face twists—shock first, then fury.

'Fuck you, Arjun,' she spits, her voice drips venom as she raises her middle finger. She storms away and into the room.

I stand there, breathing hard, my hands still trembling. I feel sick.

I should leave. Just book a cab and go. But Anurag will ask what happened. I can't let him find out. It would destroy him.

Disgusted, I wait at the stairs while she retrieves her purse.

Minutes pass. I check my watch, wondering why she's taking so long. I'm about to go look for her when she finally appears, purse in one hand, Anurag's phone in the other.

'Would you mind giving this to Anurag?' she says bitterly, shoving the phone into my hand before storming past me.

I take a step after her.

And then her scream cuts through the air.

High. Sharp. Wrong.

She is running outside.

Anurag rushes to her, stumbling slightly, his arm going around her shoulders, his hand running through her hair.

'What happened?' he asks, his voice slurred but concerned—and there's something else there too. Something cold.

'Ask Arjun,' she says, her voice sharp, full of hate.

'What did you do?' Anurag's tone turns hard in an instant. His friends look from her to me, their drunken laughter fading.

'I didn't do anything!' My voice rises in panic.

'What happened, hon?' Anurag's tone softens as he turns to her.

Reecha's shoulders start to shake. At first, it's just trembling. Then a sob breaks free, sharp and raw, echoing through the night. Everyone goes still. Even the loud music feels distant now.

She clings to Anurag, burying her face into his chest. The air thickens around us. No one speaks.

And then she lifts her head. Her voice comes out cracked, trembling.

'He ... he tried to force himself on me.'

The words hit me like the edge of a knife, cutting clean through the flesh.

The world stops moving.

The laughter, the music, the night—everything goes silent, except for the sound of my pulse crashing in my head.

Anurag looks at me in disbelief. *No. I didn't do it!*

'What the hell?' one of Anurag's friends blurts out, lifting his phone. He shows him something on the screen. I can't see what it is—just the way Anurag's face changes. The way shock twists into fury.

His eyes dart to me. Then to the phone still clutched in my hand.

'What the fuck did you do, Arjun?'

'Nothing!' I stammer. 'I didn't—'

My feet move on their own, stepping back, my breath catching. His eyes are filled with murderous intent. He's already on me. His hands slam into my collar, and before I can breathe, my back hits the wall—hard enough to knock the air out of me.

'Anurag, stop!' I gasp, grabbing his wrists, trying to pull them off. 'I didn't do anything. I swear, I didn't—'

Then her voice cuts through it all.

Trembling. Soft. But sharp enough to slice the night open.

'He cornered me in your room,' she cries, clinging to him. 'He said it was just a party, that everyone deserves to have a little fun. He told me he'd been watching me for so long—wanting me, waiting for this moment to be alone.' Her sobs deepen, but she pushes forward, her words venomous.

'I told him no. I begged him to stop, to think about you—his best friend. But he wouldn't listen. He grabbed me, whispered that no one would know, that it would be our little secret.' Her tears spill freely now, her voice shaking with rage and despair. 'When I still refused, he ... he threatened me. He said he'd take your phone, leak our private pictures, and ruin me if I didn't go along with it.'

The room feels like it's collapsing under the weight of her false accusations. She turns her tear-streaked face towards me, eyes brimming with hatred. 'And when I still said no, he did it. He sent the pictures to the entire class. He wanted to humiliate me, to destroy me for rejecting him.'

Anurag's head snaps towards me, his bloodshot eyes filled with disbelief and fury. His fists clench as he steps closer, the alcohol fuelling his unsteady rage.

'I didn't do anything!' I say, my voice cracking, my heart racing. 'Anurag, you know me. You know I wouldn't—'

But he doesn't let me finish. He grabs my collar and slams me into the wall again. I gasp, struggling to push him away. 'You tried to sleep with my girl?' he shouts, his voice rising. His breath reeks of alcohol, and his grip tightens around my shirt.

'I didn't,' I yell, my voice desperate. 'I swear, I didn't do anything—'

'Don't lie to me!' he roars, his face inches from mine. 'Why would she lie? Arjun, look at her. She's crying her eyes out.' He jerks his head towards Reecha, who's still sobbing in the corner, her hands covering her face.

'I didn't send those pictures. I didn't even touch her!' I shout, my voice hoarse, but my words fall on deaf ears.

Anurag's friend steps forward—one of the gym guys, big, red-faced.

'You disgusting piece of shit,' he spits. 'You don't deserve to call yourself a friend.'

Then the first punch lands.

A white flash.

A crack.

Pain explodes across my jaw. I taste blood, metallic and hot.

'She is lyin—' A punch landing into my stomach. I double over, gasping for air. It's Anurag.

'I didn't do it!' I manage to scream, but my voice drowns in the chaos around me.

His foot drives into my ribs. I hit the floor, clutching my side, coughing, choking on my own breath. Another kick.

'Stop. Stop it!' I plead, crawling backward, the room blurring through my tears. 'Anurag, please—you have to believe me. You *know* I'd never—'

'I thought we were brothers,' he says, his voice trembling with rage. 'How could you do this to me, Arjun? How could you betray me like this?'

'I didn't,' I scream, tears streaming down my face. 'You have to trust me. Please, Anurag, listen to me.'

But all I see in his eyes is rage and betrayal. I don't know how to make him believe me, how to undo the damage Reecha's lies have done. Another kick lands in my side, and I curl up on the floor.

It hurts—it fucking hurts.

'I didn't—' Cough. 'I swear—' A boot drives into my side again.

My tears start racing. But the blows don't stop. The kicks keep coming—each one harder, finding a new place to break. My body jerks with every hit. A punch crashes into my ribs. The sound barely registers before another lands.

'Stop ... Please ...' It barely escapes my mouth. It sounds small, like a child's voice. Nobody hears it. 'Just ... liste—' A slap tears through the air, taking my words away, my ears ringing. My vision blurs, colours leaking into each other.

There's blood on the floor. I see it for a second—dark, spreading beneath me. It takes a moment for me to realise it's mine. It's dripping from my mouth, warm against my chin.

'Please ...' I whisper again, barely a sound. 'I didn't ...'

Another hit. Followed by, 'Bastard.'

I blink, but my eyes don't focus. The edges of the room fold in and blur. The floor shudders beneath me. Everything starts spinning, becoming too loud, too painful. 'I didn't ... it.' My breath rattles; my ribs ache every time I try to pull air in.

'Please ... I ...' *Thud*, another punch lands on my face, 'I ... I didn't ...'

Then it all goes quiet.

'I didn't do it! I didn't. Please ... You have to trust me. You have to trust me!' I try one last time—this time gathering all my remaining strength.

'Wolf, Wolf! Arjun!' The voice pulls me back—soft, urgent, real. It's not part of the nightmare.

'Arjun, hey.' A hand touches my face. 'It's okay. It's okay. I'm here ...'

It takes me a moment to come back to reality. My breathing is ragged, my heart pounding. Sweat drips down my face.

Anjali is besides me, her face a mixture of concern and fear. She's dabbing my forehead with a cloth, leaning over me, her elbow propped for support.

'I'm here with you. It's okay,' she says softly, her voice like a salve to my fractured mind.

I try to speak, but all that comes out is a broken sound. My face twists, and before I know it, I'm crying harder—loud, messy—there's no strength left in me. I grab onto her, desperate for something to anchor me.

'I'm sorry,' I choke out between gasps. 'I'm so sorry.'

'It's okay. You have nothing to be sorry about,' she repeats, her voice tender. She strokes my hair gently, her touch calming me in a way I didn't think possible.

'You don't know, Huntress,' I whisper, my voice breaking. 'You don't know what happened.'

'I know,' she says, her eyes locking onto mine with unwavering certainty. Her words shock me, leaving me frozen in place. My chest tightens as fear grips me. *She knows? Is she about to judge me too?*

'They texted me the next day,' she explains, her tone steady. 'Both of them. They were texting everyone, trying to push their story. But I knew who you were, Arjun. I know who you are. And I knew you would never do it.'

Her words hit me like a flood of light piercing through the darkness. My lips tremble, my vision blurs. I struggle to process what she's saying, but then she continues, her voice soft, firm and kind.

'You're a good guy, Arjun. I know it in my heart.' She leans forward and places a gentle kiss on my forehead. Tears spill down my cheeks, harder, as I look at her, overwhelmed by the relief of being believed—by her faith in me.

Her words keep echoing in my head like they're trying to fill every empty space inside me.

You're a good guy ... I knew you would never do it.

How I've wanted someone to say that.

Just once.

That they believe me. That they trust me.

That they know who I am.

That I'm not the monster everyone thinks I am.

I hold her tightly, my body shaking as I cry into her shoulder. She doesn't flinch, doesn't pull away. She lets me release everything, lets me feel safe for the first time in what feels like an eternity.

The pain, the fear, the noise in my head—they all start to fade. Slowly. Quietly.

'Sleep now,' she whispers, her hand running through my hair in slow soothing strokes. Her voice is soft. 'It's alright. It's okay.'

And for once, I think it might be.

I close my eyes. Her face, serene and kind, is the last thing I see before sleep takes over.

No demons enter my dreams again that night.

16

I open my eyes. Huntress is right there, her face just inches from mine, and her hand resting gently on my shoulder. I can't look away. Even in the dim light, her face looks soft and beautiful. Her hair falls partially across her face, and I instinctively reach out to shift it away.

I look at her, the only person in this world who chose to trust me without question. She didn't ask what happened; she just believed me. And here I was, begging and fighting with everyone for a chance to explain myself, only to be shut out at every turn. No one wanted to listen—no one but her.

I guess the world loves being cruel, loves jumping to conclusions and labelling people the first chance it gets. Hearing both sides of the story would take away the fun.

But now, lying here, looking at her, I realise something. I don't care anymore. I don't care if the whole world stands against me. She trusts me. She believes me. And that's enough.

It feels like the weight of the entire universe has lifted off my shoulders. For the first time in what feels like forever, I feel free.

And Daisy's words from last night keep echoing in my mind: *'When are you going to tell her how much you like her?'*

Can I tell her? Can I really tell Huntress I like her? Especially when the people she's surrounded by—our entire college—see me as a monster. Even if the truth comes out someday, will they ever see me differently? And then there's Officer. She's still with him. Does she know the truth about him?

And Birdie. For the first time, I stop and really think about her—not just as someone who has helped me, but as someone who chose to. She didn't have to be there for me, didn't have to guide me through this storm, but she did. Her words carried me when nothing else could, and now, I can't ignore the weight of her presence in my life.

What does she mean to me? If I tell Huntress, *I like you with all my heart,* would that be fair? A part of me, I just realise, feels tied to Birdie, not just in gratitude but in something deeper. I want to know her, to give a face to the words that pulled me back from the edge.

I hate myself for this. I hate the situation I'm in. I hate how much I like Huntress—how incredible and supportive she is. And I hate that, at the same time, there's this part of me that's drawn to Birdie, even though I don't know who she really is, apart from being an extraordinary human being who's helped me through this journey.

I check my phone. Still no reply from Birdie. The unread messages, mostly from my sister, catch my eye. Five missed calls. That's unusual.

Call me soon. The first message reads. Beneath it are more: *Where are you? Are you asleep? It's urgent.*

I sigh. I need to call her. Knowing my sister, if I don't, she'll send a search party to comb the area. But it's still dark out, and before anything else, I need to wake Huntress. She can't be seen leaving my tent in the morning. From my own experience, I know people don't need much to twist a story.

But I wish she could stay. I wish the world didn't dictate so much of what we do. That the views of the others didn't matter as much. But they do. And I don't want that for her.

'Huntress,' I say softly, shaking her gently.

No response.

'Anjali ...' I whisper, calling her by her name.

She stirs and pulls me into a hug, her arm wrapping tightly around me, her breath warm against my neck.

I freeze. My hand twitches, almost reaching out to hold her back—but it stops halfway. I want this. I want her to stay like this forever. The way she holds me feels so comforting, soothing. It's like everything I've been craving without even realising it.

But my heart won't stay still.

Because even now, even here, it's filled with chaos. And I hate that. I hate that I can't just let myself feel this without thinking of someone who isn't here.

It's not fair—to Huntress, to me, or to Birdie.

I can't do this to her.

'Huntress,' I whisper again, gently pulling away. 'Anjali ... You need to go back to your tent before anyone wakes up.'

Her eyes open, slowly. She looks at me, sleepy but calm. 'Hmm ...' she murmurs. She sits up, staring at me for a moment before sighing. 'I wish I could stay longer,' she says softly, a faint smile on her lips. 'It's been too long since I slept without nightmares.'

'Same here,' I admit quietly, my voice barely more than a breath.

She leans in and hugs me—brief, warm, lingering just long enough to make me wish it wouldn't end. When she tries to pull away, my hands move on their own, holding her there for just a heartbeat longer.

It's not right. It's not fair.

I let go.

She smiles, her eyes soft, placing her palm gently against my cheek.

'See you soon, Wolf,' she says, before slipping out of the tent.

I stay lying there, staring at the roof of the tent, my thoughts a tangled mess. Eventually, I tell myself to let it go. The sun hasn't even risen yet. There's no point in stressing over everything now. I close my eyes, hoping for a few hours of sleep.

'Hey, pack leader. You awake by any chance?' Loosey's voice cuts through the stillness.

'Yeah, I'm awake,' I reply, sitting up. 'What's up?'

'Can we talk?' His voice is soft, almost hesitant.

'Of course.' I grab my jacket and step outside. If he's ready to talk, I want to be there for him.

He points to the bonfire, where faint embers glow. 'I lit the fire again. Wanna join?'

'Yeah, sure. It was getting too cold, anyway.' I follow him, and we sit on the rolled-out mattress he's placed by the fire.

'If you're in a pack, you shouldn't hide things from your pack leader.' Loosey picks up a can of soda from his bag, cracks it open and takes a gulp. 'And I don't want to keep anything from you anymore.'

'Loosey, you don't have to tell me anything you're not ready to say.'

'But I am ready,' he says, handing me a soda as well. 'I don't drink, but I'm pretending this is wine or beer. Just for the courage.'

I take a sip and brace myself, having a sense of where this might be headed.

'Wolf, what I'm about to say might ... shake your world. You might feel like the ground beneath your feet has disappeared, and you're falling into a sea of revelations.'

'Okay,' I say.

He turns to face me, taking a deep breath. 'Wolf ... I'm gay.'

I keep my voice calm and even. 'Thanks for telling me.'

Loosey stares at me, wide-eyed. 'Wait. That's it? Where's the shock? The gasps? The dramatic "Damn, Loosey! Really? I had no idea!" Or even the awkward "Me too" Or—God forbid—the "We can't be friends anymore." What kind of reaction is this?'

'Well, for starters, I'm not gay, so no "me too". And secondly, nothing about this changes how I see you. You're still my friend, and you're still part of the pack. As for the lack of shock ...' I hesitate. 'I kind of knew already.'

His expression falters. 'How?'

'I saw you with Officer yesterday. In the woods.'

Loosey's face pales, and he sinks back onto the mattress, lying flat on his back. 'So you know why I acted the way I did last night.'

'Yes,' I admit softly.

He stares up at the sky. 'It hurts, you know. Seeing him with her, acting all straight, picking her up and twirling her around like some lovesick fool when it should be me. I love Huntress—don't get me wrong. But I hate him for this. For hiding, for sneaking around, for only wanting me in the shadows.'

I hesitate, then ask, 'Does Huntress know?'

'She knows he's not straight.' Loosey sits up, running a hand through his hair. *She knows? Then, why?*

'Years ago, during a trek, someone almost guessed his secret. That's when she decided to help him. They started acting like a couple to keep his secret safe. It worked. It stopped the guys from hitting on her and kept him safe.'

I feel my breath hitch. Does that mean she is not with Officer? That changes everything—or maybe it complicates everything. *Shit.*

'Are you even listening?' Loosey waves his hand in front of my face.

'Yes, yes, I am,' I say quickly, trying to focus. 'But ... you were saying?'

He sighs heavily. 'She doesn't know about us. Not that there's much to know. We're not dating or anything. For him, it's just ... convenient. A fling. He tells me I'm the most interesting person he's ever met, that he can't imagine life without me. Then he goes back to her, pretending like none of it happened.'

'Have you asked him to be honest? To accept the relationship, or at least come out to the group?'

'Too many times to count,' he replies, his voice bitter. 'But he's terrified of being judged. And the worst part is ... I keep hoping he'll change. That he'll see what we could be. But I don't know if I can keep waiting.'

We sit in silence, the fire crackling softly between us.

'Loosey ...' I say after a while, choosing my words carefully. 'If he truly values you, maybe it's time to show him what it'd be like without you. Keep some distance. Focus on yourself. Live your life fully. Maybe then he'll realise what he's losing.'

'Do you think that'll work?' His voice is hesitant, but there's a flicker of hope in his eyes.

'I don't know,' I admit. 'But what do you have to lose? You'll be living your truth, being you. And maybe ... just maybe, he'll come around.'

Loosey's face lights up. He sits up straight and throws his arms around me in a crushing hug. 'You're the best, pack leader. Love you!'

I laugh, patting his back. 'Love you, too, Loosey. Platonically, of course.'

He grins, pulling back. 'Of course.'

We settle back, adding sticks to the fire as it starts to dim. My thoughts are a whirlwind as I stare at the flames.

She's not with Officer. That changes everything—or does it? My feelings for her feel lighter, less weighed down by guilt. But then there's Birdie. I check my phone—even though I checked it just some time ago. She hasn't seen it yet.

'Loosey ...' I start hesitantly. 'What do you do if ... if you find yourself liking two people at once? Both incredible, both who have changed your life?'

I wait for an answer, but there's none. I glance over and see him fast asleep, his soda can still in his hand.

I chuckle quietly, lying down beside him. Maybe I'm laughing at him. Maybe I'm laughing at myself. Either way, it's a while before the others wake up.

I close my eyes, but sleep doesn't come easily.

In my dream, I'm walking along a trail lit in golden sunlight. The air is crisp, the scent of pine sharp and grounding. A bird flits ahead, its wings shimmering in the sunlight, guiding me forward. Beside it, Huntress walks with her usual confidence, her every step radiating an unspoken warmth. She smiles at me, her face glowing softly, and gestures towards the path ahead.

The trail splits abruptly into two forks. Huntress chooses the left one, her expression inviting, her hand reaching out towards me. I take a step in her direction. But then the bird morphs into a figure—a woman draped in a flowing, colourful dress, like something out of a dream. Her face is hidden behind a dark mask, making her seem almost faceless, mysterious.

The masked woman stands on the right path, her head tilted as if waiting for me. Both Huntress and the mysterious figure call to me, their voices overlapping, each pulling me in a different direction. My feet feel rooted in place. My chest tightening as I try to decide.

Whom should I go with?

The ground beneath me begins to shift, the earth trembling violently. The air grows cold, and I glance down to see the soil crumbling away. I'm sinking, my legs swallowed by the earth. Panic grips me as the world shatters, the two paths dissolving into darkness. The voices echo, growing faint and distant.

'Wake up, Wolf!' Daisy's voice shatters the dream, pulling me back to reality.

My eyes fly open. I sit up abruptly, disoriented and drenched in sweat. Daisy is standing over me, arms crossed, looking unimpressed.

'You need to get up,' she says firmly. 'We've got to move. And you're waking up Loosey. God knows that it's impossible for me.'

Still groggy, I mumble a half-hearted 'hmm' and turn towards Loosey. He's sprawled on the mattress, one arm flung over his face, snoring lightly.

'Hey, Loosey, wake up,' I say, shaking him gently. He doesn't budge.

'Just ten more minutes,' he groans, rolling onto his side.

'Nope, buddy, we need to leave.' When he still doesn't stir, I smirk. Time for the ultimate weapon. 'Your pack leader demands it.'

Loosey bolts upright as if struck by lightning. 'Aye, aye, captain!' he says, saluting dramatically.

I burst out laughing. 'You're too much, man.'

From the corner of my eye, I notice Officer standing outside his tent, arms crossed, glaring at us. His expression is sharp, his body tense.

'Also,' I add, leaning closer to Loosey, 'don't look, but a certain someone is giving us a death glare right now. He looks like he's burning up with jealousy.'

'Really?' Loosey starts to turn his head.

'Don't look,' I snap, and he freezes mid-motion. 'Remember what we talked about? You need to start learning how to live—without going after him.'

He nods, a small grin forming despite himself. 'Got it, pack leader.'

We pack up quickly, the campsite buzzing with subdued activity. Daisy, ever the morning person, brews filter coffee and hands out paper cups to everyone—except Frost and She-Nerd. The anger simmering on She-Nerd's face, combined with Frost's dissatisfied and equally annoyed expression, is an absolute treat to watch.

Meanwhile, Huntress isn't sitting with Officer, and I can't help the small flicker of god knows what. We exchange a few smiles, our eyes meet more times than they usually do, and each time it leaves me flooded with emotions that are impossible to place.

After a quick breakfast, we set off. Loosey, still a bit sad from the previous night, walks beside me and Huntress. I tell them I need to make a quick call, and they let me fall behind.

I dial my sister. The phone rings, but she doesn't pick up. Typical. She's probably in a meeting. Just as I'm about to pocket my phone, a text buzzes through.

In a meeting. Sorry.

I roll my eyes. Workaholic. Who schedules meetings at 7.30 in the morning? Before I can reply, another message pops up.

But hey, you need to go to the location I'm sending you. There's a surprise.

Love ya.

I've always known about my sister's obsession with Google Maps, so I open WhatsApp without protest. Memories flash back to when Google Maps had just launched. Back then, she never told me where to pick her up—she'd just send her location. Always. Even now, it's the same. And when we'd drive somewhere, no matter how many times we'd been there, she insisted on asking the lady from Google for directions. It didn't matter if the route was etched into our minds like the back of our hands.

Frustrated but curious, I click the link. It opens a map, pointing to a gift shop in the city we're headed to. What now? Knowing her, it's bound to be something extravagant—it's just how we are as a family.

Catching up with Loosepants and Huntress, I pause to take in the view of the sprawling city below. It's breathtaking, a mosaic of rooftops nestled in the arms of the hills, draped in early morning light.

'Why are all the cities here so beautiful?' I ask mesmerised, the scenery stealing my attention.

'You have no idea how much I miss these hills when I'm stuck at college,' Huntress replies, her voice carrying a note of longing.

'Well, this time when we go back, you won't be the only one missing these,' I reply. I watch her smile. It's warmer, prettier, more comforting and too chaotic for my heart.

I ask everyone if we could take a small stop at a location. Everyone is okay with it since it's in our path.

The place we stop at is alive with activity. Tourists bustle about with backpacks, moving in clusters. Shops line the streets, spilling onto the narrow pathways. One side offers vibrant, handwoven shawls; the other glints with brass antiques and intricate wooden carvings. Vendors serve steaming masala milk from large pans, the sweet aroma mingling with the crisp mountain air.

Thanks to the map pin, the shop isn't hard to find. It's small but charming, carrying that quiet, antique warmth. Chandeliers hang low from the wooden ceiling, their soft glow brushing over rugs, vases and other curios stacked neatly on shelves.

'Hello, do you have a parcel for me?' I ask as I step inside.

The group decides to wait outside, wandering through nearby stalls. The man behind the counter, in his fifties and with a white goatee and matching moustache, doesn't look up immediately. He's lighting incense sticks, offering them to a small shrine of gods behind him.

'How can I help you?' he finally asks, adjusting his brown kurta.

'I think there's a parcel here for me,' I repeat.

'What's your name?'

'Arjun,' I answer.

He nods, pulls out his phone, and scrolls through something. Then he holds the screen up to my face, his hands trembling slightly as he glances between the phone and me.

'So, you're the special kid,' he says, a grin spreading across his face. 'I wish I had customers like you every day. Got a call yesterday—someone asking if I could arrange something by today. I said no at first—who could? But then they mentioned the money, and I thought, "I'd be stupid not to." Never been happier to do business!'

Special kid? His words send doubts swirling through my mind. *Is this really from Di?*

The shopkeeper disappears into the back room and returns moments later with a large parcel wrapped in brown paper. It's bigger than I imagined.

'Got the best one available,' he says proudly. 'Sent my boy thirty kilometres away to fetch it. No one makes these better than the people there. For the big money that was promised, I'd have sent him sixty kilometres if needed.'

Big money? My frown deepens, the doubts growing louder. Could this really be Di's doing? It has to be. Mom and Dad don't even know where I am—and they wouldn't care if they did. Besides, Di did say she wanted to make up for missing my last two birthdays.

I thank him and step outside, clutching the parcel tightly. Even without unwrapping it, I already know what it is. My chest feels light, almost childlike. I pull out my phone and type:

'Thank you, Di. Love you!'

A smile spreads across my face before I can stop it.

'Hey, Wolf,' Loosepants's high-pitched voice cuts through the lively chatter around me. He's standing at a cart selling salty peanuts, waving me over with one hand while stuffing his face with the other.

'Don't judge,' he says, mouth half-full. 'Overthinking or sadness makes me hungry. And right now, I'm really overthinking before I act or do anything today.'

'Not judging,' I reply, watching him shove more than half the peanuts from the paper cone into his mouth in one go. Seeing how thin he is, I can't help but think that he probably doesn't get this sad or overthink this much very often.

'Where are the others?' I ask, already picturing Huntress and Daisy's faces when I show them my surprise.

'At the inn, waiting for us to join them for the meal,' he says, offering me the rest of the peanuts. I accept a few and drag him along.

When we arrive, the group is seated on benches outside the inn. Officer's eyes are fixed on Loosepants, a faint smile—warm and trying to catch attention—decorating his face. Loosepants ignores him completely, his face showing no emotion whatsoever.

'I have to show you something,' I announce, making a point to ignore them both. Everyone turns to look, even the Nerds, who, to my surprise, are sitting close again, stealing kisses from each other. But I don't have time to dwell on that.

I place the parcel on the table, carefully unwrapping it. Even though I already have a good idea of what's inside, excitement bubbles up as I work through the layers. Loosepants starts tapping on the table as if providing a drumroll for the occasion.

And then, there it is—a brand-new guitar.

It's brown wood gleams softly under the light, the strings shining like they're waiting to be played. I run my thumb lightly over the surface, feeling the smooth polish under my skin.

'It's beautiful,' Huntress says, smiling.

'Yeah,' I breathe. 'It really is,' I echo, meaning every word. 'For years, I've dreamed of having my own guitar again—ever since my last one broke six years ago.' I pluck a string, and the sweet, rich note resonates, wrapping around me like an embrace. My heart swells with gratitude. *I love you, Di,* I say in my mind, thanking her again.

'Did you buy it just now?' Daisy asks, her eyes wide with curiosity.

'No,' I say, still admiring the guitar. 'My sister sent it as a gift.' A thousand questions fill my mind about how she managed this, but knowing her, I decide to let it go.

'What's this?' Daisy asks, pointing to a small paper tangled in the discarded wrapping.

'Probably a bill,' I reply absently, too engrossed in my new treasure to care.

Huntress picks up the paper, glances at it for barely a second, and hands it to me. It's surprisingly small. 'It's a note,' she says.

My heart skips a beat as I take it and read the only words on it: *'From Mom & Dad.'*

Everything stops. Someone says something, but it reaches me as a low, meaningless hum. It's like the world has been paused just long enough for the weight of that small note to land. I stare at the words until the ink begins to blur, waiting for them to change. They don't.

'Could you please excuse me?' I say, my voice strained. I hurriedly wrap the guitar back in its brown paper, grabbing the note, and nearly knocking over the glasses on the table in my rush to leave.

'Hey, we haven't eaten yet,' Loosepants calls after me, but I don't look back.

'You carry on for the day,' I shout, my voice sharp and unsteady. 'I'll find you later.'

There's an email in my inbox. From Dad.

> Dear Arjun,
>
> I hope you're doing well and enjoying your time hiking. Your mom and I bought you this gift, knowing you would like it. Hope you enjoy playing it, like you did in your childhood. Maybe we can plan a family trip soon. I would like that. And your mom would like that too.
>
> With love,
>
> Your Dad

I know it by heart now. How many times have I read it? I've lost count. I sit on a bench, the cold wood pressing into my back. It took a long, steep hike to get here, but I needed this—needed to be away from the group, away from the noise and the crowd.

And yet, despite the serenity around me, my mind is anything but calm. I can see through the scheme now. I hate my sister. The idea of the gift—it's hers. I'm certain. Mom and Dad must've consulted her before buying the guitar.

And then, when my Dad talked to his PA, I can almost picture how that conversation must've gone.

'Hey, my son is off on some stupid hiking trip, and my daughter thinks I should send him a gift. A guitar, of all things—not a finance book or stock portfolio like a sensible person. Find any dealer in that city. Tell them to get the most expensive one. That

should help him forget all the childhood trauma we caused. Just make sure he gets it.'

Mom would've fought with Dad over this. Maybe between rounds of arguing about how she should've got more in the property split, and him snapping back that she already got enough. Maybe she accused him of not doing enough for me, telling him to send something 'worthy of his stature'.

God, those fights. I hated them as a child, and I hate them even more now.

'You'll love it there. And the best thing is, you'll make so many friends. They will all live in the same house as you. There's a big playground, and ... so many games! You'll never get tired of playing.' I still remember the words Mom said to sell me on the idea of boarding school.

'Are you fighting because of me, Mum?' I had asked her, tears streaming down my face.

'No, honey! No,' she said, holding my face in her trembling hands. 'It's just ... sometimes people don't love each other the same way they used to. And then they fight. But it has nothing to do with you, okay? We just don't want you to get hurt.'

'Do you and Dad not love me anymore?' I sobbed.

'No! It's nothing like that,' she said, her voice breaking as she pulled me to her chest.

I didn't understand what divorce meant back then. Not until the fights grew more frequent and the lawyers started showing up—even during the rare times I was home from boarding school.

Beep.

The screen of my phone lights up, pulling me back to the present. It's a message from Birdie.

God. It's not a good time.

'Hey, how's your day?'

Terrible, I type and hit send. *Seen.* She is online.

What happened? she replies.

I hesitate before typing: *My mom and dad sent me a gift.*

Wow! That's incredible.

It's not.

Send me a photo.

Her words feel too casual for the storm swirling inside me. Reluctantly, I open the camera. The app lags, freezing momentarily. Frustrated, I shake the phone lightly, willing it to work. Finally, it flickers to life, and I snap a picture of the guitar lying beside me.

It takes a long time for it to upload. I hit send.

Moments later, her response appears: *It's beautiful. They must love you a lot.*

The words hit me like a slap. *They don't,* I reply, the words tumbling out before I can stop them.

There's a pause. Then: *They must, Wolf. That guitar might be their way of showing love.*

Anger bubbles to the surface. I can feel my fingers trembling as I type: *You don't know anything about me, okay? They don't love me. They've never cared.*

Another pause, longer this time. Her next message feels measured: *Maybe they hurt you in the past, but they're still your parents. Give them a chance.*

My frustration boils over. *You don't have any right to tell me what to do.*

I press send. The moment it delivers, I regret it.

Seen. No typing bubbles. No reply. Just silence.

Panic grips me. I quickly unsend the message, but it's too late. She's already gone.

I slump against the bench, staring at the guitar beside me. *What the hell is wrong with me?*

Birdie has been nothing but kind to me, nothing but sweet, gentle, supportive. And I lashed out at her.

I open the chat again, typing: *I'm sorry.*

No response.

I'm truly sorry. I didn't mean it. Still nothing.

My chest tightens. I slam my foot against the ground. 'Damn it!' The word echoes faintly into the empty mountain air.

I bury my face in my hands, guilt coursing through me. My phone lies idle in my lap, as still as the world around me. The guitar I hold feels heavier than ever—a physical reminder of the tangled web of emotions I carry for my parents.

Time drags. I check my phone again. No new notifications. I switch between apps, refreshing the chat, hoping for the 'seen' under my messages to change. Nothing.

I regret saying things to her. I never do that. I never hurt anyone. It's not me.

Minutes turn into an hour, the mountain breeze chilling my skin. I close my eyes, leaning back against the bench, trying to make sense of the chaos. Why did I lash out at her? Was it her defense of my parents? Her suggestion—so simple yet so impossible—that I give them a chance? Or was it because, deep down, I know she might be right?

The phone buzzes in my lap. I grab it quickly, the notification glaring back at me: *@super.birdie sent you a photo.*

My heart pounds as I tap the screen, but the image won't load. The loading animation mocks me.

'Damn you, Instagram,' I mutter. 'And fuck this network.'

I grab the guitar, swing my hiking bag over my shoulder, and take off running. I don't know where I'm going—just somewhere with a signal. Somewhere where I can fix what I just broke.

'Slow down, boy. You're gonna—' a middle-aged woman's voice calls after me, but I'm already gone, hurtling down the slope, my legs barely keeping up with the momentum.

I stop near the edge of the road, panting, two bars of network flickering on my phone. That should do it. I stare at the screen. It's a picture of a store—no caption, no context. Just a store. My heart leaps. She must be there. She's waiting for me. This is it. She's finally meeting me.

I flag down a middle-aged man and ask about the location. He gives me directions, and I'm off again, weaving through traffic, dodging people and carts.

'Look out!' I shout, narrowly avoiding a man balancing a stack of fruit on his cycle. The crowd thickens as I near the marketplace, my heart pounding not just from exertion but from anticipation. Where is she? Is she somewhere here? In this sea of endless faces?

I stop to ask someone else, a kind-looking older man, who points me towards the far end of the opposite lane. The store comes into view, and I pick up my pace, brushing past annoyed tourists, muttering hurried apologies.

Finally, I'm there, gasping for air, sweat dripping down my temple. My chest burns as I bend over, trying to steady my breath. I scan the area. There's a girl standing near the store, examining shawls. Curly hair, a red muffler, jeans and a T-shirt.

Birdie!

'Hi,' I manage, my voice hoarse. She turns around, her expression confused and slightly irritated.

'It's me, Arjun,' I say, forcing a nervous smile.

Her glare sharpens. 'Sorry,' I blurt out quickly, my stomach dropping as I realise it's not her. 'I thought you were someone else.'

'You're Arjun?' the shopkeeper calls out, his voice raspy. He's a wiry man with a dark kurta and a tobacco-stained grin that feels more sinister than friendly.

'Yes,' I reply, still trying to catch my breath.

'Someone left a packet for you.' His tone is indifferent, but his eyes glint with something calculating. 'I wasn't going to keep it—who knows what's inside—but the girl bought a shawl from me and gave it to that old beggar woman who's always pestering us. Made me rethink.'

'Can I have it, please?'

He looks me over, then smirks. 'Of course. But maybe you should buy something first. This shawl here,' he gestures to a brown one with intricate designs, 'will cost you two thousand rupees. A bargain, really.'

'Two thousand?' I echo, incredulous. 'That's ridiculous.'

'Depends on how badly you want the packet,' he shrugs.

I'm already running low on cash—and I need whatever she's left for me. He knows it—that devilish smile says it all.

'Or,' he adds, eyeing my guitar, 'that beauty there would work just fine.'

I hesitate, clutching the guitar strap slung across my back. For a moment, I consider offering it. It's not like the guitar means anything to me—it's a gift from parents whom I can barely stand to think about. But as the thought crosses my mind, a strange pang hits me. Why does the idea of giving it away feel so wrong?

'I can't give you the guitar,' I say, the words surprising even me. 'I only have a thousand rupees.'

'A thousand won't do,' he replies smugly. 'But I'll give you a final offer—fifteen hundred. Don't want to break your heart.'

I hesitate. My wallet is thin, and this trip has already drained me. But I need this. Money doesn't matter.

'Fine,' I say, handing over the money. His grin broadens as he takes it, handing me a shawl and a neatly sealed parcel.

'Who gave this to you?' I ask, clutching the package tightly. 'What did she look like?'

'I might know,' he says, his grin turning sly. 'But it'll cost you extra.'

'I don't have more money.' My voice cracks. 'Please, just tell me.'

He leans closer, eyes gleaming. 'Well, the offer stands still. This guitar would do nicely.'

His hand brushes the guitar strap, and something in me snaps in. Before I know it, I've grabbed him by the collar and shoved him against the counter. The other shopkeepers glance over but stay rooted, uninterested. This asshole is clearly not liked.

'Tell me!' I shout, my voice trembling with anger.

'All right, all right!' he sputters, holding up his hands. The stench of tobacco makes me want to vomit. 'She left as soon as she gave it to me. Said she had a bus to catch in ten minutes and couldn't wait around.'

The fight drains out of me, leaving only disappointment. She's gone. My chance to see her, to explain, to apologise, all gone.

'Now, get the fuck out of here,' he yells. I don't reply. I just turn and walk away.

Right across the street, a cemetery gate stands open, its iron bars casting long shadows in the fading light. Clutching the parcel tightly, I head towards it. My heart feels heavier with each step. *What if this is her last letter to me?*

I find a stone bench under a sprawling tree, its shade casting faint shadows on the ground. Sitting down, I clutch the sealed parcel, my fingers trembling as I try to break the seal. The glue resists, almost testing my resolve, before finally giving way with a sharp tear. Inside, a folded letter peeks out.

Hey Wolf,
I'm sorry for today.

Why is she apologising? I should be the one asking for her forgiveness.

I guess I need to tell you more about me. You already know that my parents took me on treks from the time I could walk. I was their little Birdie, always chirping about the hills, begging them to take me back up every chance we got. My uncle still laughs when he tells stories of how I'd leap out of the car the moment we parked, shouting, 'Let's go!' before my parents even unbuckled their seat belts.

You asked me once why I chose the username @super.birdie. I guess it's time I explain. It's actually a funny story.

Once, my mom and dad took me to see a Superman movie at a local theatre. On the way back, I wouldn't shut up about how I wanted to be Superman—flying around the world, saving people. (Apparently, I talked way too much back then—everyone called me Birdie because I never stopped chirping!) Anyway, my dad laughed and said, 'But if we start calling you Superman, you won't be our Birdie anymore.'

After a lot of thought, using all of my tiny brain, I announced, 'Then call me Superbirdie! That way I can still be your Birdie, but also be super.'

They teased me about it for years. My uncle and aunt did too. It became one of those stories they loved to tell, and now it's one I'll never forget.

I have many fond memories like that, just like that of the bakery I asked you to visit. I used to go there with Mom and Dad. It was my favourite place—full of magic with its rustic look, the sweet taste of those cakes and the joy of being with my parents.

And I wanted you to go there, so that you could experience that same magic.

My parents passed away many years ago—over a decade now—in a car accident. And all these years, I couldn't bring myself to set foot in that bakery. It always felt like a nightmare to go there without any loved ones around.

The car accident is also why driving a car was my biggest fear.

I wasn't going to tell you about my parents, but I thought I should. And I'm not telling you this because I want you to pity me or to seem like I'm asking for attention—I just wanted to share this because I know the pain of not having your parents around. Honestly, I'd give anything to be one of those people who get to argue with their parents, to be mad at them for their mistakes, for not being perfect, or for constantly fighting.

But I can't. They are gone, and I will never get that chance.

You, though—you still have your parents, Wolf. Even if they've hurt you, even if they've failed you, they're trying now. That second chance to get back to your parents, that's something I never got. And that's why I want to say this: give them a chance, if you can. Let them show you that they care, even if it's not perfect.

They can't erase the past, but they're reaching out now. And that means something.

Please think about it.

Yours,

Birdie

I keep sitting there, on a bench in the graveyard, the only place where there are no people around and the tears rolling down my cheeks won't be questioned.

I stare at the letter again, holding it as if it might crumble under the weight of everything it carries. Every step of this journey flashes through my mind—the first time I stumbled upon her feed and got lost in the solace it offered. It showed a way to live without worrying, without always being on edge.

I remember typing out that first message, convinced she won't reply. But she did. And with each reply after that, she became more than a stranger—someone who saw the pain I was in and chose to help me, even when she had no reason to.

She guided me—through texts, through her stories, through the way she saw the world. She advised me on what to pack, how to be ready for what lies ahead. She's the reason I met the most wonderful people like Abdul Miyan, Sharma Uncle and Aunty, each interaction leading me to the healing I didn't think was possible.

Yet, the pain I carried—the one that consumed me—is nothing compared to hers. I always wondered what life had done to her to make her so kind, even towards strangers. Now, reading her letter again, I understand ... at least a little. I reread the letter, and think about how much she must have suffered afterwards. How difficult it would have been to rise, to get on her feet, to build herself up.

I pick up my phone, opening Instagram to text her, but my fingers hover over the screen. What could I even say? How do you find the right words after learning something so deep, so painful about someone? I don't even know where to start.

Instead, I open WhatsApp and scroll to the old group my Di had created—the one she keeps alive because she feels it's her duty to keep the family together. I type:

Thanks, Mom and Dad, for the gift.

It meant a lot.

I'll see you soon.

It feels strange to write it, but I press 'send' anyway. It's a small step, but it feels like moving forward.

It was hard, growing up rushing through my childhood. Rushing to feel safe. Rushing to survive.

The chaos, the panic, the anxiety that the fights would bring—how Di and I would hide in a room, shielding ourselves under a blanket, praying it would stop.

Will I ever be able to forgive them for that? For a childhood spent always on edge?

I don't know.

But for her—that one stranger who found me when I was ready to give up, and helped me live on—I want to try.

If they really are trying to change, I don't want to be the one who stops that. I want to give them the chance to show us—Di and I—that they care, somewhere deep down.

That they understand the toll it all took on us.

And that maybe ... they're ready to put in the effort to make it right.

I go back to Birdie's chat. The blinking line feels like it's waiting for me to get my act together. Taking a deep breath, I start typing,

I'm so sorry for my behaviour, for getting angry at you. And I'm sorry for everything you've been through. I don't know what to say—I can't even think clearly. But I just want to say this: wherever your parents are, they must be looking at you proudly, seeing what a wonderful person their daughter has become.

And about being super, Birdie, you've been my superhero. You've saved me, changed my life in ways I never thought possible. That's what superheroes do, and I owe you for that. I want to thank you in person. I want to be there for you in any way you'll allow. I want to meet you, know you, stay close to you. I know I'm far from perfect—not even close.

But if there's ever a trail you want to walk, like the one I did, a magical trail that heals all wounds, I would love to walk it with you.

I press send and lean back against the bench, the letter and my phone both heavy in my hands. The silence of the graveyard around me feels deafening.

I close my eyes, letting the memories and emotions wash over me. The ghosts of my own thoughts and regrets gnawing at me from the inside. Will she forgive me? Will she give me one chance to make things right?

I quickly grab a late lunch, my thoughts circling around Birdie. After I finish, I call Loosey, but it's Daisy who picks up. Her voice is sharp, scolding me for disappearing from the group for so long. After her strong outburst—'Do you even care about us? We were scared to death'—she finally tells me where they are and demands I come immediately.

When I arrive, I see the group scattered across the bustling town square. People are browsing through shops, trying on clothes, and chatting by the small street stalls. Loosey stands out in a traditional kurta that somehow fits him perfectly. He waves when he spots me. Huntress is nearby, standing still, her eyes fixed on me.

'You okay?' Daisy asks, rushing towards me. She drops the dress she was holding and grabs my hand.

'Yes,' I reply, forcing a smile. Huntress doesn't stop watching me. I meet her gaze and mouth, 'I'm okay.' She nods slowly but doesn't look away until Daisy pulls me aside.

The rest of the day is a blur, with Daisy pulling Huntress and I from shop to shop. She holds up outfits, spinning around and asking which ones would suit her best. Loosey tells me the Nerds left after lunch; where they've gone, no one knows. Frost sticks close to the group, sulking with a dissatisfied frown. Officer hangs around Loosey, constantly looking for excuses to join conversations, but Loosey doesn't give him a chance.

As the sky darkens, Daisy leads us towards our next stop. Loosey, Huntress and I carry the bags full of Daisy's purchases. The hike to the new spot is long, winding and quiet, but the view at the top makes it worth it—a flat expanse of land overlooking the entire city below. The lights of the city twinkle like scattered stars.

We're not alone. A few trailers are parked at the edge of the ground, and several tents are already raised. In the middle, a large bonfire flickers, surrounded by mats and wooden logs for seating. A trailer strung with fairy lights adds a warm glow to the scene.

We pitch our tents and change. Despite the lively atmosphere, my thoughts keep returning to Birdie's letter. I can't stop wondering how she managed to rebuild herself after everything she went through. A part of me aches to be there for her, to help her face the fears she might hold.

To walk beside her, holding her hand, if she ever decides to step back into that bakery.

I check my phone. A notification pops up: Birdie liked my message. That's it. No reply, no hint of where she's heading, no suggestion of when—or if—we'll meet. I sigh and put the phone away.

Loosey and I grab hot coffee and rolls from a nearby stall and join the growing crowd around the fire. The warmth feels good against the mountain's chilly air.

'Do you think anyone here is like me?' Loosey asks, his voice barely audible over the crackling fire.

'What do you mean?'

'You know ... like me. Gay.'

I glance around. 'No idea, buddy.'

'What about that guy?' Loosey gestures subtly towards a man leaning against the white camping trailer, wearing a leather jacket.

'I have no clue.'

'Fifty bucks says he's into boys,' Loosey says, fumbling a crumpled note out of his pocket.

'I'm not playing,' I reply, shaking my head.

'Why not?'

'Because I don't know how to tell. I've never stared at someone and wondered if they're gay. That's just not my thing.'

'Nope, pack leader, it isn't your thing. Your thing is staring at girls, right? Like Huntress.' He grins mischievously.

How? Like, how does everyone know?

'Me? I stare at boys. Same concept, different preference. As some legend once said, love is love.' He clinks his coffee cup against mine. 'Cheers.'

'Love is love,' I repeat, smiling. Through the flickering firelight, I see the guy Loosey pointed out give us a long glance. 'Dude, he just checked you out.'

'Would you act normal, please?' Loosey's voice is a hiss, his shoulders tensing. 'You're supposed to be my wingman, not ruin this.'

'Alright, alright.' I laugh softly, taking another sip of coffee. 'He might be like you.'

'Oh, he definitely is,' Loosey says with a knowing smirk.

'How can you be so sure?'

'You see, my dear pack leader, we have an inbuilt ability to find each other. It's natural. Like a phone connecting to Wi-Fi—when we're in range, we know.'

I shake my head, laughing. 'Cool analogy.'

Another group arrives, setting up their tents behind the trailer. Our gathering grows livelier, its energy buzzing in the cool night air.

'Where is everyone, by the way?' I ask.

'Huntress found some of her friends from the last trek. She's with them,' Loosey replies, shrugging.

I don't bother asking more about the Nerds. I had found them just some time back, and they'd asked me if I was interested in trying some weed. Apparently, someone here had the 'best stuff,' and they were going to try it as a group. I thanked them for the invite and politely refused. Honestly, I was surprised She-Nerd even bothered to ask. It's not like her to try and be friends with anyone.

Loosepants rolls his eyes and gestures subtly to my left. Following his direction, I spot Officer standing with a girl, her figure outlined by the warm orange light of the fire. She's twirling her hair around her finger, laughing at almost every sentence Officer says. Damn. I'd completely ignored him earlier, assuming he'd be talking to a guy, not a girl.

I'm dumb.

But after a moment of watching, I realise something. Officer isn't just casually chatting with a girl—he's staring at us. At Loosepants, to be exact. Is this his attempt at making Loosepants jealous? If so, how does that even work when he's talking to a girl?

I guess Officer is even dumber than me.

'As if that would make me jealous,' Loosey mutters, echoing my thoughts. He tries to chuckle but the tightness in his jaw betrays him.

A man in a brown jacket and leather boots, the same guy from earlier, approaches us. 'You want a drink?' he asks.

'I don't drink,' I reply, looking up.

'I wasn't asking you,' he says, smiling directly at Loosey.

'Oh, uh, yeah. Sure. I mean, I don't drink either. But first time for everything,' Loosey stammers, his cheeks going red even in the dim light.

The man hands him a bottle, their fingers brushing. Loosey clutches the beer like it's a treasure, his face a mix of excitement and nerves.

'Mind if I sit?' the man asks, looking at me.

Before I can answer, Loosey stomps on my foot—a clear signal. *Ouch! That hurt* would have been my response, but I smile and get up, knowing it was time to leave and be a wingman. 'Nope, not at all,' I say quickly, walking away and leaving them alone.

I lean against the trailer, sipping the last of my coffee, Birdie's letter still on my mind.

'A gentleman is supposed to bring his girl a drink.'

I turn, and time slows.

Huntress stands there, wearing a short light-blue kurti embroidered with intricate floral patterns. A small black bindi sits perfectly on her forehead. I've seen her before—up close, from afar—and she's always been stunning. But this? This is something else entirely. The traditional clothes, the simplicity of it all, make her look like a dream. Prettier than anything I could ever imagine.

'Stop staring. I'm already too nervous,' she says, tucking a stray strand of hair behind her ear. My heart stumbles. She's wearing the earrings I bought her yesterday, and the sight of them, paired with her shy smile, is almost too much to handle.

'You are ...' I trail off, struggling to find words, completely lost. 'You are looking too beautiful.'

'Thank you,' she says softly, looking down with a smile that makes my world pause for a moment.

It's different now—knowing she's not with Officer. If things were even slightly different, I would've dropped to one knee right there, flowers in hand, asking her to be my girlfriend, maybe even my wife someday. But they aren't different. And someone else is occupying a part of my thoughts, someone I can't ignore.

I look away, and finally let out the breath I didn't realise I was holding—which has been happening to me too much when she's around. 'You should wear traditionals more often,' I finally manage to say.

'I will, from now on,' she replies.

'Let me get you something to drink.' I rush off towards the trailer, needing the distance to steady myself, to stop my heart from doing somersaults every time I look at her.

But even as I order, I can't resist sneaking a glance. She catches me, and that soft laugh of hers nearly undoes me. *As if the clothes weren't enough, now there's that smile.*

'Looks like Loosey has found a new friend,' she says when I return with a cup of hot chocolate.

'Yeah, he has. And it seems to be going well.' I glance at Loosey, who's clearly enjoying the guy's attention, laughing at every other thing he says.

'What are you going to do after this?' she asks after some time, her tone quiet.

It's a question I've asked myself a countless number of times. My suspension is over, and I'll be back in college soon, trying to fit in again. But who's left for me to talk to? From the calls and messages, I know everyone's heard about what happened.

And even though the version they know is a lie, for them, it's real.

'Just live my life. Ignore everyone else. Maybe use the time I save to write.'

'Do you have a story in mind?' she asks, her eyes lighting up with curiosity.

'I think I do,' I reply, smiling. 'What about you?'

'Go on with my life. I've got this wishlist, and there's one thing right at the top that I really want to do.'

'What is it?' I ask eagerly.

'Well ...' she starts, but we're interrupted by Officer, who is storming past us, headed straight for Loosepants.

'What are you doing?' he snaps, his face flushed with anger. Huntress and I step closer. I already know what this is about.

'I'm having a drink with my special friend here,' Loosepants says, hugging the guy. The man hesitates, then smiles and pulls Loosey closer.

'Get your hands off of him,' Officer demands, looming over the guy, his voice dripping with menace.

'Who the hell are you to tell him what to do?' the man challenges, standing his ground.

'I'm his ...' Officer falters, his words catching in his throat.

'Why did you stop, Officer?' Loosepants is on his feet now, trembling but defiant.

'Just get out of here,' Officer growls, shoving the guy lightly.

'Stop it!' Loosepants yells, his voice breaking.

But Officer doesn't stop. 'I told you to get out,' Officer says to the other guy, his glare sharp enough to cut.

'Just stop!' Loosepants screams, his body shaking. 'Tonight, I want to be with someone who appreciates me and isn't scared to be with me. And unless you're that person, fuck off and let me have my drink.'

The camp falls silent. The group of men drinking nearby stop mid-sip. The couples whispering sweet nothings to each other pause and turn their heads. All eyes are on Loosepants.

'Just go,' Loosepants shouts before collapsing onto the wooden log, burying his head in his hands, his body trembling. Huntress rushes to him, wrapping her arms around his shoulders.

Officer's face drains of colour. He takes a hesitant step forward but stops, realising the weight of the stares pressing into him. Without a word, he lowers his head and walks away.

'Go away.' Officer takes a big gulp of beer and hurls the bottle into the bushes. It hits a rock with a hollow *clink*, doesn't break, and rolls out of sight. 'Nothing for you here unless you're here for the drinks.'

'Can I just sit here with you?' I ask, though I don't know why. It's not like I like the guy. Hell, I even hated him.

'Fuck off, Wolf,' he snaps, but I don't move. I don't even know why I stay. Maybe for Loosepants.

'Oh, fuck you, man!' he yells, his voice cracking. 'Just ... just leave me alone.' The last words come out as a sob. Is he crying?

He grabs another beer, popping the cap off in one smooth motion, and starts drinking. I sit down beside him anyway, my back leaning against the trailer. There's already an open bottle sitting on the ground between us.

'How many of these have you had?' I ask, my voice soft.

'You here to interrogate me, Wolf?' He wipes his eyes roughly, not looking at me.

'No.' The silence stretches between us.

Away from the fire, the cold sinks its teeth into me, cutting through my shirt. I shiver, trying not to show it.

'You knew, didn't you?' he says suddenly, pushing the half-empty beer bottle in my direction.

'Knew what?'

'That I'm ...' He exhales sharply. 'Everyone else was shocked or acting surprised. But you, Wolf, you weren't even slightly surprised.'

I take a deep breath, staring at the city lights below—scattered like spilled stars across the earth. 'I saw you,' I admit, my voice even. 'In the woods. Kissing him.'

'You little snooping bastard,' his hand lashes out, snatching the beer back. 'You don't deserve to share a drink with me.'

I don't argue. I just sit there.

'Have you thought about being even slightly kind?' I ask after a while.

'Fuck off.'

That's it. I've had enough.

'Have you thought that maybe—just maybe—you constantly behaving like an asshole, and the way you treat Loosepants like he's nothing, even though you obviously care about him, is what pushed him into talking to that guy tonight?' The words spill out in a rush, my voice louder than I intended.

He smirks, but it's bitter. 'You don't know anything about me.'

'I'm here,' I say, keeping my voice steady. 'Not for you, but for Loosepants. That stupid guy who still likes you, even after all the shit you've put him through. So, help me understand, Officer. For him. Because he deserves better than your fucking bullshit.'

He sighs heavily, his hands shaking as he clutches the bottle. He opens his mouth to speak, closes it again, then finally lets out a ragged breath.

'You have dreams, right, Wolf? Like getting married, travelling, maybe finding a hot girlfriend? Well, you know what mine is?' He takes a small sip of beer, his voice barely above a whisper. 'To be accepted.'

I stare at him, unsure what to say.

'I'm sure Huntress, Daisy, me—everyone will—'

'You don't get it, Wolf.' His hand clenches around the bottle, his voice trembling. 'Let me tell you about my family. My dad—he was in the army. Used to train cadets. His job was to be tough, authoritative. And he never stopped being that guy. Not even at home. Not even with me.'

He pauses, breathing unevenly. 'He made rules—rules that are fucking taped to my bedroom wall. Wake up at five. Run three laps. Never be late for meals. Be in bed by ten. Break a rule, you get fifty squats or four more laps.' He imitates his father's stern, commanding voice, his expression tightening. 'My mom? She thinks discipline is the foundation of success. She follows his every rule without a second thought.'

He lets out a hollow laugh. 'There's a rule for everything in my house—how to talk, how to sit, how to *be*. But there's no rule for ... what I am.'

He stops, his voice faltering for the first time. 'I tried to hide it, you know? Tried to pretend. But after a while, it just got too heavy. I couldn't keep doing it.'

His voice cracks, but he keeps going. 'I couldn't take it anymore, Wolf. I had to tell someone. I thought maybe ... maybe my mom would understand.'

He gives a bitter laugh. 'But she didn't. She took me to some fucking psychiatrist. Told him to fix me. Like I was broken.'

He buries his face in his hands, his shoulders shaking. 'I told them, I'm not broken. I told them over and over. But they wouldn't listen. They just ... wouldn't listen.'

I put a hand on his shoulder, my chest heavy with anger and sadness. 'I'm so sorry,' I whisper. And I mean it. I don't know how anyone could do that—try to make someone feel like they're broken when all they're doing is being themself.

He wipes his face roughly, his voice raw. 'I decided I was going to tell my dad. Screw the consequences. But two days before I could, he had a heart attack. The doctor told us to keep him stress-free. And my mom? She uses that against me every chance she gets.'

'How?'

'She wants me married. To a girl. In two years. She wants grandkids. She wants me to play this whole straight charade so my dad can die happy.' He throws the bottle onto the ground, where it rolls away. 'She doesn't care if it fucking kills me on the inside.'

The silence between us feels heavy, suffocating. I can't begin to imagine what it's like—to have your own family make you a stranger, to strip away who you are and ask you to wear a mask for the rest of your life.

'I ... I don't know what to say, Officer.' My voice sounds clumsy, quiet. 'I really don't.' I glance at him—his shoulders stiff, eyes fixed on the ground—and it just hurts to see him like that.

'But I do know this,' I say after a pause. 'You don't need them to understand who you are. Or accept it. Yeah, maybe your mom will keep pushing for a marriage, and people will talk, but ... we'll figure something out. Somehow.' I fumble for words, my throat tightening. 'Maybe ... I don't know, maybe you tell them a story—something about heartbreak, how it made you not trust relationships. I don't know yet, but we'll come up with something. Huntress will help. Daisy too. We'll figure it out together.'

'I know it's not perfect advice,' I add softly. 'But you don't have to go through this alone. We're here. You can do this.'

He finally looks up at me, his eyes glassy, unblinking. 'And if I can't?' he whispers, his voice cracking under the weight of his fear.

'Then you need to let him go.'

The words taste bitter in my mouth, but I push through. 'If you can't love him the way he deserves, then you need to walk away. Because staying in his life and treating him like this? That's worse than losing him.'

He's quiet for a long time, his eyes fixed on the ground. Finally, he nods. 'You're right. It's cruel advice ... but it's right.'

'You've got two choices, Officer. Be honest. Or let him move on. But don't keep hurting him. He deserves better.'

—w—

'How did it go?' Huntress asks softly, her voice pulling me out of my thoughts.

'I can't tell,' I reply, shaking my head. 'How did it go with Loosey?' My eyes drift towards him, sitting alone at the edge of the campsite, his face puffy and swollen from crying.

'He was crying for most of it,' she says, her gaze following mine. 'We took a stroll outside, talked a bit and came back. He'll recover, but it'll take time.'

I nod, unsure of what to say. Her next question catches me off guard.

'You knew about them, didn't you? Did Loosey tell you?'

'Yeah,' I admit after a pause. 'He told me, but ... I kind of figured it out before that.'

'How?' She tilts her head, curiosity flickering in her eyes.

Taking a deep breath, I tell her the story—about how I had seen Officer and Loosey together, and how I had deliberately changed the path so she wouldn't notice. As I speak, her expression shifts from curious to relieved.

'I hate the situation they're in,' she says, her voice soft. 'But I'm glad you found out. Especially ... especially about Officer and me not being together.'

She looks at me then, her eyes softening. 'Keeping up that whole act—especially on this trek—has been exhausting. And I'm just relieved.'

Relieved. The word hangs between us.

She hesitates for a moment, then reaches out and takes my hand. Her touch is warm, her fingers curling around mine with a kind of familiarity that both hurts and soothes. 'I'm glad you came on this trek, Wolf,' she says. 'You've helped us more than you know.'

'Us?' I manage to say, my voice barely above a whisper.

'Yep.' Her smile deepens, but she doesn't explain.

'How ... how did I help you?' My mind is racing, trying to piece together her words.

She just smiles again, leaving me with unanswered questions.

Before I can press her further, a voice interrupts us.

'Everyone!' Officer's voice is loud and sharp, cutting through the night. Huntress and I exchange a glance, then look around for him.

'Up here!' Another call draws our eyes upward. Officer is standing on top of the trailer, a bottle of beer dangling from his hand, his figure illuminated by the soft glow of the fairy lights strung across the campsite.

'I have to tell you all something,' Officer says, his voice trembling but determined. 'Hey, Daisy, you mind recording this for us?'

Daisy, who I hadn't even noticed until now, looks up from her camera. Without a word, she starts recording.

'I have an announcement,' Officer continues. 'And I'm scared as hell to make it. But there's something I'm more scared of—losing someone who's completely weird, talks way too much, and does things so strange that no one could ever match the heights of his weirdness. But ...' He pauses, swallowing hard. 'I love him.'

A collective gasp rises. Loosepants clasps his hands over his mouth, his eyes wide, and Daisy's camera dips for a second as her hands shake in surprise.

'I know I've hurt you,' Officer says, his gaze fixed on Loosepants. 'I've bullied you, made fun of you, done everything I could to keep anyone from figuring out what we had. But now I know, thanks to these two people in front of me—my Huntress, who stood by me when no one else would, and this bastard Wolf, who pushed me to realise what I really want. Loosey ...' he says, his voice cracking, 'I fucking love you.'

Before I can react, Officer jumps down from the top of the trailer, misjudging the height and landing awkwardly. He stumbles, hitting the ground hard. I start forward, instinctively reaching to help him up, but Loosepants beats me to it, rushing ahead.

'Are you okay?' Loosepants asks, his voice shaky, his hands already brushing dirt from Officer's shoulders. Tears run down his face, pooling in his wide, disbelieving eyes.

Officer takes Loosey's hands in his own, looking directly into his tear-filled eyes. 'I know I haven't treated you right, Loosey. I know I've been an asshole—hurting you, pushing you away. And I know you have every right to throw me out of your life,' he says, his voice drops, almost breaking. 'But, please. Can you give me another chance? A chance to treat you the way you've always deserved?'

Loosepants breaks down. Tears spill freely as he throws his arms around Officer, holding him tightly, sobbing into his shoulder.

'I love you, Loosey,' Officer whispers.

'I love you, too, Officer,' Loosepants chokes out between sobs.

Cheers erupt around us, applause filling the night air. People pour out of their tents, clapping and shouting, some asking what just happened. The energy is electric, charged with relief and joy. Huntress wipes tears from her eyes, leaning into me, her head resting softly on my shoulder.

It's perfect—almost too perfect. But something stirs in me, I can make this moment even better.

'Excuse me for a minute,' I whisper to Huntress, smiling at her puzzled expression as I slip away to my tent. When I return, I'm holding the guitar my parents gave me, its polished wood gleaming in the firelight.

I sit on the wooden log near the fire, tuning the strings as everyone watches, curiosity lighting up their faces. Huntress sits down by my side, her eyes never leaving me. Loosepants and Officer are still holding each other, their smiles brighter than the flames.

I tighten the screws, pluck a string and a soothing note rings out. Smiling, I strum a gentle rhythm, letting the music flow. The sound wraps around us like a warm blanket, its melody settling into every heart. Loosepants beams at me, his happiness so contagious that even Officer grins.

'Dance with me?' Officer whispers to Loosepants, and they are the first to step into the open, swaying to the rhythm. Others join soon after, forming a small crowd of couples and friends, all moving to the gentle melody.

The fire flickers, the stars seem closer, and I play, letting the guitar guide me. The world around me fades until it's just the music, the people, and the night. I had forgotten how music could transport you to a world free of everything else, and I'm grateful to feel that magic again.

As I play, I can't help but wish Birdie was here, standing among us, watching me play this guitar—the one I'm holding now because of her words, her encouragement, her belief in second chances.

The fire crackles, the night deepens, and I keep playing, pouring everything into the music.

Daisy calls out, asking Huntress and me to look at her. We turn, and she clicks our picture, a soft smile forming on her face as she checks the shot on her camera.

'I wish we could dance too,' Huntress whispers softly in my ear. My heart skips a beat at her words, the thought of holding her making it race. But it sinks just as quickly: someone has to keep the music up.

The leather boots guy, who not long ago was hitting on Loosepants, approaches with a smile. 'Take her for a dance,' he says, nodding towards Huntress. 'I can take over. I am nowhere as good as you, but I know how to play.'

I hand him the guitar with a grateful smile, thanking him silently for the opportunity. Turning to Huntress, I extend my hand. She takes it with a smile so warm, it could melt the night. My other hand hesitates for a moment before resting gently on her waist. Her free hand settles lightly on my shoulder.

The music continues, now played by someone else, but it's just as enchanting. We sway together, moving in step with the rhythm, her presence wrapping around me like a gentle breeze. I look into her eyes, and it feels like the world fades away. They're impossibly beautiful—deep, magical and full of kindness.

She is, without a doubt, the most beautiful girl I've ever seen. Yet, my heart tightens. As much as I cherish this moment, I can't shake the thoughts lingering in my mind. Even now, with her in my arms, it feels like I'm not fully here, like I'm betraying her with the weight of my distractions.

'What are you thinking?' she asks, her voice soft but curious.

'Nothing,' I lie, smiling. I want to tell her the truth, to share the storm inside me, but instead, I lock this image of her in my mind—the way her short blue kurti sways as we move, the intricate embroidery catching the light, the delicate jhumkas dangling from her ears, and the bindi decorating her radiant face.

I push the other thoughts away. Huntress deserves this dance. She deserves to have a partner who's present, who's here completely, who sees her for the kind, beautiful and extraordinary person that she is.

So, I focus. I focus on her hand in mine, on her eyes that hold so much warmth, and on the joy radiating in her smile.

—w—

'I need to tell you something,' Daisy says, rushing over to us just as the dance ends, her face glowing with excitement. Her camera dangles in her hand, and her grin is as wide as her energy is infectious. 'First, the best pictures I clicked today were of you two together.'

She flips through the camera screen and turns it towards us. The first photo shows me playing the guitar, with Huntress sitting beside me, her eyes fixed entirely on me, carrying affection and warmth. The next captures our dance—her hands resting on my shoulders, mine on her waist, the rest of the world blurred into the background, as if the world didn't exist beyond us.

'Honestly, the pics are so good that they should be on the front page of some magazine.'

Huntress laughs softly, her cheeks pink and I am sure mine are too.

'And second,' Daisy continues, her voice quickening with excitement as if she can't wait to spill the news. She leans in slightly, lowering her voice, though it's clear she wants both of us to hear. 'Frost wanted to talk to me.'

'Frost?' I echo, my brow furrowing. 'About what?'

She straightens, crossing her arms with an exaggerated sigh, the kind only Daisy could pull off. 'He said, and I quote, "I'm willing to get into a relationship with you."' Her voice is flat, but her expression betrays her irritation.

My reaction is immediate and unfiltered. 'What the fuck? Who says something like that?'

Huntress raises an eyebrow, shooting me a look that's both amused and full of warning. 'Umm, I mean ...' I stumble, scrambling to recover. 'What did you say?'

Daisy bursts into laughter, shaking her head. 'Don't worry, my response was exactly the same—"What the fuck!"' She rolls her eyes and flips her hair dramatically. 'I told him I deserve nothing but a hundred per cent, and if the guy can't give me that, I don't want him. And I definitely don't want some guy who thinks he's entitled to my love without putting in the effort.'

'Good for you,' Huntress says with approval, her voice firm. I nod silently, but my mind is still replaying what Daisy just said.

'Okay,' Daisy says, her tone shifting to something brighter. 'Now we all have to do something special. This is our last night together, so we need to make it unforgettable.'

'Last night?' The words escape me, louder than I intended, slicing through the night air. I feel the weight of them settle heavily in my chest. This can't be true. Not now. Not yet.

I hadn't thought about this ending—or maybe I didn't want to. The trek, the people, this journey—how could this end? And Birdie ... My heart sinks. I haven't even met her. I haven't talked to her. I haven't seen her smile, heard her laugh, or got a chance to thank her in person.

There's still so much unsaid, so much unfinished.

The idea of this being over feels wrong—like waking up in the middle of a dream you never wanted to end. It's not just Birdie. It's Loosepants and Officer, Daisy and Huntress, even Frost and the Nerds. This group of people who've somehow woven themselves into my story, giving me memories I will never forget.

And Huntress ... my chest tightens as I glance at her.

I'm not ready to say goodbye to this—to her. To any of them. For the first time in a long time, I've felt something I can't quite name—connection, maybe. Belonging. And the thought of it all slipping away, of waking up tomorrow and it being over, feels unbearable. It feels wrong.

'I told you, right? In the email? I mean, the whole schedule was there,' Daisy says, shrugging slightly, as if this is just a casual reminder.

'Oh, yes ... yes ... I remember.' The words feel hollow as they leave my mouth, my mind screaming at the idea of this being over. How had nobody mentioned it while we were on the trip?

How had Birdie known this and still not met me?

'So, as I was saying,' Daisy continues, snapping me out of my spiral. 'Hello? Are you guys even with me?' She looks pointedly at both of us, her hands on her hips. Huntress scans my face carefully, as if trying to read my thoughts.

'I'm so sorry. Please go ahead,' I say quickly, forcing a smile and shaking off my thoughts. Huntress gives me one last searching look before turning back to Daisy.

'So,' Daisy begins again, her enthusiasm bouncing back, 'I brought these paper lanterns—the kind that float up into the sky when you light the lamp inside. I was planning to take them back home for my friends and family, but honestly, what better way to celebrate our last night together than to use them here? I'm gathering everyone. Let's meet at the top of the hill in ten minutes.'

She doesn't wait for an answer because, with Daisy, there's never really an option to say no. She rushes off to gather the others. Huntress and I are left standing there in the fading light, her presence grounding me even as my mind races.

The silence between us feels heavy. I glance at Huntress, her expression soft but curious, as if she's waiting for me to say something.

'You okay?' she asks, her voice gentle.

I nod, but I know my face betrays me. 'Yeah.'

She watches me for a moment, her gaze steady, and then she says softly, 'Last night.' Just those two words, but they carry a weight I can't ignore. 'You gonna miss anything?'

I glance up at the sky, the stars scattered across it like tiny shards of light. A cool breeze wraps around us, biting into my thoughts as I try to answer.

Loosepants's never-ending talks come to mind first—his endless energy and chatter. Officer too, who started as someone I hated but turned out to be just another person looking for acceptance, much like me. Even the Nerds, with their predictability, will leave a void when they're gone.

Frost? I don't think I'll miss him much. But Daisy? She's a bright, cheerful soul with a heart full of life, who is figuring out her own path.

And then there's Huntress. My chest tightens as I look at her, her eyes still on me, waiting for an answer. A cold breeze sends a strand of hair across her face. Without thinking, I reach out and tuck it behind her ear. My fingers linger for just a moment too long, my heart stumbling as I take in her eyes—wild, brave, kind and deep.

She's the kind of person who makes you believe there's more to life, just by existing.

If only things were different. If only I could ask her to stay here with me, just the two of us, exploring the life in these hills forever. But I can't.

And then there's Birdie. My heart sinks deeper. Am I never going to see her? Fear claws at the edges of my mind. I remember the first time I texted her, scrolling aimlessly through Instagram hashtags and stumbling onto her post. What if I hadn't messaged her? What would I be now? A guy at his lowest, someone who might not have made it, someone who would have probably ended his life.

She saved me, pulled me out of the darkest place. I owe her everything—my life, my hope, my ability to be standing here right now.

'What are you going to miss?' Huntress asks again, her voice breaking through the noise in my head.

I take a deep breath, trying to steady the emotions threatening to overwhelm me. 'Everything,' I say finally.

My voice is heavy, and I can feel the burn of tears forming in my eyes. 'I'm going to miss everything.'

17

Everyone has arrived. Loosey and Officer are helping Daisy with the lanterns, and even the Nerds—who I thought would be too high from the weed—are present. I can't help but wonder what changed their minds. Huntress, still as warm as ever, stands beside me, her gaze soft as she watches everyone.

I feel the urge to tell her—about how I got here, how this journey turned into more than just following a trail. How it became something deeper, something about healing, finding myself and finding friends.

And maybe I should tell her about Birdie—the person who suggested I follow this trail. But should I?

There's also this part of me that wants to tell her how I feel about her. How my feelings for her have grown, slipping past all my defences and growing into something I just can't ignore anymore. But how can I confess that when there's someone else—when my heart is still constantly thinking about Birdie?

Maybe I don't need to say anything. Maybe it's better this way, to keep it to myself. After all, it's not like she's waiting for me to confess. She might not even feel the same, and if that's the case, why risk it? It's easier to let the moment be, to just stay friends and not ruin it.

'You look tense,' she says, pulling me out of my thoughts.

'Hmm, a bit,' I admit.

'Is it about going back?' she asks, meeting my eyes directly.

'Maybe,' I say.

'You don't have to worry, okay?' she says, her voice firm yet comforting. 'Don't let what they say about you take up space in your mind. You've come so far, Wolf. Don't give them that power. And you've got me. We'll figure it out, have fun, and maybe even drag Daisy, Loosey and Officer into planning our next trip—something near our college.'

'That would be amazing,' I reply, and for a moment, the idea of having her and the others by my side gives me a sense of peace.

'So, is everyone ready?' Daisy calls out, her voice brimming with excitement as she hands each of us a lantern and a small candle. The Nerds help distribute them while Daisy suddenly remembers there's nothing to light the candles.

'We have that covered,' She-Nerd quips, lighting the candles with a lighter.

We move further away from others. Huntress turns to me as we light the small lamp inside the lantern. 'Make a wish,' she says with a small smile. 'They say wishes made while lighting a lantern come true.'

I pause, holding the lantern carefully, its folded lines slowly unfolding as the flame begins to grow. There's so much I want. I don't ever want to lose Huntress—a crush who's become a friend and so much more. And then there's Birdie, the one who saved my life. I need to meet her. I need to thank her in person.

Two wishes.

'You ready, Wolf?' Huntress asks gently, her voice drawing me back. Her eyes search mine for some sign, some silent answer.

I nod. 'Yeah, I'm ready.'

I close my eyes, letting my wishes take shape.

I want to meet Birdie—to see her, thank her, and stand by her the way she stood by me in my darkest moments. She carries her own scars, her own shadows from the past, and I want to be someone she can lean on.

And Huntress ... I owe her more than just friendship. I want to repay her kindness and support her the way she has supported me, until my last breath. Her presence has meant everything, and I want to be there for her, just as she was for me.

Two wishes. Each one carrying a piece of my heart.

When I open my eyes, the lantern's flame burns brighter, its heat spreading through the delicate walls, making them glow softly in the night. The folded edges have fully expanded now, and the warmth radiates against my fingertips. Huntress's gaze locks with mine.

Together, we lift the lantern, our movements slow, deliberate, as if neither of us wants to let go too soon. The paper feels lighter in my hands, the flame urging it skyward. Finally, we release it.

The lantern begins to rise, its flame burning brighter, casting a warm orange glow that reflects in Huntress's eyes. The folded paper walls of the lantern expand, catching the air, and for a moment, it dips. My breath hitches as I instinctively reach to steady it, but then it catches the breeze and soars upward, drifting higher and higher until it's just another point of light among the stars.

I lower my gaze to find Huntress watching me, her expression soft but searching. She steps closer, her fingers curling around mine. Her touch is warm, grounding, even in the chill of the night. My heart stumbles as I meet her eyes, and the world around us begins to blur, the distant chatter and laughter fading into nothingness. It's just us—her and me, here, now.

Time seems to slow, each second stretching as she leans in, her breath brushing my skin, her face inches from mine. My pulse races, the sound of it roaring in my ears. Her lips part slightly, so close that I can feel her breath mingling with mine.

Her eyes close, and I find myself leaning in. The space between us disappears, every nerve in my body alive, every moment like an eternity.

And then, Daisy's voice echoes in my mind. *'I deserve someone who gives me one hundred per cent.'*

I pull back.

'I'm sorry.' The words tumble out, my voice barely a whisper.

Her eyes snap open, wide with shock and hurt. Her cheeks are flushed, and she takes a step back. 'I'm ... I'm so sorry. I thought you wanted this too,' she stammers, her voice trembling, each word carrying the weight of her confusion and pain.

'I do,' I say quickly. 'I really do. Huntress, you have no idea how much I like you—how much I care about you. A part of me wants this more than anything else in the world.'

'Then why didn't you?' she asks, her voice trembling, her eyes searching mine for answers.

I take a shaky breath, the words catching in my throat. 'Because Anjali ... I can't give you my hundred per cent right now.' My voice cracks as I continue. 'There's someone else too ... someone who I want—' The sentence falters, unfinished, as if saying it aloud makes the pain sharper.

Her face drains of colour, her eyes wide with disbelief and hurt. For a moment, she just stares at me, the silence between us filled with everything I can't say. Then, without a word, she turns and walks away.

Each step she takes feels like a knife twisting in my chest. The weight of the guilt pressing down on me, suffocating me. My heart feels like it's being torn apart. Each beat grows heavier, louder, echoing in my ears like a cruel reminder of what I've just lost.

How can one heart fall in love with two?

18

I can't imagine how hurt Huntress must be. God, she deserves so much better. She deserves someone who wants her completely—for her beautiful smile, her kind heart, her bright and radiant spirit, and the way her eyes sparkle when she's about to get mischievous.

God, what have I done? Any guy would call me stupid right now—for not kissing a girl so beautiful, just because my mind is fixated on someone I haven't even met or seen. They would have just kissed Huntress and figured out everything else later. They would have chosen her—someone they've met, seen and connected with—rather than someone they've never seen before, whose warmth they've only experienced through hidden letters.

But it wouldn't have been fair—not to her, not when she deserves the best. *And not when I've just realised my heart wants someone else ... a bit more.*

I walk aimlessly, the cold wind biting at my face, sharp and unforgiving. Each step feels heavier than the last, as if the weight of my thoughts is pulling me down. My legs ache, but I don't stop, I keep going, as if I can outwalk the heaviness inside me.

Eventually, I find a bench overlooking the city. The lights below shimmer faintly, scattered like forgotten stars. I collapse onto it, my shoulders slumping under the weight of everything I'm feeling. The tears have finally stopped running down my face. I hate that they have stopped; they were a constant reminder of the pain I feel for hurting someone who has given me nothing but warmth.

I stare out at the city. *Last night.* Birdie knew this. She knew, and still, she didn't text me. She didn't ask to meet me. I clench my fists, my phone cold in my hand. Why didn't she reach out? Why didn't she want to see me?

I type out the words I've been holding back, my fingers trembling.

'It's my last night here, which I know you already know. And I really just want to meet you. There is something I need to tell you, and it has to be in person. Can we meet? Please?'

I hit send, my heart pounding as I stare at the screen. The seconds stretch into minutes, and still, nothing. She hasn't seen it. I refresh the app, over and over, willing her to respond. But the screen stays empty, silent.

I don't know how long I sit there, the phone heavy in my hand. My eyes sting—not just from the cold, but from exhaustion, from the endless replay of what-ifs in my head while staring at the screen.

What if she is ignoring me?

What if she never intended to meet me?

What if she's already gone?

—~—

'Three bun maska, three chai and a paratha—to be brought later,' the waiter repeats Officer's order. 'Anything else?'

'No,' Loosepants replies, his hand still holding Officer's since the moment we arrived. His smile is soft, content. The cold breeze from the trees outside drifts through the café's wooden frames, tousling my hair and sending a chill straight through me.

I had woken up early today, though not early enough. I awoke to a text from Birdie—a pin, a location. The moment I saw it, I ran, slipping on the uneven path and falling hard, twice. The scrape on my elbow stings with every movement, a sharp and constant reminder of how desperate I was to know what was there. Wishing secretly, all the while, that she would be there. Waiting to meet me.

But there had been no trace of her. Just a lonely letterbox, weathered and still, the final one, carrying her letter.

'I'll be back in ten,' I mumble, pushing open the café's door and stepping into the crisp morning air, her letter tucked safely in my pocket. The café's glass walls and wooden beams fade behind me as I wander to a spot on a rock overlooking the valley. The view stretches wide—a patchwork of greens and blues kissed by the soft golden light of the sun.

My hands tremble as I pull out the letter again, the paper catching in the breeze. Slowly, I unfold it, the weight of her words pressing into my chest.

> Hey Wolf,
>
> Time moves so fast, doesn't it? I still remember the first time you texted me, asking if I thought you could follow my trail. I didn't think you'd actually do it. But you did. And you didn't just walk the trail; you made it your own. It's been such a beautiful journey. But like all journeys, this one must come to an end.

I saw your messages from last night, the ones where you said you wanted to meet me, to tell me something in person. And a part of me—no, most of me—wants to say yes. I want to meet you, hear what you have to say in person.

But ... I can't.

I know this will hurt you, and I hate that. But I think it's better—for both of us—if you never know who I am.

Maybe it's best for me to remain just your Birdie from the letters.

The truth is, I'm scared. What if I meet you, and I'm not who you imagined? Real people, unlike the ones in letters, have flaws, and I'd hate to disappoint you.

So, I have a request: stop chasing me. Stop trying to find out who I am. Hold onto the magic you've found on this trail. Keep it in your heart, Arjun. And please, take care of that beautiful heart of yours. Let its kindness flow, always.

I hope I've helped you in some small way. And I hope you live a life full of adventures, even if there are no letters or Birdie to guide you.

With love,

Your Birdie

I keep looking at the letter in silence as a tear rolls down my cheek and falls onto it, smudging the words '*With love*.' Panic grips me, and I try to dab it away with my shirt, but it's too late. The words have already been smudged, turning into a blur of watery ink. The first time I read it, the tears wouldn't stop. I don't want that to happen again—not here, not now, when Loosey and Officer are having a good time.

I stare at the letter again, my eyes locked on those smudged words. My hands start to shake, and it feels like a heavy weight is pressing down on my chest, making it harder and harder to breathe. The idea of never meeting Birdie is tearing me apart.

'Damn you,' I whisper to the letter, to Birdie, to the entire universe.

'Wolf!' Loosey's voice snaps me out of it.

'Coming,' I call back, swallowing the lump in my throat. I can't ruin their day. They deserve to be happy. So, I wipe my face, straighten up and force a bright smile. It's not easy, but I've got good at hiding the pain.

When I get back inside, the food has arrived. Loosey and Officer are talking about their plans for the future. I learn they live in neighbouring cities but only met during hikes because of their fear of someone finding out about them.

As we eat, Loosey starts sharing the story of how they first met—and how he earned the nickname 'Loosepants'. He recounts how, on one of his first hikes, he'd worn a pair of pants that kept slipping down no matter how many times he pulled them up. 'It was Officer who first called me Loosepants,' Loosey says, his lips curving into a small, nostalgic smile. 'He thought it was funny, and I guess everyone else did too.'

The nickname spread like wildfire, and soon enough, everyone was teasing him relentlessly. 'I laughed at first, trying to brush it off, but then it got too much,' he admits. 'I ended up running off, crying my eyes out. I was ready to never come back,' Loosey says, his voice soft with the memory.

'But then this idiot here,' Loosey gestures at Officer with a small, affectionate smile, 'he chased me down.'

'Do you remember what you told me?' Loosey asks, turning to Officer.

Officer shifts uncomfortably in his seat. 'I don't know,' he mutters.

'Yes, you do,' Loosey presses, his smile widening. 'You told me to get stronger. You said life isn't fair, and people will always find something to tease you about. But then you said that I shouldn't let it break me.' Loosey's voice thickens with emotion as he glances at Officer. 'And then, you scolded me for being so soft, told me to toughen up. God, I hated you in that moment—for giving me the nickname, for scolding me—but at the same time, I started finding you weirdly attractive.'

Loosey's cheeks flush slightly at the admission, and Officer looks away, trying to hide the faint smile tugging at his lips.

The mood feels lighter, but I can't shake the heaviness in my chest. I take a sip of my tea, staring into the cup as Loosey and Officer continue their quiet conversation. The words slip out before I can stop them.

'Did she say anything about me?'

Loosey's expression shifts, his smile fading as he looks at me. 'I'm so sorry, Wolf, but she didn't.' He frees his hand from Officer's to rest it over mine, his touch comforting but unable to ease the ache in my chest. 'I tried to wake you up, but she didn't want me to.'

When I had woken up earlier, I found everyone sitting outside, sharing small talk and laughter. But as soon as I joined them, the conversation had died. Huntress wasn't there. I thought maybe she'd gone for a walk or needed some time alone.

It wasn't until later, after reading Birdie's letter and washing the tears off my face, that I asked Loosey about her.

'She left long before you woke up, Wolf,' he'd said in a sad voice.

Officer looks at me, his usual confident attitude replaced by quiet sympathy.

Huntress left without saying goodbye. My heart sinks deeper, the pain twisting sharply.

Huntress and Birdie ...

I've lost them both.

19

I put down my pen and stare at the journal, hoping the ink will somehow shift on its own, writing the next chapter for me. But there's nothing to write. Nothing left to continue.

I flip to the first page of the journal and reread the words Birdie had written there:

'For the time when you find a story you want to share with this world.'

'I've found the story,' I whisper, the words soft, as if she could hear me. But my heart tightens. There is no end to this story. There's no final chapter, no perfect ending where everything comes full circle.

When I returned from the trail, unsure of what to do, I found my escape in writing—starting from the beginning. *The Trail of a Songbird.* I poured everything into these pages—the texts, the letters, the adventures, the friendships I made, and the pain that followed when it all unravelled.

Maybe I started writing because the mind is an asshole. It twists memories and makes you doubt if it was all just a dream. It kept whispering that someone like Birdie can only exist in my imagination, not in reality. And that's why I needed this journal—to remind me of the truth. To remind me that it was all real, that she ... was real.

I slip the pen into the front pocket of my bag and carefully place the journal inside. I've just finished recounting last week's college annual event, when, for the first time in years, I stepped onto a stage with my guitar. I was terrified, my hands shaking, my stomach in knots.

Moments before I had stepped onto the stage, my phone had buzzed with a message from my parents.

'You'll do great. We believe in you.'

Knowing they were there, sitting in the audience, gave me the courage to keep moving.

As I began to play, the melody poured out of me like a confession, raw and vulnerable. Each note carried pieces of my heart, fragments of my story. With every strum, I secretly hoped Huntress was somewhere in the crowd, listening, even though I hadn't seen her.

When I finished, my parents were the first to stand, clapping enthusiastically in the front row. In that moment, nothing else mattered—just the joy radiating from their faces.

Now, as I sit in this empty classroom that has always been my escape, I pull out my phone and open Birdie's chat.

I've sent her countless messages. Even after the trip. Even after I knew she wasn't reading them. Little updates about my day, my life, how things were going. Sometimes just asking her if we could meet.

All still unseen.

I keep scrolling until I find the last one that she read: *There is something I need to tell you, and it has to be in person. Can we meet? Please?*

I stand and brush the dust from my pants. The sunlight streaming through the window casts a soft glow in the empty room, but it does little to ease the weight in my chest.

Outside, a bird sings, its melody drifting through the air. I try to mimic its call, hoping for a reply, but, like always, none comes.

I am not at peace. I will never be.

As I walk through the corridor, tightening the strap of my bag, I feel the weight of spiteful stares. I've grown better at pretending that they don't bother me, but that doesn't mean I don't see them. Some classmates act like nothing ever happened—when they need something, of course. And I play along, pretending not to spot their act.

A notice catches my eye: *Classes of BE B have been shifted to the second floor, classroom 22. —Class Coordinator.* Below it is another announcement, engraved in red: *Practical exams to begin next week.* Just one more week to endure.

Climbing the stairs, I enter the new classroom. The front benches are empty, as expected, while most of the students have crowded the back. I used to sit there once. My gaze lands on Anurag, who's perched on the last bench next to Reecha. He shoots me a glare, but I don't feel bad for myself. I feel bad for him, for being blind to who she really is.

The second bench, dusty and untouched, seems to be waiting for me. I slide my bag across it, leaving faint trails of wiped dust. Sitting down, I prepare for another lecture. We rise as the professor arrives—a stout man whose neck seems to disappear into his large chin. He signals at us to sit before launching into a monotonous reading from the projector.

I turn to look outside, watching a college clerk carry a notice to another classroom, when something hits me on the head. The impact isn't hard, and my head doesn't hurt, but I turn around angrily. Anurag has his middle finger raised, mouthing, 'Fuck you,' while Reecha and his group burst into laughter.

This is it. For the entire semester, I've tried to explain to him what actually happened, but he never listened. Instead, he turned into a bully, spreading lies about me and making my life hell.

I pick up the crumpled ball of paper that hit me and stand.

Slowly, deliberately, I walk towards Anurag, fully aware of all the eyes on me, including the professor's.

'I guess this belongs to you.' I hold out the ball.

'Fuck you, Arjun,' he spits, turning his head away dismissively.

'Get back to your place!' the professor shouts, his usually monotone voice now raised.

'Yeah, get the fuck out of here, snake,' Anurag sneers, not even glancing at me.

'You talking about your girlfriend?' I say evenly, my voice cutting through the tension. His head snaps towards me, fury blazing in his eyes. He rises abruptly, and I know he's ready to hit me. This time, I'm ready too. I won't back down.

'Enough!' the professor bellows, his face reddening. 'What the hell is going on back there?'

'There's a snake in the classroom, Professor,' Anurag says loudly, his tone dripping with sarcasm. 'He's trying to bite me. A second time.'

'There is a snake, Professor,' I reply, my voice steady, 'but it's the one feeding him lies. And he has been happily swallowing them.'

'Don't you dare call my girlfriend a liar or a snake, you bastard. The cellphone was in your hand. I saw you,' Anurag snarls, stepping forward, his face twisted with anger.

The room feels heavy, the weight of every stare pressing down on me. But I've had enough. I take a deep breath, steady myself before I speak, and ensure my voice is loud enough for everyone to hear.

'It was in my hands because your girlfriend gave it to me after I refused to sleep with her, and after she was done sending those pictures already.'

Gasps ripple through the classroom. Heads whip towards Reecha. She freezes, her face draining of colour. Her mouth opens as if to respond, but no words come out.

'What the hell did you just say?' Anurag barks, stepping closer, fists clenched tight.

'You heard me.' I meet his glare, my voice unwavering. 'Your girlfriend tried to frame me because I turned her down. I never—'

Anurag's fist swings towards me, but I duck in time.

I've had enough. I won't let him hit me this time. My fist connects with his jaw, sending him stumbling back.

'To the principal's office, both of you!' the professor bellows, his voice echoing through the room.

The walk to the principal's office is tense and silent. Anurag rubs his jaw, testing it with small movements. The head clerk outside the principal's office gives me a disapproving glance.

'You again?' he mutters, shaking his head. My hands clench into fists, but I take a deep breath, trying to keep my anger in check.

'The principal isn't here,' the clerk says finally, dismissing us with a warning.

As Anurag begins to walk away, I call after him, 'Anurag.'

He stops but doesn't turn around.

'I've told you the truth,' I say firmly. 'It's your choice—stay blind to it or open your eyes and see things as they are.'

For a moment, he hesitates, his posture stiff. Then, without turning, he says, 'I never knew you'd fall so low.' His voice is cold, and he walks away without another word.

—

On my way back to the flat, I take the long route. There's a river not far from the college, and I decide to stop there. I sit on the stairs by the water's edge, watching the current push through the pillars of the bridge. The sun is setting, painting the sky orange and red, slowly disappearing in the west.

'I've done my part,' I mutter to myself, watching the golden water turn darker as the sun sets. 'The truth is out.' Anurag's reaction doesn't matter anymore. I've told him everything. It's up to him now—whether he believes it or not.

The burden isn't mine to carry anymore.

As I get up to leave, I notice a couple walking along the riverside, their arms linked. They look happy, lost in their own little world. I never used to feel anything seeing couples like this. But now, it stings.

The wooden bird I carved for Birdie and the jhumke I bought for her are still in my bag. I pull the bird out, turning it over in my hand as I walk back.

Back in my room, I drop my bag on the table and collapse into the chair, covering my face with my hands. My eyes land on the mixtape I made for Huntress. It's lying on the table between my books. After the trek, I spent hours putting it together, thinking of the perfect way to apologise. I had carefully picked songs from the '70s, '80s and '90s, ones I thought she'd love.

I even printed a cover for the CD case—the photo Daisy had clicked of us, with me playing the guitar and Huntress sitting beside me.

On my first day back at college, I went looking for her. Her department is in another building, and I kept going there for nearly a week, hoping to catch a glimpse of her. I wanted to say sorry, to tell her everything. But I couldn't find her anywhere.

I wanted to ask people if they had seen her, but I couldn't. I didn't want anyone knowing that we were friends—or had been. I didn't want her to face any judgement or comments just because she *had been* my friend.

Eventually, I found out why she wasn't there. There was a notice on the board congratulating her for getting a big job—early campus placement—with a multinational company. While reading it, I overheard people saying she'd only come back for exams now.

I was genuinely happy for her—happy that she could finally chase her dreams and do whatever she wanted. She didn't have to worry about the orphanage anymore either.

Right after the trek, I had called my dad. It had been years since our last conversation, but he picked up immediately—even though he was in a meeting with an important client. He kept asking how I was, his voice filled with concern.

I told him I was okay, then told him about my journey, and asked if he could do me a favour. Without hesitation, he said, 'Anything.' So, I asked if he could help the orphanage become part of his company's CSR initiative, maybe secure some funding for them. He had agreed instantly, promising, 'I'll take care of everything.'

And when he says he'll take care of things, I know he does. He always does.

On the last day of exams, I finally saw her. She was walking into the hall, her hair catching the sunlight streaming through the windows, her face calm and radiant. For a moment, it felt like time slowed down. She looked in my direction, her eyes meeting mine. Then, she smiled—a soft, quick smile—but it was enough to send a wave of emotions crashing over me. It was the smile I had missed so much, the one that could light up a room and make everything feel okay, even if just for a moment.

I hurried through my paper, finishing it earlier than I should have, scribbling the last answers in a rush. I had to see her again. As soon as I handed in my paper, I ran back to my room, my heart racing with a mix of excitement and nervousness. I grabbed the CD—the one I had spent days preparing, the one I had hoped would be my apology, even if I knew I didn't deserve to be forgiven.

But by the time I returned, she was gone. I had spent hours searching the campus, holding the CD in my hand, but she was gone. Truly gone.

And with that, so was my chance.

Suddenly, the doorbell rings, startling me. I never get visitors. When I open it, I'm greeted by Loosey's beaming face.

'Surprise!' he shouts, wrapping me in a bear hug that nearly knocks the air out of my lungs.

'Loosey! How are you here?' I manage, astonished. Then my eyes land on the person standing just behind him. Officer.

'I wanted to give you a heads-up or at least check if you were home,' Officer says, stepping inside. 'But he wouldn't listen. His exact words were, "Where would he even go?"'

God, that's cruel ... but true.

'Please, come in,' I say, stepping aside.

I live in a tiny one-bedroom apartment, generously offered to me by one of my college teachers. He had insisted he didn't need it since he stayed in the teachers' quarters, and I'd even got a discount on the rent.

As they enter, I suddenly feel thankful that I cleaned up yesterday. Still, I rush to straighten the bed sheet and throw the two shirts lying on the chair into the cupboard. The table opposite the bed has a few books scattered on it, and I start tidying them, quickly.

'Chill, man,' Officer says, flopping onto the bed without a second thought. 'Your room's far cleaner than any of my friends' places. Relax.'

I stop fussing, obediently sitting down on the chair. It's been so long since I last saw them, which was on the trek.

'I missed you, Wolf,' Loosey says, hugging me again. He's standing next to me now, squeezing me so tightly I can barely breathe.

'I missed you, too, Loosey,' I reply, laughing.

'And I love your little Wolf cave,' he says, moving to the window. He peers outside, there's a tree filtering the sunlight, casting cool shade over the room.

'How have you guys been?' I ask.

'Really good!' Loosey replies cheerfully.

'I'm glad,' I say, smiling.

'Loosey was super worried about you,' Officer chimes in.

'Of course, I was,' Loosey says, his tone animated. 'You barely tell us what your life is like. Anytime we ask how your day went, you just say, "The usual." And when I ask what your "usual" is, you say, "College and coming back." That's it! No fun, no excitement.

He throws up his hands in frustration. 'I know you won't admit it, but you've probably been overthinking everything, brooding every single day. That's why we decided to surprise you—to remind you that you have a pack. A pack with two other members now—yes, I added Officer to it. *We'll have a ceremony later.* But you need to meet us, spend time with us and actually do something fun for a change. The pack leader can't just sulk in his room all day, okay?'

I stare at him, amazed as always at how much he can say in one breath.

'When he starts talking like that, I just let him,' Officer says with a shrug. 'It's the best course of action.' Then, turning to me, he adds, 'Oh, and Loosey was scared I might challenge you for the pack leader title. But don't worry, I'm not interested.'

'Oh, thank heavens, I wouldn't want to lose the title,' I say, laughing. 'Loosey, I'm just so glad you're here. But enough about me—tell me about you guys. The last time we talked, you said there was something exciting you'd tell me in person.'

'You should tell him,' Loosey says, nudging Officer.

'Alright, so you remember how I was scared to talk to my dad and all?' Officer begins, his voice quieter than usual. 'One day, he drives me to this nearby hill. We're on this small trek—something we've never done before, so it already felt weird. I was so on edge, my mind going back and forth between my identity, my mom pushing me to get married, and all that. It was awkward as hell.'

He pauses, glancing at Loosey before continuing, 'We stop at this spot with the most amazing view of the valley. And then, out of nowhere, my dad asks me if I want to tell him something. I don't say anything. I'm frozen, scared out of my mind. Then he says, "I know I've been harsh on you, too strict. But I'm not the kind of man to punish someone for telling me who they are."'

Officer's voice cracks slightly as he continues. 'That's when I lost it. I just broke down, crying like I haven't cried in years. I hugged him, and he hugged me back, which ... which is something we've not done in decades. Not once.'

He takes a deep breath, his emotions visibly bubbling to the surface. 'And then I told him. I told him everything. I was terrified, but he just looked at me and said, "It's okay. I've had my suspicions for a while. But it's okay to be who you are." And that's it. Everything in my life changed after that.'

'That's … that's amazing,' I say, genuinely moved. 'I'm so happy for you.'

'Thanks,' he replies, his voice still thick with emotion. 'But don't think this means I'm going soft on you, Wolf.' He tries to grin, though his eyes are still watery. 'Just because you've seen me cry or get all emotional twice now doesn't mean you're off the hook.'

I can't help but laugh. He's masking it with humour, but I can see how much this means to him. For the first time, he looks lighter, and seeing that makes me genuinely happy.

He deserves this.

They both do.

Loosey, unable to hold back any longer, throws his arms around Officer and kisses him on the cheek.

'Uh, guys … do you need the room or something?'

Loosey pulls back with a laugh. 'Nah, we're good.' Officer, his face slightly red, rolls his eyes but doesn't let go of Loosey's hand.

'What's this?' Loosepants asks, his hands on the journal I'd left sitting on the bedside table. My heart skips a beat. Amidst everything, I'd forgotten to hide it.

'It's nothing,' I blurt out, jumping up to snatch it away, but Officer is quicker.

'You shouldn't read that,' I say urgently, reaching for it. But Officer holds me back with one hand, flipping through the pages with the other. 'Seems like some sort of story?' he muses.

'Please, give it back,' I plead, my voice almost cracking. I'm not ready for them—or anyone—to read this yet. I'm not sure I'll ever be ready.

'Is this about our trip?' Loosey asks, leaning over Officer's shoulder for a peek.

I nod reluctantly.

'Am I in it?' Officer asks, raising an eyebrow.

'You are,' I admit, 'but I was just writing it for myself. I'm not planning to publish it or anything.' My stomach tightens at the thought of him finding out how many times I've called him an asshole in there.

'But you should,' Loosepants says, taking the journal from Officer and handing it back to me. His voice is soft, encouraging. 'We'd love that. And maybe you can tell others about us—the story of us all. There might be others out there, like Officer or me, or even Daisy, who need to hear it.'

'I'll think about it,' I mumble, clutching the journal tightly as Officer gives me a small nod.

'By the way, we're going camping again,' Loosepants announces suddenly, his tone shifting to something lighter. 'All of us. Next week.'

'We wanted it to be a surprise,' Officer adds. 'Everything's planned. We talked to everyone. You were the only one left.'

'Did you ask Huntress?' I ask, my heart skipping before I even finish the question. Their expressions shift. Officer and Loosepants exchange quick glances.

'She's not coming, Wolf,' Loosey replies quietly.

'Why?' I ask, the words tumbling out. 'I mean, did she talk to you? Did she say anything?'

'She did. She said she's going somewhere else. Something about finally completing her dream.'

Her dream.

The words echo, pulling me back to that evening at the orphanage—Dadaji's sad voice, his frustration spilling out. How he wanted her to fulfill her dream instead of spending all her money on the kids. How she'd said she was saving, little by little, promising she'd do it soon.

If she's finally going to achieve it, I am happy for her.

'What's this?' Officer interrupts my thoughts, his voice sharp as he pulls something from my drawer. My stomach twists when I see it. Birdie's letter.

My heart starts pounding. I jump to my feet, rushing towards him. 'Give it to me, please,' I say, almost desperate.

'Birdie?' Officer says slowly, reading the letter. 'Yours? Birdie wrote you a letter?'

'How do you know about Birdie?' I ask, my eyes wide, my pulse racing.

Officer gives me a look—somewhere between surprise and disbelief, maybe even annoyance. I can't tell. His expression is unreadable, and it's driving me insane.

'I need you to tell me about this, Officer,' I say, my voice firm despite my panic. 'Who is she?'

'Wolf, this isn't funny,' Officer replies, his tone growing sharper.

'Do I look like I'm joking?' I snap, my voice rising.

Loosepants steps in, clearly confused. 'What's going on?'

'Wolf's lost it,' Officer says, flatly. 'Probably because of the full moon.'

'Officer, I'm serious.' I start towards him, anger, desperation and panic mixing in my voice.

Loosey quickly steps in front of me, pressing a hand against my chest to hold me back. 'Hey, hey, calm down,' he says, his confusion deepening. He turns to Officer. 'Why do you say that? Why has he lost it?'

'Because,' Officer says, gesturing at me, his tone cold, deliberate, 'he wants to know who Birdie is.'

20

I cover my eyes with the back of my hand, shielding them from the snow stinging my face. I should've waited. The innkeeper had urged me to, her voice heavy with worry. But it's too late for that now. I can't stop. *This might be my last chance to find her.*

When Officer told me Birdie's true identity, it took me a long time to recover.

He had then called her from his phone, but it went directly to voicemail, saying her mobile was switched off. Not trusting the automated response, I asked Loosey to try from his phone, and then I tried from mine. No response. Holding onto reality was becoming difficult for me. Regularly pacing in the room, taking walks outside, cursing—at whom, I had no idea—none of it worked.

After Officer and Loosey left, they didn't even bother asking me when I would be arriving at the destination. They knew I had to find her and wished me luck. I texted her on Instagram, dropped messages on her number. Still, no reply.

The room—its confinement, the overthinking, dissecting every single detail, every letter, every moment—started killing me. I needed a break, a moment away, away from the place where I had turned her letters over and over, looking for any hidden clue that might lead me to her.

I couldn't breathe there anymore.

So, I went for a walk by the riverside, hoping the cold air would quieten my head. I sat by the water, watching the current carry everything away, and that's when it hit me—a way to find her without waiting. I ran back home without stopping, nearly crashing into a car on the way. I threw clothes into a bag, whatever I could grab, and booked the first flight out.

'You need to help me,' I had blurted out the moment Sharma Uncle had opened the door.

When they took me inside, Sharma Aunty insisted on making soup because, as she said, I looked like a mess—and she wasn't wrong. One glance in the mirror confirmed it: messy hair, tired eyes, a worn face. I was a wreck.

'You need to take some rest, son,' she said, gently, but I didn't have time.

'You need to tell me where she is, please,' I pleaded.

'I wish I could help you,' Sharma Aunty said, clearly torn. 'But she asked us not to tell you anything about her.'

'I know who she is,' I said, and the atmosphere instantly changed.

Sharma Aunty's eyes widened. Sharma Uncle's face hardened, his jaw tightening as the silence thickened around us. Even the clock on the wall seemed louder.

When he finally spoke, his voice was calm but heavy, caught between reason and emotion. 'That doesn't mean we'll break our promise to h—'

'I love her,' I said, cutting him off.

The words hung in the air, raw, honest and irreversible. It was the first time I had said them out loud.

Sharma Uncle and Aunty both froze, staring at me.

'You love our Birdie?' Sharma Aunty asked, her eyes searching mine for the truth.

'I do,' I said quietly. 'I love her more than anything in this world.'

A bright smile spread across Sharma Aunty's face, radiating warmth, but Sharma Uncle's expression didn't shift—except for a faint smile that I might have imagined. He walked to the kitchen counter, leaning against it, his face serious.

'If I tell you where she is, do you promise to never hurt her and to take care of her?' Sharma Uncle asked, his voice heavy with the weight of his question.

'I promise,' I said, my voice steady. In that moment, I realised—*I had never been this sure of anything before.* 'I'll never hurt her. I'll take care of her. Always.'

A smile grew on his face.

'I don't know where she is now,' he finally said. 'But I can tell you where she'll be in a week.'

He told me about her next destination and promised to send me the details of her stay if he found out. She was far away, and he advised me to wait until she returned, but I couldn't.

'At least stay here for the night,' Sharma Aunty said, concern in her voice.

'I can't,' I said, shaking my head. 'I need to get to her. I've already been away too long.'

'Pick up. Pick up, pick up.' No answer. It was 1 a.m.—he was probably asleep.

After the trip, I'd done my best to fix things at home, leaning into the efforts my mom and dad were finally making.

We were ... okay now. Better than before. Dad had offered to pay my bills and rent, but I'd said no—that I could manage on my own. That I was earning enough through freelancing.

'I'm proud of you, son,' he'd said. And then we had hugged—maybe for the first time in fourteen years.

I called him again. I needed him.

'Hey, son. Everything okay?' he answered, his voice heavy with sleep.

'I need your help, Dad.' I expected something like 'Can't we talk later? Maybe in the morning?' But he just listened. He was there for his son.

'I'll take care of it,' he said.

I'd meant to tell him I'd pay him back, but I forgot. The next day, when Mom found out about it, she told me not to say that. 'It would mean a lot to your dad,' she said, 'if, just for once, you let him help you.'

He drove me to the airport himself, asking me questions he'd probably held onto for years. He even apologised for never being there for me all these years, and he promised to fix it. When I looked into his eyes, I knew he meant it.

'Get her, and never let her go,' he said before I walked inside.

After three long days of travel—crossing borders, cities and remote villages—I had finally reached the hotel earlier this evening. When I asked the manager about Birdie, she told me there was only one Indian staying there—a girl in her early twenties. But she'd left the hotel barely an hour before I arrived.

'A girl so kind, blessed with the beauty of an angel,' the manager said, her pale skin glowing under the lobby's warm lights. Her blue eyes sparkled with sincerity as she added, 'No doubt a boy would walk to the other side of the earth for her.'

'For her, I'd walk to the ends of the earth,' I muttered under my breath, meaning every word.

I slide my gloved hands deeper into my pockets and hunch my shoulders, hoping to keep the biting chill at bay. It doesn't do much. The cold outside has already breached the layers of my thick woolen coat and sweater. It's already reaching my bones, freezing every bit of me.

But I can't let it stop me. For a year, I've spent every single day wondering who she is, if she would ever meet me, and begging the universe—*because she believed in it*—for a chance to meet her.

And now that I'm this close, I can't give up. I won't let anything stop me—not the snowflakes hitting my face like sharp needles, not the chill spreading through me, or the way it's starting to burn—too sharply—each time I draw a breath.

I scan the skies, their darkness beginning to haunt me. I remember the manager's words, 'You should wait for her, dear,' she had urged, concern softening her voice. 'They don't show up every night. And even tonight, I doubt they'll appear. When she sees that, she'll have to come back. You can meet her then.'

But I hadn't even considered it—not for a second. The thought of her being out there, so close, while I stood around doing nothing—it tore at me.

I tilt my head back, staring at the dark sky. *Let her complete her dream. Please*, I whisper to the universe. *You've taken so much from her already, been so unkind for so long. Just this once ... please, be gentle. Be kind.*

And just as I finish my silent prayer, the world lights up.

It starts faint—just a touch of green in the distance—then blooms suddenly into waves of colour that spill across the darkness. Green, blue, streaks of red and violet.

They dance across the night sky, their beauty and movements unparalleled to anything I have ever seen. It's as if something divine is being painted into existence one stroke at a time, and I am getting to witness it firsthand.

For a long moment, I just stare, breathless, admiring nature's finest creation.

They're beautiful—too beautiful—but watching this feels incomplete without her.

Because somewhere out there, under the same lights, she's waiting.

And I need to reach her. Fast.

Ahead, something dark disrupts the endless white—a lake, its surface shimmering beneath the dance of the Northern Lights. *That's where she'd be*, the manager had said.

I start walking faster, dragging my boots through the snow. My lungs burn, my heart races, every muscle of mine screaming—but I don't care. The cold is gone. The pain is gone. All that's left is the pull inside me—the fierce, aching need to meet her.

Then I see it.

A shadow ahead, still and silent, head lifted towards the sky.

Could it be her?

My breath catches.

Am I finally going to meet her?

After all those sleepless nights, all that time spent rereading our texts, writing her into existence from fading memories—am I finally here, this close to meeting her?

'Birdie?' I call out, pulling down my hood.

She's still far away—a dark figure against the shimmer of the lake, her head tilted upwards, facing the swirling lights. She doesn't hear me.

'Birdie, is that you?' I call again, louder this time,

The distance between us shrinks—slowly, painfully. The closer I get, the clearer she becomes. The outline of her coat, her hair swept by the wind.

And then she turns.

The lights from the auroras spill over her, brushing her in soft greens and violets. Her eyes find me—wide, uncertain, shining even through the distance. Her breath trembles in the cold.

'Arjun?' she says, disbelief coating the way she says my name.

And I forget everything—the aching legs, the burning lungs, the numb hands—and run.

Run to her.

To the only girl I've ever wanted.

She doesn't move. Just stands there, frozen, as if she's seen a ghost.

'It's y— It's you!' she manages again, her voice breaking.

'Yes. It's me.' Reaching her, I take her hands in mine. Her eyes swollen and red. *Has she been crying?*

'Are you okay?' I ask softly, searching her face.

'Yes ... yes ...' she whispers, but the tears spill over anyway, trailing down her cheeks. 'But how are you here? How d—?'

'It doesn't matter,' I say, gently wiping her tears. 'All that matters is that I'm here. And I'm not going anywhere.'

Her eyes carry a storm of their own, I can see that. But I will face it with her, standing by her side. She will never again have to face anything by herself.

She keeps studying my face, as if searching for proof that I'm not another illusion.

'I'm real,' I whisper, pulling her into a hug as proof.

She doesn't move right away. Her arms hang limply by her sides, her breath warm and trembling against my neck. I hold her tighter, afraid that if I loosen my grip even slightly, she'll disappear.

For a long moment, neither of us speaks.

'Is this a dream?' she finally whispers when I pull back.

'No,' I say, holding her hands in mine.

'But how did you ...?'

'It doesn't matter,' I say again, gently, shaking my head. 'None of that matters. All that matters is that I'm here. With you. And ...'

She looks up, eyes still glistening, 'And?'

'And that I ... I love you.'

She doesn't move. Doesn't react. Her expression freezes for what feels like forever. Then her breath stutters. Her lips part, but no sound comes out. Her eyes glisten, searching mine—disbelieving, desperate.

And then ...

She shakes her head—violently at first, then slower—as tears begin to well.

'You don't love me, Wolf,' she says, her voice breaking. 'You love the perfect, mysterious girl from the letters. But I'm real. A real girl who cries, who misses her parents, who saved for years to come here because it was their dream to see the Northern Lights.'

Her voice quivers, her shoulders shaking. 'A dream they never lived long enough to complete.' The tears start spilling. 'And ... And now I'm here, all alone, finishing it for them ... missing them. Hating them for leaving me!'

Her sobs grow louder, her words tumbling out in fragments. 'I'm not the strong, all positive girl who wrote those letters. I'm not who you think I am. I'm not strong. I am weak. I am ... I a—'

I move forward, trying to hold her, but she jerks away, her voice rising.

'And I was crying—crying because I wished there was someone with me, someone who loved me, here, so I didn't have to do this alone!'

'Someone who loves you is here,' I tell her, taking her trembling hands in mine, anchoring her to the present, to me.

It hurts. It hurts to see her like this. To hear the sound of her sobs—realising just how much she has been breaking inside.

She looks up at me, eyes glassy, desperate. I wipe her tears away with my thumbs, silently promising I'll never let them gather again.

'I've loved you. Always,' I whisper, my voice steady even as my chest tightens.

'Birdie ... who wrote to me. Huntress ... who stood by me. And Anjali ... who's always been my biggest crush.'

Her eyes widen, her lips trembling. I take a breath, my voice low, shaking. 'And I fucking hate myself for thinking my heart was torn between two people—when I was only ever in love with one. You.'

I cup her face in my hands, 'I love you, Anjali ...' I whisper. 'And I have been in love with you for a long, long time.'

She stares back at me, her gaze searching mine, as if trying to be sure she isn't dreaming. And then, once she's managed to catch her breath, she finally speaks, her voice trembling.

'I ... I love you too.'

Before the words can even fade, I close the distance between us and press my lips to hers.

She freezes for a heartbeat—then exhales, breathing me in, kissing me back with the same desperation, as if she's been waiting for this moment as long as I have. Her fingers clutch the collar of my coat, pulling me closer, and my hand finds the back of her neck, sliding into her hair, holding her—with no intention of ever letting go.

We don't stop—not to breathe, not to think. The snow falls harder, melting on our faces, but neither of us cares. Our lips move in sync, hungrier at first, then deeper, slower, as if trying to make up for all the moments we'd lost. Every kiss feels like a promise—of all that was unsaid, of everything still to come.

The world around us blurs—the sky, the cold, the Northern Lights.

There's only us.

A seeker and his songbird.

21

We stay there for hours, sitting together in the snow, her hand tightly clasped in mine. Neither of us speaks much, and we don't need to. The lights overhead cast a soft glow, and in that silence, it feels like everything is better, like everything is finally the way it is supposed to be.

When we return to the hotel, the manager greets us with a knowing smile. Without us even asking, she brings over two steaming bowls of soup, saying it's on the house. We sit across from each other, the warmth of the bowls thawing our frozen fingers. She finally breaks the silence.

'How did you find me?' she asks softly.

'It was Officer,' I begin, setting my spoon down. 'He came to visit me a few days ago. He saw the letter you left me, and when Loosey and I couldn't make sense of what he was talking about, he explained everything. He told me about the time before the gang formed, when it was just the two of you trekking together with random people. How his mom tried blackmailing him, and he felt like there was no way out. He was going to give up ... end everything.'

Her gaze drops, and I can see her struggling to keep her composure. I reach out, my hand covering hers.

'He said you hunted him down,' I continue, my voice steady. 'He said you nearly beat him senseless for even thinking about giving up. You made him see that his life was worth fighting for. And he told us that's when he gave you a new trail name—Huntress. Because you hunted him down and saved him when he couldn't save himself.'

She blinks quickly, as though trying to hold back tears. I give her a moment to collect herself before speaking again.

'And then there's Sharma Uncle and Aunty,' I add with a small smile. 'They helped me find you. They're the ones who gave me the location.'

Her eyes widen slightly, surprised. 'How did you get them to tell you?'

I hesitate for a moment, then lean closer. 'I confessed everything to them. How I feel about you. What you mean to me. Everything.'

And then I tell her about the promise I made to Sharma Uncle.

Epilogue
Ten Years Later

'You seriously thought that was *her*?' Daisy exclaims, shoving the phone right in my face. It's an old post from Birdie's feed—a curly-haired girl sitting near the edge of a hill. We're all sprawled around Sharma Aunty and Uncle's living room—our regular place to get together now.

'Those were the only pictures in her feed then!' I shoot back, defensive.

'Gosh, you,' Daisy groans. 'You looked at those curls and didn't even think, "that looks like Daisy"? Like, *those* curls feel exactly like mine.'

'They weren't blue and green, like your hair used to be!'

'What the f—'

'Ask him about how he thought she was a medical student,' Loosey cuts in, sitting next to Officer.

Officer looks annoyingly pleased with his partner's question. A thick beard has taken over his face since the last time I saw him, giving him an even more rugged look. Loosey, on the other hand, looks exactly the same. Still skinny. Still allergic to silence. Some things never evolve.

I glare at him and mouth a very clear 'fuck you'.

'Yes, that!' Daisy turns back to me. 'How could you even think that?'

'How could I not?' I protest. 'What else was I supposed to think?'

'That maybe she was *volunteering*? At a medical camp?' she fires back. 'You knew that was her thing.'

'Girl, how would I know that specifically?' I say. 'Like—how was I supposed to guess that she clicked *your* pictures and posted them on *her* feed while hiding your face?' I throw my hands up. 'I'm sorry for assuming people usually post their *own* photos on Instagram, not someone else's.'

Daisy opens her mouth to respond—

'Are you all troubling my husband?'

The voice cuts from across the room.

We all turn.

And thank god—*thank god*—she's here.

Anjali stands in the doorway, arms crossed, eyebrows raised in that way that makes everyone go still.

She walks towards me, then leans down and plants a kiss on my cheek. It's been years since we got together, and somehow the touch of her lips still sends the same shiver down my spine as it did the first time.

'He deserves it,' Loosey says dramatically. 'I finished reading the book last week, and I wanted to *kill* him when he thought the girl in the bus was you—you! When the you-you was standing right next to him.'

'You would've thought the same,' I argue.

'No. I wouldn't,' he says smugly. 'Also, why did you take so, so many years to publish it? Like—'

'Guys!' Huntress—Birdie—Anjali widens her eyes, and everyone falls silent.

God, my wife looks so hot when she does that.

She comes over and settles onto my lap, handing the others a plate of momo Sharma Aunty has prepared.

'No troubling my husband,' she says firmly.

'Thank you,' I mouth. For now. Knowing I'm absolutely going to take my sweet time thanking her properly later.

'Alright,' Loosey says, looping an arm lazily around Officer, 'at least tell me something the book didn't. Who fell first?'

'I—' I start.

'I did, probably in our second year of college,' Anjali says.

We all stare at her. Even me. She's never said that before.

'Yep,' she repeats with a small smile. 'Though I never told him, it was easy to fall for the guy who does so much for you without ever making a big deal out of it. Someone who notices what matters to you and tries his best to be there and support you.'

She ruffles my hair.

'And I've been falling for him ever since. For healing me. For showing me I didn't always have to be strong. For taking care of me when I'd long stopped letting anyone come close.'

I just stare at her. The one who healed me saying that I did the same for her.

I lean in, going for a kiss, and my lips just brush hers when—

My phone rings.

Why? Dear universe, why?

It's my agent.

'I'll be back,' I whisper. 'Keep that kiss reserved for me.'

She smirks and slips into my spot on the couch.

I pick up the call and step outside.

In the yard, the bonfire pit is already set—logs stacked and waiting. Tarun must've done it earlier. We've visited them countless times over the years, and he hasn't missed this ritual even once.

The agent and I talk through dates for the book tour, promotions, some interviews—for a long time. The life I never thought I would get to experience.

When I finally hang up, the kitchen door creaks open.

Anjali stands there, holding in her hands our bundle of joy, wriggling and screeching with excitement.

'There's Dada,' Anjali says with a smile, carrying our little birdie towards me.

'And there's my little bird,' I call out, raising my arms towards her.

'She woke up crying, and no one—literally no one—could calm her,' Anjali says, brushing a curl off her forehead. 'She only stopped when I said we'd go find Dada.'

'Seems like I'm her favourite,' I tease, holding our daughter close. 'By the way, I need that kiss that was interrupted,' I say, leaning in.

'You're too much,' she says, laughing and kissing me back.

'Yes, I am. I am too much in love with you,' I reply.

'Gosh, when will you stop? Anyway, you take care of our little bird while I help Sharma Aunty with the dinner.'

'Of course, Wifey.'

God, I love calling her that. I steal one more kiss before I turn towards the little one in my arms.

'You've got your mother's big, beautiful eyes,' I tell her, pressing a kiss to her cheek. She lets out a gleeful screech, laughing and wriggling.

'And I'm pretty sure you'll use those big, beautiful eyes to terrify me one day, just like your mom does.'

Another screeching giggle comes from her as if she agrees.

Overhead, birds flutter by, their wings cutting through the fresh air as they prepare for another day. Their melodies fill the quiet morning, a chorus that tugs at my heart. My little one turns her head, eyes wide and curious, searching for the source of the sound.

'Do you hear them, little bird?' I ask softly.

Then, I pause, wondering—

Should I try?

Would they answer?

They never have.

But I can't resist.

I curl my lips and mimic their call.

A moment passes, and this time, as if by some miracle, they respond.

I hold my daughter closer, her tiny hand curling around my finger, her laughter blending with the birds' songs.

A small, grateful smile forms on my lips.

I am finally at peace.

Acknowledgements

First of all, thank you for being patient with me. I know many of you have been waiting for this book for years. It's been a long journey. It took me nearly six years to bring this book to you, six years of trying to become the writer this story deserved.

I want to begin by thanking my parents, who made me fall in love with books, even when we lived in a small village where coming across a book felt like finding a chest full of diamonds and gold. To my brother, who always knew when not to disturb me while I was writing, and who has always been there for me. To Warule sir, for making me fall in love with the English language. And to Michelle, for responding to a kid's messages and guiding him into the world of writing.

Over the years, I've met countless people who supported me, motivated me, and at times criticised me, pushing me to write better. Gurunath, Gauri, Ritwik, Anurag, Sushant, Dishita, Neha, Krutika, Khushi, Partha, thank you for your friendship and for keeping me going when I didn't think I could.

I am forever grateful to the universe for the day I met Gautam sir. Without him, this book may never have found the home it deserved.

I don't know if words can fully describe my gratitude for Karthika V.K. Thank you for picking up this manuscript from the many submissions Westland Books receives, for believing in it, and for deciding it deserved to be shared with the world. I am also thankful to Vedika Mehendale, who ensured that every word and every line is right. Karthika and Vedika, thank you for your editorial insights, your patience, and for helping shape this book into what it is today.

And finally, to my readers on Instagram, thank you for being there for me more times than I can count. For supporting me through the years, for relating to my words and for staying. I must have done some good in my past lives to have found readers like you.